EVERY BREATH

Ellie Marney

EVERY BREATH

Tundra Books

Copyright © 2014 Ellie Marney
Published in North America by Tundra Books, 2014

Published in Canada by Tundra Books, a division of Random House of Canada Limited,
One Toronto Street, Suite 300, Toronto, Ontario M5C 2V6

Published in the United States by Tundra Books of Northern New York,
P.O. Box 1030, Plattsburgh, New York 12901

Library of Congress Control Number: 2014933493

Library and Archives Canada Cataloguing in Publication

Marney, Ellie, author
    Every breath / Ellie Marney.

Reprint. Originally published: Sydney : Allen & Unwin, 2013.
Issued in print and electronic formats.
ISBN 978-1-77049-772-6 (bound).—ISBN 978-1-77049-774-0 (epub)

    I. Title.

PZ7.M366Ev 2014   j823'.92   C2014-900831-7
                                            C2014-900832-5

Cover designed by Five Seventeen
Cover images: (young man) © Jovana Vukotic/Stocksy.com;
(brick wall) © Clint Spencer/iStockphoto.com
The text was set in Minion.

www.tundrabooks.com

Printed and bound in the United States of America

1 2 3 4 5 6   19 18 17 16 15 14

FOR GEOFF

A human being is only breath and shadow

– SOPHOCLES

PROLOGUE

Here I am in the photo from seven years ago – a ten-year-old rural in a blue dress.

The dress is a birthday present. I put it on over my shorts to please Mum. You can see the birthday cake in the photo. Originally a fluffy white pavlova, it looks as if it's been attacked by vultures. All that's left is the meringue carcass, gory blobs of strawberry, golden smears of passionfruit and a few stray black seeds.

I'm ducking my head in the photo. My brother, Mike, is pulling my ponytail as the flash goes off. Dad's the one holding the camera – every head is cropped except mine. I look embarrassed, because of the dress. But there's something else too: a steely glint in my eye, a tenacity. It's probably got a lot to do with the hair-pulling, but it's a glimpse of the real me. This is what I look like when I glare.

On this same day, on the other side of the world, is a boy. In this shot, from my imagination, his crazy curls are the same as now, but his face is different – younger, of course, but open, relaxed, happy.

In these imaginary photos you can see the events unfolding, like a flip-book. Here he is, catching his mother's eye from the back seat of the family car. She's smiling over her shoulder at him as his father drives through the whispering light of winter, the slow return from a family holiday.

Another photo. There's an explosion. The photo squashes all that noise and pain into one shrieking pinprick of light. Where the boy touches his mother's outstretched hand, the light blows outwards as he's knocked away. The next photos are too awful to look at, and then...the last photo shows a white room with beeping machines, soft cottonwool noise, nurses with cottonwool shoes, and nothing is the same, although the world remains the same from space.

This is me and James – Watts and Mycroft. Two people united by fate, or random chance, or the law of averages, or destiny, or a freak of nature, or pure dumb luck. Seven years from now, a man will be dead, a case will be opened, and a boy with no past may hold the key to my future.

I don't know any of this yet. Maybe it's just as well.

CHAPTER ONE

There's a *r-i-i-p* as the tape comes off.

'*Jesus Christ* – are you doing this on purpose?'

'Maybe.' I dump the scraps of bandage and keep my face neutral.

My patient sits on the paper-covered examination table, as long as a string of spaghetti, his dark hair anarchy as usual. 'Okay, I want a cigarette now.'

'Keep that thought on hold.' I press another gauze pad to Mycroft's eyebrow wound, and check that he's still putting pressure on the nosebleed.

Mycroft looks at me through one bloodshot eye. 'It's broken, isn't it.'

'It's not broken. It's just bleeding a lot.'

'It feels broken.'

'If it was broken, believe me, you'd feel worse. And you'd have two black eyes instead of one.'

'Can I just tell people it's broken?'

'Tell them whatever you want. Now shut up and hold still, or I'm gonna screw this up again.'

I whip the gauze pad off Mycroft's eyebrow with one hand and stick the butterfly closure on with the other. Before he has a chance to wriggle again, I fix a Melolin pad in place with a piece of paper tape. The tape sticks to the latex gloves I'm wearing, which is a pain in the arse, but gloves are school first-aid policy.

Mai Ng leans into my line of sight. 'So, clearly, he's gonna make it.'

I strip off another pair of ruined gloves and make a face. 'I think he'll live.'

'Principal Conroy wants to see you once the dust has settled,' Mai says. 'Both of you.'

I sigh. 'Great.'

Mai grins at Mycroft. 'Fantastic job of taking Rachel's advice, by the way. Super. And see how well it all worked out?'

I snort. Mycroft flips Mai off.

Mai presses her advantage. 'I'm curious to see how Conroy will rate this incident. You, fighting with Gary Cumberson, the six-foot-two human besser block. That's gotta score high. We should have a scale of some kind. I mean, how mental d'you think Conroy will go this time?'

Mycroft glares at her. 'I'm sure I'll find out.'

Mai muses to the ceiling, 'There's got to be a limit to how loud he can yell. He nearly went hoarse after the homemade napalm thing last year.'

'That was a genuinely useful experiment,' Mycroft says. It comes out as though he's talking underwater.

'And then there was the Bunsen-burner episode at the start of term.'

'That was an accident.'

'I'm counting on an impressive outcome, Mycroft. Serious decibels.' Mai winks and pushes up her glasses, bangles jangling down her wrist. 'I want to hear it from the English wing. Because now I've got to go to Ferguson's class and field the gossip.'

'Tell them my nose is broken,' Mycroft says.

'Yeah, tell them he cried like a baby when I reset it.' I wing a grateful glance in Mai's direction. 'And thanks for helping us get to the sick bay.'

'No problem. Oh, and you'll need this.' Mai shrugs off her enormous backpack. She rummages inside, pulls out a T-shirt and chucks it onto Mycroft's lap. 'Don't go getting attached. I want it back.'

Mycroft grimaces. 'Is that yours or Gus's?'

'Mine. Try not to add more stains.'

'It's never gonna fit!'

Mai eyes the river of red down Mycroft's front. 'It's that or take the tram home looking like one of the walking dead. Sucks to be you.'

She slings her backpack on. The straps push out her generous assets in front, highlighted by a black T-shirt with a picture of a llama driving a car, with the slogan *No, Llama, no!*

She said *English wing*. The bell must be about to ring for sixth period.

'Oh crap, can you ask Ms Ferguson what she wants for tomorrow? I don't want her to have another fit.'

'Sure.' Mai frowns and lifts a finger, doing her best Ferguson impression. 'Keep in *mind*, ladies and gentlemen, that we are *barely* halfway through first term, and you are *already* behind.'

'She's just trying to whip us into a final-year frenzy.' I crack

5

an icepack. 'Distance Ed doesn't have anything like this kind of pressure.'

'Hm.' Mai looks at Mycroft's bandaged face and waggles her eyebrows. 'Well, it's been a laugh. See you later.'

As she squeezes out of the miniscule first-aid room with her bag, Mrs Ramen arrives to check in.

'Getting along all right, dear?' Mrs Ramen holds her knitting behind herself, as if she's worried she'll get bodily fluids on it.

Her blonde-and-red tips clash with her orange eyeshadow, and she smells strongly of Rexona. The school accounts manager, Mrs Ramen doubles as the first-aid officer when required, but everyone knows she has a horror of blood. I've had my St John's Ambulance certificate for two years, so it seemed only practical to let her off the hook when we staggered in with Mycroft gushing everywhere.

'We're good, Mrs Ramen. Have you got more gloves?'

Mrs Ramen nods to a high shelf, her hair bobbing. I grab the new box of latex. Mycroft kicks his legs until Ramen leaves.

'You just *had* to tell him, didn't you?' I tear baby wipes from another packet as I eye Mycroft. 'What was it? A sudden attack of OCD, or did you think "Don't tell Gary" was open to interpretation?'

It's infuriating how Mycroft manages to look so cool and superior, even with paper tape on one eyebrow and gauze stuck up his nose. With him sitting and me standing, it still isn't enough to even out the height disparity. I angle myself between his knees to scrub the congealing blood off his face, while he presses the icepack to his cheekbone.

'Gary had...' He chucks the gauze pad on the floor. 'He had a car covered in graffiti, and no one with the balls to tell him who did it. Jesus, I was doing him a favor!'

'Yeah, and he did you a favor right back.'

'Okay, so he's an aggressive Neanderthal with no impulse control—'

'Brilliant deduction. How long did it take you to work that out?' The gloves are shitting me, so I strip them off.

'He still deserves to *know*!'

'Except for the fact that no one elected *you* to be the one to tell him. Don't try to convince me your motives were pure, Mycroft, I know you too well.' I sigh, peering at the mess. 'All right, the bleeding's stopped. Hold still.'

Mycroft ditches the icepack, lets me wipe away the dark slime on his top lip.

'Okay, fine! I wanted to tell him. But *Jesus*…' His Pommy accent has thickened; the stuffy heat of the room has burred his *r*s and toffeed his vowels. 'They were right there, talking about it, and I couldn't just *leave* it. It's not my fault that his best friend was the one with a spraycan and a grudge, and *ow*, that *hurts*.'

'Sorry.' I'm sure I don't look sorry. 'Mycroft, use your over-sized brain. Gary Cumberson's built like a tank. He could've snapped your neck.'

Mycroft snorts, but only succeeds in blowing red-tinged snot out of his nose. 'It's fine. I survived.'

'That's not the point.'

Mycroft mops his nose and shrugs.

I grit my teeth and splay one hand against his jaw while I scrub at the red-brown smears on his neck. My knuckle grazes over a sandpapery spot he missed while shaving. I rub the stubble with my thumb, feel his Adam's apple bob.

Mycroft turns his head, and now I'm getting the full stare. His blue eyes are luminous from the sunlight reflecting off the white bench surfaces. My palms suddenly go sweaty – it's way too warm in here. When my pulse jumps I have to look away.

'Anyway, thanks for doing this,' Mycroft says, his voice thick and low.

I take a breath and purse my lips. 'It's fine.'

He grabs my wiping hand. 'C'mon, Watts. How pissed at me are you, really?'

'You're officially in the doghouse.'

'Bloody hell.' He grins. 'Will I stay there long?' He fondles my fingers, his eyes sparkling. He really isn't taking this seriously at all.

I pull my hand away and dab at the split in his bottom lip. The soft flesh springs back after every touch. I flash on the moment when Cumberson's fist connected, and my stomach churns like a washing machine.

I press the wipe into Mycroft's hand. 'Here. You finish it, while I get the Dettol.' I rummage in the bowels of the fishing tackle box that serves as first-aid carry-all. 'How did you know, anyway? That it was Bruno who sprayed Gary's car?'

Mycroft doesn't reply. I glance over and there's a half-naked boy barely a foot away, taking up all of my vision. The Dettol falls from my hand.

Mycroft has dumped his own gore-fest T-shirt onto the floor and is struggling to pull on the one Mai lent him. He's all greyhound-lean muscle and stretched-out torso. His scars are puckered white serrations over his ribs and abdomen.

'Jesus, Mycroft!' I drop down to retrieve the bottle, my cheeks burning. 'Let me know when you're decent.'

'You're lucky the lid was still on,' Mycroft says. His voice has a jittery edge. 'This shirt is too small. I said that, didn't I? It's a girl's T-shirt, and it's too small.'

'*You're* lucky Mai had a spare.'

'She's done this on purpose. God almighty – can you help me with this?'

I put the bottle on the bench. My fingers flutter as I unravel the shirt at the back. His hair feathers my neck and my arms are in a weird position around him and his skin is damp, smooth, like a seal's pelt. My heartbeat is uncomfortably loud again. I step back and turn to grab the brown and green bottle and get my bearings.

'Anyway. The car. And Bruno. How did you know?'

'Hm?' He throws the wipe on the floor, messy bastard. 'Bruno's had silver fingertips for two days.'

'Right.' I unscrew the bottle cap, start spreading the joy. 'Clever.'

'Not really. It's just observing. Christ, that stings.'

'*I* observed.'

'You *saw*. Seeing and observing, not the same thing.'

'Let's observe you now the blood's stopped spraying out.' I step back to cast a critical eye over my handiwork.

Mycroft's shoulders hunch, hands squeezing the edge of the table. His curls are a dark jungle, his black jeans (extra-extra-longs) are grubby, which is perfectly normal, but he's now wearing a khaki T-shirt two sizes too small. The front of it reads *Jesus loves you – Everybody else thinks you're a wanker*. With the paper tape on his eyebrow, the black eye, split lip, red stains and bruises, he looks like a B-grade horror-movie extra.

I wince. 'God, Mycroft, you look awful. Maybe Conroy will give you sympathy points.'

'Speaking of which…'

He hops off the table. Now he's standing, I'm forced to look up to make eye contact. Way up. 'You're supposed to stay still for twenty minutes. In case of a concussion.'

'Watts, when have you ever known me to stay still for twenty minutes?'

I cap the bottle and use the stripped-off gloves to pick the rubbish off the floor. By the time I escape the room, Mycroft is standing out front holding up Ramen's knitting, a shapeless something in colors that make my eyes convulse.

'That's a jumper, is it? Lovely. Bit purple for my taste, but there you go. For your daughter's new one, Mrs Ramen?'

I wonder where he got *that* information. Then I see the photo of a woman – a younger version of Ramen – and her red-wrinkly baby, sticky-taped onto the computer monitor. Huh.

'Yes!' Mrs Ramen's smile goes full bore. 'Born last month. That's three now, two boys and a girl.'

'Congratulations.'

We exit through the sliding door and head for Principal Conroy's office down the hall. My steps slow.

'Come on, Watts,' Mycroft says. 'He's not going to eat you.'

'That's all right for you to say. You're here every week.'

'I'm not here *every* week. Anyway, Conroy's not interested in you. It's me he wants to yell at. You were just a bystander.'

I clear my throat. 'I wasn't just a bystander. When Conroy heard that you and Gary were going at it out front of the IT wing, he pulled me out of class. He thought I could...I dunno...be a calming influence or something.'

The conversation had actually gone something like this:

'You're his friend, aren't you?'

'Well, yeah—'

'And he listens to you.'

'Um, sometimes. But—'

Conroy had cut me off abruptly. 'He might listen to you now.

God knows it would ease my mind if I thought he was listening to *somebody*.'

But I'm not going to tell Mycroft the details. I sigh.

'Mycroft...have you ever thought of just keeping out of it?'

'Now you sound like Conroy.' His jaw has that unmistakeable stubborn set. 'It's not like I'm always sticking my nose in, Watts. Sometimes people *ask* me.'

'People ask for stuff all the time. They don't have to *get* it.' I feel my own face assuming the stubbornness. I shake it off. 'Look, I don't want to be your welfare worker or your emergency paramedic at school. I just want to be your neighbor.'

Mycroft grins. 'So, you've only been in the city four months and you're already the babysitter for the school's eccentric genius.'

'It's been four *and a half* months. And if you were such a genius, you wouldn't have a black eye.'

'I'm only a genius with facts. I'm an academic genius and a social moron.'

'At least you admit to being a moron at something.'

'I admit to being a moron at lots of things. Being a moron in one or two areas serves to highlight my extraordinary brilliance in everything else.'

I turn with my mouth open, wondering whether or not he's kidding. Before I can say anything, Conroy's door opens.

'You two. Finally.' Conroy glances at Mycroft's T-shirt. His gray eyebrows gather into a bushy monobrow. 'Inside, if you please.'

I shut my mouth, drop my shoulders, and walk as directed. Mycroft saunters through the doorway as if he's accepting an invitation to High Tea. It's one of the essential differences between us. I only *know* when I've been an idiot. Mycroft *relishes* it.

11

CHAPTER TWO

Dad takes off for his shift after dinner, backing the yellow taxi out of the driveway as I clear the dishes. Mike does the washing up, which is only fair considering that I cook and Mum's been cleaning other people's houses all day. I head for a shower, then dash to my room in a towel.

My room is the smallest in our new house. There are no posters or decorations – I haven't been able to bring myself to make it look more permanent. I tell myself I like the plain mushroom color of the walls.

There's not much else to it: a pine-frame bed, a desk, a wooden chair doing double-duty as a clothes horse. A bunch of novels leans like an over-stacked hamburger beneath the security-barred window, with a neighboring pile of school texts.

I culled a lot of stuff in the move. Old watercolor paintings, moth-eaten soft toys, dried flowers, special stones... anything that made me feel like a rube in the big city got the chuck. The country part of my life has been put to death. Everything that remains

– my thin photo album, my laptop, my printer – is on the desk. My guitar…I couldn't bear to throw out my guitar. It's over at Mycroft's, suffering from neglect.

I yank on cut-off jeans and a white tank, stuff my feet into boots and sling on my satchel. That's it. I'm about to walk out when I realize it's going to be another cool March night, so I grab a pilled blue hoodie to tie around my waist. It's one of Mike's that I stole and haven't given back yet.

The mirror on my wardrobe rattles as I brush past. I don't glance at it, I know what I look like. Sun-nuked brown hair, slightly ragged, falls past my shoulderblades – the blonde is starting to grow out after months in the city. If I don't tie it in a knot, it frames my face, which used to be tanned and is now just freckled. I've got unremarkable brown eyes, skinny muscled legs, strong arms. I don't bother primping; I'll look the same tomorrow.

Mum is settled on the couch in the living room with her sewing box, watching Mike watch TV. She calls out as I go through to the kitchen. 'The extra plate's in the oven, you'll want to put some foil on it. Salad's in the fridge.'

'Thanks, Mum.' She knows where I'm going.

I gather everything up, holding the plate with a tea-towel so I don't burn myself. I'm half out of the kitchen before Mum calls again. 'Has he got milk?'

'He's got condensed, that's all he ever uses.' I consider for a second, then put everything down on the yellow laminex table, grab a packet of Jam Fancies from the cupboard, stuff it into my satchel and lift the plate again.

I come out into the living room, and Mum looks up from the needle she's threading. 'That boy concerns me.'

I don't want to give her more ammunition than she has already.

'He's fine, Mum. He just needs to be reminded to eat every now and again.'

'I don't know why he won't eat here.'

I'm not going to answer this one. I know why, but it's not something I imagine Mycroft would want me sharing with all and sundry. 'He just doesn't want to impose, Mum. It's not a big deal.'

'His face looked awful this afternoon…Has he been to see a doctor?'

'Oh, bloody hell, Mum, he got into a fight at school.' Mike is bouncing his enormous nineteen-year-old self around on the couch, trying to see the NRL replay through me. 'He's a bloke, it happens. Move your arse, Rache.'

'Don't be rude to your sister,' Mum says, throwing a reel of thread at his head.

Happy for a conversational exit, I move out of Mike's way and towards the front door. Mum snags me with an accusing look. 'You took the biscuits, didn't you? I heard the cupboard door.'

'*Mum.*' I suck my thumb, which I've scorched on the plate now. 'Come on, I promise I'll replace them. Look, I'll see you later on – don't sit up till all hours.'

'Have you got your flashlight?'

'Yes, Mum.'

'Phone? Keys? Remember, put your keys between your knuckles and—'

'Mum, I'm only going two doors down.'

'She's fine, Mum, give it a rest.' Mike has showered and changed out of his delivery-driver's shirt and shorts, into jeans and bare feet. Now he's eating a jam sandwich only half an hour after dinner.

'Don't let her sit up too late,' I warn my brother. 'She'll get sucked into a rerun of *The Bill* or some other rubbish. If I come home and find her asleep on the couch again, you're cooked.'

'No worries,' Mike says.

Mum gives me a wave. For a second, I look at the two of them, Mike keeping Mum company, or vice versa. Two tired people after a long day. I sigh and close the door quietly behind me.

It's not as if we didn't all work hard before. But this is different. It used to be that we were all working together, with the common goal of keeping the farm going. But Five Mile is gone. My family is foreclosed, and ruined, and over a barrel, and we can never go back.

I put it out of my mind as I walk up Summoner Street, past the scrawl of tar lines under the flickering streetlamp, past the first house – our immediate neighbors, who sometimes have screaming fights late at night – then I'm at Mycroft's horrible two-bedroom weatherboard that looks as if it should be condemned.

I creak open the front gate and cut through the long grass to the unlocked back door.

The inside of the house isn't as bad as the exterior, but it still makes our place seem like something from *Grand Designs*. I collect a fork from the kitchen drawer and go straight for the closed door at the end of the gloomy hallway.

Mycroft's door has a hand-lettered sign, *The Stranger's Room*, taped to it along with a bunch of other crap: a poster for The Chemical Brothers, a sign saying *WARNING: Safety Glasses Must Be Worn at All Times*, and a yellow plaque with the universal black skull-and-crossbones danger symbol. I can hear the unmistakeable thump of The Knack oozing out from behind the wood veneer.

I rap twice. 'Oi! It's me!'

The door is flung wide. The music is suddenly much louder.

A fug of cigarette smoke escapes from the room, taking off for the stratosphere by way of the hall ceiling.

Mycroft stands there with a cigarette dangling from his lips, nodding along to 'My Sharona' like one of those floppy-headed dogs that sit on your dashboard. He's wearing a burgundy velveteen robe, loosely belted over cotton boxer shorts. His cuts and bruises stand out, and his hair looks particularly frightful.

'About bloody time.' The cigarette wobbles, spills ash onto the carpet. 'I'm starving.'

He puts his hands on his hips and his robe gapes.

'For god's sake, Mycroft, get your gear on. That's more than I really need to see. And take this plate, it's burning my hand.'

I close the door behind me as Mycroft sits on the wheeled chair at his desk. He grinds out his smoke, puts his socked feet up on the edge of the desk and balances the plate on his velveteen-protected knees. The foil drops to the floor and he starts devouring sausages, while I do a quick surreptitious survey.

Loud music and second-hand smoke aside, the room is so much neater and nicer than the house it's like another world. Jewel-colored Christmas lights hang around the walls, making everything seem cheery and intimate. The only other light is from the Anglepoise on the desk on the right.

Half the room has been ceded to the desk in a summary take-over. The other half is occupied by the futon mattress on pallets. The bed is covered with rumpled sheets and blankets, and there's an ashtray, a stub of candle in an old wine bottle, and a stack of books – all non-fiction – on the floor nearby.

The desk is where all the action is. There's a laptop glowing in front of Mycroft's socked toes, cords and wires sprouting out of it like some sort of intestinal disease, hooking it up to a printer, an external hard drive and a set of speakers. This is where I proofread Mycroft's Diogenes articles, ensuring they make sense. Puffy headphones – last used by me, to listen to Mycroft's current favorite by The Black Keys – hang from a red plastic model of a bloke with no skin, actually a medically accurate figurine of the human musculoskeletal system.

Pushed into the back corner of the room is a wooden dresser that seems to be less concerned with housing Mycroft's wardrobe than in being the staging area for a small microscope, Bunsen burner and other chemistry-set necessities. It's where I've stood, entranced, as Mycroft poured dissolved sodium acetate straight onto the wood, grinning like an idiot as the liquid hardened in seconds into tall, fairy-white spires.

I've also been terrified, watching him dump diluted hydrochloric acid into a beaker of magnesium silicide. When the curtains caught fire from the resulting sparks, I had to grab the chemical extinguisher from the kitchen and spray everything down.

Yes, I do worry he'll blow himself up. But he's been living this way for longer than I've been around him, so I guess if he hasn't done it yet he must be being careful.

I like it in his room – the starry lights, the feeling of sanctuary. I'm still not used to dealing with a lot of other people. I've known Mycroft, and Mai and her boyfriend, Gus, since last November, and they still feel like 'a lot of other people'. Actually, Mycroft alone could probably qualify as seeming like 'a lot of other people'. He does so much crazy stuff you could imagine more than a single offender.

After the initial desperate stuffing of food into his mouth, Mycroft looks up. I put a finger in my ear. He makes an *oh, right!* lift of his chin, and reaches to turn the music down to barely audible.

I go for a nice safe deadpan. 'My dad really likes this song.'

'Your dad is a classicist.' He vacuums up another mouthful of chips. 'Thought you weren't going to come.'

'I nearly didn't,' I lie. 'Mum looked knackered tonight. I'm hoping Mike has enough sense to shoo her off to bed before she starts snoring on the couch.'

'You don't have to be the sole voice of reason in your house, y'know.' He gestures with a chip. 'Your mum's a big girl, she can take care of herself.'

I ignore him. 'What are you doing? Working on another article?'

'Not yet.' He wipes his greasy fingers on his robe. 'Got Mai on IM. She's trying to recruit me for the Furies. Says that anyone who resorts to a headbutt in a school fight is a shoo-in for roller derby.'

I grin. 'Did you point out it's an all-girl team?'

'You try talking sense into her. I've given up.'

I dump my satchel, shift a stool from near the dresser, and clear off some of the paper litter. Mycroft lowers his feet so I can squeeze in. Two windows are open on the laptop screen, one of them the IM feed. I snort, reading over what's gone before, then start typing.

MYCROFT: Watts here. *Do you really want a team member who's so lazy he's practically comatose?*

MAI: *Hey!! Are you over there again?*

MYCROFT: (W) *The curse of neighborliness.*

MAI: *Right.*

MYCROFT: (W) *What?*

MAI: *Nothing at all. What does Mycroft's room look like in real life?*

I send her a pic of the famous garbage mountain of Rio de Janeiro.

MAI: *You're exaggerating.*

Mycroft muscles me out of the way.

MYCROFT: (himself) *Of course she's exaggerating. It looks more like this.*

He sends a pic of Frankenstein's laboratory.

MYCROFT: *The resemblance is startling.*

MAI: *Stop! I just snorted Coke out my nose.*

We chat about the Furies for a bit. Mai is on a determined recruiting drive – she even asks me to join. When I point out I've never rollerskated, ever, in my entire life, she claims inexperience is no obstacle. By the time we sign off, I'm almost convinced that having no money, no time and no rollerskates would be little impediment to a burgeoning career as a Fitzroy Fury roller-derby champion.

'I can already see you in ripped fishnets, knee pads and a crash helmet,' Mycroft says in a thoughtful voice. 'Your name would be...Whacker Watts!'

Mycroft and I are on a strictly last-name basis, but he's on a strictly last-name basis with everybody. He pointed out it was perfectly appropriate in our case, anyway. He said if Sherlock had Watson, it was only fair that Mycroft should have Watts.

Yeah, we yucked it up big time with that joke.

'Right.' I grab my guitar from its spot beside the desk, strum an aimless chord and give Mycroft the eye as he eats a few more chips. 'Salad too. Mum thinks you're not getting enough vegetables.'

'Your mum, your mum,' he mutters. He starts chewing lettuce and tomato and actually looks a bit grateful.

The pause stretches while I consider asking him again. I used to ask, when we first got to know each other, and then I stopped. But I may as well give it another try.

'You could always stay for dinner, you know.' I don't want to make it an appeal, but it's an effort to keep my voice casual. 'You're over every afternoon, doing homework with me, and there's plenty of food…'

Mycroft fixes his eyes on the plate and chews on automatic. I play another chord, but my guitar is horribly out of tune, and I know I'm not going to get a reply.

'Anyway.' I clear my throat. 'Tell me about the next article.'

Mycroft snorfles a chip and revives. 'Well, I was thinking about maybe, *possibly*, doing some follow-up on a forensics article about lividity.'

'Lividity. Right.'

'You know what lividity is, yeah?'

'Something about the way blood settles in the body after death?'

'That's very good.' He sounds surprised.

'I'm picking up the lingo from you by osmosis,' I say. 'So, why lividity?'

'Oh, you know.' He chases an olive around the edge of the plate. 'Somebody put up a rubbish article, and then Diogenes replied, and then this guy from Germany starts emailing me info about lividity rates in varied temperature conditions, so I thought I might as well write something about it. But nothing I've got's confirmed yet, and the rate this bloke's getting back to me, the whole thing'll never see the light of day.'

'So when are you going to post it?'

'Never. You know the rules. Diogenes never posts before proofing the conclusions.'

'But this bloke from Germany will reply eventually, right?'

'Don't know. It's been nine days. Thought I would have heard by now. I can't send him another email, he'll think I'm stalking him.' He waves a lettuce leaf at the laptop screen. 'It'd be okay if I was affiliated with a university or something. It's not like I can send him a reminder note on official letterhead – it's just me and my online alter ego. I'm probably at the bottom of a list of replies about twenty institutions long.'

'But Diogenes has a good reputation.' I tuck an annoying piece of hair behind my ear and trail my fingers over the guitar strings. 'He never publishes without proofing—'

'We're not saying *he* or *she*, please. Diogenes is gender neutral, as far as anyone else is concerned.'

'Fine, then. Diogenes never knee-jerk publishes, always specifies it's a hypothesis and not a theorem, never rehashes an issue, always points out something other theorists have overlooked or found too trivial to pursue…'

'Thanks very much – I'm trivial now?'

'But *you're* not Diogenes,' I remind him with a grin.

He stares back at me, a satisfied smile ghosting his lips. 'You're right. I'm not Diogenes.'

I turn my head, focus on my tuning. I try plucking out 'Spanish Melody', but it depresses me somehow. Then I remember the last time I played it was on the back verandah of our old home.

I blink away the memory. 'So, have you thought any more about compiling all the articles into one site?'

Mycroft reaches over to plink one of the strings with a finger. 'Haven't got round to it. You know my hectic schedule.'

I bat his hand away. 'No, I said *I* could do it. Remember last week, when we—'

'Oh yeah.' He shrugs. 'Yeah, I suppose. I mean, it's a lot of fiddly work.' ·

'I don't mind. It'd be a change from homework and housework.'

'If you like. Lovely dinner, by the way. Cheers.' He licks his fingers – he didn't bother with the fork. There's quite a lot of food left over, but it was a massive serving.

'So what's the plan?' I rest the guitar on my knees and pull on Mike's hoodie, scooping my hair out of the collar. Some nights we just sit in Mycroft's room and talk until I get too tired.

'Well, it's Thursday.'

'Is it?' I'd misplaced the day for a moment. 'You'll be taking the thermos in to Dave.'

He nods. 'You up for the zoo?'

I shrug.

'If you're too stuffed, I can go on my own.'

'No, no…' I check the computer – it's only eight-fifteen. If I can make it back by ten I'll be in bed early enough for school; the night will still be young as far as Mycroft's concerned. 'Train or tram? Have you got enough for a fare?'

'Tram's sooner, and I'm broke.'

'Me too.'

The idea doesn't seem to bother him. 'If we move, we can get the eight-thirty-one. There's plenty of food left, so I was thinking…'

I nod. 'I nicked a packet of Jam Fancies.'

'Outstanding.'

I put my guitar aside, promising to give it more attention tomorrow. It's my standard promise. Mycroft closes up everything on the computer and stands. He seems to take up all the space in the room when he does that, probably because the ceiling's so low. I catch a flash of his wide shoulders, the keloid ridges of his scars, as he starts stripping off his robe. I look elsewhere.

When I turn back, he's dragged on today's jeans and a non-bloodstained T-shirt. He pulls on a zippered hoodie over the top of it all.

'Gimme a sec while I make the tea.' He grabs the plate with the leftover food and slides past me to the door.

'You look like a drug dealer in that hoodie,' I call out with a grin.

He gives me the finger as he walks up the hallway.

I can hear him banging around in the kitchen. He'll be boiling a saucepan of water with five extra-strong teabags, then fishing out the teabags and dumping in about half a can of condensed milk before pouring the whole mess into a giant thermos that stands ready on the kitchen bench.

I check there's nothing burning in his room, turn off the Anglepoise, and drag Mycroft's backpack and my satchel into the kitchen. I pass the bag over so he can shove the thermos and camping mugs in. It's so large he can't do the zipper right up – the thermos pokes its white plastic lid over the top. He's organized a takeaway container with the remains of the dinner. It won't fit in his bag, so I put it in mine.

'Ready to go, then?' he asks.

'Yup.'

'Lead on.' He extends a hand for me to go ahead out the back door, as if it's suddenly occurred to him to be gentlemanly.

We hit the street, walking fast. What I wouldn't give for the quad bike now, or the paddock bomb – I could have us at the zoo in no time flat. I check behind me, looking for lights on at my house.

'Worried you'll get caught?' Mycroft's grin is wolfish in the overhanging shadow of the streetlamp.

'Mum'd kill me if she knew,' I confess.

His grin widens. 'Braving the mean streets of the big smoke, eh?'

'Just walk.'

We move briskly over broken glass past parked cars and street-lights. I keep my eye on the Sydney Road intersection up ahead, listening for the warning bell of an approaching tram.

'Your aunt doesn't mind you giving away her tea?' I ask.

I'm still curious about his aunt, who I am yet to meet. She's always either at work, or she's sleeping, or out. For a while I toyed with the idea that Mycroft's aunt was a fiction, an invention that allowed him the freedom to live independently. But I know now that there's a simpler explanation, which is just that Mycroft and Angela Hudgson have a really shitty relationship.

The fact they never see each other makes things worse. Angela works long night shifts to pay the rent and utilities on their place. Even in North Coburg, the gristly heart of migrant grunge, you pay an arm and a leg – as I'm well aware.

'Angela wouldn't notice,' he says. 'Enough tea for a drowning. It's the only thing she's always stocked up on.'

We separate to swerve around a smashed cathode TV. Mycroft walks on the road.

'I've got to get back before ten,' I say. 'The usual.'

'School-night curfew?' he grins.

'For some of us,' I say primly, then spoil it when I trip over a lump in the concrete path.

'See? The upside of being a neglected child. Knew there had to be one somewhere.'

We snort together, but it's no joke. Fortunately the tram heaves into view up ahead, so we don't have time to think about it.

'Shit, there it is,' Mycroft says.

I break into a run. 'I'll hold it for you!'

'You won't make it!'

'Watch me!' I grin, and if Mycroft could see my expression in that old birthday photo he'd catch the resemblance now.

I take off and work it to the max. My satchel whacks my hip as I wring all the energy out of my legs, the muscles previously used for quad-biking and horse-riding over dodgy terrain, for long property walks and kicking fence-posts into their holes. I brake at the corner, check for whizzing cars, then dash across the two lanes. The tram doors are just about to close.

I hear Mycroft yell. 'For *god's sake*, Watts! *Traffic!*'

I push my hair back, exhilarated by the brief run, and smile at the weather-tanned man in the driver's seat until Mycroft makes it across. He arrives puffed out and glaring.

'You know you nearly got *splattered*. You *know* that, right?' He glances at the driver as he climbs aboard. 'Oh, hi, Nick. Sorry for the wait.'

The doors close behind us and we lurch as the tram starts moving.

'No trouble.' Nick has a short-sleeved uniform shirt, a gold chain around one wrist. 'Bit dicey on the road, I saw.'

'She's a country girl,' Mycroft says scathingly. 'She's still getting used to the concept of a road with more than one set of traffic lights.'

'*Former* country girl.' My voice comes out harsh. The good feeling I got from the run dries up like a creek in January. Mike's hoodie sleeves sag to my elbows as I hold the roof strap in the aisle.

Mycroft braces against the center pole and leans towards Nick's perspex window. 'How's the car coming along?'

Nick makes a considering face as he watches the tracks. 'Not bad. Not bad at all. Did well in the last raceway meeting, but she's still dragging a bit on the turns.'

Mycroft turns to me, ignoring my black expression. 'Nick's a stock racer. He just rebuilt a 1979 VB Commodore from scratch.'

'Nineteen seventy-eight,' Nick says.

'Right. Seventy-eight. Plans to take it to the nationals in June.' Mycroft turns back. 'Nick, I haven't got the fare this time.'

'Take a seat. I'll give you a tingle if I see the inspectors.'

'You're a good man, Nick.'

'Not a problem.' Nick nods, eyes forward. 'Nice shiner, by the way.'

'Cheers.' Mycroft takes my elbow as we stagger towards a rear seat.

'Is there a tram driver in this city you *aren't* on a first-name basis with?' I ask as I flump down. I'm still stinging from the 'country girl' thing. 'I mean, there's Sharman on the school run, and Glenda on Saturdays. We had Cheryl last week—'

'Nick only does alternating months.' Mycroft checks the thermos and tries to shove it farther into his backpack but it won't go. 'The racing keeps him busy.'

'You didn't answer my question.'

He blinks at me. 'Well, Watts, I'll let you in on a secret: people, if you talk to them, often talk back. Staggering concept, I know. And not frequently applied in the city, but I'm an old-fashioned guy. Chatting's not a crime, is it?'

I think of him sitting alone in the Stranger's Room in his dingy house, with the Christmas lights twinkling and his aunt constantly absent. It might be Struggle Town at my place, but at least I've got my family around.

'I guess not,' I say, glancing down as I re-knot my hair. 'So what did Conroy say to you this arvo, after I left?'

'He said, *Rachel Watts is hot stuff, and I'd like to ask her out. Got any tips?*'

'Mycroft, don't be juvenile.'

'I am a juvenile.'

'Then don't be grotesque. Are you going to tell me, or not?'

Mycroft fiddles with his cigarette pack, loose in his long fingers.

'Nothing to tell,' he says. 'Conroy uses the same material in every speech. The *we can't put up with this behavior forever* line, and the *one more stunt like this* line. I can't figure out why he keeps recycling.'

'Maybe he thinks constant repetition will make it sink in.'

'See, that's Einstein's definition of insanity right there – doing the same thing over and over again, and expecting a different result.' He tucks the pack back in his track pant pocket. 'Anyway, stop yammering and look out the window. It's your favorite bit.'

He's right. Riding the trams and trains still has a lot of novelty value for me. It's one of the few city things I actually enjoy, especially riding at night, like now.

Peeling billboards flash past, hoardings for Al Nada Sweets and the Halal Meat Shop – the one with the dinosaur-sized helpings of beef, done in photorealist style, on the shop facade. There's Harley City motorbikes, car yards with all the colored flags reduced to dust tones, bridal shops, clearance sales. Even ALDI has a glow-in-the-dark seedy radiance. My breath mists the tram window and I'm in a bubble, one of those deep-ocean submarines that studies life at a thousand meters below.

The city is still a mystery to me – cold, unfriendly, alien. Only when I'm viewing it like this, at a removed distance, does it seem as if there's any beauty, or recognizable pattern. If I could keep the city at arm's length all the time, I'd be happy. But I'm forced to interact with it on a daily basis.

When Mycroft pushes the button for our stop, I sigh. Time to step back in. Time to engage.

We thank Nick and jump off at the south end of Sydney Road, cross into Parkville at the lights, and cut past the tennis courts on the Avenue to the bike path beside the golf course. It's much darker off the main thoroughfare, no overhead lights at all.

I look up for the stars. Here, maybe here, in the dark…but there's nothing.

I take out my flashlight, rubbing my biceps through the hoodie sleeves. 'You're sure Homeless will be here tonight?'

'I'd put money on it.' Mycroft pulls out a cigarette as we walk. He touches the split in his lip carefully, sticks the smoke into the corner of his mouth. 'He never strays from Royal Park before winter.'

'Back entrance, then?'

'Or the station.' Mycroft clicks a plastic lighter and exhales into the sky.

Homeless Dave likes Royal Park. He says he enjoys being among all the trees – it is very like the bush, some of it – and Poodle can roam around a bit, without the coppers chasing them off all the time, like they do in the CBD.

Mycroft first met Dave two years ago, when Angela began at the zoo. She used to make Mycroft come with her, so she could keep tabs on him while she was working. I can understand the logic – Mycroft's school marks might be phenomenal, but his personal judgment can leave a lot to be desired. The whole plan backfired when Mycroft began ditching his homework in favor of hanging out at the coffee-and-soup kitchen on Poplar Road, botting cigarettes off the guys who ran the place and chatting to the regulars.

The soup kitchen closed up shop last year, but Homeless Dave never moved on. Mycroft started his regular visits, bringing the guy hot drinks and the occasional meal, getting the lowdown on street-life gossip – Mycroft's very own Baker Street Irregular. The first time I came along, the smell got to me. Now it just seems normal.

Mycroft and I dawdle while he finishes his smoke, following the path near the rail line. I put the flashlight away as we hit the lit-up area, veering left over Poplar. The back entrance of the zoo looks deserted and dangerous. There's no swirling garbage – the outside cleaners have done a good job in preparation for the big queues of families in the morning – but it's still a darkened alley by moonlight.

I can hear foreign-animal yowls and squawks. Far off, the trumpet of an elephant. Somewhere inside, Mycroft's aunt is doing her rounds in the administration offices with the vacuum and the dusting rags, emptying the bins. Another tidy-upperer, like my mum.

There's no sign of our grizzled old man.

Mycroft nods. 'Check the station.'

We walk through the car park, back towards the rail line. I get that feverish feeling, from exercising in the cool air – I'm sticky with perspiration under my clothes. I strip off my hoodie and tie it around my waist again. The streetlamps blat light down over the platform, the shrubs, us. I don't see Homeless Dave, or his dog.

'Call for him?'

Mycroft shakes his head. 'He'll think it's the boys in blue. Try round the back.'

We swing around the hurricane fence, where people exit the Upfield line. There's a small stretch of vegetation between the station and the golf course. The tang of gums, the smell of clay dirt, makes me dizzy with nostalgia.

We're out of range of the streetlamps now, but I strain my eyes and see the two-wheeled pull-along trolley under the arms of a big weeping willow. Overhanging branches make a little cave, a hollow out of sight of the world, exactly how Dave would like it.

'Mycroft, there.' I reach without thinking, grab Mycroft's sleeve. His arm is warm and his teeth flash in the dark.

I push away and move ahead. There's a man slumped against the tree, leaning at an angle, legs out in front.

'That's him,' Mycroft mutters, then louder, 'Dave! Dave, you old bastard, we've brought you dinner…'

The man on the ground doesn't move.

Mycroft breaks off at the same time as I stop walking. I don't know what it is – some animal instinct, a feeling of not-rightness. We're motionless at the entrance to the willow cave, both of us glued with indecision.

'Watts…' Mycroft's voice is strangely quiet.

'What is it?' I'm trying to work it out, in the dark. There's a smell, I can't place it, and something…

'Your flashlight,' Mycroft says.

I shove a hand inside my satchel and feel for the metal tube. Both of us have our eyes on the figure of the man. There's a prickle of something on my skin, something not right, something not—

'Got it.' My voice is a whisper. I direct the bulb, switch it on.

There's a pause.

Then Mycroft's voice shivers out, hoarse and unsteady. 'Shit. Oh shit…'

30

I can't speak.

Homeless Dave is sitting on the ground, propped against the trunk of the enormous willow. His legs are splayed in front at an odd angle as he lists towards us, his chin high and his head thrown back, eyes open. His throat is a mess of red, bright and dark, all the reds there are in the world, red seeping down his neck, red bleeding over the front of his chest, staining his dirty shirt. His hands are beside him, palms upraised. The strong smell is like a new penny.

I've seen sheep and cows slaughtered for meat, seen butchery, and I know what this is.

This is the sacrificial lamb.

CHAPTER THREE

'Giss another cuppa, love?' Homeless Dave said. This was last Thursday night, and it was the last time I saw him alive.

'Sure.' I took the proffered mug. 'You want me to toss this cold stuff?'

'Nah, jus' pour it in over the top. Won't bother me.'

I unscrewed the thermos lid, poured in another half a cup of tea and passed it back.

'You're a wonder, love, cheers.'

Homeless Dave had lived on the street for fourteen years and he smelled like it. He said he used to tour the CBD, until the police got orders to keep the city center clean and mean.

'They'll move you on for nothink,' he said. 'Tryin' to find a place to kip, they'll trot over and shift ya. Make the place look untidy, they reckon. Want everybody in those bloody shelters.'

'Really?' I said. 'Is that what it's like in the city?'

I was only half-concentrating on the conversation. I was playing with Poodle, pulling a bit of cardboard back and forth as he hung on to the other end with his teeth. Tug-of-war was better than patting him, because he was covered in fleas. Poodle wasn't a poodle, he was a bitsa – bitsa this, bitsa that, more Jack Russell than anything. He gave me a pretend growl and ground his jaws on the cardboard.

Homeless Dave didn't mind not having my full attention. He was just happy to talk. He rubbed his hand across his mouth, scratched through his beard.

'That's what it's like, love.' His rheumy eyes were faded. 'Must be diff'rent, eh, where you're from?'

'Pretty different,' I agreed. I liked being identified as different, not a city person. 'Some people don't like travellers on their property. But most folks would just leave you be, so long as there wasn't any mischief and you didn't light a fire in the summer.'

'Where'd you live before, love?'

'Place called Five Mile.' I concentrated on Poodle. 'West of Ouyen. It's rural – dusty, dry. You might not like it.'

'Well, I'm a city man, y'know. All me life.' Dave slurped his tea. 'You got shelters, out that way?'

I grinned. 'Haysheds, we've got. Tractor sheds. Plenty of barns, but no shelters.'

'*Shelters.*' Dave made a face. 'Kid from your school glassed a guy comin' outta the Hub last week.'

Mycroft squinted. 'Which kid?'

'Can't recall.'

'Better out here, then,' Mycroft said. He was looking around the trees as if he was considering it as an option.

We sat on a grassy place on the golf-course side of the train station, under the eucalypts. Homeless Dave sat on an old newspaper, with his rug around his knees. His old-lady shopping trolley was parked nearby, never far away.

It was eight-thirty p.m. Mycroft had already given Dave the remains of the fish and chips he'd had for dinner. Poodle shared, of course. Everything Dave got, Poodle shared. Except booze, although I couldn't be sure of that.

'Better out here.' Dave nodded. 'Walk where you like, piss where you like. No worries about me dog. Sleep up under the trees here, over there –' he gestured towards the zoo, '– if things get a bit nippy. The RP'll take me in, last resort if I'm poorly. Bot a smoke, mate?'

'Help yourself,' Mycroft said. 'Leave me a couple, yeah?'

'Absolutely, mate,' Dave said. 'Bloody expensive. Yer a good lad.'

———

If this had been Five Mile, Homeless Dave would have been a swaggie. He'd have drifted around, done a few odd jobs in outlying places for money for booze, begged a few hot meals. Probably would have rolled into the campfire after a few too many pulls on the metho bottle, ended up dead that way. Perhaps he'd have frozen to death in the winter, if he never managed to get farther than Mildura. Or maybe he'd have died of old age and infirmity, somewhere alone in a back paddock, under a tree.

This is not Five Mile. This is not last Thursday night. And Dave is lying under a tree, dead, but not the way I'd imagined.

'Oh shit,' Mycroft says again. His voice is trembling. 'Jesus…'

We stand there, staring, in the quavering gleam of my flashlight. I am frozen. I can feel the weight of my satchel, the strap pulling on my shoulder. I'm gripping the flashlight for dear life; my feet are stuck to the ground. I realize that I'm bracing my knees, so my legs don't shake.

I make myself blink, look away, look at Mycroft standing to my right. He's white, whiter than the tape on his eyebrow. His mouth is open and his eyes are incandescent, flicking every which way.

'J-just breathe.' I try to follow my own advice. 'B-breathe in, breathe out…okay…'

'He's—'

'Just, just take it slow.' My voice is wobbly, but I'm amazed by how calm I sound.

Mycroft whispers curse words. He dumps his pack, swallows hard, can't hold it. He twists and stumbles back, bends at the waist near a hakea bush. My stomach rises – I grit my teeth, listening to his gagging sounds. I can't stand there looking at Dave's body; I turn and go to Mycroft.

He's up now, wiping his mouth on his sleeve, spitting into the dirt and leaf litter. There's a bad smell of his recently-eaten dinner, the rest of which I have in a container in my satchel…I have to bear down hard then.

Something practical. I'm always saved by something practical.

I take the thermos out of Mycroft's pack, pour tea into a mug. My hands are shaking, but I get most of the tea where it's supposed to go. Mycroft drags his pack over farther until we're on a worn hump of ground under the circle of light from the streetlamp.

He sits in the dirt. I hand him the mug, and he looks grateful. I sit beside him, pour another mug. We sit and sip hot sweet tea in the round of light, where it's safe. We stare at the shaded hollow. The tree branches are tented over the shape outlined by darkness. The dead body is our silent companion.

Mycroft sips slowly. I try to stop the shaking in my knees, my hands.

'Better?' I ask softly.

'Better.' His voice rasps like a file on a stone. 'Not great. Improving.'

35

All of his entertaining quips have disappeared. His face is getting back some color, high in the cheeks. It makes his bruises livid. I blow on my tea, feel the mug warm my hands.

'Jesus,' Mycroft says.

'Yeah.'

'*Jesus.*'

I look at the place where Dave lies. It could be a normal Thursday night, his shopping trolley upright beside him. He could be sleeping, if you don't look at him by shivering flashlight.

'This is fucked. What a fucked way to die.' Mycroft's eyes are cast in shadow. 'He didn't have anything to steal, didn't have anything. All alone—'

He looks at me, eyes widening.

Anxiety floods into my stomach. 'Where's Poodle?'

'I don't—' Mycroft says.

But I'm already getting up.

Mycroft grabs the sleeve of my hoodie. 'Wait. You can't.'

'We need to find the dog.'

'You *can't*. It's a…y'know. Crime scene. Worst thing you can do, go banging around a crime scene – you'll wreck the evidence.'

I yank myself away. 'For Christ's sake, Mycroft, this isn't your *Forensics class*. We've got to find Poodle!'

'We will. Hold on.'

He puts his tea down next to mine, then stands and holds my elbow. 'Take it slow, remember? Walk back the way we went in, take a look, then we'll check around.'

That's what we do. We retrace our steps to the place we stopped first, just inside the willow cave. I swing the flashlight beam, reluctant to see it all again, but my eyes are drawn, magnetized. Dave's throat gapes like a scream.

The dog's not near him, not on this side. I cast the beam farther out to the perimeter of the cave, to the shrubs and trees nearby.

'Poodle...' I call softly.

'Poodle...' Mycroft checks under leaves for the shivering, frightened dog we imagine we'll find. He makes a wide arc around the body, crouches on the other side. 'Toss me the flashlight.'

I throw. The flashlight arcs high above Dave's prone form. Mycroft snags it. He casts the beam along the body from his side.

'Nothing over here.'

'God, where *is* he?'

'Watts, think about it. If Poodle was here, where would he be?'

I think. Dogs don't piss off, leave their masters dying alone and friendless. Dogs stay nearby, lick faces, flip their sad tails. Dogs wait for their masters to wake up.

I nod reluctantly. 'He'd be right next to Dave.'

'Right,' Mycroft says. 'So either Poodle's been done somewhere, same as Dave, or he can't get back. Whoever did this has him, something like that.'

This idea makes me feel sick. It seems like the ultimate indignity, that Dave's dog could be in the clutches of whoever did this. The nausea rides high in my throat. I push it down with short shallow breaths.

Mycroft walks the line of his own steps back to where I'm standing.

'Who dies like this?' His eyes are savage. 'Who *did* this?'

Mycroft's gaze is fixed on Dave. We've given up looking away – Dave was our acquaintance, our friend. We stare at the shocking wound on his throat. My flashlight is back in my hand. The cool metal feels like the only real thing in the world.

'C'mon.' Mycroft pulls on my sleeve as he backs away. We

return to our tea and I get a refill from the thermos. I feel dull-headed, watching Mycroft slide his phone out of his back pocket.

'What're you doing?'

'Calling triple-0.'

I nod, dumbstruck. At least one of us is thinking straight. I was the calm one at first. Now Mycroft is recovered, taking control, and I'm the one feeling small and weightless. I don't mind – this is not a competition.

Mycroft has his phone pressed to his ear.

'Hi, yeah? I need the police.' Mycroft licks his cut lip. He looks at me as he speaks. 'Yeah, hello? I've never done this before... I need to report a death.'

I can hear the tinny voices from the phone. Mycroft explains names, location, the fact that it's a murder, because we can see it. All of this speaking seems to be coming from some kind of sky radio. The words sound brittle and nonsensical. Maybe I should have thrown up too. Maybe it would have made me feel better.

'Watts, they want to talk to you.'

Mycroft passes me the phone before I can object. Now the sky radio is in my ear, a calm male voice.

'Hello, you're Mr Mycroft's friend, are you?'

'Yes, I am,' I say slowly.

'Could you give me your details then?'

'Rachel Watts, twenty-eight Summoner Street, North Coburg.'

'That's good, Miss Watts, thank you. Can you stay there with your mate until we get a car over?'

'Yeah.' I force firmness into my voice. 'Yes. I won't go anywhere.'

'Wonderful. Okay, tell Mr Mycroft that we'll be there in ten minutes or less.'

'Okay.'

The phone is disconnected. There's only buzzing in my ear. I hand the phone back to Mycroft, but the buzzing stays. My head feels as if it's full of cottonwool.

'Ten minutes or less, he said.'

'Good. Okay.' Mycroft frowns at me. 'What's going on, you feeling all right?'

I turn my face in another direction.

Suddenly Mycroft is grabbing my hand, squeezing the fingers, chafing the palm. 'Watts... Watts, hey—'

I look back at him. I take a big breath in, feel it slide back out.

Mycroft has his raw blue eyes fixed on mine. 'Watts, you're going all pale on me now. Don't do that, yeah? Here, drink this—'

He pushes a mug to my lips. I take a swallow, although I don't want to.

'That's it. Come on, buck up now.' Mycroft's head is lowered so he can keep the thread between our eyes. 'Let's get you moving... Come on.'

He pulls me to standing. I feel his warm hands rubbing the life back into my arms. Sensation is returning. It's slow, but it's there.

He makes me take another mouthful of tea. 'Watts, the police will be here soon. You've got to help me with something.'

'Help you with what?' I still sound odd. I can feel a tingling in my cheeks.

'You've got to help me document the scene.'

'What?'

'Pictures. I want pictures. SOC.'

'What are you talking about?'

'Scene-of-crime shots.'

39

I curl my lip. 'Mycroft, that is about the most disgusting thing I've ever—'

'It's not for *me!*' he squawks. 'Jesus! What, you think I get down and dirty with this stuff late at night or something? It's *evidence*, Watts.'

I make a face. 'What, you want to—'

'There has to be something we can do. Something we might see. It could help.' He pulls out his phone. 'I'll take the photos, you just help me out.'

'The police will be here soon.'

'Then we better be quick. Come on.'

I take two deep, slow breaths. I'm not sure I'm ready to go down to the hollow again, but Mycroft is already striding towards Dave's resting place. He skirts the body, hunching his shoulders under the branches, watching his footfalls.

I walk closer, enter the grotto. Mycroft takes shots of the approach, the path we're on, the shrubs. The flash from his phone in camera mode flares everything into millisecond-brilliance. There's Dave's trolley. Dave's hand flung out, the other flopped. Dave's boots, much-repaired with cardboard inserts – I can see the holes under the sole on the left one.

I focus on the blood. It's bright red, very fresh. There's a smell of recent slaughter. Puddles of the stuff congeal on Dave's chest, on his lap, on the ground. I feel dizzy again. I swing my eyes back to Mycroft, hunkered down about a meter from the body.

'What's that, under his bum?' he says.

I play the flashlight beam over the spot. There's a scrunched-up hamburger wrapper poking out from beneath Dave's left leg. Mycroft takes a shot. I look at the trolley again.

'If they killed him, why didn't they go through the trolley?'

Mycroft takes another shot of the trolley, its tracks in the dirt.

My brain is starting to function again. 'Take shots of the...his throat. Close-ups.'

Mycroft looks straight at me. 'Go in closer. Watch your feet.'

'What do you need—'

'Hold your flashlight up there, next to his head as a measure.'

I step as close as I can without creating new footprints in the dirt. I squat down for balance and hold the flashlight close to the body. The bulb casts a shimmering shaft of radiance high up into the treetop. Where the metal base nudges Dave's shoulder, there's a soft fleshy pliability. Mycroft's camera flares.

I shiver, I can't control it. The smell is rank, overpowering. I get a sharp unsteadying memory: me and Mike and Dad, cutting the sheep we'd just hung by its back legs. We'd used the humane bolt-killer first. Dad had slashed the throat, putting a bucket underneath to catch the blood, all the blood, so much...

I breathe through my mouth, force my hand still.

'That's good.' Mycroft takes another shot. 'Now I'm going to take it from the other side.'

'Hurry,' I say. I can feel the hurry in my voice.

Mycroft takes rapid shots three-sixty degrees around the body. He even holds the phone up from behind the tree. He stays the requisite few meters away, no closer.

'I wish I could get in there...'

'Don't,' I say.

'Do you think he's in rigor mortis?'

'How should I know?' But I look anyway. Dave's lips are relaxed over his teeth, his hands uncurled. I remember the press of the flashlight at his shoulder, the lack of resistance. 'I don't...No. I don't think so.'

41

'Me neither. So he's either been killed in the last one to five hours, or he's been dead like this all day.'

'How do you know all this stuff?'

Mycroft scratches a hand through his hair. He looks rattled. 'From forensics research. Rigor gives an approximate time of death. It sets in within about five hours, and lasts about twenty-four hours, then the body relaxes again.'

Surely the police are taking longer than ten minutes to arrive? I bite my lip. 'Back off. It must be nearly time.'

'Okay, that's it. Wait, one more.'

Mycroft steps in to the place where I held the flashlight and takes close-ups. He backtracks quickly and we both return to the spot where we left our mugs.

'Do you really think he's been dead like this all day?' I ask.

'No. Someone'd notice, wouldn't they?'

'I don't know.' I scan the skyscrapers in the distance, feeling disoriented. Where are the stars? 'It's a big city. Who'd notice an old bloke lying against a tree in the park?'

'It's too close to the station.' Mycroft waves a hand back towards the platform. 'People coming past here all day. Plus there's no insects, and the smell and color of the blood...'

'I was thinking it reminded me of when we butchered a sheep last winter.' I tuck my arms around myself, look away. 'God, that sounds awful.'

Mycroft's eyes are grim. 'I think he was killed in the last few hours.'

There's a sound of sirens, far, near, nearer, the flash of red and blue.

'I guess we're about to find out,' I say.

———

I could tell you what happened from start to finish, but the first part was kind of boring. Which sounds ridiculous, like I've been questioned by police so many times that I'm jaded or something. That's not true.

One officer was a woman, hair in a dark plait. She wanted all the details – names, addresses, dates of birth, time we found the body, phone contacts. She asked us what our business was with the deceased. Mycroft shot back that it was a bit impersonal, saying 'the deceased', as if he didn't have a name. But then Mycroft had no idea what his real name was, apart from just 'Homeless Dave'. The female officer gave him a look, and went to speak to the next car that arrived, a Highway Patrol vehicle.

More cops in uniforms. I've only had a couple of dealings with uniformed police. Once when our hay shed in Five Mile got torched by a local hoon and once when the property was being foreclosed. The bank had heard that Dad was getting edgy, so the cops showed up for the final move out. Nothing came of it, of course. Dad went meekly in the end.

But the Five Mile cops are just Jared Capshaw and Derrin Blunt, and everyone knows them. They wear their sidearms, but they're mostly for show. The shotgun in the squad car is for shooting half-dead roos or livestock on the side of the road.

These cops aren't Jared or Derrin. Their shirts are well pressed, their caps are square, and the men are clean-shaven. They stand stiffly, and their flashlights are a lot bigger and heavier than mine.

Mycroft and I work our way through the thermos of tea. Mycroft smokes, answering questions in a billow of exhale and picking at the tape on his eyebrow.

A third car arrives, then a fourth, unmarked. I realize this is going to be a long night, for them and us. I check my phone.

No messages, but I see the time and swear under my breath.

'What's that?' asks another officer, with a thin body and long face.

'I said I'd be home at ten.' I'm fretting, because I'd said no such thing, hadn't actually given any indication that I was *going* anywhere. Mum and Dad are going to kill me, but I don't want to call. The sound of Mum's frantic voice would make everything worse.

'That'll have to wait.'

The man who says this is about Dad's age, taller than me. He's stocky, thick in the waist, like a high-school footy player run to seed. His carroty-red hair is unflattering – he's already dealing with a pockmarked face and a knobbly, bulbous nose. His suit looks as if he's been wearing it all day and his tie is crumpled. But he seems alert, observant, maybe because of the takeaway cup of coffee he's carrying.

'You're Mr Mycroft, is that right? And Miss Watts?'

We nod in unison. The man wears the serious Face of Authority.

'My name is Detective Senior Sergeant Vincent Pickup, from St Kilda Road station. I'm going to ask you a few questions now, if you don't mind, and you'll feel like you're repeating yourselves a bit, but that's just the way we do things I'm afraid.'

He takes a sip from the hole in the plastic lid of his cup. Blunt fingers on his other hand open his police notebook.

'James Mycroft.' He glances at his notes, pointing his cup at Mycroft, then at me. 'Rachel Watts. Both of Summoner Street, North Coburg, is that right?'

'Yes,' I say.

'Boyfriend, girlfriend, is it?'

'No!' I balk at the same time as Mycroft gives a 'hah' of expelled breath.

Pickup stares.

'We're not going out.' My voice is firm. 'We're just mates.'

'Neighbors,' Mycroft adds.

'Neighbors,' I say.

Pickup waits to see if there's more. When there's nothing forthcoming, he moves on. 'Right. Came down by tram, you said?'

Mycroft nods and takes a drag on his smoke. He drops the glowing filter and stands on it, then picks up the butt and puts it in the back pocket of his jeans.

Detective Pickup blinks. 'You'll get the nod from the SOCOs, doing that stuff.'

'Scene of Crime Officers?' Mycroft asks.

'That's right. They like neatness.' Pickup takes a swig from his coffee. 'You drop any other butts nearby?'

'No, sir.' Mycroft is using his best polite voice. It comes out slightly more plummy than his usual speech. 'Did the same for all of them. Back pocket.'

Pickup nods. I can't tell if he's approving or just noting. 'I'll ask one of the SOCOs to see you. They'll want one.'

'Ash testing?'

I can see Mycroft's absorbing everything. I suppose that stands to reason. Some of his online papers have covered exactly this scientific ground.

'Yes.' Pickup narrows his eyes. 'Got an interest, have you?'

Mycroft nods. 'Forensics class. At school.'

'And where'd that be?'

'North Coburg Secondary. Watts, too.'

'Right.' Pickup turns his dark-red brows towards me. 'Miss Watts. No connection with the zoo, other than coming here to see this bloke, the one we're all staring at?'

'No.' I backpedal. 'But there's Mycroft's aunt. She works in the zoo, cleaning staff—'

'We'll speak to her,' Pickup says. 'Dave hasn't got a longer name?'

'Not that we know of. He's always just been Dave. Homeless Dave, we call him. We bring him something to eat and a bit of tea sometimes, I've still got the…um, his dinner, here…'

I start rooting in my satchel. There's the hard edge of the container and the crinkle of cellophane when I hit the Jam Fancies. Detective Pickup waves a hand that brings me to my senses.

'That's fine.' He tilts his head at me. 'Bit shocking, I imagine.'

'Pardon?' My brain still isn't functioning properly, apparently.

Pickup has noticed. 'Shocking. To come upon something like this.'

'Yeah. Well…' I feel my face blank out. Suddenly I'm reliving the feeling I had when I first saw Dave's body. My lips go cold. 'I've only known him for a few months. But he…he was a friend.'

'Hm.' Pickup glances at Mycroft. 'You've known him longer?'

'Yeah. About two years.' Mycroft can't help looking over to the body. People are moving around the edges of the scene. Someone is unrolling blue-and-white tape around the tented branches of the willow cave. It looks like a ribbon around the hem of a crinoline ball gown. 'He wasn't, y'know, desperate. He was a bit of a boozer, but not too bad. Not off his face all the time.'

'And here's his regular spot?'

'He moved around a bit. If it got too cold in the park, he'd shift closer to the station, the zoo, even go over to the tram stop on Elliott Avenue.'

'Not odd, you reckon?'

'Odd? He was a homeless, sure he was *odd*—'

'No,' Pickup says. 'Odd, as in a couple of teenagers making pals with a homeless bloke.'

Mycroft squints, as he does when he's deciding whether you're taking the piss. 'Not really. I mean, you chat to the postman, don't you? The lady at the checkout? I used to come with my aunt, hang out at the soup kitchen. Soup kitchen moved on, Dave didn't. So I started coming with the thermos every week...'

'Making your rounds, so to speak.' Pickup's eyes are very still and bright.

'So to speak.'

'And nobody else loitering around, taking an interest.'

'No.'

'No other mates of yours, making pals with Dave...'

'No.'

'What happened to your face, son?'

'Some wanker at school.'

Mycroft's voice has a steely quiet. I glance back and forth between him and Pickup. I'm hoping I won't need to intervene, explain how truly harmless my eccentric friend is, despite all his bruises.

Pickup looks away first, to the notebook again. 'You'd chat to him, then?'

'Yeah, mostly. He'd cadge a cigarette, chat. You know.'

'Chat about what?'

Mycroft sighs, as though he's sick of it. We're taking turns being on our game tonight. He rolls his head on his neck, looking exhausted. I'm feeling more alert than when I first arrived.

'Chat about what, Mr Mycroft?' Pickup says.

'You know, just crapping on. About being on the street, places he'd been...'

'He has a dog,' I interrupt. 'Poodle, it's called. It's not a poodle.'

Detective Pickup puts his cup down in the dirt between his feet, takes a pen out of his breast pocket. He writes *DOG? Poodle – name*, in careful letters in the notebook.

'A mutt, is it?'

'Yeah.' I feel like saying that calling someone's life companion a 'mutt' is a bit rude. 'Bitsa. Small, short-haired, Jack Russell-cross-everything else. We had a look for him, but he's not here.'

'Hm,' Pickup says.

'I mean, unless something happened to him, he'd be here. That's just what I think.'

'Okay.' Pickup makes the face that says, *thank you for providing this useful information*, the one he must use for the general public. 'Look, this is going to go on for a while. Hours, probably.'

He looks over as yet another police car arrives. This one parks right up on the verge. Three guys get out in jeans and clean shirts, and start pulling on blue plastic overalls. They swathe their legs, arms, velcro themselves up to the neck. Blue hoods go on, white paper face-masks.

'Right, SOCO's arrived.' Pickup checks his watch, the pages of the notepad flopping. 'I'd like you both to stay here, if you don't mind, just a bit longer. Then we'll assist you to get back to your homes. Anything you need?'

'I really need to go to the loo,' I admit. I've been having trouble stopping myself from jigging from one leg to the other. All that tea.

'Right. I'll get Officer Costas over, she can take you to the public toilet.'

'I need to see my aunt,' Mycroft says.

'Costas can take you both over to the zoo entrance. Use the toilets there, see your aunt – two birds with one stone. That okay?'

48

'Great,' I say with relief.

'Back in a minute,' Pickup says.

Then he's gone, and Mycroft and I are standing in the same spot we've been occupying for what feels like the last twenty years. I can't help myself, I jig a bit, hug my arms across my chest.

'You don't really need to see Angela, do you?' My knees are goosebumped. I'm glad I have Mike's hoodie, because the temperature's dropped about ten degrees.

Mycroft has his hands bunched into the pockets of his hoodie, stretching the fabric down. The tape on his eyebrow is starting to come loose where he's picked at it.

'No,' he says. 'Prefer not to, actually. She'll be in a total flap because it's the police. But I need to get the hell out of this place for a bit.' He looks up as the SOCO people brush past us. 'Right, here we go.'

'What's that?'

'Don't know,' he admits. 'Just want to see what they do.'

What they do is start with photos, from every possible angle. They collect dirt and soil samples, everything into paper bags, plastic bags, ziplocked. They scour the scene around the body before they even go near Dave.

Pickup goes over to speak to one of them. The man he speaks to, full moon suit on, walks back to us slowly, as though he's on a planet with lighter gravity than ours.

'D'tective s'd y'ad—' He stops, pulls the face-mask down, smiles. He's a nice-looking guy in his twenties, with slightly bulging eyes. 'Sorry. Detective said you had something for us. Some cigarette butts?'

'Oh, yeah.' Mycroft fishes in his back pocket and pulls out nearly a dozen butts. 'You want the lot?'

'One's plenty,' the Scene of Crime Officer says cheerfully. 'Thanks. And we'd like to say a general thank you, as well. Didn't touch anything, didn't move anything. A good neat crime scene.'

'Except for the puke in the bushes.' Mycroft's voice is listless.

'Yeah. Except for that, you did great.' The guy grins. 'We saw how you retraced your footprints. Even some of the police didn't do that.'

'Mycroft does Forensics in school as an extension course,' I say lamely.

'Well, it certainly makes things easier. Cheers.' Then the guy registers Mycroft's bleak face. 'Um, sorry for your loss, by the way. He was someone you knew?'

'He was a friend,' Mycroft says, voice soft.

The SOCO guy bobs his head. 'Right. Sorry again. Thanks for the cigarette end.'

He doesn't seem to know what else to say then, so he retreats. We stand there and watch the SOCOs gently touching the body. They open the bloodsoaked collar of Dave's grimy shirt. As they turn his hands to put paper bags over them, we see how his fingers have stiffened, started to curl.

Mycroft sighs. 'Rigor mortis. One to five hours.'

'You knew that.'

'Yeah...' His head is down, his eyes closed. He touches the sore spots on his face with the pads of his fingers. 'I don't know what I know anymore. Shit.'

I uncross my arms and put one hand on his back. It feels awkward at first, then more natural. My hand lifts as Mycroft breathes deep into his ribcage. We stand like that until the uniformed officer, Costas, comes to lead us away.

CHAPTER FOUR

Mai nudges my shoulder. 'So what did your parents say? Did they go completely mental?'

'A bit.' I wince. 'A lot. Mum started crying when she saw the police. I had to do a total song-and-dance number before she calmed down. You can imagine.'

'I can *imagine*, yes.' Mai stretches, hugs her knees. Today's T-shirt has a picture of a zombie in a business suit. 'If I showed up at home, middle of the night, with the cops in tow, my mum would have an aneurysm.'

I'm plonked on the bench seat under the big scribbly gum near the school library. Mai is sitting beside me in knee-high striped socks. Her boyfriend, Gus, slouches on the brick retaining wall near the footpath, folding a gum leaf carefully into halves, quarters, eighths. His skin is so dark the filtered light from above is reflected in it.

Last night has taken on an unreal aspect, like something I watched on TV once. Now I'm just getting the odd unnerving flare of the flashlight, shades of red. The feeling of panic is evaporating in the glossy heat of the morning.

Mai waves at another senior girl walking by. Junior kids wander past holding their clingwrapped food. There's an empty chip packet flapping near the leg of the bench seat. When I have to focus on something, I focus on that.

'At least your mum doesn't lapse into unintelligible Vietnamese when she's stressed,' Mai says.

'No. Mine just goes apeshit in English.'

Gus selects another leaf. 'What about your dad? And Mycroft's auntie wasn't upset?'

I can't speak for Angela, Mycroft saw her while I was in the loo. But Dad was okay – he's always better with emergency stuff. Mum's not a complete hysteric, but when it comes to me and Mike she can get herself in a lather. I spoke to Dad this morning, after his shift, then called Mum's cleaning outfit and explained she'd be in late. Dad pointed out that a few more hours of sleep wouldn't hurt her, given the circumstances.

I felt a bit annoyed. It was me who saw the horrible dead body, but Mum was the one who got to have a sleep-in.

Which must be what Mycroft decided to do as well. Since we said goodnight to each other in the back of the police squad car twelve hours ago there's been no sign of him.

Mai squints at me, mind-reading. 'Where's Mycroft?'

'You tell me and we'll both know.'

'Probably using the whole thing as an excuse to skip. Bastard.' She rolls her eyes, possibly wishing that she too could use the brutal murder of a friend as an excuse to bail from school. 'He should be here. He's studying fingerprints and crime scenes all the time in class, he should be used to it.'

I think of Mycroft walking carefully around the willow circle, Mycroft holding up his phone as the flash exploded...Mycroft heaving into the bushes.

'I don't think so,' I say. I look at the chip packet. 'I don't think you get used to it. Not when it's like that.'

Mai nudges my shoulder again. 'Rubbish way to spend your Thursday night, anyway.'

The bell rings. I'm relieved to change the topic. Mai is heading for Legal Studies, and Gus for PE, and I won't see them again until lunch. I just have to worry about my Chem homework now, something more mundane. Mundane can be quite good, I'm discovering. Quite calming.

———

I keep my eyes open for Mycroft in third period, then fourth. He doesn't walk in late, doesn't walk in at all. The bell rings for lunch. I'm thrusting crap into my locker when I get a tap on the shoulder.

I jump like a rabbit. 'Jesus!'

'Watts, you've got to learn to relax.' Mycroft grins at my furious expression. 'Not a guilty conscience, is it? You been offing old duffers out in the park again?'

'That's not *funny*.' I slam my locker shut and spin around. 'Where have you been? I've been fielding bloody Twenty Questions from Mai and Gus all morning. The least you could do is arrive on time to help.'

The paper tape on his face droops as he makes eyebrows. 'Sorry. I had a pressing need to sleep after being kept up half the night by the police. And then I had something to do. But I'm here now.'

'What did you have to do that was so important?'

'Tell you later. But now I want you to explain what I missed in

53

Chem, so I don't get my head bitten off by Mr Knox on Monday.'

'Come on then,' I say dully. 'I'll summarize on the way.'

I'm always so obliging. I wonder where I get it from, which gene code it was written into: *Rachel will be polite at all times.* Even when she doesn't want to be polite. Even when she wants to clobber something, such as the tall boy walking next to her down the concrete path to the sports oval.

Mai and Gus are waiting for us underneath the big tree. At least they have the consideration not to look too eager.

Mycroft gives them his version of events, surprisingly underplayed. I lie on my stomach on the warm grass, propping up my chin with my hands. Maybe the lack of sleep from last night is starting to get to me.

'What, they kept your *cigarette butts*?' Gus's forehead wrinkles up.

'Forensic procedure.' Mycroft manages to look knowledgeable as he scrounges in my satchel for something to eat.

'My god.' Mai pushes off Gus's chest to sit upright. 'And you two were lurking around before the police even came. The guy who did it might have still been there!'

'We weren't there long before the cops came,' I say. 'And we didn't see anyone.'

But my mind starts racing. *Was* someone there, who slipped away? We weren't in any fit state to notice. I squeeze my hands into the grass, trying to get the chill off my fingertips.

'But he *could* have been there,' Mai insists. I wish she'd shut up now, but there's no stopping her when she's on a roll. 'It's common, isn't it, for murderers to hang around near the place where they did the deed? To see what happens – I read about it.'

'That's true.' Mycroft crunches into the apple I had left over from morning recess and speaks through a mouthful. 'But you don't know about the *he*, it might've been a *she*.'

'Statistically, that's rubbish,' Mai says. 'It's so completely *random*, though. I mean, killing a homeless man that way... What's the point?'

'There is no point.' I hunch my shoulders. My voice sounds toneless and odd. 'It was horrible, and pointless. That's what makes it so awful.'

'No.' Mycroft nudges me with his foot. 'Horrible, and awful, yes, but not pointless. Murder's never pointless. People who kill other people have a reason buried inside their heads somewhere. You just have to figure out what it is.'

Mai snorts. 'And *you're* going to figure it out, is that it?'

Uh-oh. I push off the grass to sit up, frowning at Mycroft's calm expression. I'm getting an uneasy feeling in my stomach.

'Mycroft, you've got nothing to go on,' Mai says. 'You were there, you saw what you saw, but now the police have to sort it out.'

'Well, that sounds very logical.' Mycroft chucks the half-eaten apple over his shoulder. 'Except we've got something the police haven't got.'

The feeling in my stomach becomes a roiling mass, like a big bag of eels.

Mai curls back onto Gus's chest. '*Right*. And what's that? A written confession from the killer? Next you'll be telling me you've hacked into the police database, and I'll know you're full of shit.'

Mycroft smiles broadly, looks at me.

'Actually, he's telling the truth.' My face is tight, but I force the words out. 'We have got something.'

Mai stares. 'What?'

'We've got *this*,' Mycroft says.

With what strikes me as unnecessary dramatic flourish, he whips his phone out of his back pocket. He brandishes it high, as if he's holding the Olympic torch, or the sword of Excalibur, or something equally ridiculous.

Mai looks at him as though he's lost the plot. 'Your phone. Against the murderous forces of criminal evil.'

Mycroft nods, grinning stupidly. 'Yes!'

'It's not just the phone,' I say. 'It's the photos he's got on it.'

Gus makes a noise which could be a swear word in either of his two native languages. 'You took photos of the *murder*?'

'Seriously?' Mai's eyes goggle.

'Well no, we didn't take photos of the *murder*.' Mycroft waggles the phone, losing some of his sense of theater. 'We took photos of the *scene*, before the police arrived. First documentation, y'know. It's important.'

'That's just…' Mai is flabbergasted. She stares at Mycroft, switches to me. '*Both* of you?'

I point at Mycroft. 'It was his idea!'

'That's gross.' Gus grimaces. I guess he's been thinking about what taking crime scene photos might involve. 'Smart, but gross.'

'Gross, but useful,' Mycroft says.

'Illegal, but audacious.' Gus grins.

'So where are the hard copies?' Mai asks.

Mycroft looks over innocently. 'Of what?'

'The *photos*?'

'Oh. They're still printing, at my place. They were taking ages, so I thought I'd drop in at school for a bit.'

'School being a mere distraction from your more pressing duties.' I sound waspish.

Mycroft glances at me. 'At the moment, yes.'

Oh god. I've seen this before, and I know the signs. Mycroft is well and truly committed now. He's got an idea in his head, and everything else has faded into background wallpaper.

If you looked inside his brain at this moment you'd see all the little synapses, Catherine wheels and penny bangers and skyrockets, all firing off into space in some sparkling display of gathering momentum. I don't want to look into his brain. Looking into his eyes is bad enough.

'So, you two are going the full Conan Doyle on this now?' Gus asks. 'Living up to your names and everything?'

'Pardon?' Mycroft thumbs his split lip.

Gus speaks more slowly. 'You two are *investigating* this now, are you?'

I say 'No', quite firmly, at exactly the same time Mycroft says 'Yes'.

Mycroft gives me a sharp, surprised stare. 'Watts—'

'Look, can we not talk about this anymore?'

I just want to walk away, go to class, not think about gaping throat wounds, or congealing blood, or the look on Mycroft's face.

Mai grins at Mycroft. 'You know that's slightly ridiculous, don't you?'

He smiles. 'Why?'

'Because...because you're teenagers.' Mai's expression says it should be obvious. 'Mycroft, this isn't like figuring out who spray-painted some guy's car. This is *murder*.'

'The principles are the same,' he insists.

'But you're both minors. And you have no access to police information, no experience, no forensics lab, no authority...'

'Mai, are you trying to bring me down or something?'

Gus, who usually only gets emotive about things like soccer, suddenly leans forward.

'I think you should do it.' He glances at me and Mycroft in turn. 'This homeless guy, it's not like his death is going to be a major priority, is it? The police won't bend over backwards to bring his killer to justice or anything. He was a derelict with no family. So you two are the only ones who even care.'

I feel like hitting him over the head. Great – just what Mycroft needs, more encouragement.

The end-of-lunch bell peals. Thankful for small mercies, I get up, dust off my arse, and break the spell.

'Well, it's been a laugh. I'll see you all in English.'

I burn off towards the edge of the oval, slinging my satchel over my shoulder, aiming for the Biology wing but really just heading for anywhere, anywhere with a little distance. Images of camera flash, darkness, tumble around in my head. The tang of copper hovers on my tongue. I clench my fists, try to blank everything out.

I've almost made it to D Block when Mycroft sprints up behind me.

'Watts!'

I don't answer.

'Watts! Come on, Watts, wait...'

His ridiculously long legs make short work of my trailblazing march. 'Hey, slow down. Jesus. Think of my smoker's cough.'

'Mycroft, I really need to get to Biology.'

'No you don't.' He grabs my arm. His touch is warm but insistent, and strong enough to stop my forward momentum. 'Hey. I thought you were on board with all this.'

'Whatever gave you that impression?' I shake my arm loose.

My tone is so caustic it's a wonder my tongue doesn't drop off. 'And by *all this*, you mean investigating Dave's death?'

'Of course that's what I mean. What's your problem?'

I glare at him. 'Is this some kind of game to you or something?'

'What?'

'Last night we saw a *murder*, Mycroft. Not a bloody traffic accident, or a, a—' I lose the thread, my hands flailing.

Mycroft puts his hands on my shoulders. 'You were scared. It was full-on, I *know* that, I was *there*. I was scared too—'

'It's not *about* being scared!'

I pull away, tramp up the concrete stairs to D Block. More people are around now. We're getting a few curious looks; they probably think it's some relationship drama. That I can't correct their impression is just another irritation.

'So what *is* it?' Mycroft says. 'Jesus, Watts—'

I fling around.

'You don't get it, do you?' My eyes are getting hot but I blink it back. 'This isn't some kind of intellectual puzzle. It's not another bloody article, or a news headline, *Vagrant Killing Still Unexplained*. Dave is *dead*. I thought you cared about him—'

'I do care!' Mycroft's voice explodes off the walls nearby. 'Bloody hell, if I didn't care why would I bother trying to figure out who killed him?'

He stops, breathing hard.

I examine his face, wanting so very much to believe him. 'So that's all this is?'

'Yes!'

'And it's not just something for you to obsess over. Like your newsfeeds.'

'No!'

'Like Gary's spray-paint problem.'

'That hardly took up any brain-space at all...' He sees my look. 'Again, *no*.'

I twist my satchel strap in both hands. 'Mycroft, tell me this isn't about you writing a few papers for Diogenes to post on some online criminology journal or something.'

'It's not. I swear, Watts, that's not what this is about.'

'Tell me this isn't—'

Tell me this isn't about your parents, I nearly say, but I pull back right on the precipice.

'What?'

'Nothing.' I close my eyes and sigh.

Mycroft tilts his head. 'Watts, don't you think we could do something to help? Something good?'

'Yes. No. I don't know.' I can't believe I'm vacillating like this. My god, I am just as mental as he is.

'C'mon, Watts. Help me out.' Mycroft's face is imploring, which is almost gratifying. 'Because I could do this on my own, but... I don't want to.'

'Right.' I roll my eyes. 'You need me to be your Watson.'

'That's right.'

'Because your genius doesn't work unless it's being lavished with attention.'

Mycroft just grins. 'Come on. I'll walk you to Biology.'

———

Mycroft takes off from English as soon as the bell goes, saying he needs to do some research. Mai and Gus want to spend some time canoodling before Gus catches his train.

It will be a great relief to everyone, particularly Gus, when

Mai gets up the guts to tell her mother that she's going out with a Sudanese boy. Right now she's paralyzed by the idea that her mum will go off her rocker – the much-vaunted Vietnamese aneurysm. I guess all the zombie T-shirts in the world can't overcome the terrible power of parental disapproval. I can sympathize.

The afternoon seems infinitely more boring without my regular routine with Mycroft to look forward to. I get off the tram at Summoner Street and walk fast, past the tomato garden in front of Mrs Gantinas's (another Mycroft contact), past the telly carcass. I walk straight to the house. For the past four and a half months this white-stuccoed horror has been like the Watts family way station.

I still have dreams about our old home. The bleached verandah timbers and corrugated iron roof glowed in the distance during the final roundup, when the bank managers came in.

The air was ripe with dust and the smell of sheep shit. I was skirting woolly legs, jumping fences, whistling dogs – basically working my arse off. Mum had started the billy fire over near the ute. Dad made the chirrup, flapping his hands like he was shooing flies, to get the rest of the cut into the stock pens. Mike waved his hat at a bolting ewe, to head her off. I loved the fact that we were all working together, a team, a unit, even though it was the last time.

Even though I felt like I was being stabbed in the heart.

I used to believe that a home was forever – a place you've worked to make nice, a comfy nest you return to at the end of the day. Thinking of what we've lost makes me feel bruised inside, like a ram has thumped me in the guts before running out of the stockyards.

Anyway.

I dump my bag in the kitchen. Normally Mycroft and I would be doing homework at the yellow table, but now I'm thrown. I head for my room. My much-abused laptop whines when I open it up. There's only one email, from Carly.

Carly was my best friend when I was living in Five Mile and doing Distance Education. Our friendship has survived bushfires, stock theft, essay deadlines, and boyfriend dramas. Which is pretty amazing, considering we've never met face to face.

Since I've moved to the city, though, her emails have developed a certain tone. This letter has the same feeling, a disdain for the fact that I'm living in the big smoke. It hurts, too, to hear about her family's property. The hurt's been creeping into my own replies. It's not as if I *want* to live in Melbourne, or I ever had a *choice*.

Things have changed a lot in four-and-a-half months. Ether-space doesn't have the same weight as meat-space, as Carly used to say. I'm not isolated anymore, not desperate for contact – I get as much contact with people in meat-space as I can handle. I'm no longer part of the internet education crew. A distance is starting to develop between us, which is weird when you think that distance was the thing we originally had in common.

I answer her email anyway, finish it before I get too depressed. I head back out to the laundry, put a load of washing on, then start plowing through my homework in the kitchen. It's nearly five-thirty before I realize I'd better get dinner on.

I've just finished slicing the gravy beef for the casserole when Dad wanders into the kitchen from the backyard, sweat-covered and bristly. His KingGee shorts are grotty with mud; he has dirt on his face and hands. It all looks so achingly familiar and out of place.

'Hey, love.' He gets himself a drink from the tap, drains the mug in four long swallows, grimacing at the chlorine taste. 'God almighty.'

Dad's been waging a one-man war against the barren eyesore that is the yard of our rental house. He's barely stopped mowing, clipping, pruning and composting since we arrived. Right now, he's obsessed with pulling out the abandoned stump of a Hills Hoist planted – for maximum ugliness – in the dead center of the backyard. He's been worrying at it like a dog with a bone.

'Hit a rough patch?' I sauté the beef and attack the onions.

'It's always the same patch,' Dad says, resigned. Then something registers in his eyes. 'Hey – what about that business from last night? You hear anything about it?'

'Nothing.'

'Bloody hell. What a thing to happen. You all right?'

I shrug. It's the standard response in our family when you can't explain what you're feeling.

'No collywobbles?'

'A little bit,' I admit. 'I try to leave the collywobbles to Mum.'

Dad rolls his eyes and takes off his hat to rub more sweat into his head. His salt-and-pepper hair stands up like a galah's crest.

'Ay caramba.' The way he pronounces the phrase, you'd never recognize it as Spanish. 'Yeah, your mum got into a flap. She's just worried, you know.'

'Yeah, I know.'

'She already thinks the city is a black pit of iniquity…' He looks around absently. 'Where's Mycroft? Thought you two were study buddies?'

'Oh, he's off on some project.' *Project Catch Dave's Killer* – I can't say that to Dad. 'Anyway, it's Friday. We can get some study in over the weekend.'

'Right.'

'I can't believe we've got practice exams in four weeks.' I'm chopping the carrots now. 'It just seems bizarre.'

'Well, it's your last year, isn't it? Given any thought to what's gonna happen after school?'

'What?' My knife is arrested mid-chop. 'Dad, we've only just arrived *here*. I'm not really thinking that far ahead.'

Dad's eyebrows come together. 'Well, Rache, I think maybe you should. What if you want to go to uni?'

'Can we afford that?'

The air between us goes still.

Dad puts down his mug. 'Rachel, if that's what you want to do, then we can afford it. You let me and Mum worry about the finances, okay?'

I nearly say *Yeah, and look how well that turned out last time.* I bite my lip. 'Well,' I fumble, 'there's some ag courses I was thinking about. You know – farm management.'

'You don't want to…y'know, aim a bit higher? A profession? Your marks are pretty good.'

I concentrate on cutting potatoes into neat cubes. 'Farming's a profession. I know farming. And I want to *do* something, something physical—'

'You want to get out of the city.' Dad sounds doleful.

'Is that such a bad thing?'

Dad chooses his words carefully. 'No, love, that's not a bad thing. But just…give it some thought, okay? Will you do that?'

'Sure. Sure, Dad, I'll give it some thought.'

I've given it some thought. I gave it some thought on the day we loaded up the truck and arrived here. My thought process lasted about two seconds.

I try a change of topic. 'So how's the Hills Hoist going?'

Dad seems as relieved as me to move on to something else. 'Well, it's getting there. Bit slow, y'know, with just the mattock and shovel. Whoever installed it overdid the cement. But I reckon I can get it out by the end of the weekend.'

'Dad, I know you're not on shift tonight, but you're working all day tomorrow and Sunday. When are you gonna get the time to attack the garden over the weekend?'

'I want to get it out.' He runs the tap for more water. 'I'm sick of it. It's sitting there like a big sore thumb...'

'So let it sit. It can wait a few more days, can't it?'

'*Rachel.*' Dad fixes me with a glare. 'I tell you what. You take care of your business and I'll take care of mine, okay?'

Without drinking his water he plonks the mug down, slaps his hat back on and stalks out of the kitchen.

The world's gone all watery. I swipe at my face with the back of my hand as I fry the vegetables, make a gravy, and pour it all into the casserole pot. I shove the whole thing in the oven, give the timer a vicious twist.

Dad and I agree on things. We don't *never* fight, but we're like-minded. We see eye-to-eye. Except for today, apparently, when we've just disagreed with each other twice in the space of one conversation.

I think about having a shower, washing the whole day away...then I hear Mum letting herself in. A shower is always the first thing she wants straight after her cleaning work.

I retreat to my room, kick off my boots and lie on my bed. Suddenly the tiny space doesn't feel cozy. It feels like a cave. More than anything, I want *sky*, open air. I want to walk out of the house, get on the quaddie. I want to go tearing up to one of the back paddocks, where I can have a good howl and nobody will hear me. But I can't do that anymore.

Through the bars on the window shines a limited view – part of a tree, a corner of the house next door, a patch of licorice sky. I'm lying there, feeling as if ants are crawling under my skin, when my phone dings.

Mai says her place tonight ok? 8pm

I frown at the screen, the stupid smiley and the *M*. I can't seem to work up the same aggravation now, about Mycroft's crazy vision for solving Dave's murder. At least it's something concrete. Something I can focus on.

Something not *here*.

CHAPTER FIVE

Mai lives in a flat with her aunt, her aunt's son, her mum, and her two little sisters. When I knock on the front door, Mai's aunt opens it. Her little boy winds about her legs like a jungle liana as she hollers over her shoulder in Vietnamese.

Mai comes into the hall, says something to her aunty, rolls her eyes at me. 'Whole circus is still up. Come on, the boys are already here.'

'I had some trouble getting away,' I say, shouldering past the tall sideboard and kids' toys and clutter in the hall.

Mai grins at me. 'Your parents didn't want you gallivanting off into the night, after what happened last time? What a surprise.'

Over dinner, Mum had fussed about my 'ordeal' and Dad had silently chewed the tough bits of casserole beef. When I'd said I was going out, Mum had sighed in that time-honored way parents do before they pull the rug right out from under you.

I give Mai a glance. 'Mum's getting paranoid about Mycroft. She asked if I was going to be "hanging around" with him tonight.'

'Seriously?' Mai stares. 'But he's got the best academic record in the whole school! And you're neighbors, you see each other every day, in classes even. It's not like you can drop him off your list!'

'Yeah, I did point that out. I almost said she was being ridiculous, but I thought better of it.'

Mai grins. 'So what word *did* you use?'

'*Unreasonable.*'

'Ouch.' Mai pats my arm. 'Family. God.'

'Tell me about it.'

'Glad you came, though.'

'Me too.' It's true, even though I'm nervous about the whole murder investigation business, even though I was just desperate to get out of the house for a while.

'Some of the other girls from school don't get the whole extended-family-squash thing.' Mai's bangles glitter as she waves at the messy flat. 'You get it. Plus, I have to confess, you make great camouflage.'

I lower my voice. 'For you and Gus?'

Mai rolls her eyes. 'For me and anybody. Mycroft used to drop over to study more, but Mum spat the dummy about me having a boy in my room. There's safety in numbers. Sorry, but you're doing double-duty as my chaperone again.'

'Happy to oblige. But d'you really think you can keep the whole relationship thing off your mum's radar?'

Mai sneaks a glance at me. 'Maybe she thinks Mycroft and Gus are seeing each other, I don't know.'

I snort a laugh.

We walk into her room, where her speakers are wafting out Triple J, and close the door. Mycroft and Gus are occupying the cramped space like an invasion of the barbarian hordes. Gus is lounging on Mai's bed and Mycroft is pacing, wearing a path in the tiny floor rug.

Mai's a bit of a neat freak, which is understandable given that her room is about the size of a cupboard. Any larger and she'd be sharing with one of her younger sisters, so in this case, less really is more.

If I was her sister, I wouldn't be in any great hurry to share Mai's room. It's completely given over to Mai's exotic taste: tidy racks of weird manga, posters of even weirder bands and tattoo flash, and one shelf crammed with disturbing dolls.

Mai's infinitely more fashionable than me. I still find it bizarre, that people in the city are so hung up on how they look. Back home, who would I have ever dressed up for? There was only my parents, my brother, and a whole load of sheep.

But Mai keeps wanting to paint my nails in black polish, or try out a cherry-red lipstick she's just bought. Sometimes I let her do her thing, but mostly I just like being me. I don't think she minds having a friend whose only nod to trendsetting is to avoid wearing flannie shirts too often. She did say I was a wimp for not getting a nose ring, but just the once. When she tried wheedling me into cutting my hair into a shag crop, Mycroft growled at her to lay off.

I like that Mai and Gus are together, though. Mai puts up a good facade of being in control, but she's really a bit insecure. After what he and his family went through in Sudan, Gus is very sure of who he is. And he's kind – right now, for instance, he's patting a spot beside him for Mai to sit down, like he's saved her a space. It's her own bed, but I still think it's cute.

Mycroft merely turns to see me, and rolls his eyes. 'Finally.'

'I had to do the dishes.' It comes out a bit stilted. In our last conversation we were yelling at each other. 'What's happening?'

'We were talking about why you'd kill a homeless guy.' Gus

puts an arm around Mai's waist as she forgoes the bed to sit on his knee. 'Mycroft is explaining about sport killing. Apparently, some people kill for fun.'

I shiver. I've only just arrived and already I'm plunged back into it. I hug my knees on the end of Mai's bed.

'That's right,' Mycroft says. He sinks down cross-legged onto the floor. 'There's only a limited number of reasons why you'd off a homeless, yeah? The first reason is, you're a sicko who likes preying on vulnerable people. Then there's a subcategory of that, which is called "sport killing".'

'Did you google this or something?' Mai says.

She passes me a bowl of popcorn. I take a handful before passing the bowl to Mycroft, who takes some and then with great consideration leaves it in his lap.

'Yes, thank you, I did.' Mycroft gnaws on the popcorn. 'In the US, it's how a lot of homeless people get murdered. They're just hanging out, being homeless, and someone goes all *Clockwork Orange* on their arse. Usually it's teenagers, local college jocks after the big game, that kind of thing.'

'Okay.' I'm picking at my popcorn. I'm trying to think about this logically, to stop thinking about Dave's face. 'But that's sort of spontaneous, isn't it? Unorganized. Which would make it hard for the police to investigate.'

'Exactly. Unless there's a string of similar murders that can be traced to a particular area or street gang or something.'

'And has there been? A string of similar murders—'

'No.'

'Oh. Okay.' I cross my legs under myself. 'So what's the next reason?'

Popcorn bits fly off as Mycroft waves his hand. 'Well, the next reason is homeless people being killed for their organs.'

Gus snorts. 'Does that even happen in Australia?'

'Not that I know of,' Mycroft admits.

I dump my popcorn with a grimace. 'And Dave wasn't all...y'know.'

'Sliced and diced...'

'Yeah. Just his throat. So that can't have been the motive.'

'My thoughts exactly.' Mycroft gives me a sly glance. 'See, you're thinking about motive. That's a good sign, that's—'

'Just keep going.' I sigh. 'What's next?'

'Okay. Well, there've been a couple of one-off incidents like the Michael Malloy case, where homeless people have been murdered because they were actually rich. As in, they were rich but loony, so they were offed for their money. But cases like that are pretty rare.'

Gus helps himself to popcorn out of Mai's hand. 'Who'd live on the street if they were loaded?'

I frown. 'Dave wasn't the kind of guy who'd have a secret bank account, or a stash of millions in his shopping trolley. Anyway, the trolley didn't seem to be touched.'

'Exactly,' Mycroft says. 'So that leaves only one other reason why homeless people are done away with. Get this – historically, it's very common for poor and vagabond people to be used in scientific experiments.'

'Bull,' Mai says.

Mycroft shakes his head. 'No bullshit. It used to be that if you wanted to try out a new medicine, or poison, or some crazy medical-slash-scientific quackery, you'd go off and kidnap a couple of itinerants. People who won't be missed, yeah?'

Mai curls her lip. 'But that sounds like something that hasn't been done since, what, the nineteenth century?'

Mycroft adopts an odd, far-seeing expression. He ticks off on his fingers.

'Tuskegee syphilis experiments, 1933 to 1972 – the American government sanctions giving syphilis to poor and vagrant black men in order to test the progress of the disease. Cincinnati radiation experiments on charity cancer patients from 1960 to 1972. Grigory Mairanovsky in Russia, 1940, used political prisoners for experiments with poisons like mustard gas...'

'That's bloody horrific,' I blurt out. 'Anyway, nothing like that happened to Dave. I mean, he didn't have a disease, or any sign of...well, anything, except that he'd been slashed up.'

'Well, we won't know, will we, until we get the autopsy results.'

I want to say *What autopsy results? How the hell are we getting* autopsy results *now?*

'All right, fine. There are all these weird reasons for killing homeless people,' Mai says, shuddering. 'Do we have to choose which might be the most popular option?'

'Dave didn't get a choice.' My voice comes out flat, heavy.

Gus is looking somewhere else, at the mangled dolls on Mai's shelf. 'We did that in English, last week. The quote by that *Fight Club* guy: *Live or die. Every breath is a choice.*'

'Palahniuk,' I say automatically.

'I don't think he was talking about murder.' Mai touches Gus's cheek with gentle fingers.

'It's not about choosing. We don't have to choose.' Mycroft wriggles, impatient. 'It's about examining the evidence and coming to a logical conclusion.'

Mai rolls her eyes. 'But Mycroft, this isn't like one of your research papers. God almighty – it's a homicide investigation.'

She reaches down to pull on a drawer handle under her bed. I see Gus's eyes linger on the way her shirt rides up at the back, exposing a flash of pale skin and the edge of her tattoo.

Mai sits back up with three thin beer bottles. Mai's place, Mai's bar. We all chip in, except for Gus, who doesn't drink. The booze inside the bottles fluoresces in the dim light of the bedroom lamp. Mai keeps talking as she gets up to position them on the night-stand, scratching for the bottle opener in the drawer.

'I mean, they'll have detectives on it, won't they?' She pops a cap and offers one in my direction. 'Legspreader?'

I always grin when I hear that name – gross – but I take it anyway. 'Thanks. Yeah, that's true. We met one of them, Detective Pickup.'

I swig from my bottle, make a face: it tastes like vodka-flavored cough medicine. Mycroft doesn't seem to care. He's gulping his like a thirsty horse.

'Right.' Mai curls back up on the bed next to Gus. 'And it's not like the police are going to keep you posted on the investigation as it proceeds.'

'That's why these come in so useful.' Mycroft sets aside his drink and the popcorn bowl and yanks a gold A4 envelope out of his backpack. 'I finished printing them up. I think I've got something.'

The hairs on the back of my neck lift. I put my bottle down and stand up to reach across Mycroft for the photos. 'You've got something? What've you got?'

He waggles his eyebrows and holds the envelope away. 'Patience, my dear Watts.'

'Mycroft, I don't *have* patience, you know that. Stop dithering and show me.'

'Fine.' Mycroft uncurls to stand beside me and hands me the envelope. Before I finish fumbling open the flap, his fingers circle my wrist. 'Watts, they're not pretty.'

His voice is very low, and I shiver. 'It's okay,' I say, but my words come out small and a bit unsteady.

73

I'm nervous, but I want to just deal with it. It's like getting hurt when I was a kid – I always wanted to just yank the splinter out, or put the stinging antiseptic straight on, or tear the flap of skin right off. Better to get it over and done with.

When I look at the photos it's a bit like reliving it all, but only for two or three seconds. The backs of my legs hit the edge of Mai's bed. Mai scoots over closer to Gus to make a space as my knees lose concentration.

But it's okay. There's not that same sense of absence I felt when I nearly fainted last night – the feeling of wind rushing through my hollow head, blowing clean through my ears. Mai asks me if I'm all right.

'It's not that bad,' I say. 'Not as bad as last night, I mean.'

Mai peers curiously. 'Geez, it can't be any worse than—' She recoils with a grimace. 'Oh. Oh god, that's…yeah.'

I'm surprised at her reaction, considering that dark'n'twisted is kind of her oeuvre. I see Gus's face. He's not saying anything but his eyes are serious, with a guarded sadness I haven't seen before.

'Yeah, I guess it's pretty bad,' I admit.

Mycroft flomps down on my left, between Mai and me. Gus ends up squashed up near the headboard with Mai practically sitting on him again.

Mycroft squints at the top photo. 'I printed them on decent paper for better resolution. See, this is the one I thought gave you the best example. But if you take the wider shot—'

Mai groans and buries her face in Gus's shoulder as Mycroft rifles through the photos, making a gory picture book.

He picks a couple out and thrusts them under my nose. 'Here. You can see it here too, but the hands are less visible.'

I frown, switching from one photo to another. 'I don't know what I'm looking at. Apart from all the blood.'

74

Mycroft gives me his best *Are you a total moron?* expression.

'You said it – *all the blood*.' He waits for a beat. When my expression doesn't get any less mystified, he continues. 'Watts, we did this last term. Biology? Poulette's formula. It's not ringing any bells?'

I do a mental gear change, feel the smoke coming out of my ears. 'It was to do with, um, liquids expelled under pressure? Er, something about the rate of pressure. And...I can't remember what it was, because Miss Paulsen had this enormous pimple on her nose in that class, and I just couldn't take my eyes off it. Seriously, I didn't know a pimple could interfere with your concentration like that—'

'I remember,' Gus says, coming to my rescue. 'Not everything, but it was to do with the rate of pressure equal to the combined equation of volume and viscosity of liquid, and the diameter of the expelling aperture.'

I lean around Mycroft to stare at Gus. It makes a change from staring at gore. 'How did you remember that?'

'Because he wasn't looking at pimples during class.' Mycroft whips the photo out of my hand, his expression scathing. 'Anyway, even if you can't recall a basic scientific fact, you should at least be able to remember *one* thing...'

I'm looking at the photo in Mycroft's hand, my eyes burning holes into the paper. Dave reclines against the tree. Where his throat should be, there's a wide, revolting slash, a bloodstained maw. I can see the meat of his scrawny neck exposed, the white of muscle, tendon. Blood has pooled in the bottom lip of the wound, clotted like a crimson jelly. The blobs on his front are all red, red, red, variations on the same awful theme, all the way down to his waist.

The human body is like a big plastic bag, full of blood, and here are the tones and shades arranged...

And I remember one thing about Poulette's formula.

'Wait.' I tug the photo closer, making Mycroft lean. 'Where's all the blood?'

'Oh my god.' Mai rolls her eyes, takes a fortifying slug of her vodka cough medicine. 'What do you mean? There's blood every-goddamn-where.'

Mycroft has his eyebrows raised. He's waiting for me to continue to the obvious conclusion.

I start slowly. 'No. Actually, there's hardly any blood on the ground around him. And I can see shirt color here, at his waist. And here. Big patches all over. His trousers are dark green corduroy...I can see his *zipper*, for god's sake—'

'Yeah.' Gus is nodding, craning over Mai's shoulder to see the photo. 'You're right. His shirt is a kind of khaki color.'

Mai waves her bottle. 'What has his *shirt color* got to do with anything? For god's sake, the poor guy's *dead*.'

'Sorry, look.' I turn the picture to explain it to the only person in the room who doesn't study either Biology or Physics. 'Okay, the human body has a total blood volume of about five liters, yeah?'

'I know *that* much.' Mai hates being made to feel dumb.

'So if blood pressure operates as normal...' I nod quickly to Gus, '...allowing for variations in the diameter of the cut vessel, you'll still lose your entire blood capacity in something like, oh—'

Mycroft robs me of the big reveal.

'Sixty seconds.' He leans back, propped on his hands. 'One minute. Or less.'

Mai finally gets it. 'That's fast. Holy crap. Five liters in one minute? That's like—'

'Like pouring a bucket of water down the front of yourself,' Mycroft says. 'No, wait, a better analogy. Have you ever gone to the cinema and accidentally spilled an extra-large cup of Coke on your shirt? Well, imagine if you had *five* of those cups, and they all got spilled on you at the same time—'

I ignore Mycroft and hold Mai's gaze.

'Your shirt wouldn't be khaki. Your shirt color wouldn't even be *visible*. The volume of blood would be too huge.' I slap at the photo. 'We shouldn't be able to see the color of his shirt, or the zipper on his pants, or anything at all except a big wash of red. And there should be a big pool of blood on the ground around him, he'd be swimming in it, like a, a...'

I get a sudden spin of nausea, remembering the sheep we hung, how the blood had splashed out of the bucket like the red crest of a wave. I'd jumped back so I wouldn't get it on my boots...

'So, not all his blood was expelled when his throat was cut.' Gus catches my eye, fully aware of where this line of reasoning is going.

'But that doesn't make sense.' Mai pushes her glasses back up her nose. 'If your throat is cut, that's your carotid artery, right? So wouldn't you just lose *everything*, like—'

She sticks her tongue out sideways and makes an explosive gesture with one hand, as if she's spewing blood everywhere. It's funny, in an off-joke kind of way, and it brings me back to life.

I nod. 'Yes. There's actually only one reason why you *wouldn't* lose a massive amount of blood from a wound like that.' But I'm already looking for more evidence. I search the photo in my lap, can't find what I'm looking for. 'Mycroft—'

He pushes up to lean beside me again. 'The one underneath. You can see his hands.'

'Right.' I examine the shot. 'Okay. Yep.' I look straight into Mycroft's face, amazed. 'You're right. You're totally right. How did you work this out by yourself?'

His expression should be smug, but it's more exasperated. He's had to wait for everyone else to catch up. 'It's observing, isn't it?'

Mai leans across, fighting her distaste. '*What's* observing? What are you looking at?'

'More proof.' I point to Dave's hands in the photo. 'The photos aren't conclusive, but it looks as if his hands are unmarked. No defensive wounds. He can't have been attacked from the back, because the tree behind him is too wide to reach around. So they must have come from the front. But if someone's being attacked like that, they raise their hands to defend themselves. Dave should have marks – cuts, probably – on his hands. But there's nothing.'

Gus gives Mycroft an admiring look. 'That's impressive. You really are Sherlock's much-smarter brother.'

Mai glances from Gus to Mycroft to me, and shakes her head like her brain is hurting. 'If you're saying what I think you're saying, then...it just sounds crazy.'

'It might sound crazy,' I say, 'but I think Mycroft's right.'

They're all looking at me as though I should be the one to say it. Mycroft, because he wants to feel validated. Gus, because he usually lets other people do the talking. And Mai, because to her the whole thing doesn't seem quite real.

I turn my face away from all of them and look down at the photos, explaining it to the only person for whom it has any real meaning. Dave stares out at me from the shots, sightless and pleading.

'Dave's heart had already stopped beating when he was slashed,' I say softly. 'Whoever killed him...killed a dead man.'

CHAPTER SIX

It's half an hour after my Saturday eight-till-twelve shift at Tognetti's mini-mart, and I'm dying inside from a combo of hunger and a glow-in-the-dark-alcopop hangover. I did the shopping after work, so now I labor into the kitchen carrying four bags of groceries. Mike and Mycroft are eating cereal at the kitchen table.

'Sounds bloody terrible,' Mike says, as he shovels Weetbix in. 'Mmf...sorry, mouf-ful...anyway, yeah, sure. Be happy to do it.'

I dump the groceries near the fridge. 'Be happy to do what?'

Mycroft is hunched over his bowl, in black jeans and a white T-shirt under a red shirt. The damage to his face is healing. He's picked all the tape off his eyebrow, revealing the dried-black laceration underneath. But the split in his lip is improving, and the bruises on his cheek and nose are fading to yellow.

'Remember what Mai said last night?' He chops at his cereal with a spoon. 'We've got corroborating evidence now. That's why I've come by. We should do it.'

79

'Pardon?'

'We should do it, what Mai said. We should take it to the cops.'

I sag. 'Could this not wait until after I've had Panadol and a coffee?'

'It's a murder investigation, Watts. *Murder*. Time is of the essence.'

'Mycroft, we have to take Gus along, or someone else, a concerned adult. If the police want to talk to us now, it'll have to be in the presence of—'

'Your brother's offered to come to the cop shop with us. Said he'd drive – how flash is that? Bit of an improvement on a tram.'

Mike takes a look at my face. He swallows his mouthful of cereal and talks fast.

'It's not like that, Rache. Mycroft's not twisting my arm or anything. He told me more about what happened with that poor bloke the other night…' He examines me as if he's making a careful stock assessment. 'So you're all right, are you?'

I open my mouth, but my throat has closed up. It's not post-traumatic shock. It's just that it's Mike asking.

There's a lot to be said for having a brother two years older. Mike never had any great interest in my 'girly stuff' while I was growing up, but he's always looked out for me. He's picked me up when I got knocked over by a ram, carried me screaming to the house when I cut myself on roofing iron, dusted me down when I fell off the quaddie. What Dad didn't teach me about wire fencing, or repairing the pump, or snakebite, I probably got off Mike. Plus a few extra things Dad would never have told me about, like why boys always try to see who can piss the farthest, and how to hawk a really big spit.

Now that our schedules make us all ships that pass in the night, I miss Mike more than anything.

And now it's Mike asking me if I'm okay. I get a bit sniffly, but I blink it back. If there's anything my brother taught me, it's that crying won't fix it. And his other favorite saying – if there's no blood, there's no point blubbing about it.

In this case, there's blood, sure, but it's not mine.

'I'm fine,' I say. 'And it's nice of you to offer, Mike, but we don't really need a lift.'

'Watts,' Mycroft says, 'it's not just the ride. Mike can be with us, as an independent supervisor.'

I look back and forth between them.

'Did you two have a nice little conversation while my back was turned or something? Mycroft, are you *insane*? What could possibly have given you the idea that I'd want my own brother mixed up in all this?' I turn my gaze on Mike. 'And *you*. Encouraging him. He's bad enough when he just *thinks* he's right, let alone when people agree with him.'

'Rache, Rache…' Mike says. 'Look, it sounds like this bloke Dave is just gonna get his whole life put on some dusty cop-shop shelf if nobody does anything. Don't you reckon it's worth it?'

I boil inside for a second. Then I puff out a big breath, let my shoulders flop.

'Of course it's worth it. I just…' I flail a hand at him. 'It's your day off…'

Mike's grin is enormous. 'It'll be awesome. All the places of police interest in the great city of Melbourne.'

I cast around for something, anything. But I'm running out of excuses. 'I've just finished work. I'm starving.'

'So make yourself a sandwich and you can eat in the van.

Come on, Rache. Murder investigation, remember? Time is of the essence!'

I look from Mike to Mycroft. They grin and high-five each other. I make a mental groan.

———

I'm sitting high in the cab of my brother's white delivery van, feeling like a budgie in a glass cage.

Mike's nonchalant, holding the wheel as though he could let go at any moment if he chose. Mycroft is on my left, folded into a seat designed to fit a normal-sized person. I'm squashed between the two of them. Mycroft's arms fly out occasionally and catch me on the forehead as he and Mike argue over the navigation.

'Take Sussex to Bell, then go on from there.'

'I'll take Sussex, but not Bell. Like a bloody cattle stampede. On-street parking's a joke – anytime of the day or night, you're dodging some wanker's hotted-up Mazda.'

'But it's direct. There's through traffic.'

'Forget it, mate. I take Sussex then Bruce, take the back way to Brunswick Road.'

'So you're basically trying every street in Coburg.'

'Ha bloody ha. My truck, I drive.'

'Why not just turn from Albion Street?'

'You think we want to get onto Sydney Road in a hurry? Not so, mate.'

'What, you're going to turn right from Brunswick Road? You, sir, are a bloody madman.'

I brace my hands on the dashboard and raise my voice over the comedy routine. *'THERE IS NO HOOK TURN AT BRUNSWICK ROAD, FOR THE LOVE OF GOD—'*

'Right, I knew that.' Mike pats my knee. 'Relax, sis, we're home and hosed.'

At this rate we'll end up with a police escort to the station. I'm also horribly nervous. I have no idea what to expect when it comes to dealing with police detectives.

I tug on Mycroft's sleeve. 'Will he even be there on a Saturday, d'you think? Detective Pickup?'

Mycroft shrugs. 'Don't know. Imagine so. I mean, he could've gone fishing for the day or something, but he *is* the lead officer in a murder investigation.'

Mike takes the corner, cresting the gutter on two wheels. I can't think for a moment, let alone formulate a witty reply.

Ten minutes later, we're approaching the place we need to be on St Kilda Road. Mike indicates left near the Shrine of Remembrance, swerves in front of a car, and pulls up so hard that all our foreheads leave faint grease marks on the windscreen. 'There we go.' He slaps the wheel with a satisfied grin. 'Perfect parking.'

I blink at Mike with my mouth open for a second. I have believed, for so long, that my brother is a competent if slightly daring driver. My opinion must have been colored by all my memories of being with him as he drove paddock bombs around Five Mile. I'm still wiping the sweat off my palms as we cross the road.

St Kilda Road Police Headquarters rises up in front, a seventeen-story edifice of beige concrete and dull glass. We stand on the footpath, chins tilted high to take it all in.

Mike's hands are jammed in the pockets of his jeans. 'Glad I don't come here regularly on business, if you know what I mean.'

'Bit intimidating, isn't it?' Mycroft doesn't look as certain of his plan as he did twenty minutes ago.

I bump him with my elbow. 'Well, this was all your bright idea.'

'No it wasn't. It was Mai's. It was Mai's bright idea.'

There's uniformed police and people – non-uniformed police, civilians, criminal masterminds, god knows who – going in and out of the main entrance. Mycroft and Mike and I dawdle near the concrete disability ramp.

'What do you want me to do?' Mike takes his hands out of his pockets. Then he changes his mind, jams them in again. 'You want to me do the talking?'

I pull my satchel strap over my head, scraping my hair out of the way. Being unfamiliar with police-station fashion etiquette, I'm wearing khaki camo pants with a black tank and my boots.

'Well, we want them to think you're the mature one, so maybe you'd better do as little talking as possible.'

Mike gives me the *oh, ha har-dee ha* face.

Mycroft takes a deep breath. 'Come on, let's do it.'

We walk up the grubby stairs with the watch-your-step fluoro strips, and go through the automatic doors together. Mike and I trail Mycroft to the main desk. Except for glass security checkpoints blocking the way on our right, the place looks like a normal office. I'm trying not to look around. It's hard to avoid wondering who's under arrest and who's not.

Mycroft is already talking to the young guy in uniform behind the L-shaped expanse of buffed white counter-top. The officer's nametag reads *Houli* and he reeks of aftershave.

Officer Houli makes a phone call, then puts down the phone and frowns at all three of us. He points to our left. 'Take a seat over there, please. Someone'll be down shortly.'

We park ourselves on the cushioned bench seat by the wall.

I wish I had a coffee. Damn, I *deserve* a coffee – I've worked since early this morning after a late night out and I haven't eaten anything but a cheese sandwich, scoffed in anxious gulps in the van. I settle my satchel on my knees, nudge Mike over.

Mycroft uncrumples a packet of chips from out of his backpack. He takes a fistful before shaking the packet my way. 'Salt and vinegar? I hear it calms the nerves.'

'No thanks.' I pull the hem of my tank top down over my hips.

'Suit yourself.' He shoves the chip packet across towards Mike. 'Convenience food?'

'Cool,' Mike says.

Mike grabs for chips. The packet makes a loud crinkling scrunch, like an accident in a sheet metal factory. The entire population of the foyer seems to look in our direction.

I stare at Mike and Mycroft in turn. 'Are you two quite finished? Trip to the police station not interrupting your picnic or anything?'

'Nah, we're good.' Mike grins at me.

In less time than it takes them to finish eating their chips, Detective Pickup is standing in front of us. He looks barely altered from when we saw him on Thursday night. He's changed his shirt; his collar looks less crumpled. The effect is not a good one – the fresh white of the shirt collar only shows up the shoddy nature of the suit.

He doesn't smile, or do any of the traditional greetings. He crooks a finger.

'Come.'

We come. Mycroft wipes his oily fingers on the leg of his jeans. Mike and I exchange glances. We walk through the glass checkpoint, our bags are examined and returned to us, then we're directed towards a bank of lifts.

Disapproval is emanating off Pickup in waves, and I can see more details now that I didn't notice before. Pickup is about fifty, his face dark and driven. He has burned-looking cheeks from a recent shave. His skin is so pocked with old acne scars that it looks like the surface of the moon – I can imagine it would be hard to shave. His dark-orange hair is atrociously vivid, and his eyebrows are the same color. He must have gotten heaps of shit in school.

Pickup herds us into an lift and punches the button. When we reach the twelfth floor he waves us out, like he's shooing cattle. We move along the corridor until we get to the door of an office.

It's not an office. The room has a table, chairs, beige walls, no windows. There's a distinctly claustrophobic feel.

I balk at the threshold. 'Why are we going into an interrogation room?'

Pickup's eyebrows furrow. 'This is an *interview* room, Miss Watts. This is where we go when we need to talk to people.'

'Oh,' I say. 'Well, I guess…'

'And we have to do this by the book,' Pickup continues. 'We got your preliminary statements on Thursday night, but if this is something new, we need to get a proper record. I'm assuming this *is* something new?'

'Yeah, it's new,' Mycroft says.

'Right. And we don't need to make arrangements for independent supervision, which is a bonus.' Pickup looks curious. 'How'd you know to do that?'

'A friend.' Mycroft clears his throat. 'She's…she does Legal Studies at school.'

'My word.' Pickup's voice is dry. 'Legal Studies, Forensics… Seems you can do anything you want in high school these days.'

He does the shooing thing with his hands again, until everyone's inside. 'Right. Mr Watts, you sit there. Mr Mycroft, Miss Watts, just here.'

He switches on a mini-recorder and goes through stuff like names and suburbs again. He asks Mike to identify himself formally, then turns his eyes straight on me.

'Now. What did you want to tell me?'

I shift on the hard folding chair. 'Um, nothing. I mean, I'm mainly here for moral support. And I wanted to say I'm really interested in seeing this through, and finding out who killed Dave.'

'As we all are, Miss Watts.' Pickup puts a finger into his collar and yanks, maybe to make room for a bit more fortitude there. 'So Mr Mycroft, you're the one who has additional information?'

'Yeah. Yes. Although what Watts says isn't quite true. I had this theory, and then she and I kind of worked it out together—'

'Certainly. I'm sure we can sort out the correct attributions later. A theory. Right. So what was this theory?'

Mycroft glances at me. I nod my chin at him, encouraging.

'We think Dave's throat was slashed after he was dead,' Mycroft says. 'That he was killed twice, as it were.'

'Killed twice.' Pickup leans forward and uncrosses his arms. 'What makes you think that?'

Ah, the tricky bit. Mycroft and I have already discussed how we're going to phrase this. We don't want to admit to having photos of the crime scene, which could be some kind of crime in itself.

'We were talking about it…' Mycroft begins.

I nod. 'Talking about what we saw. On Thursday night. And we realized—'

'We remembered that there wasn't enough blood. You could see the color of Dave's shirt, and there wasn't enough blood on the ground, in his lap…'

'And you know this how? From watching telly?' Pickup seems to have forgotten about the pen in his hand. The notepaper in front of him bunches up as he puts his elbows on the table, his attention focused on us.

'From class.' Mycroft sits back. He looks slightly miffed that anyone would think he's cribbed a theory off the telly. 'I've been taking extension studies in Forensics for two years. And let's face it, the physics is pretty elementary—'

'This isn't something off the television,' I cut in. 'We did it in Biology too. A person's entire blood supply comprises about five liters. Blood pressure is based on Poulette's equation. So if you get your throat cut when you're alive, there's just a massive…gush, like a—'

I suddenly think of the striated muscle inside Dave's throat, the jellied red. I dig my nails into my knee under the table and the vertigo passes.

'The blood loss would be sudden and immense,' I continue, 'and you sure wouldn't see the color of someone's shirt afterwards. You'd be lucky to see the color of their trousers, maybe even their shoes. And there'd be a huge mess of blood on the ground. This is just basic physics.'

Mycroft takes over. I'm happy to let him.

'From what we can remember, there were no defensive wounds on Dave's hands or arms,' he says. 'No slashes to suggest he'd tried to fend off his attacker. The blood-loss pattern and the lack of defensive wounds suggest that Dave was already dead when he was assaulted.'

'What if he was drunk? Or under the influence of something else?'

My estimation of Detective Pickup climbs a fraction higher.

He's asking us real questions, genuine questions. He's not fobbing us off.

'Was he?' Mycroft's eyes glitter. This kind of information is like a worm on a hook, wriggling deliciously right in front of him.

Pickup squares himself in his seat. 'I'm not currently authorized to release any of those details. The autopsy findings haven't been made official. We're proceeding with the idea that your friend was killed in a sport-killing attack.'

This jolts me. I remember what Mycroft said yesterday.

'Have there been any similar cases in the area?' I try not to wilt under Pickup's hairy eyeball. 'I mean, any other bashings or—'

'No,' Pickup says, curt.

I frown. 'So this is a vicious murder that just occurred out of the blue, and there've been no other attacks reported on homeless people in the general area of where Dave was found?'

'Yes, that's correct.' Pickup looks thunderous.

'Bit odd, isn't it?' Mycroft's wearing his most innocent expression. 'Don't these things usually come on like a rash?'

'Sometimes there's a run, sometimes not. Your friend might have been the first in a new spate, for all we know. We're fairly confident that's what this is, and that's how we're going to investigate it.'

'What about the dog?' I ask. 'What about Poodle?'

'We haven't found the dog yet,' Pickup says, laying the emphasis on *yet*, 'but we're sure it'll turn up. Let me remind you that this is a homicide case, and regardless of the victim's status, we investigate all these things with the utmost—'

'We want to see the body.'

Mycroft's voice cuts through the standard line. My head snaps around.

'We do?' I take a peek at Pickup; he's giving Mycroft the full glare. I'm supposed to be providing back-up support here. I better start backing up fast. 'Uh, yeah, we do. We'd like to, y'know, say good-bye. Dave was our mate.'

'That's right,' Mycroft says. 'Our mate. And we were his regulars. We might not get another chance to give our regards, especially if you catch up with his real family.'

'We need closure.' I nod, ladling it on. 'Our school counselor, Mr Fossum, reckons that's the most valuable part of the grieving process, closure.'

Pickup seems at a loss. He turns to Mike, who's looking at me and Mycroft with eyes as big as goose eggs.

'And you're approving this? These two informed you that they wanted to view the body?'

Mike does a quick drop-catch. 'Uh, yeah. They were talking about it on the drive over, and I wasn't too convinced, I said, y'know, Rache, if you wanna see this dead guy…'

He starts spinning it a bit. I give him a quick bulging-eyes glare, to make him shut up. A lie is always better if it's not embellished too much.

'…anyway, I said, uh, yeah, that they should do it,' Mike concludes lamely.

Pickup glowers at each of us in turn while he sucks on his teeth.

'Providing information is one thing, but viewing the body's a totally different story,' he says finally.

I lean forward. 'Detective—'

'But you could talk to the pathologist,' Pickup continues, ignoring me. 'No harm there. Explain your little theory and see what he says.' He turns off the recorder and stands up. 'I have to make a call. Stay here and don't do anything.'

Pickup leaves, pulling his mobile out of his trouser pocket. I'm wondering what he thinks we could possibly do in this bare-walled room in his absence. Once the door closes behind him, Mike whips around. He glares at me and Mycroft with a face that's turning a faint shade of puce.

'What the bloody hell are you two playing at? Are you *serious*? I thought we were just going to come here, talk a bit, have a cuppa or something and then—'

'We need to see the body,' I say. I suddenly know in my gut this is true, whether I want it to be or not. It's the only way to confirm what Mycroft and I suspect. 'Maybe we can make a case with the pathologist, I don't know. But we've got to try. Even if we don't find more evidence, it'll be good. I do need closure, and not in a Dr Phil way. I want to see Dave. It's important.'

I try not to look too pleading. Mycroft opens his mouth to say something. Before he can, the door opens.

Pickup walks back in. 'Right. It's approved. Come with me.'

CHAPTER SEVEN

The room is white, full of lab tables. It's in another building, in Kavanagh Street – Pickup had to drive us, and I was disoriented as soon as we turned off St Kilda Road.

I look around. The benchtops are arrayed with microscopes, beakers, chemical hoods, and drip trays. There's a whole lot of machines I can't even identify.

I feel something brush against my left palm, almost jump before I realize that it's Mycroft's thumb. I look at him. He waggles his eyebrows at me, but his eyes are electric, intense.

A tall man well past middle-age stands up from his stool. He has a long jaw and a pointy head. Thin graying hair peels back from his crown; what's left nestles around his ears like the grass skirt on a hula dancer. Everything about him is rangy, angular. He's wearing a white coat, glasses on a string, and a benign expression.

'Ah, Pickup.'

Pickup glances around the empty lab room. 'Quiet, is it?'

'Saturday afternoon, that's fairly normal,' the man says, smiling.

'You'll find most of the staff at the Farmer's Arms. Stout, or the convivial house red, I'm told.'

'Wish I was there.' Pickup seems keen to get the professional chit-chat out of the way. He angles himself to include us in the conversation. 'The ones I was telling you about. Miss Watts, Mr Mycroft, this is Professor Emmett Walsh, forensic pathologist assigned to this case.'

Mycroft gives a little wave. I smile tightly. Professor Walsh folds his arms across his chest.

'Bit irregular.' He doesn't seem angry or bothered. He's just stating the obvious.

'A little outside normal channels, but we've got independent supervision.' Pickup jerks a thumb at Mike. He turns to Mycroft. 'I want you to tell Professor Walsh what you just told me.'

Mycroft's expression is wary.

'About the, uh…?' He makes a gesture – flattened fingers slashing at mid-throat that is quite understandable to everybody.

'Yes.'

'Oh. Okay.' Mycroft glances at me. He looks at Walsh. 'Right. Um, in a nutshell, we think that Dave—'

'John Doe from Thursday night,' Pickup says, talking across Mycroft's shoulder. Walsh nods his understanding, nods for Mycroft to continue.

'Um, me and Watts found the body. And we think Dave had his throat cut post-mortem.' Mycroft straightens, drawing on some inner resource. 'There wasn't enough blood lost at the scene. He wasn't in rigor when we found him, so we're guessing the time of death was close to time of discovery. He was cut at the carotid, so obviously he lost some. But not enough – I mean, the throat wound was large, and you'd think he'd lose total capacity within

93

sixty seconds, if he was alive when it happened. But there just didn't seem to be a large enough...'

He loses the thread when he can't bring the right word forward. Professor Walsh, who's been looking at Mycroft with a reserved fascination, cuts in at this point.

'"Blood pool" is the term you're looking for.'

'Yeah.' Mycroft expels a relieved breath. 'The blood pool wasn't large enough.'

'But the ground was soft dirt, there could have been some absorption...'

'True, but not that much, not if you consider the timing. There was hardly any ground stain. Plus, the bulk of it would have gone on his clothes, given his position, right? There was some in his lap, but you could see his trousers...'

'Yes.' Professor Walsh stares at Mycroft a second longer. Then he gives Pickup a grin. 'Goodness. I didn't know you'd brought me a sharp one.'

Pickup rolls his eyes. 'Sharper, we'd be getting paper cuts. Me, especially.'

Walsh is still grinning as he unfolds his arms and pats down his lab coat pockets. 'Mm. I've got a...somewhere...Ah.'

He fishes out a wallet, extracts a worn business card and passes the card to Mycroft, before folding himself into his hunched posture again. 'Contact details. Future reference for you.'

Mycroft takes the card, blinking. He licks his lips, glances at me, then back to Walsh. 'Actually, we were hoping—'

'Oh no. I'm afraid there's a limit,' Pickup says. 'Saturday afternoon, two minors, and there's a limit—'

'We'd like to say good-bye to Dave,' I say, cutting Pickup off. I speak only to Walsh. We're in his jurisdiction now. 'We've got independent supervision, and we *knew* him, we wanted—'

'*Miss Watts.*' Pickup's eyes are blue agates.

'It's all right, Vincent.' Walsh looks at Pickup. 'Quite under-standable, really.'

Pickup's eyebrows shoot up. 'You're okay with a viewing?'

Walsh nods and uncurls himself, opens out his hands. 'Let's go to my office.'

He ushers us out of the lab area. We all walk down a pleasant hallway – subtle artificial light, tapioca-colored walls, like the corporate places my mum cleans every Wednesday. We enter another lift and go down.

The decor on this level is different. No carpet – polished concrete, splashback walls, and the doors are double swing. Walsh walks through a smoked-glass entry on the left, waves for us to follow. The room is tiny, no wider than a hallway. To our right is a waist-to-ceiling glass wall.

We've walked into a viewing area. Through the glass I can see a larger, partitioned room. Close to us on the other side of the glass there's a section a meter or so wide that's fenced off with a light-green curtain. The curtain is gathered at the top onto rings that follow a runner along the ceiling.

Behind the curtain lies the rest of the room, which we aren't supposed to see. There's a foot-wide gap in the curtain, though, and I realize what goes on in the larger room by the furniture.

It's not your normal furniture. I can see tables, but they're all steel, on rollers. The cement floor has drains down the middle. There are metal sinks, and benches with jugs of chemicals, hooks for rubber gloves, hoses, trays of instruments.

I shiver. Mike gives me a quavery smile and that tilt of his head which asks me if I'm okay. I swallow and nod. Mycroft is absorbed in what's beyond the glass. Pickup is standing close by, watching us, his face like a death in the family.

Walsh has passed through a single door at the end of the viewing room and entered that strange other universe of the morgue.

He thumbs an intercom button on his side of the wall, and his echoing voice enters our glass holding pen. 'When you're ready, I'll bring him in. Are you ready?'

Pickup looks at me and Mycroft. I'm holding my breath. Mycroft nods, I nod on automatic.

Pickup pokes the button next to the door on our side. 'Go ahead.'

Walsh steps behind the curtain. He pulls it aside a little and rolls a table into the curtained-off area. He steadies the table in front of the glass and pulls the curtain neatly closed behind himself.

I'm staring at the table. It's a long trolley, a metal one, like the others I glimpsed. There's a large shape laid out on it. The shape is covered by a long hospital-blue cloth, but I can see the lumps and bumps under the cloth. The contours suggest a head, a nose, a barrel-chested torso, legs, feet propping the cloth at the bottom end.

I feel a bit swimmy. Mycroft stands beside me on the left. His breath, like mine, is frosting the glass.

Professor Walsh is standing near Dave's head. He looks up at us. He doesn't use the intercom to ask the question, just asks with his eyes.

'Are you ready?' Pickup's voice is loud in this space.

'Yes,' Mycroft says.

I don't trust my voice to come out right. I just wobble my head.

Pickup nods at Walsh. The pathologist takes the top ends of the cloth and gently, so gently, folds the cloth down.

I rear back. There's a person, a man, from the head to the mid-chest. The head is tufted with ragged hair, the face strewn with beard. The cheeks are sunken, so that the beard seems stuck on, fake. The flesh is gray, sickly-looking. There's a broad, slashed line across the throat, held together with butterfly closures. A grotesque caterpillar track of stitches seals an incision that's been made from the point of each shoulder, meeting at the base of the throat and stretching down the torso to a point somewhere under the cloth.

This is not Dave. This is not a person I knew, not a friend or acquaintance. This is just a wax figure, not animated, not alive, not of the real world at all.

My body relaxes a little. I've been holding on to Mike's hand. I release him now and stand alone. I can do this. I'm not unaffected, but it's okay.

I let my shoulders ease down. I suddenly realize that Mycroft has his hand on my back, between my shoulderblades. I remember the night we found the body, how I put my hand on his back and felt him breathe. I look at Mycroft. His face is suspended in front of the glass as if he's smelling it.

'Are we done, then?' Pickup sounds as if he's trying for gentle, but it's come out abrupt.

'I want to get closer.'

I gasp when I realize it's me who's spoken.

Mycroft looks at me, a fast, hard stare. He turns to Pickup. 'Me too. We need to get closer. Can we do that?'

Pickup glances at both of us as though we've spoiled his dinner plans.

'Let me ask.' He jabs the button. 'They'd like permission to enter.'

Walsh considers. 'I'm going to buzz you in. Just the two, please.'

'Two is fine.' Pickup seems quite happy to remain on this side of the glass. The door buzzes, and he ushers us to the opening.

I suddenly notice the smell. The puff of air from the morgue is awash with unpleasant chemical scents. I distinguish bleach, cleaning agents, the sickly-sweet smell I associate with hospitals… plus something else.

It takes me a moment but I finally place it. It's the same stench I remember from the day I went into the east paddock with Dad and we found the ewe that'd died giving birth. She was hidden under a massive clump of gorse in the winter-creek gully. The lamb was half-in, half-out of her, and they'd both been dead a while. It was in the autumn – hot days, cool nights. The smell of decay stuck inside my nostrils for ages after.

No matter how it's scrubbed and disguised, that same smell exists in this room.

Then Mycroft steps over the threshold and I can't turn around and go back. It was me who asked to go in. And I want to know – I *need* to know. Going into the morgue is the only way to find out.

I step through the entrance.

Walsh positions us on his side of the body. It'd be easy to look up and see Mike and Pickup through the glass. I don't, though, because Mike would see my longing to be out of here and he might do or say something silly. I just keep my head down and do what Mycroft's doing.

Up close like this, in full smell-o-vision, Dave's body still looks like a funeral effigy carved from wax. I clasp my hands piously in front of myself. I'm supposed to be saying good-bye.

But I don't think Professor Walsh is under any illusions about closure or our grieving process. Mycroft certainly isn't making any effort to hide his interest. He's leaning over the body as much as he can without falling over. His thick eyebrows are screwed up and his bottom lip is sucked between his teeth, and he's examining, examining.

I move closer. I can detach and examine too. Like a test, an experiment at school. I can study what's obvious in this picture, draw conclusions...

'The throat wound...' I start hesitantly. 'It's clean, not ragged.'

'Not a serrated edge.' Mycroft's eyes are darting, studying minutely.

'Something very sharp,' I say.

'I don't know.' Mycroft's voice is soft. 'A hunting knife?'

I shake my head. 'They have serrations at the bottom edge.'

I know this from when Mike and I have shot foxes on our property.

'Right.'

I glance up. Pickup is staring. I put my head back down, bite my lip. 'A kitchen knife. A filleting knife.'

Mycroft is going with me. 'Maybe a box cutter?'

I'm looking at the way the lips of the wound join together neatly at the edges. 'Something like that, something thin. A razor, a scalpel.'

Mycroft leans in, centimeters from Dave's neck. I move my head closer, ignoring the smell of chemical preservative. We could be back at home, huddled over the kitchen table, working out a Chemistry problem. Examining, making observations. I try to ignore the feeling that Walsh and Pickup are doing the same to us.

'Has to be.' Mycroft frowns. 'The edges are almost seamless there. And there. No tearing.' He points. 'But see that? The thin line above the left edge?'

'An earlier cut. First try?'

'False start.' Mycroft nods. 'Hesitation mark. An unpracticed killer. Not his regular occupation.'

'You said *he*.' I nudge him with my shoulder.

'Don't tell Mai,' he says. His mouth turns up at one corner. 'So the knife, scalpel, whatever, it starts on the left...'

'False start, then the cut is highest on the left. Right-hander.'

'I think so. Remember the body position? Back against the tree.'

I'm thinking fast. 'And the tree was too wide to reach around. So he can't have done it from behind.'

'I'm guessing.' Mycroft leans back a little, makes a mime of his hands. Right hand forward, grasping something, thumb out. It comes to an imaginary throat somewhere in front and draws across slowly from left to right. 'Like that.'

'Interesting.' I blink. 'But apart from the issue of the blood loss, we haven't completely established that Dave was already dead.'

'Then we need to rule out—' Mycroft suddenly looks across me to Walsh. 'Hands. Could we please look at the hands?'

Walsh appears to have been studying us as closely as we're studying the dead man. He steps forward and eases the cloth down farther to lift Dave's arms. He bends one elbow gently, letting the hand emerge. Walsh is wearing latex gloves – I hadn't registered that before.

He moves to the other side of the body and repeats the process. The way he can manipulate Dave's arms means that Dave has passed out of full rigor. How do I remember all these details from Mycroft and his endless research papers?

Mycroft has been watching Walsh do his thing with Dave's hands. Now he steps around Walsh without a word of thanks and leans close, backs up to gain perspective, close again.

'Okay. Here.' He reaches across the table to tug on my wrist.

I put my hand on his, to keep his enthusiasm from pulling me off-balance. The last thing I need is to end up half-sprawled over a dead body.

'What? There's nothing.'

'That's my point. It's confirmation – no cuts on the fingers or hands. No defensive wounds. Dave's already dead before the cut, or he would try to defend himself.'

'What if he was out of it, like Pickup said?'

Mycroft looks at Walsh again. 'Alcohol?'

Walsh makes a small headshake. 'Not enough.'

'Right,' Mycroft says. 'Not pissed. What if he was just, y'know, knocked unconscious?'

It's the first time I see Walsh look uncertain. 'We'll examine for evidence of petechiae and haematoma that would indicate he was rendered unconscious during the attack. He sustained long-term damage, from a number of sources – alcohol abuse, prescription drugs, other things. He'd had a hard life. We're trying to rule everything out.'

'But there's no bruising, like a bashing, or—'

'No.'

I look at Dave's face. There's the calmness of absence, of complete surrender...I get a sudden brainwave.

'What if he was sleeping?' I say.

Walsh doesn't smile; his face just has a faintly pleased expression. I think he's pleased with me.

'It's a good idea. Might explain the lack of defensive wounds, if the perpetrator was quick and quiet enough. But it still comes back to the blood-loss issue. You're absolutely right on that count, of course. The blood loss was insufficient for a catastrophic

101

throat wound pre-mortem. He was dead before he was cut.'

'And the number of assailants?' God. *Assailants* – I do watch some crime shows. 'Did more than one person attack him?'

Walsh shakes his head. 'Not according to SOCO.'

Mycroft and I share a glance. That's more information than we would have got out of Pickup.

'So we're looking at the work of one person.' My voice sounds so calm. But I'm not calm – I'm angry. One guy, girl, whatever, decided they'd like to see how it'd feel to slide a knife across someone's throat.

Mycroft nods. Then his expression melts into a frown. 'That just brings us back to the original question.'

'What's that?' I ask.

'The one I first came in with. Why do you cut a guy who's already dead?'

Walsh makes a little cough. I realize that we're standing beside a *pathologist*. How could we be so stupid?

'Professor Walsh, what did Dave die from?'

Walsh's eyes are kind. 'Well, there's no mystery about that, really. We've established that he suffered cardiac arrest. He had a heart attack, Miss Watts.'

It all starts to come together in my head and I get a terrible feeling. 'You think he was startled by his attacker.'

'Basically, yes. It's likely the cardiac arrest was brought on by shock or fright, just before his throat was cut.'

The feeling gets worse. I look at Mycroft. He's leaning over, eyes still intent on the body. He glances up at Walsh. 'What about stomach contents? Tox screens?'

'Complete toxicology will take some time to come back,' Professor Walsh says.

This dawning realization presses on me, my heart slowly flattening in my chest. I know why Professor Walsh is being so calm, so gentle. I even know why he's allowed us in here, bypassing the protocols. He's seen this before – a thousand different permutations of the questioning, the search for answers, from sad friends and relatives coming to the morgue every day.

Dave will never get the opportunity to explain what happened to him. And Mycroft...he just can't deal with it. He might think he's on some dark quest to find a murderer, but in reality he's just looking for the same answers that everyone who loses somebody looks for.

Because the questions aren't *How did he die?* or *Who killed him?* They're much simpler. *How can this happen? How can someone who was alive suddenly just not be there anymore?*

Walsh doesn't look at Mycroft and me and see a couple of half-arsed detectives. He sees two traumatized teenagers who've witnessed the aftermath of a terrible event. Who need to see, to examine, in order to understand and accept what's happened. I can't argue with his perception of us, because for god's sake, that's exactly what we are.

A terrible lassitude rises through my body, as though I'm filling up with quicksand. I realize that I'm standing beside the gray body of a man, an acquaintance, a friend. A man who will not rise up. Who didn't even have the chance to go down fighting. Suddenly it's all I can do to stay on my feet.

'Mycroft.' I put my hand on his back. 'Mycroft.'

'Cardiac arrest...' He's looking down at the sad, sunken face. 'But why do you—'

'*Mycroft.*' I understand now. Mycroft's in the grip of something much deeper and more personal than logic, and I'm not going to

103

be able to reason with him. I turn to Professor Walsh. 'I'd like to go out now.'

Mycroft lifts his head. 'But Watts, we're nearly there! We just have to—'

I close my eyes. 'Mycroft, I want to go. I think...'

I am too tired to say it, to speak the truth. Too tired to confront Mycroft. I turn to the tall, thin man at the head of the trolley. 'I want to go now, Professor.'

Walsh nods and goes for the door. Mycroft's eyes are darting between my face and the face of the dead man. But I have nothing left for him right now, not even the strength to persuade.

I look down at Dave's body. My eyes start to swim. I put my hand, my bare hand, over Dave's cold one. This is probably against regulations. It doesn't matter now.

'Bye, Dave,' I whisper.

I don't know what else to say. *We'll keep your spot warm for you*, or *We'll think of you*...It all seems so cheesy. Dave is dead. He can't hear me. My words are for myself alone.

I clear my throat and walk to the door – Walsh offers me some gel for my hands and I chafe it in. Mycroft must be going through the same routine behind me.

Mike walks across the viewing area and takes my hand. His, at least, is warm. Pickup studies me gravely. When he speaks, his voice isn't abrupt or terse, for a change.

'Come on,' he says. 'I'll give you a lift back to the station.'

———

The smell of smog from the CBD is foul in the late afternoon. We cross busy St Kilda Road but I'm still too numb from the viewing to pay attention to my feet; I stumble as I hit the pavement on the other side. A man is circling a ride-on mower round and round the park lawns. I watch him spin the wheel, skirt bushes, play hide-and-seek among the tree trunks. My brain only comes back to life when Mycroft's voice floats in. '...still doesn't answer all my questions.'

I so want this conversation to happen later, not now, but I must have used up all my luck in the police station.

'Mycroft, Pickup was right.' I have to say it. I have to speak sometime. 'It was a sport killing.'

'You're joking.' Mycroft grins. Then he sees I'm not grinning back.

He stops so abruptly that Mike nearly walks into him. 'Watts, tell me you're joking.'

Mike pulls his keys from his pocket, looks from my face to Mycroft's, squares his jaw. 'Right. I'll wait for you in the van.'

I'm as drained and exhausted as I used to be after shearing time, but I open my mouth anyway. 'I'm not joking, Mycroft.'

There's a pause. '*Bullshit.* I don't believe you believe that. You can't—'

'I can. And I do.'

'Watts, you were standing *right there*, next to me! We *saw* it, we saw the same stuff—'

'Yes, but we came to different conclusions.'

'Oh, come on! How can you *say* that?'

Suddenly my own voice flares to life.

'Walsh felt *sorry* for us, Mycroft, don't you get it?' I rake my hands through my hair, wanting to pull something out by the roots. 'He let us in the autopsy room so we could do our little "investigation", and he stood there and watched, and let us ramble on, because he knows *that's what people do.* Don't you think he hasn't seen it

105

before? Don't you think every poor bastard who dies violently like that hasn't got someone who thinks, "well, gosh, maybe there's something more to it than just some random assault"?'

'But this time it's *true*! Dave's murder *wasn't* a random assault—'

'It was a *sport killing*, Mycroft. Think of the evidence—'

'*What* evidence?' Mycroft's eyes are sparking, blue as the after-image of an X-ray flash. 'There's no related cases, there's no pattern, they're only speculating about how he came to have a heart attack before he was cut, they don't even have the *tox screen* back! They're trying to tell us it was some amateur youth, who took it into his head to go out and—'

'*Yes*, because that's exactly what happened! Mycroft, you're trying to beat this up into a murder mystery, but there's just *nothing there*! For god's sake, we only got in there on a pity vote!' My words come out sharp. 'Maybe what Pickup said is true, maybe there'll be more, maybe Dave was the first—'

'And do you always believe everything the cops tell you? Come *on*, Watts, *think* for a minute!'

'I *am* thinking!' My breath comes short and tight. 'He was frightened to death and then cut, that sounds exactly like what Pickup said they know about—'

'They *don't know*. That's the whole point! And what about the dog?'

'*What about the dog?* You're basing your whole bloody theory on what happened to a *dog*?'

Mycroft's hands are squeezed into fists. 'It's not just that and you know it! Pickup's accepted this sport-killing theory with open arms because it's *easy*, it's a bloody easy answer—'

'And sometimes the simple answers are the right ones.'

'Oh, *piss off.* That's fucking pathetic reasoning if ever I heard it! I thought you had a better brain than that.'

'Mycroft, *Dave's dead.*' I can feel my eyes tearing up, fight for control. 'He's dead. And he's not coming back.'

'*Don't you think I know that?*'

Mycroft has two flushed spots high on his cheeks and he's breathing hard, like he's been running.

I push past him to the van. His next words are aimed at my back.

'Jesus Christ, you just don't *want* to care, do you? You don't want to care about anything in this city, or any*one*—'

It's as if I've been slapped. I feel all the blood drain out of my face. And in the back of my throat, what should remain unsaid swirls and rises up inside me. My mouth floods with an acid taste, as if I've been sucking on a battery, and the pressure is too intense, and the dam breaks.

'*Don't you make this about me!*' I turn and stumble towards Mycroft, screaming into his face. 'This is about *you,* it's *always* been about you! This is *not* an investigation! And I am *not* your Watson! And Dave is *not your parents!*'

Mycroft freezes in front of me. All the color dies from his cheeks. I hear my own heart galloping in my chest. Blood thumps behind my eyeballs, as though someone has kicked open the back of my head.

I want to clap my hands over my mouth, but it's way too late.

Mycroft's voice comes out still and soft and dangerous. 'Do you want to say that again?'

My lips part, but all that escapes is a thin gasp. I'm left standing, staring, wondering how this will ever be put right. But I don't think it ever will. This is too much. I've shattered something important, something crucial, and I can never, ever, put the pieces back in place.

He takes a step and leans in close, so close. I am too paralyzed to move. I can feel the heat radiate from his body. His lips are dry and trembling, and his cheekbones jut out. His eyes are electric blue maelstroms.

'Mycroft…' My voice shakes so hard I can barely hear myself.

He takes two slow steps backwards, then breaks away. He walks off, gaining momentum, up the green hill that the mower man has made so neat and tidy, so pristine.

Then he is gone.

CHAPTER EIGHT

A memory steamrollers into me, from last December.

It was my birthday. Remember my birthday? Pavlovas, blue dresses, brothers that pull your hair, the works. Only this birthday was different. I was seventeen, so no blue dresses and no hair-pulling. And not a lot of anything else, as it turned out. No cake, because Mum was working, and Mike ran out of time after his shift to buy one. Dad was delayed getting home, so we didn't have my birthday dinner until eight-thirty.

I'd said I didn't want a present. I knew we couldn't really afford it. All I'd asked was that someone else make dinner for a change, so that'd been Mike's job. A right balls-up he'd made of it, too. Burnt chops and soggy beans and lumpy mashed potato...

Normally, it would have been something we'd laugh about. But this time, it mattered. Singing Happy Birthday to Me with my family, around a single lit candle in a cup, it suddenly hit me – the full force of all the shit that had happened to us. Of where we were, and why, and how horribly and irrevocably our lives had changed.

No birthday presents. Burnt dinners. Everyone freaked out about their jobs, the money side of things. All of us twitching like nervous horses. One wrong step and the whole set-up comes tumbling, crashing down...

I realized how close we were to the knife-edge that night, my birthday night.

I hadn't seen Mycroft all day – he'd had another 'personal day' off school – and I wanted more than anything to feel that, if I had nothing else, at least I had new friends. So, I'd gone two houses down.

The noises coming from the house were audible from the graffiti-swathed telephone box. I didn't realize it was Mycroft making them until I got through the back door. There was a yell, the smash of glass...

I ran through the darkened house, wondering where Angela was, not realizing at that stage that Angela never was.

I got to the door of his room just as the noise reached a crescendo. There was a godawful crash and I panicked, pounded on the door, knocking off the skull-and-crossbones sign.

'Mycroft!'

'*FUCK. OFF.*' His voice sounded tarred and harsh.

'*Mycroft*, for god's sake—'

The door flew open. '*What part of FUCK OFF don't you—*'

We both froze. His eyes were red-rimmed, hollow, his face pallid, his dark hair corkscrewing every which way. He was in jeans but no shirt or shoes. The skin of his flat stomach goose-bumped in contact with the cooler air from the hallway as he gripped the door. It was the first time I saw his scars.

His heavy-lidded eyes fixed on me. His fingers wove a cigarette to his lips. The reek of alcohol was overpowering and I realized that he was deeply, deeply drunk.

110

'What part of *fuck off*,' he said, enunciating slowly on the exhale, 'don't you understand?'

My cheeks bloomed with heat and my whole body went rigid. At the exact moment I was about to fling around and walk back out, Mycroft lurched forward.

'Oh shit,' he slurred. 'I didn' mean…'

Then he keeled over.

I managed to catch him as he slid down the edge of the door. Part of me was still wishing I'd turned and stalked off, but it was too late. He was lolling all over me, a tangle of arms and legs and heavy sweat-soaked boy. I pushed him up with a groan, got an arm around his waist and prayed he wouldn't throw up.

His room was another shock. The place was completely trashed – bedding everywhere, books, papers. I couldn't see his computer equipment or his chemistry set – I didn't know until later that he'd carefully packed them away where they wouldn't be damaged. Smashed glass glittered beside the overturned desk. Everything stank of vomit and whisky.

I lowered Mycroft to a clear space on the floor, then hauled his futon back onto the pallets, laid a blanket over the bare ticking. I half-rolled, half-lifted him to where he needed to go. At some point during the process, he came back to life.

'What're you…doin', you shouldn't…' He struggled, slapped at my hands. His accent had thickened with the drink, and his eyes were drifting in and out of focus.

'Mycroft, you're pissed. You need to—'

'YOU SHOULDN'T BE HERE!'

He staggered to his feet and immediately collapsed again. His bare shoulder crunched against the zigzag of glass near the desk.

I stepped closer but he squirmed backwards on his bum, pushing with his heels to get away.

'You jes'... You stay there!' His finger jabbed in my direction, and his voice was hoarse and cracked. 'Don' you... You stay... *Don't you come here!*'

I could see over his shoulder – he had a long shallow scratch across one shoulderblade. The scar ridges on his body stood out in blanched relief. I'd been angry when I first arrived – now I just felt bad. He looked pitiful.

I sank on my knees on the booze-sodden carpet, as though I was trying to make myself seem less intimidating to an injured animal. 'Mycroft, take it easy.'

'No, you jes'...'

'Hey.' My hands were up, palms out. 'It's okay.'

'There was...so much blood...' He bowed his head.

'It's okay, Mycroft. Let me look at your shoulder. I'll wipe off the blood, it'll be okay—'

'Too much. You can't. There was too much. They were...' He looked up, took a deep breath. 'They were dead before the police came.'

I felt a chill. 'Who were dead, Mycroft?'

'I couldn'... There was nothin' I could've...' His eyes were wild. 'Tha's what they said. But what if I could've helped? I could've done the...whassit...breath of life. The *breath of life*. One of them might have...stayed with me...'

The chill turned into permafrost, all over my body.

Mycroft's head dipped down. He looked as cold as I felt. I snagged his burgundy robe off the floor, slid closer and opened it around his shoulders.

'Who might have stayed with you, Mycroft?'

'I couldn't choose,' he mumbled. 'Don' make me choose—'

'No one's going to make you choose, Mycroft…'

I sat there, rubbing his good shoulder, until I could tell from his limp heaviness that he'd passed out again. I drag-pulled him onto the bed, where he started snoring.

Satisfied that he was in a position where he wasn't likely to choke on his own vomit, I went into the kitchen and made up a thermos of black tea. I put it on the floor beside the bed, and fetched a bucket and a roll of toilet paper for the aftermath. Then I started sorting out his room, putting towels down for the puke and whisky on the carpet before righting the desk, the chairs, putting the bottles in the bin, along with the glass shards from the floor.

That was when I found the album.

———

'Rache.' Mike shakes my arm. *Rachel.* We're home. Come on, let's get you inside.'

He manhandles me into the house, sits me down at the kitchen table, makes me a cup of tea. The mug is hot in my hand, and the warmth travels up my arm, spiralling through the rest of me. The dull waxy feeling inside me melts, and I start to cry, proper crying, bawling crying.

Mike moves his chair so I can lean against his shoulder and howl. Once the noise has settled, once my breathing starts to hitch and slow, he fetches me a paper towel so I can mop myself up a bit.

'Thanks.' I blow and swipe and generally make more of a mess.

Mike gives me a sad, sideways look. 'Your eyes are as red as tomatoes, you big duffer.'

'Shut up.' I flatten my arms on the table, sink my face onto them. 'I mean, sorry, you don't have to shut up. I just…'

I swallow hard over the incredible tightness in my throat and try again. 'You drove us all that way, did the witness thing as well... That was a really nice thing to do. You didn't have to do that.'

'Yeah, I did.' My brother scrapes his chair back again and plonks himself down.

I finally look at him, with his dark hair tufted up, delivery driver's shorts, Redbacks making brown scuffs on the dingy kitchen lino. 'You saw a dead bloke. For me.'

'Yeah, that was weird.' His eyebrows give themselves a shake.

'Are you gonna tell Mum and Dad?'

'I think I might keep this one on the down-low.'

I stop shredding the corner of the paper towel. 'Like that time I kept on the down-low about you and Della Metcalfe and her dad's ute?'

'Well, I knew you could keep a secret. You had a good track record.'

It feels strange, and very adult, me and Mike talking about keeping each other's secrets. I lick my dry lips as Mike continues talking.

'Hey, don't worry about Mycroft. He'll come round. And even if he doesn't, well... Maybe that'd be for the best.' He looks to some random point near the fridge.

'What do you mean by that?'

Mike meets my eyes. 'While you and him were cozying up to the dead bloke in the other room, your Detective Pickup was having a word in my ear. Confidential info for interested parties, you might say.'

'Like what?' My instant frown turns into a flush of realization. 'Wait a minute. Pickup told you stuff about *Mycroft?*'

'Well, yeah.' Mike shrugs, bites his lip. 'He said he had form.'

'Form? What the hell is form?'

'It's like a criminal rap sheet.'

'A criminal…' I cross my legs, push back from the table. 'Like, for what? Something serious?'

'Not really. Just pissant stuff – but there's a fair bit of it. Shoplifting, trespassing, public drunkenness, vandalism, that sort of thing.'

I cross my arms to match my crossed legs. I'm cross all over. 'So what do you want me to say? Mycroft's only been caught for doing the same kinds of stupid shit you got up to back at home. Like when you took Pat Righetti's tractor that time, and tore up half her bloody paddock when you accidentally put the ripper down.'

'Jesus, Rachel, why are you *defending* him?' Mike's back stiffens. 'He acted like a total shit after you came out of the station. Not to mention that you wouldn't even be *in* all this crap if he hadn't dragged you off to the zoo that night—'

'I was the one who decided to go!'

'—and now this copper's telling me he's got a rap sheet half as long as my arm—'

'Well, don't you reckon *you* would have done some crazy stuff if your parents had been—'

I stop, clap my hands over my mouth. It's what I should have done earlier, but Mycroft's words were too hurtful for me to exert any control. Well, I can exert some control now.

'What?' Mike's eyes narrow. 'His parents *what*? Shit, Rachel, what *is* it?'

'I can't tell you.' I move my hands to my hot cheeks. 'I *can't*. I'm sorry, I'm sorry, really. But it's not my story, it's not my place—'

'*Rache*—'

'Mike, *please* understand! I would totally tell you if I could, but I *can't*.' My hands flutter as I shove hair out of my face. 'It's Mycroft's personal stuff, and...I only found out by accident, and it would damage him beyond repair if he knew I'd been telling people.'

Mike is glowering. Considering we've just been talking about sharing each other's confidences, I may as well have given him a punch in the guts.

'Mike, *please*. I bury my head in my hands. 'Oh god...'

I can't go on then, because what did I care about Mycroft's privacy this afternoon? What did he care about mine?

'So is that what you two fought about this afternoon?'

Mike's voice is so gentle. I wrench my head up, look at the ceiling as the tears spring out again.

'Oh bugger...' I rough my face with my hand. 'We just...We said some awful things. It's like we know too much painful stuff about each other, so we both know where to stick the knife.'

My whole body's aching from tiredness and emotion. I lift my feet up on the chair, wrap my hands around my knees and let my head drop down.

'So this...whatever it is...' Mike pats my hair tentatively. 'It happened when Mycroft was a kid?'

'Yeah.'

'So he cops it in the teeth when he's a young fella, and now his homeless mate gets offed. And maybe he did all his wild criminal stuff a while ago, maybe he was getting shit out of his system or something...'

I nod at the logic of it all.

Mike gently takes my chin in his fingers. '...but you know what, Rache? Whatever happened to him – I don't know, I don't

116

wanna know – he's *still* getting it out of his system. Any half-blind idiot can see that.'

'But that doesn't mean—'

'Listen to me. I'm not claiming he's a bad guy. He's not. But I don't think he's right, either. D'you get what I'm saying?'

'You think I should stay away from him.' My throat is tender as I swallow. 'You're as bad as Mum and Dad.'

My brother ducks his head. 'Ah, look, I don't want to come down like that. I mean, remember me and Harris Derwent? Mum chucked a fit about us hanging out together, because Harris was such a local toerag. But he was an okay bloke. You just had to keep an eye on him.'

I push my hair behind my ears. 'So you think I should just...keep an eye on Mycroft.'

'I guess. It's a bit different, though, because of the girl-guy thing...'

'What girl-guy thing?'

Mike gives me a long hard stare. I'm the first to look away.

'Cheer up, Rache. It'll be okay. You might not have to worry about it.'

I wince. 'You mean, Mycroft may never want to talk to me again, right?'

'Yeah. So it's win-win!' He grins at me.

Even though it's hopeless, even though I still feel like there's a massive hole throbbing deep in my chest, something about Mike's presence lifts me up. Somehow he always manages to give me the calming feeling that no drought lasts forever.

My back is like wood. I stretch, sigh, and pull up out of the chair.

'Okay, I'm stuffed. I'm gonna have a shower. Whatever you say about city living, at least you don't have to worry that the tank's gonna run dry.'

'Too right.' Mike stands up and collects the mugs. 'It's okay, I reckon.'

'What's that?' I lean my bum against the table, trying to muster enough energy to move. 'You mean the city?'

'Yeah. I don't mind it here, apart from it being a bit cramped, and Mum and Dad busting their arses with work.'

'Don't you get that...claustrophobic feeling?'

'Nah. You know me. I'm pretty happy anywhere, so long as I'm keeping busy.' He rinses the mugs, props them on the drainer. 'You don't like it, though, eh? I've seen you, looking out the window with the sads.'

I sigh. 'I'd give my right arm to get back to Five Mile tomorrow.'

Mike stands, gives me a quirky grin. 'And what use would you be on the property with only one arm, eh?'

———

I'm in the same spot where we discovered Dave's body. The curtain of willow branches cuts off the grotto from the rest of the world. Dave lies in the same way, with the same dreadful injury. But this time his arterial blood isn't dribbled and congealing. It gushes from his neck like a fountain, creating an ever-widening pool.

I can't move. My feet are glued to the dirt. The syrupy scarlet life-blood sloshes over my boots. I look desperately skyward – the lights from the city have canceled out the stars. That terrible smell rises up, and I'm knee-deep in blood.

Dave's eyes spring open, milky and dead.

'*No shelter,*' he rasps. '*No shelter.*'

I wake up with a gasp.

I'm covered in sweat, panting. Sunlight is streaming in my window, heating up my tiny room. My bedside alarm clock reads nine a.m.

I flop back in bed, remembering yesterday. I torture myself for a while, replaying that moment. Over and over in my mind, I scream, '*I am not your Watson, and Dave is not your parents!*' into Mycroft's face. Again and again, I watch his cheeks bleed to white and his whole expression crumble...

There's a choking, hollow feeling in my chest. If only I'd done things differently yesterday. I think of all the ways it might have gone, the apologetic words I could have said. I kick off the quilt and drag myself to the shower.

Mycroft's scathing voice still rings in my head—'*Jesus Christ, you just don't* want *to care, do you?*'

But he's right. I don't want to care about this city. About any of it. Why should I? After December, I'll be eighteen and I can do anything, go anywhere.

I know where I want to go. I close my eyes, envisioning it: the shadows under the gums in the backyard, the smell of clean dry air, splashing in the cool creek in the afternoon, walking up the back hill, just walking and walking...

I want to go *home*.

The image of Dave's gray body lying on that gurney swims up in my memory. Dave and I had more in common than I realized. Both of us, homeless.

As I make myself some toast, I wonder why Dave never just up and quit it. He'd said he was a city man, but he was always in the margins, always sticking to the bush-corridors near the zoo. '*Better out here*', he'd said. '*Walk where you like, piss where you like... Sleep up under the trees here, over there if things get a bit nippy...*'

Something snags in my memory, like a ripple on the glassy surface of a river...I spread my toast with a slow knife, getting jam on my fingers.

I try to remember Dave as he was. Not wax-like and unreal in the morgue. Not – even worse –with his throat cut and bleeding in a grotto of willow branches. I squeeze my eyes shut, reaching for an older memory. Dave under his tree, having a cuppa. Botting smokes off Mycroft, watching me and Poodle play tug-of-war with a piece of cardboard.

Sleep up under the trees here, over there if things get a bit nippy. The RP'll take me in, last resort if I'm poorly.

The RP.

I abandon the toast and go to my bedroom, coax my computer to life.

I bring up a map of Parkville – the zoo, the Avenue, Poplar Road. I trace over the spot where we found Dave's body. My finger leaves a grease-mark on the screen as I follow the line that takes me to...

The Royal Melbourne Hospital, Royal Park Campus.

That's it. That's where Dave meant. I'd thought he meant Royal Park station, that he would take refuge under the eaves there if things got nasty for him. But he wasn't talking about the train station. He was talking about the *hospital*.

I tap for more information, hear the 'hah' of my sudden exhale. Royal Park Campus has one of the biggest mental-health units in Melbourne.

What if Dave had been a patient there? Maybe that's why he considered it a safe place in times of crisis. Even if he wasn't a patient, if he just needed somewhere quiet and sheltered...

They'd know him. I'm sure of it. They might only know his full name, but even that would be something. Something more than we have now.

Only there's no 'we' anymore. There's just 'me'.

Stuff it. I close the laptop, twist my hair into a wet, straggly knot and reach for my boots.

Mycroft might think I've got the whole 'not caring' thing down pat. But he's wrong.

———

'Good morning.'

'Hi. Um, sorry, I know this is Sunday…'

'It's okay.' The woman at the counter is wearing a shirt-and-slacks uniform that emphasizes her tiny waist above generous hips. She's about twenty, dark hair in a long ponytail, with a very calm smile. 'We still work on Sundays, you know.'

'Oh, right. Yeah, of course.' I smile back tentatively. 'Well, um—'

'Why don't you start by telling me your name,' the young woman suggests.

'Sure. I'm Rachel Watts.' I clear my throat. It was extremely weird, coming in here on the train and getting off at the station near the zoo. I kept looking over to the spot where Dave had died. I forced myself to keep walking, past the golf course to the hospital campus. Now I've made it all the way to reception I'm not going to waste the effort by turning into a stammering idiot.

'Look, I'm not sure exactly who I should talk to about this. But I'm trying to get some information to help a friend.'

She gives me a nod, and I realize that phrasing it that way makes it sound as if I want to pick up some pamphlets or something.

'No, not like that,' I correct. 'Okay, sorry. You know there was a homeless guy killed around here a few days ago?'

The woman nods again. 'Yeah, I heard some of the night staff talking about the police being up near the zoo. Was that right?'

'Yeah. Well, um, me and a friend found him. He'd been murdered.'

'God.' Most people would back away. This woman leans forward, her face full of concern. 'That's pretty awful. And your friend wants to get some counselling after that? Is that why you—'

'No. Sorry.' I sigh. I'm going to have to explain the whole thing. 'The thing is, we knew this guy, Dave, before he died. The police are trying to get the person who killed him, but the problem is, they still don't seem to have much of a clue about Dave's identity. And I remember him saying that he sometimes took shelter here at the hospital. So I thought I'd come and see if anybody here could recognize him from a description.'

She takes it all in. This is a mental-health facility, after all – perhaps she's used to hearing weird stories.

'You think he might have been a patient here at the hospital?'

'I don't know. Maybe. He said he only ever came as a last resort.'

The woman – her name tag reads *Azzopardi* – rubs the back of her neck as she considers. Then she plants her hand firmly on the counter-top.

'Okay. If this guy – Dave, you said? – if he was a patient, he'd be on file. Now, that kind of information is only available to relatives of the person here. We're not allowed to pass on anything, not even a full name. That's a legal requirement, you understand, as well as a privacy issue.'

'Oh. Okay.'

I'm deflating as she says all this. It seems stupid to withhold information about a man who's dead if it would help identify him. And I can't call Pickup on a mere hunch.

My trip here may have been a huge waste of time.

'But,' she goes on, 'if Dave ever came here casually, and was just given a bit of support, like a cuppa and a bikkie, then he wouldn't have been visiting as a client. Not checked in or registered. So you'd need to talk to someone who's met him – a long-term staffer.'

'I'd be allowed to do that?'

She bites her lip and leans across the laminex. 'Would you be able to stay for a bit? I'm working for another half hour, but I can contact the staff member who I think can help. You're lucky he's on shift. He's been here long enough to score the prime spots on the roster.'

'Sure, I can stay.' I nod eagerly. 'That would be fantastic. Thank you.'

'No problem. I'm Alicia, by the way.' She holds out her hand and we shake. 'There's a little smoker's garden around the back, to the right of the building. Could I meet you there?'

I walk around until I locate the smoker's garden, then leave the hospital grounds. I'm starving: I forgot to eat my breakfast toast and now it's midday. I can't recall eating dinner last night, either.

My fingers chafe my satchel strap as I walk slowly up the bitumen path towards the railway station. It's a close walk.

There's the metal railing that leads to the Upfield platform. As pedestrians from the zoo and the station wander past me, I stand there looking towards the place where Dave last rested.

Blue-and-white tape still flaps around the scene. Some of it has blown loose. Now all the photos have been taken and the squad cars have driven away, the whole place looks abandoned.

Gus was right. No one is going to push the matter of Dave's murder, because there's no one around to care. He had no family. The police probably think of him as another statistic, just some vagrant the city swallowed up.

There's the hillock where Mycroft and I sat and drank tea with trembling hands. The memories rise unbidden in my mind: Mycroft smoking as he answered questions, cigarette-hand lolling in front of his face; Mycroft sitting with his knees up, staring at the willow cave and rubbing his thumbnail across his torn lip.

Another image: Mycroft passed out on his bed, puffy circles around his eyes, pale under the Christmas lights of his room, the night I found out what really happened to his family...

The ache in my chest is back again, and my stomach hurts. I move, because I have to move, have to do something. I find myself walking over the zebra crossing to the zoo back entrance.

The sun is so bright I'm sweating, and the light thrown off the pavement is making me squint. I lean against the sandstone wall of the zoo, in the one shady spot I can find. Suddenly my legs are tired. I let my satchel hang down and my head loll back, then I'm sliding down to my bum.

I close my eyes. My stuffing's been removed all of a sudden. Going back to the murder scene was a mistake – just a reminder of how full-on these last four days have been. I've seen a man with his throat cut, the same man lying on an autopsy table. I've been grilled by police. I've fought with my best friend.

I suppose that's a lot, but didn't I used to be tougher than this? I used to have more mettle. Now I have one stupid argument with one stupid boy, and I'm...

'Excuse me, but are you all right?'

I look up with a start. There's a man standing in front of me, but the sun is so high I can only see his black form limned by a halo of diamond-light. I lift my hand to shade my eyes.

'Miss?'

He shifts, and I can see him now. The guy is about thirty, with blond hair and a slim build. He's got the standard chinos and zoo-logo shirt of an employee, with slightly grotty runners. His worried eyes peer from behind gold-rimmed professor glasses. Perspiration glints at his hairline.

'Sorry.' I blink, shuffle myself upright. Suddenly I'm aware of how I must look: a bedraggled teenage girl flopped in the shade near the zoo entrance. 'Sorry, I'm not...I mean, I'm not lurking. I didn't mean to—'

'It's all right,' the guy says. 'I was coming back from my car, and I saw you here... I thought you'd passed out. Are you okay?'

'Yeah.' I try to stand straight. 'Yes. I...It was just the sun.'

I realize that my legs are shaky, and press my palms against the wall for support.

'The sun is a bit much today, isn't it?' The zoo guy is speaking lightly. 'Do you need a drink or something?'

'I've got water in my bag.' I fumble with my satchel, pull out the bottle and take a sip. It does make me feel a bit better.

'Okay. That's good.' The man moves from one foot to the other, at a polite distance. 'What about something to eat? If your blood sugar gets low in the heat, you can get a bit—'

'I've got money for food,' I say stiffly. God, he thinks I'm a beggar loitering around the zoo.

The guy puts up a hand. 'I'm sure you do. But the nearest shops are over the other side of Brunswick Road, it's a fair way to go. Why don't you come into the zoo and go to the cafe?'

There's no way I can afford to go into the zoo. I'm mortified again, but I force myself to meet the man's eyes.

'Thank you, but it's okay. I'm good. The water is making me feel better. Honestly.'

The zoo guy scratches the top of his head.

'Yeah, but I think you should eat. It'd make *me* feel better.' He glances at the ticket gate, then back to me. 'Look, I've got an employee pass, I can get you through the gate. Then the cafe is only twenty meters away.'

I bite my lip. My stomach really is hurting. This guy seems nice, genuine. He's just being a good Samaritan.

'Um…'

'Great.' He smiles. 'This way.'

We walk the few meters towards the gate. He's still keeping his distance, which I think is pretty chivalrous. He says something to the woman at the ticket gate, then we're through to green grassy hillocks, and shady trees, and the tang of hot chips and vinegar from the cafe. My stomach makes an involuntary groan.

'Okay, there it is.' The guy waves a hand towards the cafe. 'I'll leave you here. I'm afraid I have to go back to work. You sure you'll be all right?'

'Yes. Thank you.' I turn to him, feeling a strangely melancholy sense of gratitude. There are nice people in this enormous city, people who'll stop and help a total stranger. I thought I'd left that behind in Five Mile. 'Really. Thank you, heaps. You've been really decent.'

'That's fine.' He smiles suddenly – he has a shy, pleasant smile – and holds out his hand. 'I'm John.'

'Rachel.' I shake his hand and smile in return.

'Nice to meet you, Rachel. Hope you start feeling better. If you have any problems, just, y'know, ask for me. John, in the labs.'

'John in the labs.' I nod. 'I will. Thank you again.'

He gives a kind of sweet, self-effacing shrug. Then he turns and walks away to the right.

I stagger to the cafe, where I'm disappointed to find that all my loose change won't buy me a bucket of hot chips. But I can afford a small choc-chip biscuit and a kiddie-sized carton of juice, which is better than nothing.

I sit on the grass under a tree and eat my biscuit and drink my juice, feeling some energy return. A complete stranger did me a kindness. Maybe the city isn't a soulless void after all. Maybe it's not populated totally by murderers and their victims. There really are individuals living in the city who have a heart. Mai, and Gus, and Nick the tram driver, and Professor Walsh. And now John-in-the-labs, and Alicia Azzopardi...

Alicia Azzopardi.

I check the time, bin my rubbish, bump through the exit, run.

CHAPTER NINE

I'm sweating by the time I make it back to the tiny hospital smoker's area, with its small raised bed of bright geraniums. There's a park bench, but I don't have a chance to sit down before Alicia Azzopardi arrives, with a man walking beside her.

'Hi, hi, sorry I'm a bit late.' Alicia has changed from her staff uniform into civvies, a messenger bag slung over her shoulder. She holds out a hand to the man at her side. 'Rachel, this is Graham Jetta. He's been a ward nurse at the hospital for about as long as I've been alive, and I think he might have had some contact with your Dave.'

Graham Jetta is a raw-boned Indigenous man. With his upright posture it's hard to tell how old he might be, but his short hair is sprinkled with white. He has a merry face, and there's a cigarette tucked behind his ear – he whips it out and lights up. When we shake hands, I feel the gnarled lumps of age and hard work in his fingers.

'Hey, nice to meet you. Call me Gray, that's what everyone

calls me.' He grins. 'Sorry about the smoke. I've gotta go back to the wards, so I take my opportunities when I can get 'em.'

'No worries.' I can't help smiling at this man. He seems the kind of person who makes everyone feel like a friend. 'Thanks for speaking with me, I'm Rachel Watts. I guess Alicia already explained why I'm here.'

'You're the girl who found this bloke, then? And you reckon it was Dave Washburn?'

Dave Washburn. My breath catches. The man I've shared thermos tea with, whose dog I've played with, whose body I've seen mutilated and anatomized...Suddenly that man has a name.

'We only knew him as Dave – Homeless Dave, we used to call him.' I lean forward. 'Mr Jetta, if you think it might be the same person...'

Gray speaks on an exhale. 'Well, geez, I hope it isn't him. But he's about sixty, gray hair, bit of a beard, usually gets around with a little trolley. He has this dog, a terrier—'

The world goes a bit washed out. I have time to think that obviously this isn't about my blood sugar, and then I have to sit down.

'Rachel.' Alicia has taken my arm. 'Here, the bench seat's right behind you. Just take a second, get your breath back.'

'I'm...' I blink for a minute. 'I'm fine. Sorry. I'm okay, honest.'

Gray Jetta goes down on one knee in front of me. He's flicked his smoke away and I feel bad, because he said he doesn't get many smoke breaks.

'Ah, hell.' His brown eyes are full of compassion. 'So it *was* Dave, eh? Jesus, that's awful. Alicia says you saw what they done to him... Well, Rachel, I'm sorry as I can be.'

It takes me a moment to get my voice back.

'He...he was a nice bloke.' I'm getting clogged up. I swallow so

129

I can talk properly. 'He used to talk about how he liked living out in the open.'

'Yeah, he didn't like being cooped up, Dave.' Gray's eyes are focused right on me. 'Liked the action in the city, but he never could handle sticking in a shelter. He used to come here maybe once, twice a year, only when he was really up the creek. He never would check in, we'd just sit out here and have a smoke – smokers together, you see? I'd give him a hot drink, find him a place to go, give him a blanket. He'd always take off the next day…'

Graham Jetta's words wash over me like a slow-moving river. After a few minutes of listening, the cold tingle in my cheeks starts to fade.

———

I dump my satchel in my room and bolt for the kitchen.

I pull strange food combinations out of the fridge while the kettle boils. The end result is a carrot, two slices of white bread, a few cuts of chicken loaf, pickles and mayonnaise. Hardly gourmet, but I'm ready to chew off my own arm.

I should be happy, getting the information about Dave's identity. I *am* happy. After I've put my stomach out of its misery, I'll call Pickup with the news. At least then I'll have someone to be happy with.

There's something else bugging me, though. In any murder mystery I've read, the identity of the victim always provides some link to the perpetrator. Finding out Dave's backstory hasn't pushed me any closer to discovering his killer, because as far as I can see, there's no links to anyone or anything.

But really, what was I expecting to find? Mycroft is treating

Dave's death like it's something straight out of Conan Doyle. Only this situation isn't like that. Dave's murder was a random act, I'm sure of it. The only reason behind it was the desire to tear something to pieces – dry red aggression, and the sight of a soft target.

Mycroft's wrong. Isn't he?

Being right, winning out over Mycroft's usually unerring logic, gives me no feeling of satisfaction. It just makes me feel crummy, and cold, and alone.

I take my cup back to my room. Mike's at his friend Patrick's place, and Mum and Dad aren't due home until five. I sit and slurp my tea. Kick my legs. Turn on my laptop.

And because I'm avoiding emails from Carly, and because I haven't got anything better to do than be pathetic, I go looking for Diogenes.

'Okay, Mycroft, what've you been getting up to without me?' I mutter, then stop. Talking to yourself – never a good sign.

I gasp when I check my search results from the last twenty-four hours. There are Diogenes refs all over the place. My neighborhood eccentric genius has been a very busy boy.

I scroll through a longish article he's posted at *Homelessness International*, where he's provided a new and grisly listing – murders of vagrants reported in national online newspapers and police dailies over the past eighteen months. A summary after each name relates the circumstances of the death and whether there was any arrest or prosecution of suspects.

He's cross-linked that to a piece he's written in the comments field of an article in *Psychology Today*, covering sport killing in greater detail. The summary of his findings has been underscored – that in really brutal cases, there's a lead-up period that involves assaults of increasing ferocity. He cites a few cases where a singular attack has resulted in murder; these are always associated with a gang or group of attackers.

If I'm reading this right, Mycroft seems to be putting together an argument to counter Pickup's theory that Dave was killed by a lone individual, the first attack of a new spate of sport killings.

In fact, if I'm reading this right, Mycroft's saying that cold-blooded killings like Dave's *always* start earlier with serious assaults. He's added a link to another article about criminal escalation in homicides, written by a professor of forensic psychiatry in Michigan. She says that if you're a solo offender, you don't start your spree by slitting someone's throat. Rather, you build up to it with increasingly violent strikes – bashings, weapon assaults, then intentional homicide.

In other words, you graduate to murder.

There are enough links and source material to make Mycroft's argument convincing. It's an impressive effort from someone who I last saw furious and hostile, who burned off into the distance like he was hell-bent on raging destruction. He's taken his wrath and channelled it into something useful.

Mycroft hasn't just been sulking in a corner somewhere. Now I think about it, apart from finding out Dave's name, *I've* been the one moping, the one who lay on my bed and howled.

I'm contemplating whether or not this makes me the idiot in the equation when my arse pocket starts ringing. I put down my cup and answer my phone.

'Yo,' Mai says. 'Rachel, I'm sorry, but I didn't know who else to call.'

'Anytime. What's up?' I frown at the wall. Mai sounds churned up. 'You haven't been chucked out of your mum's or anything, have you?'

'No, god, no. Rachel...Mycroft's been arrested.'

———

The afternoon is still glorious with sun, too glorious for me to be standing in the car park of the Fawkner police station. Mai starts talking as soon as I slam the door of the cab.

'Well, it's not looking as bad as first glance suggested—'

I stop her right there. 'Does it look, at first glance, as if Mycroft broke into school grounds last night, wrote *TWAT* in two-meter-high letters in hydrocarbon on the wall of the Science wing, and then set this artwork on fire?'

Mai grimaces. 'That's, um, the overview.' She smooths down the back of her tartan miniskirt. 'Yeah, okay, it's looking pretty bad. But he's caught a break, because Principal Conroy already inspected the site, and he's not pressing charges.'

'You're kidding me.'

'Totally not. I didn't get to ask him why, because he came and went before I arrived. And they can't charge Mycroft under the Graffiti Prevention Act, because he wasn't using spray-paint, just some kind of colorless flammable thinner. I downloaded a whole swag of court-case references on my phone on the way here, and I didn't even need to use them.'

'That's a good thing, right?'

'Right.' She looks disgruntled about the references, though.

'So he's been in the lockup all night and all day?' The mental image gives me a pang.

'I know.' Mai winces. 'But it happened at about three a.m. He passed out in the cell as soon as he arrived, so he never even made

133

a phone call until eleven this morning. Apparently, I'm the only person he knows with any understanding of law, although why he didn't just call Legal Aid I have no idea...'

Because he's punishing himself. The realization curdles in my gut. I have to zone back in to Mai's voice as we pede-conference through the doors of the station. '...And he called his aunt, of course, but it went straight to voicemail. At this rate, he'll be released by the time she arrives.'

'I'm sure he'll be devastated about that,' I say.

Mai rolls her eyes. 'I don't know her from soap, but *really*. She *is* supposed to be his legal guardian.'

'I've never met the woman, but going by the way he lives, I wouldn't give her guardianship over a pot-plant.' I rap on the security glass near the front desk. 'Excuse me? Hello?'

A middle-aged woman, the desk sergeant, appears through a door behind the counter. She puts down a cup of coffee.

Mai tucks a black strand of fringe behind her ear. 'Hello again, sorry to be a bother...'

The police officer gives a tight smile that says, *Please spare me from any more high-school lawyers*, but she nods gamely.

'I didn't get to speak to our school principal, Mr Conroy, before he left about...' Mai checks her phone, '...half an hour ago, but apparently the school isn't going to press any charges, is that right?'

'That's correct.'

'Great,' Mai says. 'Only, I was wondering—'

We never get to hear what she was wondering, because someone walks into the station and straight up to the desk. It's the last person I would want to see, except for maybe my parents.

'Detective Senior Sergeant Pickup, St Kilda Road,' he says to

134

the policewoman, flashing his badge. 'You're holding a juvenile – Mycroft, James Whelan – who's a person of interest in an ongoing investigation—'

I interrupt with as cheery a tone as I can muster. 'Hello again, Detective!'

Pickup's expression withers on the vine. 'Miss Watts. Fancy seeing you here, of all places.'

'Yes, fancy,' I say, keeping up the cheer for as long as possible. 'I hadn't realized that Mycroft was a *person of interest* in Dave's murder. Isn't that a term you usually reserve for suspects?'

'Miss Watts, if you don't mind, I'm in a bit of a hurry—'

'That's fine, so are we.' I turn back to the desk sergeant. 'So what my friend Mai here was trying to say is that if Mycroft is ready to be released and he hasn't been charged, then perhaps we could speak to him?'

'Um, yeah, that's right.' Mai is quick on the uptake. 'There's a mature person on his way here, who'll be capable of signing any forms necessary for Mycroft's release. He should be arriving some-time in the next fifteen minutes, so if we could just have a few minutes with our friend before this person's arrival, it would be—'

'—it would be an interference in an ongoing investigation,' Pickup says over the top of her. His fox-tail eyebrows are meeting in the middle again, not a good look. 'A *homicide* investigation.'

The desk sergeant straightens and makes an *O* with her mouth. I think we're in trouble. I decide to put my foot down.

'*Detective.*' I push my shoulders back, wishing I wasn't wearing yesterday's clothes. 'I'm not sure how you managed to hear about Mycroft's arrest, but Dave's case has nothing at all to do with this situation. Mycroft and I answered all your questions when we were at the station with our independent third person.'

135

Pickup points at me. 'You two came in yesterday under the dodgiest of pretexts—'

'We had a theory. And it turned out to be a pretty good one, considering that the forensic pathologist agreed with it—'

'*The dodgiest of pretexts.* And we won't even discuss the matter of how you got in to examine the body.'

'You saw the *body?*' Mai sounds disgusted.

'Yes,' I say to her quickly, before turning back to Pickup, 'and it was important we did that, for a whole lot of reasons, which I think Professor Walsh figured out before he even took us in. But the point is, we answered all your questions then, and we answered all your questions last Thursday night, and there's no real reason to question Mycroft further, unless you—'

'Unless we have information that leads us to believe his alibi for last Thursday night is less than solid.'

'Unless you...what?'

Pickup has an unpleasant smile on his face. 'We've been back over the statements, Miss Watts. You said that you and your *neighbor* were at your home until six-fifteen p.m., and then he left. You met back up with him just before eight p.m.'

'So? That's—'

'That's a window of nearly an hour and a half, Miss Watts.'

My eyes bug out. I know Pickup isn't in love with Mycroft, but I never suspected he would stoop to this level of stupidity. 'You think *Mycroft* killed Dave?'

Pickup says nothing, just looks smug. Mai plucks at my sleeve, suggesting caution. I brush her off.

'Detective, that's so totally illogical it sounds insane! Mycroft *threw up* when he saw the crime scene. D'you get that? It made him physically ill. What motive could he have? What possible purpose would be served by—'

'A seventeen-year-old boy, making friends with some homeless bloke? What purpose is served by *that*?' Pickup's eyes get this icy fire. 'And what *motive* could he have? I'll tell you what motive. He's a bloody loony delinquent kid, who gets his jollies from looking at crime scenes and examining dead bodies. He's got a history of erratic episodes, to which our current presence here testifies. He's got form, he knew the vic, he had time and opportunity, all of which adds up to—'

'—absolutely nothing at all,' Mai says suddenly, 'unless you've got testimony or evidence directly linking him to the murder. Excuse me, Detective, but I have to butt in at this point.'

Her expression is very firm. She's pushed her glasses up, which lends her an air of professionalism, even if the grotesque *Death Note* T-shirt is a bit distracting.

Pickup turns to Mai with a look of incredulity, as if he finds it unbelievable that he's being back-talked by a short Asian chick in a punk anime-schoolgirl outfit. 'You have to butt in at this point. Right. And you are?'

'Mai Ng, a friend of both Rachel and James.' How she can say it all so casually is beyond me. 'Anyway, as I was saying, you need some kind of testimony or evidence. And I'm happy to tell you that I can account for Mycroft's whereabouts on the night of the murder.'

'Why?' Pickup peers from underneath his bushy eyebrows.

'Because you contend that Mycroft had an hour and a half, between six-fifteen and seven-forty-five p.m., in which to commit murder. But I was Instant Messaging him at frequent intervals between seven and seven-forty-five p.m. that evening. Mostly we discussed homework, but at about seven-thirty we had quite a long conversation about whether or not he would join the Fitzroy Furies roller-derby team. If you check both laptops you'll find a history of the contact.'

'Fitzroy Furies. Roller derby.' Pickup's eyes bulge. Three obnoxious know-it-all teenagers in one week – how is that even statistically possible?

Mai gives him a sweet smile. 'Yes. It's really just good luck that I'm here to tell you about it.'

'But you didn't actually speak to him on the phone? Just emailed him?'

'It's true that I didn't speak to him.' Mai's being very careful with her words. 'But IMing isn't like email. It's more like a real-time conversation. I messaged his account. There'll be a record. It's true he could have been anywhere, but I don't quite see how he could have been murdering someone and conducting a complicated long-distance conversation with me at the same time.'

'We could search his house and find the laptop, check his account,' Pickup grinds out. 'That would corroborate this lovely story.'

Mai shrugs. 'Or you can just ask him about his activities during the time window. I'm sure his story and mine will match up. Is there anything else you'd like to know?'

She does the sweet-smile thing again. Pickup looks as if he wants to beat someone to death with their own arm. I'm amazed. I had no idea Mai was so brilliant. Smart, and a bit anal, but not this brilliant. She's practically *glowing* with brilliance.

Pickup's face is livid. He spins around to the desk. The sergeant, who's been watching and listening to all this with confused disbelief, snaps to attention.

'Sir?'

'I'll speak to the suspect. *Now.*'

I wish we'd been able to do that. The sergeant whips some keys out of her belt and she and Pickup bustle through the access door.

Mai is glowering. 'He can't do that. We should make a complaint. He's skating right on the edge.'

'What do you mean?'

'He can't call Mycroft a suspect unless he's been arrested for the crime. And he's not legally allowed to question a minor without an independent witness, unless there are grounds to think that waiting for a witness might cause a danger to other people. And considering that Mycroft's being held, I don't think there's really any cause—'

'I think we'd better leave it,' I say. 'The stuff you just told him has thrown him already – putting him in a corner might only make things worse. You were really incredibly good with the legal stuff, by the way. I had no idea.'

Mai beams, then shrugs. 'I suppose that's what I'm here for. Seriously, though. He can't stand Mycroft, can he?'

'Mycroft seems to bring out that reaction in a lot of people.' I'm thinking it's a dangerous habit to have when the police are involved.

We pace around the station reception area. I really can't believe Mycroft's done this – I'm going to kill him with my bare hands. To stave off boredom and anxiety I examine the fake mustaches and composite pictures on the A4-sized Wanted posters, until there's movement outside in the car park.

Mai looks up from her phone. 'Oh great, here's Gus.'

Her happy expression gets even happier when Gus comes striding through the door. They don't hug, they just stand there, looking happy at each other. I suppress the urge to roll my eyes.

Gus takes his enormous hands out of the pockets of his hoodie. 'Okay. So what do I do?'

'You sign a few forms, saying you're a concerned adult who'll take official responsibility for Mycroft leaving the station,' Mai says.

Gus looks pained. 'I have to take responsibility for Mycroft? What if he screws up again, will I have the police on my doorstep or something?'

'No, no.' Mai pats his arm. 'It's just to get him out of here. His auntie is too pathetic to come and get him, and they won't release him into the wild without the presence of a responsible adult.'

'And we all know how responsible you are,' I say, grinning. 'Hey, Gus.'

'Hey, Rachel.' Gus smiles. He nods towards the desk. 'So let's do this, and then we can all get out of here.'

'There's a hiccup,' I say. *And his name is Pickup.* 'We're waiting for Mycroft to finish talking to the detective. As soon as they're done, we should be able to go.'

We don't have to wait long. Five minutes later, Pickup appears around the corner of the desk. His scowl makes the whole room seem overcast. He stalks towards me until I start backing up.

'*You,*' he says, finger pointing, face working. 'You...can take him home. Get out of here. I don't want to see you, or your boyfriend, at any point in the near future.'

He's not my boyfriend, I want to say, but don't. 'So Mycroft's version of events was the same as Mai's?'

'Yes,' Pickup snarls. 'Like I said, *I don't want to see you.* Make sure he gets the message.'

'I'll try to make sure that Mycroft behaves himself.' I keep my tone nice and even. Then I remember that I forgot to call

Pickup earlier. 'Oh, and there's something I have to tell you. About Dave.'

Pickup breathes heavily out his nose. I force myself to continue.

'His name is David Washburn. I talked to someone at Royal Park hospital, and they said they knew him. I just thought it might help with the...identification thing...'

Pickup blinks a few times. His frown softens the teeniest bit.

'David Washburn. Royal Park hospital. Right, I'll look into it. Thank you.' He has to force the words out from between his teeth. 'Now you do something for me. No more amateur sleuthing, d'you get it? This is a police matter. Go home. Listen to pop music, watch TV, do homework – whatever it is that normal teenagers do, okay? Stay *out* of it.'

'Right. Stay out of it. We will.' I make a tight bow with my lips, refusing to think about what Mycroft may or may not do once he discovers I've dug up a lead. 'Absolutely.'

Pickup nods at the desk sergeant, then takes in Mai and Gus with an appraising eye. I think he's about to make his point more emphatically. Instead, he walks out. Just like that.

My shoulders, everything, deflates. I can breathe normally again. I catch Mai's *what the?* glance and give her a shrug.

Then another duty sergeant walks Mycroft into the foyer, and my attention is grabbed by the scruff of the neck.

CHAPTER TEN

Mycroft's dressed in a threadbare white T-shirt and gray track pants, and socks but no shoes. Even his hair looks slumped. He has dried blood under one nostril. And he's thin, I realize: thinner than I remember him being in a while. My god, how did I not notice this?

His hunted eyes glance around. He sees me, and his face lifts.

I walk up and stand in front of him. A tiny tsunami lurches in my chest – this is going to be the first time we've spoken since our argument. But what am I going to say?

I think of the word *TWAT* blazing its way into last night's starless sky.

'Yes,' I say. My voice wobbles. 'You are.'

Mycroft licks his lip. 'Yeah, I know I am.'

I stare into his eyes. 'But so am I.'

He blinks, lets out a soft breath. Gives me a worn, cracked smile. 'Please tell me you've got a cigarette, before I kill myself.'

I punch him in the arm.

'Ow! What'd you do that for?'

'For being a complete idiot. Now go over to the desk. After Gus signs your forms, you can get your smokes back.'

———

We're in the back of Gus's uncle's station wagon, driving back to Summoner Street. Mai and Gus are in the front, being happy together. Mycroft and I are maintaining an uncomfortable distance from each other in the back. He's fidgeting because Gus won't let him smoke in his uncle's car. I've got the police-station paperwork in my lap.

'What about your nose?' I say.

'S'okay. Another ding for the collection.' He picks at the blood above his lip. 'And not assault by a police officer, if you're wondering. I knocked it on the railing when I fell. Hurt like crap, but it's all right now.'

'Oh, good. So I can still punch you in the face a few times without causing any lasting damage.'

'C'mon, Watts, I've said I'm sorry at least fifty times…'

'Keep saying it until, oh, maybe *Christmas* and it might make an impression.'

'Jesus, please, *I'm sorry*, okay?'

'You broke into the school. You *torched* the side of a building—'

'It was a high-grade propellant! It won't even leave a scorch mark!'

'—you got yourself *arrested*. I had to pay for a taxi to the cop shop. Gus had to borrow his uncle's car, and we wouldn't even be here *talking* about it without Principal Conroy's benevolence and Mai's gift for legal mumbo-jumbo—'

'She is pretty cool, isn't she?'

'—*and* she confirmed your alibi for the night of the murder. Pickup went ballistic. He's told me to keep you out of trouble on pain of death.'

Mycroft's eyes gleam. 'Yeah, that jail-cell chat with Pickup was quite entertaining. I didn't even know he was out to screw me until he started getting all antsy about the IM thing.'

I punch him on the arm again. 'For *god's sake*, Mycroft, it's not funny! How can someone so smart be such an utter moron? What on earth were you *thinking*?'

'*I WASN'T BLOODY THINKING, okay?*'

Mycroft's voice cracks. He glances towards the front, his expression rippling as he struggles to lower the volume.

'I wasn't...I just couldn't...*breathe*. And I tried just getting smashed, because sometimes that helps, but it didn't help, and I tried working it out...' His hands are clenching, squeezing the gray fabric over his knees. 'I got all these articles together, but I still didn't feel like... And all that stuff I said, about you not caring...'

I'm ripping inside, my moorings coming loose. It was *me* who made him feel that way, by screaming at him about his parents. I want to say something, touch his hands before he ties his fingers into knots.

'...and then I saw the spray thinner so I just...I just did it.' He's staring out the car window as if the explanation is out there on an autocue somewhere, if only he could see it. 'The fire was nice. It looked like...'

I can't stand it. I put my hand on his forearm, and he startles.

'You did all that Diogenes stuff while you were plastered?' I say softly.

'Yeah.' His eyes return to mine. 'You...you saw that, did you?'

'Yeah.' I try to smile. It's a shit attempt at a smile. 'Your spelling is much better when you're drunk.'

'Is it? God.'

He snorts, but it's not funny. It's horribly unfunny.

I need to say something, what I should have said yesterday. I want to return his honesty. But I can't look him in the face when I do it.

'Mycroft, you were right. Everything you said is true. I *don't* want to get attached to this city, or anything about it. I *hate* living in the city.'

I glance up. His expression is crestfallen. I keep going, fast.

'But I do care. I care about what happened to Dave. And I care that I hurt you, talking about your...' His face tightens, so I veer quickly, '...about your history. I wished I could bite my tongue off as soon as I'd said it, and I'm sorry. Mycroft, I'm sorry.'

I examine the minute details of the vinyl interior until I hear his voice.

'At least you didn't go off and get yourself arrested.'

'No,' I say. 'But I just went home and had a big bawl. You actually did something useful.'

'Useful. Right.'

'No, you did. All those articles...'

He sighs. 'I went to the zoo, as well. I walked around looking for that bloody dog for ages.'

'You looked for Poodle?'

'Yeah. But I was too smashed, I could hardly stand up properly. That was just before I went to the school and...'

I catch his gaze as he trails off. 'So you didn't find him?'

'No. But I will.' Mycroft's eyes are lit by some deep burn, lava-hot beneath the surface. 'Watts, he's the key to *all* this. Don't you get it? Poodle is the most important fact of the whole case.'

I don't get it. I don't even agree with him about Dave's murder, although his work on sport killing and escalation in homicides has made me think in disturbing new directions.

'Look,' I say, 'there's something you should know. I went to Royal Park hospital, because I remembered something Dave said once, about taking shelter there. And I talked to someone, and found out his name – David Washburn. So he has a name now.'

Mycroft gapes. 'You went to Royal Park?'

'Yes. I told Pickup. He needed to know, if only so they can stop calling Dave "John Doe" down at the morgue.'

'David Washburn.' Mycroft tries out the name.

'Yeah. And I've got the name and address of the guy who knew him. I've arranged to go over to his house tomorrow and get some more information. I'll have to skive off school, but I think it's worth it. Do you…' I pause and push my hair back. 'D'you wanna come? It's not far on the train.'

Mycroft's smile starts slow, builds until it's radiant. He's got no shoes, a bloody nose and a hangover, but the effect on me is still devastating. I look at the scuffs on the car mats – plain things, sane things.

'Absolutely,' he says. 'Definitely. And my social calendar is free for, oh, about five days, so…'

'Oh shit. Conroy suspended you?' I don't know why I'm surprised.

'He was pretty decent about it.' Mycroft waves a careless hand. 'It's fine. My home-suspension schoolwork should take about ten minutes and then I'll have five days free for anything.'

'Pickup told me that if he catches us "amateur sleuthing" again, he'll throw the book at us.'

'Yeah…' Mycroft looks out at the passing glisten of shop windows. His expression is lost again, like when he first emerged from behind the desk at the police station. 'I'm pretty crap at it anyway, aren't I? Dave's still dead, and we're not any closer to figuring out why he was killed. I just wish I could…I dunno.'

'What?' I say. 'So you're not the world's most perfect detective. Give yourself a break.'

'I *want* to be,' he says fiercely. 'I want to be Sherlock-bloody-Holmes.'

'You're not Sherlock.' I reach over and squeeze his hand. 'You're Mycroft, the much-smarter brother, remember? We'll work it out. Dave Washburn won't have died for nothing. It'll all come together, I swear.'

Mycroft squeezes back, and I think, *oh shit, what have I done?* I've agreed to help him work out the truth, when half of me doesn't believe there's any more truth to find. I must be barmy.

Mai chooses this exact moment to turn around and lean her head over the back of the seat. I give her a look.

'Did I hear my name mentioned earlier? Part of a heartfelt praise of my brilliance, I hope. And guys, we're here – Summoner Street. You're home.'

———

Gus and Mai drop us off near Mycroft's house. I was very specific about not being dropped off near mine. It's nearly three-thirty – I don't think Mum and Dad will be back yet, but Mike could arrive home at any time. I prefer to err on the side of caution.

We get out and make our effusive thanks. Mai and Gus drive off and we walk on.

I don't even think about it when Mycroft swerves into his

front yard – I swerve too. We fight our way past the weeds, along the side to the back entrance.

Suddenly, Mycroft stops. I collide into his back and bruise my nose.

A woman is exiting the house by the back door. She's skinny, late thirties. Her jeans, runners, and green T-shirt are all worn and faded. She's tied a bandanna around her head, from which lank strands of blonde are staging a desperate escape.

When the woman hikes up her shoulder bag, I see her face. She's aging badly, with that gray complexion that fair-skinned people get when they're unhealthy. Her mouth is pinched; her eyes, scanning over me, are tired, angry.

So…this is Angela?

She and Mycroft give each other a wide berth on the path, with wary glances and thin tight lips. I immediately think of cats who reluctantly share territory.

'You're off early.' Mycroft's voice is so neutral and forced he sounds like one of those pre-recorded phone messages.

Angela keeps her tone similarly blank. 'Didn't finish vacuuming one of the admin blocks last night. Got to make it up.'

'Righto.'

They veer around one another. I stick behind Mycroft as though I'm glued to his shoulderblades.

Just before Angela disappears around the corner, she looks back. 'There were messages about you on my phone. From the police.'

'What, you couldn't be bothered picking up?' Mycroft sounds off-hand, but his face is a stiff mask.

'I was sleeping.'

'Right. Of course you were.'

'Were you even going to tell me?' Angela's voice is taut as she scratches for a cigarette from the pack in her jeans pocket. 'Or was I just supposed to mind-read again?'

'I didn't want to stress you out,' Mycroft says evenly. He shifts his feet, looking at the back door.

There's a pause thick enough to slice through.

'You didn't want to stress me out.' Angela stares at him, holding her cigarette in a pincer grip. 'Is that all you're going to say, then?'

'What do you *want* me to say?' Mycroft chews his lip so hard I'm worried he'll make a hole. 'Anyway, I'm here now, aren't I? Look, it's over. Just...go to work.'

'James—'

'*Don't call me that!*'

The snap in his voice makes me jump, but Angela doesn't even react. Her gaze travels from me to Mycroft, taking the measure of both of us. 'Fine. Just mind how you and the girlfriend go. I'd rather not have any more unexpected phone calls.'

'She's not my girlfriend,' Mycroft grates out.

Even though I was about to blurt exactly the same thing, the way he says it makes my ribs squeeze together painfully.

'Right.' Angela's definitely glowering now. 'Just mind how you go, like I said, or Social Services will be on our doorstep again, and I think I've had just about all I can take for one week.'

She sticks the cigarette in her mouth, digs in her pocket for a light as she turns on her heel and stalks off. If she really was a cat, her tail would be whipping from side to side.

Mycroft stands there, staring, his jaw clenched. Just as I'm about to say something, anything, he puts his key in the lock and his shoulder against the back door and shoves it open. He leaves me to close up as he barrels down the hallway. When we're safely in his room, with all the Christmas lights twinkling, I can still see the flare in his eyes.

'So.' I cross my arms around my chest, like I've caught a chill. 'The fabled Angela.'

'Yes.' His voice is tight as he strips off his dirty T-shirt and hunts for a clean one. 'She of legend. Songs have been written, et cetera.'

'Right. Well. Have you considered just...leaving post-it notes for each other or something? That would eliminate the need for face-to-face contact.'

'I've considered *many* things.' He actually cracks a smile, pulling a blue long-sleeve over his head. Then he lets his head hang back, closes his eyes. 'Four months. Four more months, then I'm eighteen, and I can get the hell out of this dump...'

He thumbs the button on his laptop. I take a look at him in the blue glow of the resolving screensaver and put a hand on his arm.

'Mycroft, wait. Stop.'

'I have to pull up the records for David Washburn.' He fumbles with the mouse. 'Check out the Royal Park angle. There's heaps of—'

'Mycroft, take a break. Ease down.' I shift my hand to his shoulder. It's rigid with tension. 'Come on, you just got out of jail, you're hung-over, and you've hardly slept. Have a rest.'

'But we can't—'

'Yes, we can. Dave's already dead, he can wait. He'll understand.'

I close the lid of the laptop and steer Mycroft towards the bed. He flops down onto it, hands squeezing his forehead. While he pulls off his filthy wet socks, I get some paracetamol and a glass of water from the kitchen. Once he's sculled the medication, I push on his chest until he falls backwards.

'You're very competent at this.' His voice is a slurring breath and his eyes are already closed.

'Well, it's not the first time I've gotten you squared away.' I glance elsewhere as I pull the blanket up. I don't know if he'd appreciate me reminding him.

I stand up and walk to the door. Just as I'm about to go, I hear Mycroft's voice, barely audible.

'Thanks, Watts. For getting me squared away.'

'No worries.' I give him a smile. 'I'll be back later. Get some sleep.'

———

I feel strangely buoyant after leaving Mycroft's place. By five-thirty, I'm thoroughly pleased with myself. I've vacuumed, swept, done dishes, cleaned the bathroom and put on a load of washing. The soup I've made for dinner is bubbling away on the stove when Mike and Mum walk in the door simultaneously.

'Is there any meat in there at all?' Mike views the insides of the pot with suspicion, gives the contents a bit of a stir.

'You had lunch at Patrick's,' I say. 'Barbeque, wasn't it?'

'Yep.'

'So you've had your steak-and-sausage RDI. Stop fussing, at least it's made for you.'

'But I'm a carnivore,' Mike complains.

'Meat's expensive.' I pull out a Tupperware container and ladle some soup into it. 'Tell Mum I've put the kettle on for her.'

'I'm right here,' Mum says. She's pulling a brush through her damp hair. 'Thanks, love. What's that for, are you freezing some?'

'No, it's for two doors down. Last day of work for a while, hey?'

I'm aware that I'm talking fast and not mentioning Mycroft by name.

Mike gives me a funny look. 'Thought you and Mycroft weren't on speaking terms.'

'We worked it out,' I say curtly. I give Mum a cheery look. 'So, you ready for the weekend?'

It's a running joke that Mum has a mid-week weekend, because she works all day Saturday and Sunday. But she's not taking the bait today.

'Yes, I'm well ready.' Her voice is very even. 'And I must say I'm getting a little bit tired of the fact that I'm working my bum off to feed someone who never bothers to stay for dinner. What's wrong with Mycroft eating at our place?'

There's a little frozen moment as the kettle starts whistling.

I don't look her way as I make the tea. 'Oh, come on, Mum. You've never objected before.'

'No, I haven't, and I think I've been incredibly patient. If Mycroft's not going to do us the courtesy of staying to eat, then I think he'll just have to fend for himself. I'm sick of you delivering takeaway every night.'

I stop dunking the tea bag and turn. 'Mum. You've seen his house. He'd be eating at the Salvos if we didn't help him out occasionally.'

'But he has his computer, and his bills paid for him, and all the rest of it – it's not as if he's completely—'

'He's not going to hock his laptop for groceries, is he?' I pour the milk, knowing my voice is too sharp, trying to soften it. 'His aunt pays enough to keep the place going, but she's working too hard to be much good at the regular stuff, like meals and—'

'Well, why doesn't he eat here? And if they're in such a bad way, why hasn't the welfare stepped in? Rachel—'

'Why are you bringing this up now? And what's with all the Scrooge stuff, I thought you were always into being charitable?' I plonk Mum's tea on the kitchen table. My fingers feel cold despite the warmth of the mug. 'What happened to all that community spirit you used to preach? Like when Ellen Davies's husband passed away and you made all those frozen meals for her?'

'Ellen was one of my closest friends.' Mum's words are stiff, her face an echo. Her hand holding the hairbrush has dropped to her side. 'And at the moment, this family is just about bordering on a charity case as well. I'd like to know, I really would, when someone is going to start being charitable towards *us*.'

'Well, that's the city for you, Mum. No one gives a shit about anybody. Maybe you and Dad should have given it some thought when we moved here.'

I turn around to thump the lid on the Tupperware container. My face feels like granite when I turn back.

Mum is staring at me. Mike is standing near the doorway to the kitchen. His expression says he'd rather be anywhere else in the world, back at Patrick's perhaps.

'*Rachel*—' Mum swallows hard, presses her lips. 'I honestly don't understand where all this attitude comes from. I *know* you don't like being here. I *know* you don't like the city. But *we're* not the city – we're your *family*.'

'I know that.' I squeeze the edge of the table with white fingers.

'These last four months, it's like you've had a total personality change. Your father, your brother, me…we're no different from when we lived in Five Mile. It's just the scenery that's different—'

'*I know that!*'

'*Then why are you behaving like this?*' Mum lifts her hairbrush, like she's going to strike out with it. 'I feel like I'm working as hard as I can to keep this family together! And then I come home to *this* – all this *hostility*, bad feeling... It's like you're angry *all the time*, Rachel! It's bloody *exhausting!*'

'You started this!'

'Rachel—'

'My god, aren't you ever *happy*?' I fling out my hands, hardly recognizing the raw raised voice as my own. 'I do all the housework, all the bloody washing and tidying up, make all the dinners... Can't you just be satisfied with that? Do you have to give me the third degree about how I'm hostile, and get stuck into my friends as well?'

'Rachel—'

'It's not *fair!* This whole bloody thing is unfair!'

I turn, blindly grab the Tupperware, wrap a dishtowel around it, operating on automatic. Mike dodges clear as I push out of the kitchen, out of the house, out and out...

It's not until I'm on the footpath that I remember my original destination. I clasp the Tupperware full of hot soup to my chest. It's the only warm spot on my entire body.

CHAPTER ELEVEN

Summoner Street looks almost peaceful in the gloaming light. I close the back door to Mycroft's house behind me and walk through the dismal hallway until I come to the Stranger's Room.

I carefully tiptoe through the open door into the kaleidoscopic twinkle of the Christmas lights in the half-dark. I set the Tupperware container full of soup down on the desk and glance behind me.

Mycroft is snoring gently, one arm thrown over his face, his long body twisted in the sheets except for his bare feet, which stick off the end of his too-small mattress. It's almost exactly the same position I left him in that December evening. My *'What part of FUCK OFF don't you understand?'* birthday evening.

I get a seasick, déjà vu feeling so strong I take a step back. Then almost without thinking I reach up to the shelves above the desk, to the highest shelf, and bring down the large blue-covered photo album.

The book is heavy in my hands, as though all the grief

contained inside gives it extra weight. I sink down on the floor, the book inside my crossed legs. I look at Mycroft again. Then I open the cover, just like I did before.

The first few pages seem normal, like an album you'd have at home. There are photos of a man and a woman, both separate and together.

The man is tall, lean-muscled but pale, with very dark curly hair. He looks serious, although in several shots there's the hint of a wicked smile. In some photos he wears nutmeg-colored cords and a waistcoat, like a university professor, and rimless reading glasses.

The woman is slender and her hair flows around her face in a blonde cascade. A resemblance to Angela Hudgson is subliminal, but this woman is like a summer sunset on Bondi beach. Her piercing blue eyes are instantly recognizable.

The man and woman together make a striking couple, dark and fair. In each snapshot you can see the soft looks they bestow, the way their bodies lean together. In a wedding photo, the man has a protective arm curled around the woman's waist. I'm reminded of twin saplings that twine around each other as they grow.

Then there's a tiny newspaper cutting and a lock of very fine blond hair, tied with a scarlet slip of ribbon. The cutting says: *'Edward Whelan Mycroft and Katherine Josephine Mycroft (nee Hudgson) are proud to announce the birth of their son, James Whelan, 8 pounds 7 ounces, on 23 July. With thanks to the midwives and staff of Barts and the London Hospital Maternity Service, and with great joy.'*

And then there are the baby photos, of course, and they're funny, and unbelievably cute, the way baby photos are. I would smile, looking at them again, only I know what's coming, so I can't smile. It's all too awful, too poignant. Even the other photos – of a toddler with darkening curls, a boy grinning on a trike, the same boy in school uniform with a soccer ball under his arm – just make me sad.

After a page with photos of a family on holiday (dark-haired father throwing snowballs with his curly-haired son; mother cuddling her son inside a firelit living room), there's a gap, where the pages are blank.

My hand shakes as I turn to the next part.

The first item is another news cutting. It's much larger than the birth announcement, and the headline is black, dramatic:

MOTORWAY TRAGEDY DESTROYS FAMILY

A shocking accident on the A1 just outside of London yesterday afternoon has claimed the life of promising academics Edward and Katherine Mycroft, of Paddington, and left their young son in a critical condition in Royal London Hospital's paediatric intensive care unit.

While returning from a holiday, tragedy struck when the family car – a white late-model Volvo sedan – veered and struck a road pylon at a speed greater than sixty-five kilometers per hour. Witnesses said the car was traveling normally until…

There's more, but I've read it before. There are so many other articles, clippings, letters, and essays that I only read the excerpts this time.

My eyes flick through the file – because that's what it's become, a case file – and catch short sentences, scatterings of detail. Other headlines, such as *Police Deny Shooting Attack Caused Academics' Deaths* and *Investigation of A1 Crash* jump out. The different typefaces form a dizzying waterfall of jumbled text.

...police are yet to release details of the crash, and are appealing for information...

...the couple's ten-year-old son with internal injuries. Hospital sources have described his condition as grave. Any information can be provided via the police hotline...

...CCTV footage of the crash has not been released by investigators. While bullet fragments were recovered from the scene, the police have no theories as to...

...Police are baffled by what they are now describing as 'a carjacking gone wrong', which killed a prominent academic and his wife, and has left their young son recovering...

Then there's an entire collection of articles and correspondence, with titles such as 'Carjacking: legal definitions and frameworks' and 'Case Histories – Carjacking, Vehicular Homicide 1990–1999/2000–2010' that look as if they've been obtained by request.

There's loads of legal jargon and some information that reads as though it's come out of a manual or online encyclopedia. I flick through that briefly, picking up things like *Carjacking is a form of hijacking, where the crime is stealing a motor vehicle and so also armed assault when the vehicle is occupied... and increasing carjacking cases in the UK there has been some discussion whether specific carjacking laws are... a man who authorities say was a passenger on a motorcycle, who fired a shotgun through the window of a car on the Eisenhower Expressway ...* and I'm starting to feel as though I'm in a vortex, reading it all.

Only a few things stand out under the onslaught of all this. The first thing is the sheer volume of information – the album is big, and the papers are bulging out of it. I wonder if, once this album has exhausted itself of available pages, there's going to be a second album, or even a third… The idea is terrifying, because I think I already know the answer.

Another thing that catches my eye is a printed email, in which a professor emeritus from Durban, South Africa, has written: *In reply to your inquiry, in most carjacking attempts the objective is to steal the victim's car in a blitz-style attack. Firing into a car while it is traveling at speed would typically be considered counter to such an objective, as the car would be written off in the resulting crash. I would be wary of any attempt to catalog an attack of this nature as a carjacking. What it resembles more closely is an assassination, a deliberate homicide of the car's occupants. You can see my refs here, dated…*

The reason this stands out is because the original email inquiry is included below the reply. In the email address field is *diogenes@gmail.com,* the first time I've seen the use of Mycroft's professional pseudonym in the file. It has a timestamp from three years ago.

But what I return to, as I reverse my momentum and turn back pages the way I've come, is a short quote from a newspaper item early in the initial reporting on the accident. It's the only mention of what happened to the boy, the one whose 'condition is grave', and who 'suffered internal injuries', and 'was airlifted to hospital'.

…the hospital is not willing to comment. The boy, who has been operated on twice since Wednesday, will now fall under the care of his closest living relative, a maternal aunt.

I trace the lines with my finger. Then I close the album, encase it all back in its heavy covers. My knees ache from being in one position for so long. I'm about to get up and return the album to its shelf when the click of a lighter makes me jerk.

'Do you often snoop around in my stuff while I'm asleep?'

Mycroft is propped on one elbow, rumpled sheets pooled

around his waist. He tosses his lighter and cigarette pack onto the carpet beside the mattress, and gives me a cool, appraising look as he exhales smoke.

'Only when...' I swallow and smooth the cover of the album with my thumb. 'Only when you're asleep, yes.'

'Okay.' His eyes are the blue of a lightning storm. Except for the dark raccoon-circles around them, their resemblance to his mother's is very strong. 'I only get that down for anniversary days now.'

'I know. I've seen it before. That night...'

'That night you came over. Yeah, I remember.'

'I'm surprised you remember,' I say slowly. 'You never even mentioned it the next day. You just arrived with those enormous sunglasses on—'

'I remember,' he says. His voice has a flat finality.

I don't think, I just speak. 'That was my birthday.'

He stops in the act of raising his cigarette to his lips. 'That night? The twentieth of December?'

'Yes.'

'That's your birthday?'

'Yes.'

Smoke curls out of the glowing tip of his cigarette as he stares at my face.

I always want to ask, and there's never an appropriate time to ask. This moment seems as inappropriate as any, but I do it. I ask.

'Do you think you'll ever know what happened to your parents?'

Straight away, I'm appalled that I said it. But Mycroft's face shows no expression at all.

'I know what happened to my parents,' he says. His hand trembles, just faintly, as he ashes into the saucer by the bed. His

160

voice comes out raspy and very quiet. 'They were people. And they died.'

He looks at me and my mouth goes dry. There's nothing I can say, and what I've already said I can't erase. This is worse than when we fought, because he's so calm about it. I've jabbed my finger into a bleeding wound, and although Mycroft's not flinching I can feel the pain in him, ghosting around us in the smoke.

Oh my god, I'm on a roll tonight. This was supposed to be my sanctuary, and now I've ruined it. I've done my usual great job of stuffing everything up. I stand, dizzy, the blood throbbing in my face.

'I . . . I'll put this back.'

It's a relief to turn around. I lift the album to the shelf, stretching on my toes to lodge it in place. My tank rides up at the back and I'm self-conscious, sure Mycroft is watching me.

Then there's a rustle, and suddenly Mycroft's breath is right next to my ear.

'Here.'

CHAPTER TWELVE

Mycroft's hands cover mine and his long body stretches up behind me. He is still warm from his bed. The warmth combines with my flush of humiliation and fans out inside me like tongues of fire.

Our legs and arms are tangled, root and branch. Mycroft reaches higher, traps me against the desk, his hip against my bare back. He smells of cigarettes and sleep, and suddenly this other awareness licks through me that I shouldn't be feeling now, and my palms are sweating, sliding on the album as our hands fumble together, and the damned album is, like, *stuck* or something…

I swallow and my voice comes out breathless. 'I don't need your help, I can—'

'It's done.' When Mycroft speaks, I feel the vibration against my shoulderblades. The album is in its spot. Our arms lower together and his hands gently turn my shoulders. 'Watts…'

I keep my eyes focused forward and my body stiff. I don't want to meet his gaze, but it means that now I'm staring at his chest, and I don't know which is worse. His muscles curve gently beneath the thin blue fabric of his T-shirt. If I put my hand there, I could feel his heartbeat. The urge is so powerful my hand lifts of its own accord, floats in space.

There's only one thing I can do, what I should have done in the first place. Mycroft's palms are hot on my shoulders, and I've got this strange light-headed feeling, but I just have to push through it.

'Mycroft, I'm sorry. I…I didn't mean to offend you.' My breathing is tight and I rush to the finish. 'I shouldn't have looked through your album or asked about your parents, it's none of my business—'

'*Watts.*'

He moves one hand to lift my chin, his eyes darting across my face. I'm staring at him now, and his expression seems to fold through so many different emotions I can't keep up. It's the same intensity he had the day we argued, but this time he doesn't look angry. His cheeks are colored high, and he seems to be holding his breath.

Then he swallows and licks his lips, drops his hands, steps back.

'It's fine. I'm not offended. You've seen it all anyway. You know what it means.'

He turns and recovers the cigarette he's left in the ashtray. He's not looking at me anymore, and I wonder if he's telling the truth. He has every right to be furious.

But when he speaks again, his voice is completely normal. 'What are you doing over here anyway? I thought you were going to let me sleep?'

I blink at the sudden reprieve, my legs unsteady.

'I have. I mean, I did.' I grope in my jeans pocket for my phone, check the screen. 'It's nearly seven. I've brought you some soup. I mean, I made soup, so I thought—'

Mycroft dabs out his cigarette, turns to frown at me. 'Watts, is there something going on over at your house?'

I look away. God, am I that easy to read? 'I had a fight with Mum. I just…I needed to get out. I didn't think… I hoped you wouldn't mind.'

'Mind?' Mycroft scratches both hands through his hair. 'God, I don't mind.'

'Mycroft, I really am sor—'

'I said it's fine. You brought soup. I could eat a horse. A soup made from horses.'

'It's only vegetables,' I say limply.

'Not to worry. I want tea. Do you want tea? I'm desperate for a piss, so I'll make it on the way back.'

He rubs his stomach through his T-shirt, walks out of the room on bare feet. I get up the guts to call through the open door, 'Make sure you wash your hands.'

He gives me the finger, and a weight lifts off my heart. He's okay. I'm okay. We're good, we're normal, and I am absurdly grateful just to be here.

———

The room is dark. Starry twinkles on the walls fold us into our own galaxy.

In a curious reversal of our usual positions, I'm the one at the desk, typing on the laptop, one foot tucked beneath me. Mycroft sits on the floor with his back against the wall and his long legs stretched out in their regulation black jeans.

'Do you want all the forensics articles split up into something more manageable?' I backspace, then cover a yawn with my hand. 'Mm, sorry. I can put some under organic chemistry, or

164

we could just break it up into different sections.'

'I'm not sure.' Mycroft's strumming my guitar, which sounds terrible because it's so out of tune. 'You don't have to do this, you know.'

'I'm going to keep them together,' I say. I make a few clicks, unkink my neck. 'Mycroft, we've been over this. I said I would do it, and you said I didn't have to do it, and I said I wanted to do it. Can we just—'

'No, it's fine. I meant you didn't have to do it all in one night.'

'It's nearly done.' I'm close enough to want to keep at it now. '*Diogenes* is now an official site. I've put up a counter, so you can see when people are looking at stuff, and there are comments fields at the end of every article. You'll be able to log people's ISPs in case you get any idiots who want to hassle you. And it's all completely gender-neutral and anonymous.'

Mycroft fiddles with the guitar pegs. 'I said thank you, didn't I? God, I hope I said thank you.'

'Yes, Mycroft. You've said thank you at least half a dozen times now.'

'I mean, I could do it myself. I'm not averse to doing things myself. But you seem to be doing it much quicker than I would, so—'

'I'm much better at this than you.' I smile at the screen, content with imagining his expression. 'Come on, I have to do *something* better than you. You can't have the complete monopoly on *everything*.'

Mycroft plucks a string, gives it the full reverb. I look over. He shakes the neck of the guitar and bites his lip with his eyes screwed up, like a heavy metal soloist. I snort. The note twangs into silence.

'What else do you like to do?' he asks suddenly.

'What do you mean?'

'You know what I mean. Stuff you like to do. You *know* all the shit I like to do. And I know you're good with computer stuff, and you like reading, and you like music, and you can play guitar—'

'Badly.'

'Better than me, at any rate. What else?'

I tap and click and I don't know how to reply.

'I dunno. Stuff.' I think about it. 'I used to like hiking. And horseriding. And dirt-biking. I used to do that with Mike.'

'Can't do that stuff in the city.'

'No.' I brush an annoying moth off the screen. 'Anyway, when would I have time to do all that now? I spend most of every day doing either schoolwork or housework. There isn't a lot of room in the margins.'

'You probably need to sort that out, then.'

'Probably,' I say, but I'm not really focused on the conversation because I've completed uploading everything. 'Hey. Come and check it out.'

The guitar dongs mournfully as Mycroft clambers to his feet. I turn the laptop so he can see the home page headed by *Diogenes* in electric blue on a black background. He props himself on the corner of the desk.

'The layout's very simple,' I explain. 'It'll be easier to maintain if it isn't fancy.'

'It's *fantastic*.' Mycroft smiles fit to burst. 'Watts, this is awesome. I can't believe you did this in...' he checks the screen, '...oh shit, four hours. I guess that's a while.'

I lean back in the wheeled office chair as far as I can go, dig my fingers into the small of my back.

'Yeah. Ah god, that hurts.' I let my head loll backwards, close my sore eyes. 'I think a hot shower would be perfect now. Or a full-body massage.'

I open my eyes. Mycroft is staring down at me. He has a very strange expression on his face.

'What is it?' I sit back up and check the screen. 'Did I screw something up?'

Mycroft opens his mouth, closes it, shakes his head. 'No. It's...nothing. It's great.'

'Oh, good.' I push the chair away from the desk and unfold my leg, which has gone to sleep. 'I don't suppose I could trouble you for a cup of tea?'

'Aren't you up past your bedtime?'

'Yes, but I'm procrastinating. I don't want to go home. Which is stupid, because Mum's probably in bed by now.'

Mycroft has moved to pick up my guitar and settle it gently back against the wall. 'You could crash on my couch, but I don't have one.'

'Thanks for the offer, but I haven't done a sleepover since I was in primary school.' Then I realize what that sounds like and I blush. God, I really must be tired.

Mycroft snorts and grins. 'Tea it is, then.'

He pours me a cup from the thermos near the bed, comes back to hand me the mug. We swap places so I can stand up and stretch my legs.

'You know, this is really going to be fantastic. If there's a query, I'll be able to—' He stops scrolling down the list of articles. 'You put all the homelessness references on the site.'

I nod.

'I thought you didn't want me to post anything about Dave's case?'

'I know that's what I said. But I've been thinking about it. I think you should publicize it. That homelessness data and the sport-killing stuff...It's important.'

He blinks at me. 'Well, what about the murder?'

'Put that up too. Get the information out there, maybe it'll help somebody. And...Dave should be remembered. When we figure out who killed him—'

Mycroft stands up from the chair, staring from the screen to my face.

'You think we can really do this? Solve this case?'

'I know we can,' I say.

And for the first time since all this started, I believe it to be true.

———

The tired red brick of the Science wing wall looks unremarkable on Monday morning. There are a few blackened edges at the top of what I assume was the *TWAT* artwork, but I can't see the letters. Whatever chemical Mycroft used to make his grand statement, it hasn't done any lasting damage.

'He's certainly a man of extremes.'

Mai has walked over to check out the wall as well. She's eating an icypole, which must surely give you brain-freeze at eight-forty-five in the morning.

She's wearing red-and-yellow striped tights under black denim shorts. Today's T-shirt has a picture of a woman with an Alice band in her hair, one hand raised to her cheek and the other brandishing a fifties-style ray gun. The slogan says *Flash! Flash, I love you! But we only have fourteen hours to save the Earth!*

She checks out my stunning wardrobe combination of – you

168

guessed it – white tank top, blue flannie and jeans. At least I wore my Cons today, for some variety.

I point at the wall. 'Extreme is kind of Mycroft's middle name.'

'If Extreme was his middle name, we'd still only be allowed to call him Mycroft.' Mai offers me some icypole, which I decline. 'What is it? Are you worried about him?'

'I don't know. Do you think I should be? Maybe this is the price you pay for hanging out with fledgling geniuses.'

'Did you know that Einstein got expelled from school?' Mai gestures with her iced treat. 'And apparently Edison was a complete jerk. And Sherlock Holmes—'

'Was fictional.'

'Don't interrupt. Sherlock Holmes was a total nightmare, shooting holes in the walls, and not talking for days, and playing violin until all hours, and being a general pain in the arse to live with.'

'Maybe I should consider myself lucky,' I say.

We stand and look at the wall.

Mai tilts her head. 'You know, I think it's kind of romantic.'

'What?'

'You don't think so? The fiery sweeping gesture, the emblazoned apology, the—'

Gus runs up, panting, and stands with his hands propped on his knees. 'Conroy's on the warpath. He's looking for you, Rachel.'

'For me?' I clutch my satchel. 'Where is he?'

'English wing, last I saw.'

'Great.' I turn to Mai. 'I'd better go.'

'You can't dodge forever.' Mai passes what's left of the icypole to Gus. 'Conroy knows where you live.'

The bell's gone. I almost manage to collect my junk from my

locker and get clear, but then a booming voice echoes down the hall.

'Rachel Watts!' Conroy is barrelling in my direction. 'A moment, please.'

I turn slowly and paste on a compliant smile. 'Yes, Mr Conroy?'

Conroy is red-faced, but not out of breath. The same can't be said for the small, overweight man in the caramel-colored cardigan trailing in his wake. With a sinking sensation I recognize Mr Fossum, the school counselor, whose name I bandied about at the St Kilda Road police station only two days ago.

'Miss Watts,' Conroy says. 'I understand you were instrumental in helping with Mr Mycroft's release yesterday.'

I nod warily. 'It was good of you not to bring charges, sir.'

Conroy's eyebrows look stuck together.

'Well, *good* would be conditional on Mycroft never again doing anything so unbelievably stupid, which I can in no way guarantee.' Conroy gestures to his side. 'In any case, I'd appreciate if you could talk to Mr Fossum here. He'd like to know a bit more about Mycroft's outbursts.'

I frown. 'Outbursts?'

Mr Fossum is blinking at me with watery gray eyes magnified by the lenses of his glasses. 'Rachel, you live next door to James, is that right?'

I lied when I told Detective Pickup what Mr Fossum said about closure. I've never been to see Mr Fossum. Not even the day after I saw a dead body.

'I live two doors down,' I correct.

Mr Fossum adjusts his cardigan. 'And does James seem troubled outside of school?'

The way Fossum calls Mycroft 'James', like they're best buds, really gets up my nose. My polite expression is thinning out.

170

'Well, I know Mycroft gets fantastic grades, with no effort at all. But if you want to know about his mental state, I'm not sure what to tell you. Is it even ethical you're asking me?'

Conroy glowers to one side. 'Miss Watts, *you* get some of the best academic results in your year level as well. But I haven't had you in my office anywhere near as often as Mycroft.'

I stare at each of them in turn. 'Can I make a suggestion? Stop treating Mycroft like he's a head case. Maybe he's an eccentric genius or something. Do you really want him case-managed and medicated until he's a "normal" person? Mycroft's not a "normal" person. Maybe you should just... get over it.'

Conroy's frown repertoire seems to have extended – the gray shrubs have turned into an entire hedge. Mr Fossum's eyes bead up eagerly.

'Miss Watts, do you think the school was unfair to give Mycroft a suspension?' Conroy seems to actually want my honest opinion.

'No, sir,' I say with a sigh. 'I think you were well within your rights to do that, but—'

Mr Fossum thrusts his head forward. 'So does being an eccentric genius excuse any kind of behavior, no matter how antisocial or self-destructive?'

I ignore him. 'Mr Conroy, I'm sorry, but I've really got to get to class.'

Conroy waits a beat, then jerks his head sideways. I'm dismissed.

Once I'm away from the locker area I feel like I can breathe again. I try to put the conversation from my mind, but Fossum's comment is like the worm in the apple, gnawing through my brain.

Does being an eccentric genius excuse any kind of behavior, no matter how antisocial or self-destructive?

———

171

Slipping out of school early proves a lot less troublesome than I thought it would be. When I go to the reception office at lunch to get a pass for the 7-Eleven down the street, Conroy is there. My heart is in my throat until I discover that douchey Mr Fossum has provided me with a get-out-of-jail-free card.

'Well, Miss Watts, your time with the counselor has made some kind of impression. Mr Fossum feels that you're under stress, and would benefit from having time out of the school environment.'

Is that armchair-psycho speech for 'have the rest of the day off'? Apparently it is, because Conroy gives me a pass to go home.

'We'll see you tomorrow, when you're feeling a bit refreshed. All right?'

I'm amazed. Teachers are so weird. Fossum and Conroy are giving me time off because they think my friend is a nut-job? What would they do if they knew about the whole murder-case thing? The possibilities are endless.

Out of school, I find Mycroft lurking near the rubbish skips at the car-park entrance. Maybe he thinks his black jeans and navy T-shirt make him 'one with the shadows', or maybe he just doesn't care.

'Jesus, Mycroft, if Conroy sees us together outside school grounds—'

'It's too late for you now, Watts.' He grins. 'Conroy's already tagged you as one of my known associates.'

'You're supposed to be on suspension. As in, nowhere near the school.'

'It's a stupid system. Giving me five days holiday – that's supposed to be some kind of punishment? I'll be back in a week, so what's the point?' He gazes dolefully at the school, then gives himself a shake. 'Anyway, have you got the address?'

I pat my satchel as we walk. 'I checked it out last night. It's only three stops on the train.'

'Are you gonna tell me who this bloke is that we're visiting? He's not a recently-released psycho patient who's going to come after us with an ax or something?'

'No psycho axes,' I say. 'He's a nice guy. But you'll have to wait.'

Mycroft rolls his eyes. 'Come on. If we leg it, we can make the one-fifteen train.'

Mycroft is quiet on the train ride, cogitating over something. I rest my head against the window and alternate staring at the city landscape, and at the other passengers.

I surreptitiously watch two very black young women, Ethiopian maybe, with cornrowed hair that swishes over their shoulders like a beaded curtain. One's steadying a pram. They're both incredibly slim and tall, and their clothes are like a sexy rainbow. Three Asian guys, one of whom is severely overweight, commandeer the facing seats near the door. A broken-looking white woman about Mum's age, with straggly limp hair, chews on her lips and gazes out the window. On the other side of the aisle two boys are melted into each other, making out so passionately I have to look away.

Where are all these people headed? There was never such a variety of people in my hometown. Five Mile is very white and very straight – farming people who've lived there for generations. They would view any one of the passengers on this train as an opportunity for raised eyebrows and gossip.

But here, in the big smoke, variety is everywhere. It's startling, disconcerting and, in some ways, a bit of a relief.

I'm contemplating this when I realize Mycroft's fixated on the carpet. I give him a gentle nudge with my elbow.

He blinks back to life. 'Are we there yet?'

'One more stop.'

'Sorry, I was just thinking…' He cracks his knuckles, like he's getting ready to do some heavy lifting. 'We're missing a lot about this case. Modus operandi, identity of the killer, motive.'

'So what's our theory?'

'We only have speculation. We don't have enough facts to work out a theory. All we've got so far is Dave's real name and a suspicion about his death. That's bugger-all. We need more information.'

'Well, if we can find out more about Dave's circumstances it might give us a lead. So today might be useful.'

'And the dog. We need to find the dog.'

I sigh. I've given up Poodle for dead long ago. I don't like being reminded of the horrible things Dave's attacker might have done to the dog. I change the subject.

'Well, no matter what we do, we can't ask the police for help. Pickup clearly doesn't want us anywhere near the case. He really seems to hate your guts. At the police station yesterday he was talking about getting a warrant to search your house.'

Mycroft folds his arms, digging his fingers into his biceps. 'Let him. I'm not hiding anything from that bastard.'

My eyebrows shoot up. 'You're not?'

'No. Why would I?'

'I thought you, er…Maybe in your room…' I clear my throat. 'Well, actually, I thought you might have something pharmaceutical.'

'What?'

'Recreational.'

Mycroft knits his dark eyebrows. 'I don't think so. Should I?'

'You *are* a chemist.'

'I'd never thought about it.' He regards me with an amused expression.

'Shit, I've gone and given you ideas now, haven't I?'

'Well…'

'Shut up.' I put my hand in front of his face and look out the window. 'Just don't say anything for thirty seconds.'

'This is our station.'

'*Thirty seconds.*'

We exit the train station together, Mycroft looking at me with this funny, entertained face and me with my lips clamped together. I check the address of Gray Jetta's house, and the map on my phone, and we head off in the right direction. Occasionally Mycroft tries to say something. I just put up my hand, and he chuckles.

Finally we're at the right address. The house is tiny, a neat weatherboard with westringia and bottlebrush and saltbush and lilly pilly planted out the front in heaped beds. This guy obviously knows his gardening.

It's just after one-thirty, by my phone, so we're at the door on time. I can't hear anybody moving around inside the house. I knock, but there's no response.

'Maybe he's busy axing something,' Mycroft says.

I head towards a brick path that wanders around to the right of the house. 'I'm gonna see if he's out the back.'

'What about the ax?'

'Shut up, Mycroft.'

'What if he's doing a spot of nude sunbathing or something?'

'Shut *up*, Mycroft!'

I walk along the path. It's lined all the way with pink correa in full bloom. Hardenbergia riots over the wooden fence. I think my dad would probably like to get together with Mr Jetta and discuss composting.

At the rear of the house there's a small paved area bounding a low deck made from rail sleepers. It's lovely carpentry – the smooth redgum glows like toffee in the midday sun.

Gray Jetta is sitting on the edge of the deck, transferring vegetable seedlings into pots. A half-smoked rollie lolls from the corner of his mouth. His soft brown pants and worn white shirt have dirt wiped on them.

When I step forward he sees me and stands up, a pot in one hand. 'Ah geez, Rachel! Sorry, sorry, when I'm out the back I can't hear nothing, even if you're banging on the front door like crazy. Come in, sorry.'

'I'm sorry to bother you, Mr Jetta,' I say. 'It's really nice of you to see me. I've brought along a friend who knew Dave too, if that's all right.'

'For sure, no, you're not bothering me at all. And you brought a friend…' He looks over my shoulder and his expression transforms. Amazement blooms into a smile that creases all the laugh lines in his face.

I turn to see Mycroft – weary, resigned, dark around the edges. He lights a cigarette and smoke swirls around him, obscuring his features.

'Hello, Gray,' he says.

CHAPTER THIRTEEN

I'm gaping. This does not compute.

I stand between Gray and Mycroft, glancing back and forth between them. I'm saying something like '...but what...how'd you...'.

Mycroft finally breaks the pause by walking over with his hand out. 'Nice to see you again, man.'

'Likewise, Mycroft, likewise.' Gray shakes Mycroft's hand, beaming up at him like this is the best thing ever. 'You got tall, mate.'

'Yeah.'

'Said you would, didn't I?'

'Yeah, you did.'

I still have *no idea* what is going on. *You two know each other?* is obviously completely redundant, so I try for something original.

'I should have guessed this. I don't know why I didn't guess this.'

'What's that?' Gray asks.

'Mycroft knows everybody,' I say. 'I mean, *everybody*.'

Mycroft and Gray look at each other.

'Didn't you tell her?' Gray says. 'Nah, I guess you wouldn't tell her...Do you want me to?'

Mycroft shakes his head. 'No, it's okay.'

He finally meets my eyes. 'Me and Gray know each other from about three years ago. When I was in Royal Park.'

My mouth drops open. 'When...you were in Royal Park?'

'Yeah.'

'As in, you...'

'As in, I was an involuntary patient at a mental-health facility, yes.'

I squint. 'What does that mean? An involuntary patient is, like—'

'I didn't check myself in, is what it means. I had a pretty bad anniversary, Angela called triple-0, and a triage team took me in.'

Mycroft's expression is detached, but he's looking away from me and sucking furiously on his cigarette. He walks to the edge of the deck, leans down to grind the butt into the saucer. His hands are shaking.

I don't know why I'm so shocked. Mycroft has let his guard down with me on other occasions. But this fresh information is a landslide. I feel as if someone took my head and shook it, and all the pieces of my brain have tumbled around inside before settling back into a new order.

Except it's the right order. Suddenly, so much is starting to make sense.

Mycroft looks at me and his face contorts. 'So now you know what kind of head case you've thrown in with.'

'Mycroft—'

Gray's voice is soothing.

'That's not it, mate. She's just sorting it out, that's all. And fair enough, yeah, if you didn't say nothing? Don't get your hackles up.' He grins at me. 'He can get himself into a lather over nothing, this bloke. I'm sure you know the story.'

I nod, dumbstruck.

Mycroft's face grows less angry, more tentative, as he glances over my way.

Gray waves a hand. 'Anyway, it's no bother. Come on through, I'll put the kettle on and we'll have a cuppa. Too hot to be moving those seedlings anyway.'

He puts out his cigarette, bangs his shoes against the wire mat at the back door, and goes on in.

I stand on the deck, shifting my feet. I do the maths – Mycroft would have been fourteen when he was admitted to Royal Park. Only four years after he arrived in Melbourne. Four years after the awful deaths of his parents.

I realize that meeting Gray Jetta wasn't something he expected to do again in this lifetime. That Gray's a reminder of a time he's probably tried really hard to forget.

I'm monumentally unsure of what to say next.

Thankfully, Mycroft takes a big breath and goes for broke.

'I was in the hospital for three weeks. It wasn't a fantastic time.' He's talking fast, as if he wants to get it out of the way before we move on to something more important. 'Gray was working there, and he was a nice guy. He helped take my mind off where I was.'

'Did being in hospital help?' I blurt. As soon as I say it I feel like sticking my hand in my mouth.

Mycroft just raises his eyebrows and looks at me, shrugs.

'Yeah, I guess it did help. They gave me medication at first, which was pretty dire. Makes you feel like you're moving on goldfish time.' His thumbnail scours his bottom lip as his eyes focus elsewhere. 'But once we sorted out the meds issue, and I started being a bit more cooperative, things picked up. It wasn't so bad. I mean, living with Angela's never been a party either, so it was a break from that.'

He gives me a weak smile.

'Why didn't you tell me?' I ask softly.

'Why do you think? I haven't told anybody at school. It was before I transferred from my last school, so I don't even know if it's on my file. Well, maybe it is, from the way Fossum the Possum has been talking around it. I haven't told Mai or Gus.'

'But then you haven't told them about lots of things,' I say. He knows what I mean by 'lots of things'.

'That's right.'

He stares straight at me, his blue eyes swirling with dark matter. There's something else he's trying to say, beneath the words. I'm not sure what it is, but his expression makes my mouth go dry.

Before the pause gets ridiculous, Gray Jetta sticks his head out the back door. 'Oi, you two. You coming in for a cuppa or not?'

Mycroft recovers first. 'Absolutely. And I want all the hospital gossip.'

'In yer dreams.' Gray smiles and ducks back inside.

Mycroft gives me a grin. 'He'll totally tell me. You watch.'

He's totally right. By the time we're on our second cuppa, Gray and Mycroft are yacking about whether this client or that client has had a repeat visit, and what the staffing conditions are like at the hospital now, and various clients (Gray considerately refers to them as 'this young bloke we had' and 'this lady') who've been up to mischief.

Gray's house is a humble widower's pad. Blanched floral curtains drift above the kitchen sink, and a framed photo of Gray and a silver-haired woman graces the top of the telly. We drink tea at the bench in the neat kitchen as Gray talks about his work.

'Gotta have the right temperament – balanced, calm, no quick temper. I've always been good at that. Take your Dave. He needed a bit of calm when he came in.'

I rest my mug on the kitchen counter. 'So he was never a regular client?'

'No, god no. Couldn't stand being inside, Dave.' Gray pours himself another mug from the pot. 'Speaking of which, let's take it out on the deck. Smoke and talk.'

Mycroft perches on the edge of the deck with one long leg off the side, and Gray sits opposite, his tobacco pouch in his lap. I cross my legs on the redgum, loving the smell of resin and oil from the timber. I turn my face towards the sun and soak up the rays.

'You're a country girl, aren't ya?'

I startle, open my eyes to Gray's brown ones. 'Uh, yeah. From over Ouyen way. Me and my family haven't been in Melbourne long. Just since the end of last year.'

'You've still got the look.' Gray sticks the unfiltered rollie end between his teeth. 'Like you're not sure which planet you're on. That's okay. I'm a high-country man, originally. Still feels a bit strange, living in the city. But it's a bit like high country here, yeah?'

He gestures out. Over the fence we catch a glimpse of the city backdrop, steel Lego towers in the distance. The high country.

I have a sudden urge to ask him how's he's managed it, going from living in the mountains to living here, in the Melbourne suburbs. Mycroft cuts in before I have a chance.

'So Dave wasn't a regular. But he'd drop in when he was tight. He didn't get assessed or anything?'

'Bless me, no,' Gray says. 'He was never a bother, but he wouldn't have tolerated the ward. Especially not with that dog of his. Man, he looked after that dog – half a bikkie for him, the other half for Poodle, remember?'

'I remember, yeah,' I say. It hurts to say it, but it seems to hurt less, talking about it with Gray.

Mycroft squints at the yellow passionfruit on the vine to his left. 'I just...I still don't understand.'

'The murder thing?' Gray's hand is tucked under his elbow, supporting his smoking arm. 'Happens, doesn't it? Vulnerable man, soft target.'

'No. A bashing, I could understand. Almost normal, if you look at the statistics on homelessness. But this was different. It seems he was cut *after* he was dead.'

'Sounds like a mystery, all right. You checking it out, are you? Diogenes rides again?' Gray grins.

'How do you know—' I stammer.

Mycroft throws me a lopsided smile. 'Gray's the original Diogenes fan. My first supporter, I suppose you'd say.'

'Helped you come up with the name, didn't I?' Gray ashes his butt. 'That was Sherlock's brother's club, Diogenes. A space just for thinking, working things out.'

'And it was the name of a Roman philosopher,' Mycroft adds. 'Diogenes the Cynic.'

My mind really can't get any more expanded today or it's

going to explode. 'You were already doing this stuff back then? When you were in the hospital?'

Mycroft picks a leaf off the passionfruit vine and twirls it between his long fingers. 'Yeah, well, once I mostly came off the meds and could think straight again, I had to have *something* to do.'

'Or he was going to go out of his mind,' Gray says, and the two of them crack up.

Once their laughter tails off, Mycroft turns back to me. 'Yeah, so I started writing these little papers, and when I got computer access I posted them. It was pretty amateur stuff, just basic chemistry problems and research. Then I started branching out – mathematics, physics…and forensics, of course.'

'Of course,' I say lamely.

Gray nods in Mycroft's direction. 'You done good. You were one of my success stories, y'know. You still living with that auntie of yours?'

'Angela. Yeah.' Mycroft winces. 'I never meant to lose touch with you, man. I'm sorry about that.'

'That's all right, I understand. It wasn't an easy time.' Gray waves a hand. 'I still check out what you're up to sometimes, if I'm browsing on the computer. Last thing I saw, you had some paper on, what was it? Composition of natural acids or something – I couldn't even pronounce half the words!'

Mycroft grins and Gray grins back.

I check my phone. I'm shocked to discover it's nearly two-thirty. 'Uh, Mr Jetta—'

'Gray, just Gray.'

'Gray. So is there anything else you could tell us about Dave that would help us figure out who he was, or why someone would want to hurt him?'

Gray shakes his head. 'I wish there was, Rachel. But he was usually pretty sick or weary when he came in. Nothing we talked about would have had much bearing, I don't think. Just how he was feeling, how's the dog, stuff like that.'

I slump a little with the disappointment of it.

'Maybe we're coming at it from the wrong angle,' Mycroft says softly.

I look over. 'What do you mean?'

'If there wasn't anything particular about *Dave*, maybe it was something else.' He narrows his eyes at Gray. 'You said the last time he was in at the hospital was about six months ago. So was there someone he might have come into contact with around then?'

'Nobody would have come into contact with him but me,' Gray says firmly.

'Well, has there been anything? Anyone out of the usual, giving you trouble, someone with a violent history...'

Gray sucks his teeth as he thinks. Mycroft glances at me, then back at his old mate.

'There was one patient.' Gray speaks slowly, as though he's contemplating how much to tell. 'Been in and out a lot over the past couple of years, stayed for a spell when Dave came round. Not that they knew each other or anything. But we had real problems with her...'

Her. I remember Mai's words, *Statistically, that's rubbish*, and give Mycroft a significant look, which he ignores.

'Yeah, she was a handful,' Gray continues. 'Ran with this crowd...well, this older bloke came in to see her a couple of times, gave us grief. He used to wind her up, she'd be in a terrible state after his visits. Bad business, it was. She was an involuntary, too. Her dad checked her in, some bigwig at the zoo...'

Bad business. The zoo.

My head lifts. Mycroft has that rapt expression he gets when he's really paying attention.

Gray notices and his gaze hardens. He cuts himself off with the flat of his hand. 'Nope, sorry. I can't say nothing more. Legally it's not the right thing to do, give out patient info.'

Mycroft lets out a tiny breath. 'Gray—'

'Nope.'

'Gray, please. There's a man who's died—'

'I *know* that, but there ain't nothing more I can say. I'm sorry, really I am.'

Mycroft's face works. Then I think of something, something good.

I put my hands on my knees and lean forward. 'That's fine, Gray, we understand. We don't expect you to give out information like that.'

'Not the right thing to do. Cost me my job if people found out, yeah?'

'We know, and it's okay. We're just trying to discover as much as we can to help out the police.' I hope Gray can read honesty into my face. 'But can you think of *anything* you can say? Any little link, anything you can think of, and then we could follow it up ourselves. Whatever we find out, it won't have been something that you told us, yeah? It'll just be us, speculating.'

'Speculating, huh?'

'Yeah. And you won't come into it at all. It'll just be something we've worked out for ourselves.'

Gray frowns at the wood grain on the deck, sucks on his bottom lip.

'Any little clue,' I prompt.

Gray considers for a long time. I'm about to burst from holding my breath. Mycroft is stock-still across from me, as if he doesn't dare move.

Gray opens his pouch to roll a new smoke.

'Roof monkeys,' he says.

Mycroft squints. 'Roof monkeys?'

'Roof monkeys. Ocean flower.'

Ocean flower?

'That's it. That's all I can say.' Gray finishes rolling and looks up. 'I know it's thin, but it's the best I can do.'

Mycroft's expression tells me his brain is already hard at it.

'That's, uh, pretty cryptic,' I say.

Gray smiles, lifts his chin towards Mycroft's strangely absent look. 'He's a smart lad. He can work it out.'

———

We end up running to catch the three-fifteen train. Out the train window the high-country skyscrapers of the CBD are hazed with smog, blocky gray outlines on a tissue-paper background.

Mycroft has his phone out, searching for any combination of roofs, monkeys, oceans, and flowers that he can think of.

'Ocean. Sea. Coast. Cove. Quay…'

I'm leaning over his shoulder. 'Inlet. Estuary. Tide…Could it be seaweed? An ocean flower is a kind of seaweed, or coral, isn't it?'

'Seaweed. But what does that have to do with Dave?'

'Damned if I know. Your mate Gray has a funny way of being subtle.'

'Roof monkeys…' Mycroft glances at me. 'Yeah, he does. He used to be into crosswords and that sort of stuff. Maybe this is just his own brand of mystery.'

'Great,' I say.

'Perceptive, by the way. How you brought Gray round to the idea of giving us something.' Mycroft's head is tilted, as though he's considering me from a new and more interesting angle.

'I just didn't want him to get into trouble, that's all.' Mycroft is still staring, so I press on. 'He seems like a good guy. He *wanted* to help us. He just needed to find a way to do it.'

'He is a good guy. I don't know what would've happened with me at the hospital if he hadn't...' Mycroft trails off, looks at his phone. 'Yeah. Anyway. I should've stayed in contact with him. I feel like a bit of a bastard now.'

'It was fate. Now you're back in touch, you can fix it.'

'I guess so.' He's still searching. 'Well, I'm not getting anything relevant from ocean, or flower, or anything in combination.'

'Gray said her dad was some bigwig at the zoo.'

'Yeah, that was a slip on his part.' His thumbs tap a staccato. 'I'm sure this girl is important. There's nothing else about Dave to suggest why he might have been targeted, apart from the fact that he was vulnerable. So we have to imagine the motivation came from someone else.'

'And the connection between the hospital and the zoo, with Dave smack in the middle...'

'Yeah.' He suddenly stops tapping. 'Wait.'

'What?'

'Here, check this out.'

He turns his phone to me. The resolution is crap, but I can see a painting on the side of a large concrete wall. The mural is startling. It's a blaze of fiery swirling background color, like a nuclear explosion, with a foreground of black silhouettes.

'What am I looking at exactly?'

'The *name*, Watts. Roof Monkeys. I thought Gray was getting at a zoo reference, or a band or something, but that's not it. The Roof Monkeys is a group of graffiti artists.'

'*Graffiti?*'

'Yeah. It says…' He scans the article, resizing the text. 'Okay, so the group has been getting into strife with the cops for redecorating some prominent corporate buildings in the CBD. Apparently they've been hard to pin down, because their tag has gone viral. But this is their signature style.'

I crane over his arm to see. The details of the mural remind me of a shadow-puppet play I saw on telly once. But these silhouettes are more unnerving.

Emaciated black figures with spikes for hair and gaping mouths filled with shark teeth. Cut-out eyes that burn with the background reds and yellows. Figures that are chewing each other up, and feeding each other into machines that churn out something like black mince. Black stick-children roasting each other on spits. Monstrous black factories and sparking black fires.

All around the edges of each tableau, long strings of words dribble together to form circling slogans. The slogans speak about corporate greed, the enslavement of poverty, how consumerism is destroying society.

'Wow.' My voice is hushed.

'Yeah. I can see why the cops and the businesses involved are going right off.'

'That's…well, I guess you'd call that confronting.'

'Now, consider. This mural was done on the side of a bank high-rise.'

'And?'

'It's ten meters up.'

My eyes pop. 'Seriously?'

'Seriously. The cops think they use window-washing equipment already onsite to do it, or possibly rock-climbing gear. It's risky stuff. Large pieces, done quickly in areas that are so high up you'd go splat if you fell, right in the middle of the CBD. These guys have quite a reputation.'

'Not just guys,' I remind him.

Our stop is coming. I glance out the window and have one of my infrequent moments of sheer genius.

'Mycroft, where exactly is that mural?'

CHAPTER FOURTEEN

We don't go to the most recent mural, because it's so prominent we'd be noticed. We go to one the Roof Monkeys completed about two weeks ago, done in one night. It's about nine meters above our heads, a fire-bright accusation plastered on the bluestone wall of the city branch of Mutual Systems Incorporated where it backs onto a lane.

'It's rather high up, isn't it?'

Mycroft tosses his cigarette butt into the gutter and cranes his neck. I'm suddenly reminded of his queasy expression when he faced the glistening tower of St Kilda Road Police Headquarters. I'd thought it was the prospect of doing battle with Detective Pickup, but maybe it had originated from another source altogether.

'Mycroft, are you afraid of heights?'

He lowers his chin to glare at me. 'Everyone has issues with *something*, Watts. Mai hates blood, Mr Conroy has an allergy to bees, you can't deal with spiders—'

I gawk at him. 'How did you know about that?'

'What, that time at your place when you saw the huntsman on the wall and practically climbed into my lap wasn't enough to tip me off?'

I blush. 'I did *not* climb into your lap.'

He grins. 'I'm not saying it was a *bad* thing. I'm just saying it wasn't hard to draw the obvious conclusion. Anyway, fine, the mural is high. Maybe the Roof Monkeys climbed onto the top of the building and used rappelling gear or something.'

'We'll need to get up there. I can't see the tags from here.'

Mutual Systems Incorporated obviously feels that a mural on the topic of corporate greed isn't doing wonders for their public image, because they've hired a cleaning crew to get rid of it. The bluestone looks like a pain to clean. I nod towards the equipment, which includes a concertinaed platform lift and a jungle-gym of gray scaffolding.

Mycroft pales. 'Well, I'm not climbing *that*.'

'Relax,' I say. 'I'll climb it.'

'No, you won't. You'll die.'

'Please. I was always the one who used to climb up and clean the dead possums out of the rainwater guttering at home.'

'Lovely. But I'm sure it doesn't cover climbing twenty feet of dodgy scaffolding in the CBD.'

'Do you want to find out what's going on with this mural or not?'

Mycroft frowns, hands patting his jeans pocket. 'Can I have a cigarette before we start?'

'You just had one. Look, it's after four, and there's no other equipment – I reckon the cleaners have decided it's beer o'clock. We should do it now, before they get rid of it.' I walk over to the scaffolding, eye off the heights and distances between the joints in the gunmetal-gray poles. 'Just stay on the ground and tell me if you see someone coming.'

'Hey, I'm not being the lookout. If you're going to climb this bloody thing, then I'm going to climb it too.'

I shrug. 'Suit yourself.'

We drop our bags inside an industrial bin farther down the lane, in case we get sprung and all our identifying material is found sitting on the footpath underneath us. Then I walk back, quickly scan for onlookers, and grab the first scaffolding poles.

The metal is grainy, not smooth, which helps. The poles are a bit larger around than my grip, though, so I've got this disconcerting not-quite-hanging-on feeling.

I shin up the diagonal, then chin-up to the first horizontal length. I slide my legs over so I'm straddling the pole.

Mycroft is pulling himself up to sit beside me, looking ungainly. His height gives him a higher center of gravity – he's hanging on for dear life, and we're only a couple of meters up in the air.

'You're doing great,' I say.

'Fantastic.' Mycroft's breathing is shallow. 'Possum disposal. What other talents do you have that I'm not aware of?'

'I can shoot a rifle. And I can fix a water pump, and run a chainsaw without cutting my foot off.' I look up to assess the route. 'Does this all fall into the stuff-I-like-to-do category?'

'No.' Hair curls over his forehead as he licks his lips.

'Are you ready for the next bit?'

'Just keep going, before I fall off.'

I use a jointed corner of the scaffolding to lever myself up to the next section. The crossbar is just out of reach, over my head. I make a little jump, less than a hand's-length, and grab the crossbar. I hear Mycroft groan behind me, as though he's in pain.

I have to use sheer muscle to get to the point where I'm waisted over the bar. After that, it's fairly simple to sling the rest of me over. I straddle this bar too, and lean down to Mycroft.

'Come on,' I say. 'Give me your hand.'

Mycroft is staring up at me. The whites of his eyes are showing. 'I think I'm going to be sick.'

Good grief. If he hates heights so much, why did he come? 'You're not going to be sick. You're going to get up here with me. You said you wanted to climb, so stop whining and do it.'

Mycroft maneuvers himself up very carefully, reaches high for the crossbar. At full stretch he can grab the bar comfortably. He clutches my hand with his free one – his palm is sweaty, his long fingers desperately grasping. By the time he's sitting with me, he's mint chocolate: gray-green face, eighty-per-cent-cocoa hair.

'Is there anyone coming?' I crane my head over my shoulder.

'No. There's no one.' The muscles in his arms are trembling with tension. 'Jesus Christ, we're fifteen feet above the pavement.'

'It's okay, Mycroft. Look up.'

'If I look up I'll topple over.'

'Mycroft, look up.'

He does. A short way above our heads is the bottom edge of the mural. I can see this corner, the right-hand one. The spray-paint burns like embers, the color is so bright.

I think I admire the Roof Monkeys – their art, their philosophy, but mainly their guts.

'Where are the tags?' Mycroft says. Faced with the object of his interest, his voice is losing its choked wobble.

I point at the mural. 'Well, they've started cleaning from the center, so that's a plus. The artists' tags should be in one of the corners, I guess.'

'Can you see anything on this side?'

I stand up on the crossbar and step out lightly to the next horizontal, which makes the corner. Mycroft makes a strangled noise as I put my hands on my hips and balance there.

'I can't see anything that looks like a tag,' I say. 'Just words from the message – corporate hegemony and the destruction of blah blah blah. There's more as it goes higher.'

'It must be on one of the other edges,' Mycroft says. 'And could you please get down from there, Watts, because it's making me ill just looking at you.'

He's sitting on the crossbar with both knees pointed to the wall, holding another upright and swearing under his breath. In his dark jeans and T-shirt, he reminds me of a black cockatoo perched on a wire.

'Mycroft, I hate to break this to you, but I've got to get to the other side of the scaffolding.'

'Right. Of course you do.'

'I have to get over *there*.' I point at the upright he's holding on his left.

It forms one side of a makeshift ladder. Two rungs before the top of the ladder, a long length of hardwood planking extends out over the drop. This reconnects with more scaffolding on the far side.

'If I want to see the other corner of the mural, I'm going to have to get over that plank,' I explain.

'Fucking hell.'

'You don't have to come. In fact, it might be better if you don't, because I'm not sure how much weight that plank will handle. I don't think it's designed to be load-bearing.'

'Watts, this is a bad idea.'

'No, it's not. It's fine. You just sit there and I'll call out if I find anything interesting.'

I lower myself back to straddling the first crossbar. I frown, considering the logistics. This part is going to be tricky.

'I'm going to have to get by you. Just stay exactly where you are, and I'll do the moving about, okay?'

Mycroft nods, like he's beyond speaking.

'Look, I'm going to reach across you, and grab that pole you're holding. Then I'll swing over. If you hold on tight you won't overbalance.'

He squeezes his eyes shut. 'Just do it.'

'Okay, here goes.'

I wriggle a bit more until I'm pressed in tight to Mycroft's right side. I brace my left hand on Mycroft's shoulder, then ease my left foot up onto the bar. I take a breath and reach out blindly with my right hand for the vertical pole on Mycroft's other side.

For a moment, as I'm stretched across his body, I can feel how he's shaking. Then I've grabbed the pole, and in one smooth movement I swing my right foot over and stand up.

Now I'm standing with one foot on either side of Mycroft's lap, holding on to the upright with my right hand.

I wobble for a second – I have to keep my left hand on Mycroft's shoulder for support. His face, I belatedly realize, is just level with the crotch of my jeans. I'm glad he's too scared to look up, or he'd see me blush.

'You know, this isn't as bad as I thought it would be,' he says. His voice is muffled, because his mouth is squashed against the top of my thigh.

'Don't get too comfortable,' I warn him. 'I'm going to swing over in a second. Just let me balance.'

He does look up at me then. He's still pale, but he's grinning. 'Take as long as you need.'

I squeeze my fingers into his shoulder and he gives a little 'yikes'. Then I feel his hand, hot and damp, circle my ankle.

I gasp. 'Mycroft, don't do that!'

'Do what?' His fingertips trail lightly over my skin, between the top of my sock and the hem of my jeans.

I shiver, wobble. 'That! Stop that. I'm going to swing over.'

His hand moves away. I try to refocus. Swinging – I'm swinging over to the ladder. Okay.

I pirouette on my right foot, and reach out for the ladder as I spin backwards. Now I've got two secure handholds and it's easy. I pivot in to the ladder and climb the first two rungs. Then I'm at the plank.

'Watts, are you sure about this? That plank looks tired.'

It does look tired, actually, craggy from overuse and bristling with long splinters. And there's no guard rail. Clearly, when Mutual Systems Incorporated decided they wanted to get rid of the mural, they decided to go with the Dodgy Brothers route.

'It's the only way across,' I point out. 'We want to find out about these tags, right?'

'Not if you're going to fall to your death,' Mycroft says. 'In that case, no, we don't.'

I move before I lose my nerve, standing up on the plank and lightly touching the wall.

'Watts—'

Ignoring him, I walk one foot in front of the other, careful but fast. The plank is horribly uneven, wobbling beneath me.

I have to keep an eye on my feet, so I need to look directly down. I try to block out the fact that I'm much higher than I'd originally thought. If I fell off here, I'd make a very messy raspberry-jam blob on the footpath.

The human body is like a big plastic bag, full of blood...

I'm nearly at the other set of scaffolding. With one palm on the wall, I check the mural. The goal is so close – I take the steps. Suddenly I can see the mural's edge.

There's a crimson square painted in the corner, its sides decorated with a razor-wire pattern. Inside the square are a series of squiggles, the maker's marks.

There's an elaborate title, *Roof Monkeys*, and three tags – no, four. I can make out a scrawl that looks like a hieroglyph, a jackal head. Another tag says *Nidra*, in harsh angular letters. Another one I can't read, it's so elaborately spiked. The last one is straight text, letters that look like newspaper print. The word is very clear, ink-black: *Madd*.

'Watts, for god's sake!'

Mycroft must have been trying to get my attention for a while. I've been too focused on the tags, trying to work them out. But I don't have to do that, I realize.

'Hang on! I'm going to take a photo!'

I ease my phone out of my back pocket and hold it up. Two shots are probably plenty but I have to use my left hand, so I hope they're not going to be blurry.

I return the phone and put both hands on the wall. I'm pretty ready to get down now. The air up here seems rarefied, thin. Maybe it's the city smog.

'I'm coming back.'

'About bloody time,' floats across the divide.

I walk back the way I've come. The plank bounces under me. I try to slow my steps, keeping my hand on the wall. The chipping paint flakes away under my fingernails.

'Come on, Watts. You're nearly there.'

I don't look up at Mycroft. I can't. I need to focus on my steps.

'A little closer and you can come and sit in my lap again, okay?'

'Mycroft—' I can't help it. I glance up at his sweating, grinning face.

Which is a mistake.

There's a sudden tug on my foot as I bring it forward. I stumble and look down. My shoelace has caught on a massive splinter.

'No. Shit—'

But my hand has already parted company with the wall. I totter, then my body takes over. My arms wheel. Panic tears through me like a wildfire.

'*Watts!*'

Mycroft's cry is drowned out by the rush of blood to my head. My body weight goes back – I wrench my chest forward, try to reverse it, throw my arms toward the wall.

My feet lose contact with the plank and I *scream*.

CHAPTER FIFTEEN

My arms and chest hit the plank with a thud, and oh *god*, it's agonizing, a heavyweight punch in the ribs. I slip down, almost let go of the plank, but I don't, I *can't*.

Salty blood spills into my mouth. I'm gasping, winded, with a ringing in my ears. I struggle, get my elbows across the plank. Something's cutting into me, but I'm hanging on, and I'm not letting go. *God*, I think, *please don't let me let go.*

Okay, I have to get my leg up. No, I can't. *Concentrate.* Fuck. I'm nearly ten meters up in the air, with no crash mat underneath. If I lose my grip, I'll die.

My heart is pounding out of my chest. I'm making noises, stupid noises, but the pain is almost unbearable. I wheeze in air, wriggle for a better hand hold.

'Watts, I want you to look up and come to me.'

I blink my eyes open. Mycroft is half-sprawled across the plank, his feet still on the ladder. He's got one arm holding the pole and one arm stretched for me, his hand reaching, his fingers star-fished out. His face is dead white, cheekbones like twin slashes, blue eyes intent and over-bright.

'Easy for you to say.' My voice is rasping. It hurts to talk, and I gasp again, cough. No, coughing is bad.

Tears leak out of my eyes, but I can't brush them away. My arms are trembling and my hands feel slick on the wood. *Oh Jesus—*

'I'm going to come closer,' he says.

I shake my head furiously. 'No, the plank's not strong enough—'

'It's okay. I'll hold the ladder, and I'll get close enough for you to grab me. Come on, Watts.'

He eases his body across and grabs my left arm in a vice-grip. I'm so grateful for that one handhold, that one contact, that I wail a little.

Whatever it is that's cutting me, it's really hurting now – my eyes are swimming, my legs dangle and kick in space. They feel heavy, my whole body is heavy, like an enormous sack of sand.

'Watts, you've got to move now. Just grab onto me, and I'm going to pull back.'

'*Mycroft*—'

'Come on, you can do it. I've got the ladder. Come *on*.'

I've got no choice. With a gasping cry, I let go of the plank with one hand and grab for Mycroft's shoulder. His T-shirt bunches in my grip as I wrap my arm around his neck, hooking on with my elbow.

'I *can't*, fuck, oh god, I'll pull you down, I can't do this—'

'Easy now, I've got you,' Mycroft whispers.

I yell, and sling my other arm around him. Suddenly he's dragging us both back. I kick my legs and get a purchase with my knee. I get my other leg up and shuffle forward until my thighs hit the rungs of the ladder.

My arms are hugging Mycroft's neck like I hugged the plank, and I'm gulping in air, crying. My ribs are on fire. My whole body is shaking, and Mycroft is shaking too; we're both shaking like leaves in a gale. He's murmuring something in my ear, but I can't really hear what it is.

I'm making this weird, gasping *huh…huh…huh* noise. Mycroft rubs his free hand up and down my back soothingly, his other hand holding on to the ladder.

'Okay.' I still can't seem to catch my breath. 'Okay. Okay, we…we have to get down.'

It takes Mycroft a minute to reply.

'Great idea,' he says. His voice is thick, gravelly.

After having my face tucked into the warmth of his neck and shoulder for so long, the air feels icy on my cheeks. I unwind my arms from around his neck, slow careful movements, as if one of us might crack. He starts to slide his arm from around my waist and I grab onto him.

'*Stop*. Just…leave your arm there. I think I need you to help me down…oh, this stupid *shaking*.'

'Okay, okay.' He squeezes my waist gently. 'Watts, it's all right. I understand. I'll help you down.'

'Just…slowly.'

He helps me inch the rest of the way off the plank. I can't get off it fast enough, but I can't go too fast either.

Getting off the scaffolding feels so much harder than getting up, even with Mycroft's hand on my waist. My arms are stiff and shaking, and my palms feel like raw meat. We take turns easing down the crossbars and along the diagonal poles. Finally Mycroft is standing on the footpath, reaching up to brace me as I swing down to ground level.

Once my feet hit the concrete I get a sudden reeling dizziness. I reach for a handful of Mycroft's T-shirt as my legs turn to jelly and I sink onto my knees.

I lean all the way forward, trying to avoid throwing up. My head touches the concrete as the feeling washes through me.

'Can we please not do anything like that ever, ever again?' Mycroft kneels in front of me, strokes my back as the dizziness fades. 'Watts, you're bleeding.'

I sit up slowly. There's a trickle of blood on the pavement in front of me.

'My ribs are...god, my hands are so sore...' I look at my sandpapered palms, wincing. My wrists and inside arms are covered with scrapes. 'I-I bit my lip, I think.'

Mycroft touches my bottom lip with the pad of his thumb and I shiver. He holds up his thumb so I can see the red blot-mark on it.

I lift the rolled-up sleeve of my flannie away from the crook of my left elbow and finally see what was cutting me. I've got a huge splinter pushed into the soft meat of my inner arm. The skin is torn. Blood leaks in a thin line down my arm, dripping onto the concrete.

'Jesus,' Mycroft gasps.

'Good thing Mai's not here.' I squint at where the piece of wood has broken off. 'I don't think I can get that out with my fingernails.'

Mycroft shakes his head. 'Let no one say you aren't stoic.'

He reaches over and starts undoing the few buttons I have left on the front of my flannie shirt.

'Field bandage,' he says when I startle.

He tugs the shirt, gently peels it off me. He wraps it around my

202

left arm. The bleeding is staunched, but I feel a bit cold in just a tank top.

Mycroft gets me to my feet. 'Come on. We'll do a proper job when we get you home.'

I wait for him to come back with our bags. I blink, remembering, and check my jeans pocket with aching fingers. My phone has survived, thank god. I look up at the scaffolding, the mural.

'It really is quite high up, isn't it?' I say.

Mycroft shudders, puts his arm around me. I don't feel so cold now.

'I fell *off* the roof once, getting the possum.'

Mycroft rolls his eyes. 'You country people are insane.'

———

'Okay, I've downloaded the photos off your phone,' Mycroft says. 'Now let's have a look.'

He's sitting at the desk in the Stranger's Room. I'm bunched up on his bed, swaddled in an enormous jumper of Mike's. Mycroft's pillow has a flannelette cover, and smells a lot like him. A hot water bottle I snagged from home is tucked under my aching ribs.

I got the splinter out, had a shower and cleaned myself up. I worked on maintaining the illusion that this was a normal day, putting on a load of washing before starting the dinner.

It was hard work, moving and talking as usual to Dad and Mike, when my body felt like one giant bruise. When Mum walked into the kitchen with the groceries, I carefully walked out. Confronting Mum, even *talking* to Mum, in that terse way people do after they've had a fight, was just more effort than I could sustain.

I'll admit to having taken quite a few analgesics. The hot sweet tea I'm sipping goes down smooth, and I've got a nice little buzz coming on as my body settles into a liquid shape.

'Watts? Oi – the photos?' Mycroft's voice seems to come from some distance away.

'You look at them. I looked plenty before, when I was standing on that bloody plank.' My eyelids are heavy blast doors held open by the toothpick of my will. Even leaning over to put my mug on the floor feels like a gargantuan exertion.

'Are you right over there?' Mycroft glances over, still tapping the keyboard. 'Don't get too comfy, or I'll have to carry you home.'

'Mm,' I say as I lose the battle with my eyelids.

With my eyes closed the room turns slowly under me, but not in a vomit-inducing way like this afternoon. It feels appropriate; something has shifted, I think. Somewhere between the revelations at Gray Jetta's house and the near-disaster on the scaffolding, I've had a change inside. I'm not sure exactly what it is yet, or what it means. But I remember something, something important.

'I never said thank you. For getting me down.'

'Come again?'

'Thank you. Really. Because I would have...you know. Died. And it was very brave, especially because you hate heights so much...'

'Watts, are you sure you didn't hit your head on that plank?'

'I'm sure.' I yawn hugely. There's a sparkling display, fireworks or something, just behind my eyelids. Whirls, and harlequin colors, and...

———

Someone is gently shaking my shoulder.

'Watts. Watts, come on, wake up.'

I surface slowly. Mycroft's face is right in front of me. He has those dark hollows under his brows again, and his cheeks are smudged with stubble. He looks washed out. But his eyes are so excited they seem to be animating his entire body.

'Watts, you're not going to believe this.' He's practically bouncing on the bed. 'Come on, snap to it.'

'What—' I push myself up and gasp. There's incredible stiffness, and a lancing pain inside my left elbow. My arms feel like soggy newspaper. I scrape my fingers through my hair. 'Did I sleep?'

'Of course you slept, you were bloody comatose. Come on, look at this.' He's thrusting papers under my nose.

I bat them away. 'Mycroft—'

'The *tag*, Watts. The Madd tag.' The papers crackle as he shakes them. 'I crossed it with all these references and got nothing but graffiti sites, and then I tried to…Look, it doesn't matter. *I've found her.*'

'What?' Still foggy, I sit up properly. 'Who? Mycroft, what are you talking about?'

He shuffles papers. 'Look, look. Gray said her dad was a bigwig at the zoo. Here – the names of all the zoo administrative staff. The director – Ronald Maddison. Maddison – *Madd*. Do you get it?'

'I…I don't know.' My eyes aren't even focusing properly yet.

He's got this elated grin. 'He has a daughter, she's an art student. And there's her name, d'you see? Rosemarina Maddison. *Rosemarina.*'

Something swims back to me then. 'Rose…marina. Ocean flower…'

'Yes!' He flops back on the bed, his weight warm on my legs, his hands behind his head. He's still wearing the navy T-shirt and jeans from the afternoon. 'Bloody internet research, I tell you. You'd be better off going to Town Records and just examining the files. Bloody hell, I can't believe it took so *long*.'

'How long did you—' I angle my head to look through the crack in Mycroft's curtain. The sky outside is a watery cyan, the color of stained glass. The color of dawn. 'Mycroft, what *time* is it? Oh my god, have I been sleeping here all night?'

He smiles, curls flopping over his forehead. 'You look very cute when you're asleep. You snore a little, but that doesn't—'

'Mycroft, for god's sake!' I throw off the blanket, onto Mycroft's face, and pitch upright. A lightning strike of pain in my ribs, down my legs, makes me stagger. 'Oh *shit!* Shitshitshit—'

I find one shoe, yank it on, cast around for the other one.

'Watts, it's okay—'

'It's not okay! It's most definitely *not okay*! Oh *Jesus*, my parents are going to have a total—'

I check the time on the computer and make a wailing noise, before finding my other shoe.

'Watts—'

I'm trying to stuff my foot into my other runner while hopping on the spot. 'Mycroft, how *could* you? You let me sleep all night in your room, and I'm—'

'Watts—'

'—going to catch absolute *living hell* from Mum and Dad when they find out that I—'

'*Watts.*' Mycroft has pushed off the bed to stand in front of me. He grabs my shoulders with both hands. 'Calm down. Just don't tell them.'

'What?'

206

'Think about it. It's quarter to six in the morning. Who's going to be up?'

My eyes dart around, the way dragonflies zip over the surface of a creek. 'Huh. No one. Mum...Mum'll be sleeping in. It's her last day off.'

'And nobody will expect you to be up for a while yet, will they?'

I blink hard, push a hand through my bed hair. 'No. Not for an hour and a half.'

'Your dad won't be in for another hour. What about your brother?'

'He...' I try to make my brain work. 'He gets up about seven.'

'Right. So just go home before your mum wakes up, and before your dad and Mike make an appearance, and no one will even notice.'

I stop holding my breath. He's right. With my bedroom door closed, no one will know I'm not there. Mum will sleep like the dead, and Dad gets back with the taxi about seven...

There's only Mike, if he topples out of bed early for work, which is unlikely. So I have a forty-five-minute window, during which I'll have to pray that nobody decides to poke their head into my room to see if I'm awake.

'I...I've got some time,' I say.

Mycroft's face is bemused. 'Obviously.'

'But if they find out...I'll have to *lie*.' I look up at him. 'I don't...I mean, I haven't done that before.'

'Lied to your parents about where you spent the night?'

Mycroft's eyebrow is arched. His lips curve in a way that makes me flush.

'You make it sound like we—' I cut myself off before I say something embarrassing.

'Like we what?'

I know he's teasing me, but his eyes have darkened to an intense blue. He's dropped his hands from my shoulders and he's standing very close. I can still feel where his hands touched, and I'm finding the whole thing very... distracting.

I slip away from his personal-space circle to stand at a nice safe distance near the desk, while I pull my runner on the rest of the way.

'Tell me about Rosemarina Maddison.' I rub at the grit in my eyes. 'No. Actually, tea. First, get me tea, then tell me about Rosemarina Maddison.'

Mycroft grabs a hoodie off the floor and pulls it on.

'Bossy, aren't you?' He's grinning as he heads for the door. 'Stay over one night, and it's all *do this, do that, get me tea*—'

'And toast,' I call, as he walks up the hallway. 'If you have any.'

I can hear him doing 'get me tea, get me toast' impersonations as he bumbles around in the kitchen. He's being quiet with the crockery, and I suddenly remember that Angela will be in her room, asleep. There are pips, and a mumbling from the laptop speakers, and I realize that he's got the BBC World Service on in the background.

I can't believe I *fell asleep*. I can't believe he didn't *wake me up*. I'd hate to lie to my parents, who have always trusted me up until now. Not that that's saying much – miles from anywhere on the farm, with no driver's license and no friends close by, there wasn't really anything I could *do* until now. Until the city.

It's not as though I've never been kissed, but there's a gaping chasm between kissing a guy and staying out all night in his room. But I'm not sure why I'm thinking about the kissing thing, because it's not even *relevant* in this case...

Mycroft comes back with the tea. He thrusts a mug in my direction, dumps a plate balanced on his own mug onto the desk. 'Toast, tea, as ordered.'

'Thanks.'

'Shove over and I'll show you what I found.'

I shift my chair back a bit, and start slurping and crunching. The tea makes me feel human again, so I'm vaguely alert when he opens windows on his laptop.

'Here we go – list of zoo staff. I kept it to central administration because I had to start somewhere.'

'So who's this Maddison guy?'

'Here.'

He brings up a window with a picture. I peer at the screen – a bull-necked man, florid, with a buzz of thick black hair. Zoo director Ronald Maddison looks like an army sergeant who's muscled his way up to business prominence.

'It was a *guess*.' Mycroft's mouth squirms with the admission. 'But a logical guess. Maddison, Madd, and the art student daughter. The ocean flower clue pretty much clinched it. Can't find a photo of the girl, for some reason.'

'And you didn't get a hit with any of the other tags, like the Nidra one, or the jackal?'

'Not a whistle.' He stops clicking the mouse and warms his fingers around his mug. 'But clearly they're linked through something. The daughter's art school, maybe.'

'Where does she go?'

'Don't know.'

'Then we should find out and, you know, talk to her.' I'm getting toast crumbs down my front.

'And say what?' Mycroft crunches a mouthful of crust. 'Excuse me, miss, but we heard you'd been in the loony bin and we were just wondering if you've been off butchering old men in the park? That should go down well.'

'I thought you'd have a plan?'

'Gimme a sec.' Mycroft stretches one shoulder. 'I've been up all night researching, I'm completely out of plans.'

'Okay, fine. Then we go with my plan.' I gesture with my mug. 'We just need to get a look at her. Tell her we're writing a paper for school. Poke around a bit.'

'Find the blood-splattered murder weapon, is that it?'

'*I* don't know.' I stand up to alleviate the anxiety still lurking inside. 'But she's the link, isn't she? There's her, there's Dave, and there's the zoo. Somewhere inside that triangle we've got the reason he died that way. We can't rely on the police to make the connection, so we have to figure it out ourselves.'

Mycroft looks up at me as I'm pacing. 'You'll have to skip school again.'

'I'll slip back before lunch. There's only study hall after third period anyway. Conroy and Fossum gave me a half-day stress leave yesterday. If they catch me, I'll just say I'm feeling stressed again.'

'You are feeling a bit stressed, aren't you?'

'Yes, I am.' I dump my mug. 'Right now, actually. Because I have to get back into the house to get my satchel, and the idea of running into my folks is giving me the heebie-jeebies.'

'You better go then. It's nearly six-thirty.'

Easing back into the house is not as fraught as I thought it would be. I'm familiar with the way certain doors creak, and which floorboards groan when you step on them. I go in the back, which I know will be unlocked to allow Dad to slip in early without disturbing the rest of us. It's when I get to my room that I hit a snag.

I'm turning the doorhandle, ready to feel the jubilation of a sneaky act well done, when Mike shuffles out of his room, rubbing his rumpled T-shirt. He stops dead.

'Um.' I swallow hard. 'Good morning.'

'*Where the hell have—*' Mike glances towards Mum and Dad's room, lowers his voice, steps closer. 'Where the hell have you been? And don't tell me you just got up, because we both know that's *bullshit*.'

'I…' I don't know what to say. I'd been expecting to justify myself to Mum and Dad. Not to Mike, who can smell a leg-pull from a mile away, given he's told so many himself. My shoulders slump. 'How did you know?'

Mike's hair stands up in all directions. He has a three-day growth, I notice with a pang. I'd feel a wash of sisterly affection, if he didn't look so incredibly angry.

'How do you *think*? I waited until midnight, ages after Mum went to bed, and you never came back.' He gives me his patented thousand-yard stare. 'Were you at Mycroft's house? All night?'

I nod. It's not as if I can do anything else. 'Yeah. But it was an accident, I—'

'Jesus, Rachel – what the hell?' Mike squints at me as if I'm a complete stranger who just spewed on his shoes. 'Since when do you pull this kind of shit?'

My voice enters that weird register somewhere between yelling and whispering. 'I didn't mean to! For god's sake, I was going to come home, but I—'

'*Don't*. Christ, Rachel, just…' Mike reels back and then refocuses on my face. His expression is very dark. 'So are you sleeping with this guy?'

'*No!*' Then I remember who I'm talking to: it's not my parents, or a teacher. It's *Mike*. I grab for the doorhandle to my room. 'No. I *fell asleep*, Mike. That's it, not that it's any of your business.'

'Well, actually, you being my little sister makes it my business.' His eyes are stony. 'And I *saw* you last night, walking around like you're made of glass. What do you call this, then? And this?'

He grabs my wrists and turns them over, so my palms face up. I gasp, because his grip on my sore arms really hurts. The places where my skin is scraped raw stand out in red. Bruises mottle my forearms. It looks as if I've been fooling around with Mum's purple eyeshadow, the way I used to when I was little.

I know how it must seem, but I almost laugh.

'Mike…Mike, it's okay. What, you think Mycroft's been bashing me up or something? I had an accident. I nearly fell off a ladder. That's how I got the bruises, okay? But it's fine. I'm *fine*.'

'Falling off ladders doesn't sound fine.'

'Mike, Mycroft was the one who stopped me from falling. He *saved* me.' I don't think it's worth mentioning the height of the ladder at the moment.

Mike's eyes are still hot, but some of the fire seems to have dulled. He heaves out a big breath. 'Christ, Rachel. You really take the cake, you know that?'

I recognize the phrase; *You take the cake* is one of Mum's.

'Yeah,' I say. 'And I'm supposed to be the responsible one, remember?'

'You're catching up way too fast.' Mike gives me a grim look. 'This isn't exactly responsible, though, is it? Coming home before seven in the morning in the same clothes you had on last night, and that's *my* jumper, by the way—'

'I *told* you. I fell asleep. End of story.'

'So one minute you and Mycroft are screaming at each other,

and the next minute he's saving your life and you're sleeping in his room... Are you *sure* you're not shagging this bloke?'

'God, Mike, will you *stop*? We're not...' I get a sudden visceral memory: Mycroft's hand on my ankle, on my shoulders. I shake it off. 'We're just...not like that.'

'Why not? What's wrong with you?' Mike rubs a hand across his mouth, obviously realizing what he just said. 'Okay. Fine. Jesus.'

I raise my eyebrows. 'Wow. You're, like, mini-Dad.'

'Funny.'

I look at him, still in his bed-wear, and something occurs to me. 'What are you doing, anyway? Aren't you getting ready for work?'

'Nah.' Mike turns so I can't see his face.

'What?' I frown. 'What is it?'

'Got the flick, didn't I?'

'What, they didn't sack you?' I move so I can see his eyes. 'Oh my god, they *did* sack you?'

'Yeah.'

I get a twisting feeling, deep in my gut, and it has nothing to do with ladder flashbacks. 'Since *when*? Bloody hell, Mike, you were having barbeques at Patrick's on Sunday, and now you're—'

'Patrick. Yeah, well. He's the roster manager, isn't he.' Mike clears his throat, still looking at the hall carpet. 'That's why he got me over. Said he didn't want to just call me out of the blue, which was nice of him, I guess. Kind of spoiled the whole barbeque thing, though.'

I'm stunned. My hands flutter in the air as I talk. 'But you... You never said anything on Sunday. Or last night. All through dinner, you never even seemed upset—'

Mike glares at me. 'Well it wasn't like *you* were going to notice, was it? I could've been walking around with my head on fire, I don't think you would have even looked up.'

He wheels around and stalks down the hall to the kitchen. I stand still for a moment, before deciding to hell with it and trailing after him. By the time I get into the kitchen, he's putting the kettle on.

I walk up and put a hand on his shoulder. 'I'm sorry, Mike. I didn't know. And yeah, I've been kind of wrapped up in myself lately.'

He sighs, gets out another mug, another teabag. 'That's okay.'

I fetch the milk from the fridge while the kettle boils. 'You haven't told Mum and Dad?'

'Not yet.' Mike looks about as low as I've ever seen him. Even after the foreclosure, he didn't look this depressed. He picks at the grouting on the edge of the bench. 'I didn't go to work yesterday. I went to the park. I'm trying to figure out what to do, Rache. I need a job. We need the money. I thought it'd be easy, getting work in the city, but it's not.'

He pours the hot water, and I do the milk and stirring. I take my tea to the kitchen table. Mike's still standing, shifting on his feet as if he's too agitated to sit.

'What about getting a taxi job, like Dad?' I suggest. 'Or a—'

'A what? There's plenty of shit-kicking contract jobs around, but I need something regular, something that helps with the rent. You need to be qualified to be a bloody checkout chick these days, and I've only got high school.'

I bite my lip. 'You could...you know...'

'I'm *not* gonna go on welfare, so don't even mention it.' Mike glowers, purses his lips. 'Rachel...'

'What is it?'

'I've been thinking…' He closes his eyes. Opens them with a sigh. 'Don't be mad, okay? But I've been thinking I should go back. I could get picking work, get farm work…'

My stomach does a full three-sixty and drops to somewhere near the soles of my shoes. My face feels frozen.

'You're going back to Five Mile?'

Mike blows into his mug. 'I dunno. Maybe to Ouyen, somewhere I could get cheap rent. Or if I get farm work, there are places I can get board.'

My field of vision has dimmed to blurry grays. 'You're going back to the country?'

Mike finally looks at me. His expression is pained, as if he's hurting just watching me. 'Shit, Rachel, don't look at me like that…'

I swallow to clear my sludgey throat, but my voice still comes out small. 'But you *like* the city.'

'Yeah, I do. I want to stay, but I've got to *work*, Rache. I've got to support myself. The city's bloody expensive.'

'I could help. I could get more hours at the mini-mart. Sundays, even after school—'

'Rache, I love you, but you shouldn't have to do that. You shouldn't be working to help me out when you're supposed to be studying. And I need to *do* something. At least in the country I wouldn't be shelling out for costs so much. I can't stay on here, putting a burden on Mum and Dad, if I can't pay my own way.'

My mug is still in my hands – I'd forgotten about it. I slide it away from me.

I can feel my forehead creasing, my mouth tightening up. 'I can't believe you're getting to go back. I hate it here. I'd give anything to go back to Five Mile.' I know I'm being selfish, but I can't help it.

215

Mike sounds like he's trying to be gentle. 'But Rache, you're still in school. And you've got opportunities here that you wouldn't have in the country—'

'Like *what*?' I'm amazed by how bitter my voice is, as if I've been sucking on wattle seeds.

If this were Mum or Dad, they'd be all softly-softly about it. But it's Mike, and he suddenly raises the volume.

'Like a bloody decent education, for one thing! Jesus, Rachel, open your eyes! You're so set against living in the big smoke you can't see past it, and I'm damned if I know why. You're doing great in school, you could do anything—'

'I *want* to do *farm work*.' I set my face. 'That's what I want to do! I want to get out of the smog, and the traffic, and—'

'And *what*? Marry some local yokel and pop out a few babies and live in rural poverty your whole life?' Then he softens. 'Rachel, you could do so much more.'

When I open my mouth again, my voice has a pathetic, plaintive quality that makes me cringe. 'But…but I've never wanted anything else.'

My brother tilts his head. His stare goes into my eyes, into my heart.

'Then start looking around. You know, I'd give almost anything to have your brains. Don't waste it, Rache. Please.' He sighs, and puts his half-full mug into the sink. 'Okay, stuff it, I'm going back to bed.'

'Right,' I say thickly. 'No point being laid off if you don't take the chance to have a sleep-in, huh?'

CHAPTER SIXTEEN

Mike's going back to the country. He's leaving me here, alone, with Mum and Dad working around the clock, and he's going back to the place I want to be more than anywhere else in the world. And he doesn't even *want* to go.

The unfairness of it, the pain of it, hits me like a sledgehammer. I crumple over in my chair, bow my head until it's resting on the tabletop. My arms hug my chest. I can't see; I can't *breathe*. I can't breathe in this place, this *goddamn place*—

I hear the noise of the car and boots on the concrete side pathway. I suck the feelings and the need to cry back inside, almost gagging from the strain. I scrub my hand across my face just in time to hear Dad let himself into the house.

'Hey, Rachel, morning, love.' Dad rubs my hair and walks heavily to the sink in his taxi-driver's uniform, reaching for the kettle. 'Mum still out to it?'

'Yeah, I think so,' I say.

I haven't seen Mum since last night, so the words come out

forced and unnatural. I stand up from my chair – I've got to get out of here before Dad notices. 'I'm going in a bit early, Dad, okay? Study hall with Mai. I'll see you later.'

I walk back down the hall, towards my room. I change clothes and brush my teeth, grab my satchel, and get out of the house as though stockwhips are cracking at my heels.

———

'Right, we're nearly there. Earth to Watts…'

My feet are tucked up on the seat, and one arm's around my knee so I can chew my thumbnail. I was doing a pretty good impression of my normal self until we got on the train. Then I had to just sit.

Streets and buildings scurry by out the window, but I'm not really seeing anything. Mycroft's voice seems foggy, distorted, as if my head's underwater in the bath.

'Sorry.' I sound like a zombie. 'Nearly there. Right.'

Mycroft has peeled a mandarin, and is stuffing the last segments into his mouth.

'Watts, you're doing it again – that whole contemplation of the arid urban landscape thing. You'll get yourself all depressed, and then I'll have to be entertaining and funny to snap you out of it…' He catches sight of my face and swallows his mouthful. 'What is it?'

I don't look at Mycroft. I don't want to hear myself, or relive this memory, but I do it anyway.

'We put all our dogs down when we left, you know.' I rip away a piece of thumbnail, down to the quick. 'Working dogs aren't like pets. They're trained to behave a specific way, and if you take them out of their work environment they get aggressive.'

After a pause, Mycroft's reply drifts over like smoke. 'I didn't know that.'

'Nobody we knew was able to take them in, because Tilly was getting old, and Hoob…He was a younger dog, but there just wasn't anywhere for him to go. We couldn't take them with us, not to the city. So we put them down.'

I'm not here right now. I'm miles away, back in time and space. My throat is jammed and I *remember*. It's not a memory for sharing, but I have to get something out, have to release something, before I self-combust.

'I mean, *I* put them down. Mum and Dad couldn't bring themselves to do it, and Mike was driving the moving van to Melbourne, so I did it. I took them out into the east paddock, because that was their favorite. I tied them up to the big scribbly gum and let them lick my hands for a while. Then I got Dad's twenty-two rifle, and I—'

I can't keep going. My eyes blink with a dry heat, as if I've woken up with a fever. We're going by a rail siding, and I can see Mycroft's face reflected in the window.

'Watts…what's going on? This isn't about you sleeping in my room, is it, because you've got that—'

'It's not about that.' I look over, make a short, unpleasant laugh. 'It's not about you. Sorry, I'm just in a bad mood. I'm fine. I mean, I'll be fine.'

Mycroft stares into me. His eyes are a rich ultramarine, like the sea on a Hawaiian beach, the long dark lashes a vivid contrast.

'You don't have to pretend with me, you know.' He reaches out and tucks a strand of my hair behind my ear. His expression is so open and honest I feel it like a sucker punch. 'I used to pretend, all the time, so I can spot it a mile away. If you're feeling shit, then

219

just say so. I don't need to know the reason, it might be none of my business—'

'I'm feeling shit.' The words fall like toads dropping from my mouth.

'Okay.'

'Mike's going back to the country.'

'Ah.'

'He's lost his job and he's going back, and he doesn't even *want* to go back, and—' I look blindly out the window. 'I can't really talk about this right now.'

'Fair enough.' He waits a beat. 'I'm sorry.'

'It's not your fault. But I just can't—' I push down on my heart as hard as I can. 'What did you mean about pretending? You said you *used* to pretend.'

'Yeah. Sure.' It's Mycroft's turn to look away. 'But it was a crap idea in the long-term, because I got too good at it.'

'How's that?'

'You know.' Mycroft shrugs, watches the 'arid urban landscape' move out the window of the train. 'In the hospital they tell you to soldier on, keep smiling, stuff like that. You end up just faking being happy all the time, and it does your head in. If I feel like that now, I just take the day off to be miserable.'

I think of Mycroft's 'personal days' off school, the ones Mai loves to gripe about. Since I found out about his parents, about his stay in the RP, Mycroft's erratic behavior is becoming more and more understandable.

'So you don't pretend anymore?'

Something in the way he scans my face – my eyes, my hair, my lips – makes me feel restless all over.

'I still pretend with some things.' He glances away fast. 'I'm the master at pretending. Come on, this is us.'

At Royal Park station there's a smattering of people walking towards the zoo entrance. Employees, I think, considering it's only eight in the morning and the zoo doesn't open for another hour.

Off the train, I feel oddly better. Not great, but not like one of the undead anymore. My heart is still bleeding, but I shove it to one side.

I pull at Mycroft's sleeve to get him to slow to my pace. 'How are we even going to get in? I don't know about you, but I'm about twenty bucks shy of the entry fee.'

'No problem.' Mycroft scans the back entrance area. 'I have a plan of action.'

'Great.' I sigh, but I follow him up the path.

There's no one in the ticket booth, and the big gates are shut. But there's a matronly woman in a zoo-logo polar fleece buzzing herself in.

Mycroft snags her before the door closes. 'Hi! Excuse me, hi there!'

With his bruises and lacerations mostly healed up he can get away with this more easily. It always amazes me to see the way Mycroft's face transforms when he puts on one of these performances. After our conversation on the train, I guess I shouldn't be surprised.

He explains that his aunt, Angela Hudgson, works as a cleaner in the zoo and that last night she left something behind in one of the admin blocks – 'A ring, about so big, silver, with a little diamond?' – and he said he'd pick it up for her before he headed to school. When the woman vacillates, Mycroft turns on the full-wattage smile.

'Please, I know *exactly* where it is. I swear we won't be a bother – straight in, straight out, yeah?'

The woman blinks under the onslaught. 'Oh…all right. Fine. Just quickly, okay?'

'Thank you *so* much,' Mycroft says, pulling me through the gate behind him.

We walk straight towards the top entrance. Past the picnic pavilions I glance back; the woman is still watching Mycroft.

'That was kind of mean, don't you think?' I keep a hand on my satchel to stop it from bouncing.

'D'you think so?' Mycroft says. 'I was perfectly polite.'

'Yeah, but then you gave her the three-thousand-volt smile.'

He laughs, and his face goes suddenly brilliant. I put my hands over my eyes, as if I'm dazzled by the glare.

Past all the decorative plantings, the functional rectangles of the zoo admin block heave into view and we stop goosing around. There's a ramp to a glass door labeled *Office*.

I hang back as Mycroft twists the doorknob. 'Now what do we say?'

'Haven't the foggiest. Don't you know I'm just making this up as I go along?'

He does the smile thing again on the woman behind the foyer desk there. 'Oh, hi, my name is James Mycroft, and this is my friend, Rachel Watts. We're here to speak to Ronald Maddison.'

The woman, a no-nonsense sort, doesn't seem as affected by Mycroft's charm. 'Right. You'll need an appointment to see Mr Maddison, and he's not in the office at the moment. Can I take a message?'

Two men enter the office area behind us.

Mycroft slogs on. 'Actually, I don't think so. We're trying to find out how to contact his daughter, Rosemarina, and if we could just speak to him for a minute or two—'

'Excuse me, good morning, yes?'

One of the men pushes forward to stand behind the woman at the desk. He's about forty-five, with a sunburned face and sandy hair, and looks as though he keeps fit religiously. His eyes are like green cellophane, and when he squints I know we're in trouble.

'Pardon me, but are you here on zoo business?'

Mycroft spares him a glance. 'Well, like I said, we're trying to get in touch with Mr Maddison's daughter...'

He flounders and I step up. 'We're doing a paper on ten significant graffiti artworks, featuring some of Rosemarina Maddison's work. We'd like to interview her about it, but we aren't sure how to contact her. If Mr Maddison would give us a moment of his time—'

'I'm sorry, but this is completely irregular.' Squinty-eyes has one hand on the back of the receptionist's chair and the other out in a *Stop, Do Not Pass Go* gesture. 'If this isn't a zoo-related matter then you really shouldn't be here.'

'I'm sorry,' I say, as though I really am. 'Excuse me, Mister...?'

'Illingham. It's Ian Illingham, and I'm the operations manager. Now, how did you two get into the park, if you don't mind?'

'Mr Illingham, we didn't think this would be a problem. Our teacher, Ms Ferguson, suggested that we speak with the artist. As there's no listing for Rosemarina Maddison, we thought it would be simplest just to contact her through her father. Mr Maddison's contact is through the zoo—'

'I'm sorry, this is not the way to go about things. You'll have to call and make an appointment. If Mr Maddison agrees to see you, then you can proceed from there.'

'Mr Illingham, we need to speak to Rosemarina Maddison sometime in the next few days. I'm sure if her father knew this was about her artwork—'

'His opinion on her artwork is common knowledge.' The guy's face is so stiff you could bounce a penny off it. 'You haven't said how you got in here yet.'

Mycroft leans forward. 'It was a very nice lady, who let us in from the train station entrance. So you can't tell us where to contact Miss Maddison at all?'

Illingham's cheeks bloom with twin spots of flamingo pink.

'Right. Mr Harrow, please escort these two people off the premises. I'm going to call the Rail Gate to make sure they exit.' He bestows a cutting glare on Mycroft and me, before turning to the receptionist. 'Claire, could you get me the extension for Human Resources? We're going to need to draft a memo on employees abusing their gate privileges. And then the Rail Gate, if you don't mind…'

I don't hear the rest of it. The other man, who's been standing behind us the whole time, suddenly comes around to the front. He smiles tightly, extending his hand to the door.

I blink. It's John – Good Samaritan John, John-in-the-labs John. He's wearing identical clothes to the ones he had on Sunday, even the grotty runners.

I'm preparing to speak when his eyes flick across to Illingham. I close my mouth so fast my teeth click together.

John adjusts his glasses with one hand, his other still outstretched. 'This way, please.'

Mycroft balks. 'But we haven't—'

'Come on, Mycroft.' I pull on his hand.

My eyes water in the morning glare when we emerge. We walk

224

down the ramp, John leading. Once we're a safe distance from the admin building, I break into a grin.

'God, talk about luck. Good to see you again.'

John smiles as we all keep pace together. 'Well, it's nice to see you too, but I wasn't expecting to find you facing off with Ian. Thought we'd bump into each other at the elephant exhibit or something.'

Mycroft is walking on my other side, wearing a slightly flabbergasted look. 'Excuse me, but we haven't been—'

'Introduced, sorry, yes,' John says. His gold rims flash as he reaches across me to shake hands, still walking. 'John Harrow, pleased to meet you.'

'Mycroft, likewise,' Mycroft says. He's still looking between me and John. 'But how do you know…'

John smiles. 'Oh, yes. I, ah, came across Rachel the other day.'

'I was half-comatose outside the zoo.' I laugh until I see Mycroft's raised eyebrows and realize how it must sound – like I've been some kind of feeble, delicate flower in his absence. 'I mean, I'd been at the station and I just forgot to have breakfast or something, and the sun was a bit hot…'

I can see I'm digging myself in further, until John chips in to help. 'Actually, you were fine, weren't you? Just a touch of the sun. Nothing a bucket of hot chips couldn't sort out.'

'Yeah.' I don't bother to say the chips had been beyond my budget. 'So anyway, John let me in to get something from the cafe. Very kind. But hey, you said you were in the labs, not zoo admin.'

'I *am* in the labs. That is, I'm usually in the labs.' He waves towards the huddle of offices near the Reptile House. 'But I help out from time to time – everyone here multi-tasks to some extent. I had to chase Ian around this morning.'

'We weren't trying to get in trouble with Mr Illingham,' I say, 'but we need to talk to Ronald Maddison.'

'Good luck with that.'

'We're trying to contact his daughter, Rosemarina,' Mycroft says. 'It's for a...project.'

'A paper – yes, I heard. Art students, are you?'

'Yeah.' Mycroft smiles, loping along as if he's taking a nice stroll around the park. 'Mr Illingham doesn't seem to like questions about Rosemarina Maddison, does he?'

'He's not much of art aficionado.' John grins. He steers us towards the bottom gate as he chats, hands in his trouser pockets. 'Sorry, I shouldn't speak out of turn. But it's true Maddison's daughter's self-expression isn't hugely popular here.'

'Why, are they worried she'll start painting the Zoo walls with murals about corporate greed?' I ask.

John laughs. 'Maybe. I'd hate to see Maddison's reaction though.'

'I wouldn't have thought the zoo walls would be high enough for Rosemarina to bother.' Mycroft's eyes fix on John as we pass the entrance to the platypus exhibit. 'So, she and her dad have...artistic differences?'

John lifts a mild eyebrow. 'Let's just say her artwork probably won't be displayed in the foyer anytime soon. I've met her and she does tend to enjoy ticking people off. Bit embarrassing for her father, really. Looks bad.'

He scratches under his shirt collar.

'Look, I don't want to make waves around here. You're not going to put what I've said into your paper, are you? I mean, everyone's aware of the boss's relationship with his daughter, but—'

I hold up a hand. 'Hey, no problem. We're not going to quote you.'

John's expression clears. 'Good. Thank you. I mean, you could say she was "volatile" and that would pretty much cover it. I'm sure you'll understand better when you meet her.'

'Which will be never, at this rate,' Mycroft says. 'Unless Mr Maddison can squeeze us into his busy schedule this week.'

The Rail Gate is just below us, the path gently sloping towards it. John slows as we approach the giant turnstile.

'Sorry about this. You know, guard duties aren't my regular thing. It does seem a bit ridiculous that you have to make an appointment and come back in just to get a phone number...' He ushers us towards the turnstile. 'Have you tried contacting her through the art school?'

Mycroft's face lifts. 'We couldn't find out which one.'

'Ah. It's the Hundertwasser School.' John shrugs. 'Who knows, maybe with all that exclusive tuition she'll turn out something her dad can hang in his office one day. Nice to meet you, anyway. Best of luck with the paper. Good to see you again, Rachel, glad you're feeling better.'

We spin through the revolving cage of the turnstile and are disgorged onto the footpath. Mycroft is already madly thumb-typing on his phone.

His mouth has an odd quirk. 'Didn't know you'd been having fainting spells outside the zoo.'

I snort. 'It wasn't a fainting spell. You make it sound like something out of Jane Austen.'

'That was the day you came to the RP?' He glances at me, and I know he's thinking *The day after we fought.*

'Yes. But it wasn't—'

'He seems agreeable enough, your mate.'

'Yes. He was very—'

'Kind, yes. You said. And a good source of info.'

'That isn't—' My arms hurt when I cross them. 'Can't you spell Hundertwasser?'

'Hundert... H-U-N-D...'

I spell it for him. He glares at the screen, then smiles.

'Got it. The Hundertwasser School. It's right off La Trobe Street.' He winks at me. 'Come on, Watts. The game's afoot!'

———

'Are you sure we're in the right place?'

'This is it.' Mycroft checks his GPS app. 'Yep. Definitely. Doesn't look very exclusive, does it?'

A walk north from Melbourne Central station has brought us to the front of a crumbling three-story facade. The building was probably impressive about a hundred years ago.

'It looks like a run-down hotel,' I say.

'I guess so. Still, it's in the heart of the CBD. The rent must be staggering.'

We let ourselves in through the paint-peeled double doors. The foyer is dusty, unlit, cold; it leads directly toward a gloomy set of stairs. Mycroft lowers his voice to suit the tone of the place as we climb. 'What's the definition of *artistic*?'

The stairs are killing my stiff muscles. 'Enlighten me.'

'Likes to sleep and drink.' Mycroft waggles his eyebrows. 'What about *cubism*?'

I snort, pull myself up by the railing. 'I'm sure you're going to tell me.'

'Paintings done after smoking chicken stock cubes.'

Suddenly another voice chimes in from above us. 'What's the definition of *avant garde*?'

There's a stocky young woman at the top of the next railing at the third floor. She's wearing overalls and wiping a collection of paintbrushes on a rag. Her strong arms end in worn hands with surprisingly delicate fingers.

Mycroft seems unperturbed. 'Avant garde. Isn't that something you should like until it's popular?'

'Right.' The woman grins, a slow sunrise. 'Are you here about studio time?'

'We're here to see Rosemarina Maddison.'

The woman jerks her head back to a point behind herself. 'She's working. But I don't think she'll mind an interruption. Welcome to HundieVee, come on up.'

She walks off. Mycroft and I glance at each other before taking the next set of stairs two at a time.

We arrive at a bare high-ceilinged corridor with a single wooden door. Faded gold words, *Fine Art – Painting,* are embossed on the door. Mycroft shrugs and offers me the lead.

When we enter, it's into such light and space that the gloom of the hallway and stairwell seems like a bad memory. White-painted walls with enormous multi-paned windows soar to a vaulted ceiling. A forest of wooden easels sprouts from the floor. There are tables with equipment, drop cloths, paper sketches in various stages of completion, battered stereos, mugs, a camp stove, and various bottles. Canvases lean haphazardly against the walls, or are stacked in geological layers on the floor. Everything in the space is splotched, splashed, dripped and drizzled with color, standing out in high relief against the pristine walls.

The woman from the top of the stairwell is standing near an easel on the left, stuffing the rag into her front pocket. She's shorter than I realized, and she's wearing a white tank underneath the overalls. Her dark brown hair is an asymmetric punk bob and hieroglyph tattoos circle her tanned biceps.

'If you want to talk to Rosemarina, you probably don't have long. She has the attention span of a budgerigar when she's working. Hey, Rose! Rose!' The punk-artist woman sighs and walks into the easel forest.

I scan the walls behind us. There's a canvas that looks like a conflagration right out of Hell – burning tombs and blackened bodies, shocking and familiar. I tug on Mycroft's shirt to point out what I've seen. He doesn't respond.

When I look back at him, the expression on his face pulls me up short. I follow the line of his gaze and look past the woman we've already met to another figure approaching close on her heels.

At first, I think of an exotic butterfly, with dramatic banners of color. The girl walking towards us could be in her late teens or early twenties – her manner and outfit blur her age.

Rosemarina Maddison is dressed in the dragon-fire colors she seems to favor in her murals. High-soled black boots buckled all the way up to her knees make her taller, and she's been poured into her black jeans and blood-red tank. Draped over this outfit is a sleeveless scarlet dress, tied like a smock at her chest but left open the rest of the way.

The dress swirls around her calves. She pulls a slim paintbrush out of the bun at her nape as she approaches, so her black hair falls around her pale face and shoulders in glossy waves, almost to her waist. Her lips are full and her eyes are dark and large. She is, in a word, gorgeous.

Then I realize that she's not looking at me at all – just at Mycroft. I revise my opinion. She not like a butterfly. With her skinny angular limbs, and those colors, she's more like ... a spider.

That's it. A redback spider. I glance over at Mycroft, so we can share a mutual raised-eyebrow moment.

Mycroft's face is lit with fascination, spots of color tinting each cheek. His mouth is open, definitely gawping.

I feel a sharp twist in my chest, and alleviate it by leaning forward casually and stepping on his foot. He comes back to life with a gulp.

'Oh, right.' He steps forward with his hand out. 'Miss Maddison, hi, we're sorry to be a bother, but—'

Which is all he gets out before Rosemarina Maddison walks right up to him. In one smooth motion she fists a hand into his shirtfront and pulls his lips down to her own.

CHAPTER SEVENTEEN

I feel as though I'm standing in the middle of a thundercrack. Rosemarina drops her paintbrush and lifts her other hand, twining it into Mycroft's thick curls as she kisses him.

After the initial shock, when his eyes widen like saucers and his hands levitate out to the sides, Mycroft's whole body seems to go limp. His eyelids shimmer down, the lashes dusting his cheeks.

And I...am completely gobsmacked. Blood rushes in my ears. My cheeks are blazing. My ribcage has gone tight and I can feel myself gaping.

A movement off to the side is the only distraction. It's the woman we met earlier, who's watching Rosemarina with a wry expression. When she sees me, she snorts and rolls her eyes. I can only assume the eye-roll indicates that pashing complete strangers is a regular feature of Rosemarina's behavior.

But really, I can't look away from the kiss for long. Mycroft appears to have melted. His hands run like candle wax down his sides. Just as I think bitterly that maybe I should sneak back down the stairs and leave them to it, Rosemarina slips her hand out of Mycroft's hair and pulls back so she can stare at his face.

'The only person who calls me Miss Maddison,' she says, voice throaty, 'is my father's PA. And you don't look old enough to be his new employee.'

She smiles, releases Mycroft's shirt and pats out the wrinkles she's made in it. She saunters towards a bench on the far side of the studio, where a camp stove is parked. An espresso pot sits on the burner.

'Coffee?' She glances up at us. 'It's Caribbean roast, honestly it's wonderful, you should try it. Anna, you won't have some?'

The last comment is directed at the woman who invited us in. A connection links in my brain – *Anna – Anubis – jackal-headed Egyptian God of the Dead – hieroglyphs…*

The woman with the hieroglyph tattoo is one of the Roof Monkeys. I'm sure of it.

However, I'm less interested in that useful bit of info than in watching how Mycroft blinks at the floor and gives his head a careful shake, as if he's just been concussed.

'I'm good,' Anna says, pulling a tube of oil paint out of her front pouch.

'I was just wondering when I get mine.' I rock back on my heels and make flint-eyes at the delightful Miss Maddison.

She strolls back, one hand offering a coffee mug in my direction. 'Two sugars, and there's no milk, I hope you don't mind.'

'I wasn't talking about the coffee.'

'Oh.' Rosemarina's smile doesn't extend past her lips. 'Sorry, I don't kiss girls. Not on first meeting, anyway. I have more respect for them.' She blows into her own mug. 'So, it's nice to have visitors, but I'm assuming there's a reason you dropped by?'

She steps back and perches on a low-backed bar stool near the closest easel, sipping her coffee. She seems quite aware of the fact that in those clothes, with her incredible looks, she could be posing for a portrait.

Mycroft has regained the power of speech. Somewhat. 'We, um, want to...that is, er—'

I take a slurp of coffee, which really is good, push the mug into his hands to shut him up, and turn to Rosemarina. 'We want you to make a mural. At our school in North Coburg.'

'A mural?' Rosemarina seems entertained by the idea. 'I have done larger pieces, but a—'

'We're not representing the school. We want a mural done by the Roof Monkeys about the soullessness of education, and we want it painted on the outside of the IT wing.' I glance at Anna, who has gone still. 'And I know you're part of the group too, so you might want to listen in.'

Anna's eyes sharpen.

Rosemarina rests her mug on her thigh. 'Well, goodness, this is very interesting, but—'

'We worked out the tags,' Mycroft has finally come up for air. 'From another mural in the city. We know you only do corporates, but we'd like you to consider this as a one-off piece. We could pay you.'

'Like a commission,' I say. 'Not much, but something. Think of it as an inspiration to your legions of fans trapped in the factory-high-school public education system.'

Anna takes a step closer, her paint tube twisted in her hand. 'Not that we're saying we're involved at all, but how did you hear about the Roof Monkeys?'

I shrug. 'Like he said. The tags. And we know a few people who

234

have an interest. We have a contact at the zoo. That's how we got the information to come here.'

Rosemarina has looked up from her coffee. Now she is holding herself very still.

'Rose—' Anna says quietly.

'The mural content would be totally up to you,' Mycroft interrupts, ad-libbing freely. 'And we could give you details about onsite security, all that stuff.'

'The wall is about four meters high.' I force a grin. 'Not much of a challenge, I know.'

Rosemarina stares at me for a moment and I'm praying she can't see that I'm faking. Her gaze is so hypnotic it makes my palms sweat, and I'm reminded of why we're here. This woman might be linked to Dave's death. There's definitely *something* going on with her. After seeing that kiss, Rosemarina's beauty seems to me like a thin veneer: the chocolate coating some bitter fruit.

She and Anna look at each other, then Rosemarina turns back to me. 'Anna and I would like to chat. In private, if you don't mind.'

'No problem.' I bob my head. 'We'll just…um, do you mind if we look around? This place is pretty amazing…'

'Go ahead.' Rosemarina waves a hand.

Mycroft and I wander casually into the easel forest, as if we're checking out the other artists' work. Apart from the low murmurs of Anna and Rosemarina behind us, the place is quiet. I guess it's too early for other art students to have crawled out of bed to the studio.

Mycroft nudges me, talking in a whisper as we move around the exhibits. 'What the hell are you *doing*?'

'Hey, *I'm* not the one *macking* with the suspects.' I elbow him out of the way. 'I'm making it up as I go along, remember? We wanted to get a look at her, check out the place. It was all I could think of at the time.'

'I had a plan!' he protests.

'I think your plan went out the window when she kissed you, along with your *brain*. Here. This looks like her stuff.'

I recognize the color scheme – vibrant crimsons, inky blacks, all the pigments of flame and death. Rosemarina wants to burn it all down, whatever it is.

I bump Mycroft again. 'Don't loiter. Go see what else you can find.'

'Her stuff's all over the place.' He glances at a collection of aerosol cans dumped haphazardly on a nearby bench. 'Hold on a sec.'

He trots off around another easel to explore. I examine a trolley near Rosemarina's easel. A tray on top holds a random mix of paintbrushes, rollers, spraycans, dirty rags. There's a palette knife there. I reach out to test the edge – too blunt.

I see something more interesting: on the edge of the tray, a box cutter. I snick out the blade. It's thin, sharp, and heavily stained. Is that paint or something else?

Mycroft has been swallowed up in the forest. I step past the painting that Rosemarina is still working on and go to the collection of canvases leaning against the bench. I lift the dropcloth tentatively.

My eyes widen. I look again. Look at the next one. And another. And another.

I pull back each canvas, feeling a revolted astonishment.

All the canvases are large. The smallest is about a meter square. The black silhouette style is instantly recognizable. I'm viewing the same furious explosion of nuclear colors and distinctive characters: the vacant red eyes, emaciation, long tendinous limbs, all bone and gristle.

But there's more substance to these images, more fine detail and more pain. And there are characters here that haven't appeared in the Roof Monkeys' hastily sprayed murals. Girls with enormous eyes and whipping black hair, held in chains made of their own flesh. Thick bull-necked men with beefy hands, performing acts of torture. The images get progressively more graphic, more perverse, with each canvas.

The messages about world poverty and consumerism are conspicuous by their absence. These works aren't political, but highly personal. In vivid ghastly color, Rosemarina is telling people everything...everything about her relationship with her father.

Nauseated, I pull out my phone and snap a few hasty photos of the images. I return my phone to my pocket; my hands are shaking as I lean the last canvas back into place.

'Find anything you like?'

I whip around.

Rosemarina Maddison is standing with her arms crossed, close enough that I can see the fine tracery of her eyeliner.

'I didn't...I...' I swallow hard. 'I don't think you're supposed to like them.'

Rosemarina's beautiful mouth twists. Did she see me take the photos? And where the bloody hell is Mycroft? There's a pause while I hold my breath...then she leans across me to pull the drop cloth over the paintings before stepping away.

'No, you're not,' she says. 'They weren't painted for exhibition.'

In the second it takes me to recover, I remember the only

thing I know about artwork. 'Do they have a title?'

Rosemarina's expression distorts again. She's laughing at a horrific inside joke.

'Yes. They're called *Patronymic*.' She glances around. 'Where's the tall Brit?'

God, I wish I knew. 'Er, he's—'

'Watts?' A mop of dark-brown curls bobs over the top of a nearby easel. 'This place is like a maze of paint and fumes. Where are—'

Mycroft makes it around the corner, spots me and Rosemarina in parley, and pulls up short. 'Oh. Hi. Is the discussion over, then?'

'Yes, it is.' Rosemarina reaches to roll her hair against her nape. She fixes it in place with a paintbrush she snags from the tray. 'Naturally we can't confirm or deny anything, but we think that your project may be something the Roof Monkeys would be interested in.'

'Well, great.' Mycroft smiles all over his face. He really is much better at pretending than me. 'So do you want more information about the school? Or we can—'

'What you can do is give me a contact number.' Rosemarina reaches to another easel and tears paper from the edge of somebody else's sketch, then scrawls on it with a texta. 'And here's a number to call if you change your mind or there's some other problem.'

Mycroft plucks the paper from her fingers. I find a piece of scrap paper on the floor and lean it on Mycroft's back to write my own mobile number on it.

'That tickles,' he says.

I ignore him, and pass the paper to Rosemarina. 'There you go. Will you be contacting us soon?'

Rosemarina examines my squiggles. Her long fingers, holding

the scrap of paper, have all their nails bitten down to the quick. It's the only thing about her that isn't elegant and sophisticated.

'Soon. But it won't be me who gets in touch. This should be the only time we ever have to speak face to face.' She tucks the paper down the front of her top. 'In fact, it might be better if you just forgot all about this little meeting. It's been lovely to chat, but please don't drop in again, do you understand? You might not get such a friendly reception next time.'

'Oh.' Mycroft blinks. 'Right. Well, it was nice to—'

'Yes. Delighted.' Rosemarina waves a hand towards the door. 'I'm sure you can see yourselves out.'

She turns away from us, slides on a set of headphones and starts unscrewing tubes of paint.

We've been dismissed. As far as Rosemarina's concerned, we no longer exist. Which suits me right down to the ground.

'Come on.' I pull on Mycroft's sleeve. 'I wanted to get out of here about fifteen minutes ago.'

We weave through the forest, emerge onto the bare floor space before the door. Anna is stewing something at the camp stove; she makes no move to acknowledge our existence either. I keep my hand on Mycroft's sleeve as we make our way out of the studio and down the flights of stairs.

Mycroft squints as we enter the harsh daylight outside the Hundertwasser School. I just feel an almighty sense of relief.

'Well,' Mycroft says. 'What do you think?'

'What do I think?' I cross my arms, then realize it's the way Rosemarina stood in front of me bare moments ago and uncross them. 'I think we're in. I think Rosemarina Maddison is definitely disturbed. And I think there's a real possibility that she killed Dave.'

———

239

Senior study hall is in a quiet room at the far end of the English wing. Mycroft points out that it's miles away from the admin block and the large windows are open at ground level. Also, there's no regular teacher supervision. Therefore it's perfectly reasonable for me to let him sneak onto school grounds and climb in, so he can touch base with Mai and Gus.

After a minute or two of arguing with him about it, I give up. Now we're all talking near a table in the corner. I'm extremely thankful that Mai and Gus and I are usually the only students who bother to attend study hall.

There are plenty of gaps to fill in. Mycroft and I give an amended version of our visit with Gray Jetta and explain the cryptic clues that led us to check out the mural. Mycroft glosses over the disaster on the scaffolding and I report on the zoo. Finally we get to the main event: meeting Rosemarina Maddison.

By the time we've finished giving them the basic outline, Mai and Gus are both sitting with their mouths open. Then we move on to theorizing.

'So she encounters Dave somewhere between the RP and the zoo.' Mycroft twirls an abandoned plastic ruler in his fingers. He's lounging on one of the armchairs beside the study tables, which I personally think are an invitation to study yourself into a nice afternoon nap. 'She threatens him, or maybe Poodle, with a knife, which brings on a heart attack. Then she cuts his throat.'

'It's thin,' Mai says.

'It's very thin.' Mycroft taps the end of the ruler against his forehead. 'There's still the issue of motive. We need more information on Rosemarina. Where she's been, what she was doing on the night of the murder...'

I showed him the photos of Rosemarina's ghastly incest

paintings on the train. Even though I would love to go straight to Pickup with it, it's all circumstantial; we'd agreed to keep quiet until we find out more. I think of Rosemarina, abused and angry, admitted against her will to a psych ward…It gives her manner and her appearance a whole new meaning.

I've never known anyone who's gone through something as awful as that. I've been so protected. Rosemarina channels some of her rage into her creative work. But would anger like that also make you want to lash out, tear something down, rip it to pieces? Would it make you want to destroy something, someone?

Someone like Dave?

Some of these puzzle pieces are still not fitting together, and it's giving me a headache.

'I don't know, guys. You've got no hard evidence. You're really just hypothesizing.' Mai is slouched against the table, her *Fitzroy Furies – Fresh Meat!!* T-shirt riding up above the waist of her flip-skirt.

'We're missing loads of things.' I talk with my eyes on the notes I'm scrawling from Mai's originals. I'm actually trying to work. It's probably an insane idea, but I'm behind in three subjects. 'Not to mention proof.'

'Which is quite important in a court of law,' Mai says, nodding.

'The dog.' Mycroft throws down the ruler and steeples his fingers. 'We're still missing the dog.'

'Well, you've made a lot of progress. Sounds like this Rosemarina chick is good for the murder.' Gus is losing focus, too busy ogling Mai's exposed skin from where he sits behind her.

Mycroft hauls himself up. He studies the lint on the carpet as he paces in short, tight steps.

'There's something else, though. Something I'm not getting,

and I just can't…' He stops pacing. He leans his bum on the table between me and Mai, too absorbed to notice he's getting in the way. 'I've been trying to work it out. It was something I remembered, just after Rosemarina kissed me in the studio—'

Gus's attention snaps back. 'What?'

'She *kissed* you?' Mai looks up at Mycroft, appalled.

'Yes,' Mycroft says, testing the scab on his eyebrow with a finger.

'What, she just walked up and—'

'—grabbed him by the shirt and planted one right on him.' I glance over. 'Again, yes.'

'For god's sake!'

'She had quite hard lips,' Mycroft says to no one in particular.

'Well, don't get too excited.' I return my head to my notes. 'I got the impression that's her standard greeting for any male of the species that she wants to mess about.'

'When do I get to meet her?' Gus grins for about one second before Mai elbows him in the stomach.

'Never, apparently.' Mycroft smiles at them both. Then he glares down at me. 'And I didn't get *too excited*, thank you very much. It was weird.'

'You didn't seem to complain at the time.' I push my hair behind my ear with the end of my pen, then stand up and shove Mycroft over, start undoing the straps on my satchel. Seeing the kiss once was enough – I don't need a recap.

'No,' Mycroft says. 'It *was* weird. Like kissing my sister.'

I can feel Mai's eye-roll without needing to see it. 'Mycroft, you don't *have* a sister.'

'Like kissing you, then.'

'Well, you're not kissing *me*.'

'That's right,' Gus says, quite vehemently, 'you're not.'

'Like kissing Watts, then,' Mycroft says.

'*Right*,' Mai says.

I really only come back to the conversation when I hear her inflection. I turn, frowning. 'What are you talking about?'

'A scientific demonstration,' Mycroft says, and he reaches out and grabs me.

There's no fanfare, no warning at all. My eyes widen and my hand startles out, dropping my pen.

Then Mycroft's mouth is on mine and my eyelids close of their own volition and all my thought processes dissolve.

My whole body stops in a giant gasp. Everything inside me is suddenly reduced to *feeling*. That's all there is, just pure sensation. It's too much, overpowering. My back arches as part of me fights for control...

But I can't fight.

Mycroft's lips are swollen-soft. I feel the rasp of the old cut on his bottom lip. He tastes a little of citrus, faintly of cigarettes, but mostly just of *boy* – something so alien and interesting that everything inside me springs to attention, wanting to know more.

He's pressed up against me; one of his arms is snaked firmly around my waist. His body is wiry and muscled and *warm*, so warm. He's running at a hotter temperature than me, than anyone else on the planet.

My body ignites. I lean in, deepening the kiss. Mycroft makes a soft noise, low in his throat. I feel it on my lips. Something suddenly floods through me, like superheated mercury...

...and then his lips are gone, and my eyes slowly open. I'm standing there with my cheeks on fire, and what must be the stupidest facial expression of all time.

'There,' Mycroft says. But his voice sounds unsteady and strange. His eyes are dark, dazed.

There's a pause, during which I notice that I've got my arm around his neck and he notices that his other hand has slid up to squeeze my shoulder. We extricate ourselves in a fumbling way. I dither between saying something and turning back to my satchel, before I realize that I can't really speak.

Mai clears her throat. 'That was ...very scientific.'

Mycroft blinks.

'It was, wasn't it?' He picks up my pen from where it fell onto the table, puts it down again. Presses his lips together. Frowns. 'Right. I'll...I better go.'

He walks off.

I gather up everything I've left on the table in a huge armful, thrust it into my satchel and squash it all down. I drop the flap and leave the straps to fend for themselves.

'Right,' I say. My voice sounds weird, even to me. 'Right.'

I look up to find Mai and Gus staring at me.

'What?' But I don't really want them to answer that question, so I plow on. 'Okay. I'll see you in...' I remember that I won't see them again after lunch. 'I'll see you.'

I walk off in the opposite direction to Mycroft. I even use the door.

CHAPTER EIGHTEEN

The rest of the school day goes on, obviously, but I don't really exist in it. I walk around inside a fog.

Mycroft kissed me.

Rosemarina is the most likely culprit for Dave's murder.

Mycroft *kissed* me.

I spend too much time frowning off into the middle distance, occasionally raising a hand to touch my lips. In History class Mr Abboud asks me if I'm feeling all right. At some point I realize that my eyebrows are getting tired from being scrunched together for so long.

Mycroft kissed me.

It's not something that I ever expected to happen. And really, it should never happen again, because it will screw everything up. We have such a comfortable arrangement, where he studies at my place and I treat him like another brother. Then I go over to his place and we hang out, as friends, as mates. And it's so *easy*, the way we are when we're together, listening to music or talking rubbish. There's no stress, and I can ignore the fact that I'm attracted to him and he can do stupid science experiments and smoke and lounge around in his socks and boxers, and it's all so *simple*, uncomplicated. We can be simple and easy and uncomplicated, together.

So it should never happen again.

But I only have to close my eyes for half a second and it all comes rushing back: the way I caught fire, the leaning, and the feel of his body, and his hands, and his lips and his taste, and *I want it to happen again*. God, I want it to happen again. And again and again, and *all the time*.

And if it was like that with Mai and Gus watching (oh my god), if it was like that the first time, what would it be like if it happened in his room, with the door closed behind us and nobody else around? And what would it be like if it was deeper, stronger… What would it be like with his shirt off, the two of us pressed up against the wall near the bed, and what would happen if he made that noise again, that noise that felt like a rumble in my mouth, a whimper—

'You should stop doing that thing with your eyebrows,' Mai says. 'You'll give yourself a headache.'

The tram seat feels stiff and scratchy under me. I come back to earth to realize that I'm one stop away from home. Mai has her legs crossed, sitting opposite mc. I feel too jumbled up inside to care whether I miss my stop. Maybe a brisk walk back a few blocks would even help.

'God. It's bad, isn't it?' Nobody else is watching, thank goodness. I don't have to fight the urge to bring a cold palm up to my cheek and press away the blush.

'Yes, it is.' Mai grins at me. Her wrist tinkles as all the bangles slide down. 'No, it isn't. It's fan-bloody-tastic. Stop looking so stressed.'

'I can't help it. It's stressful.'

'Really? Because it didn't look that stressful to me. It looked kind of sudden, and unrehearsed, and wow, kind of raunchy, all on the first go—'

'*Mai.*'

'What? It was great. I've never seen Mycroft totally lose it like that before. Clearly he needs to get you alone somewhere and work out some of his control issues.'

The idea sends a pulse right through me. 'That is *not* going to happen.'

'For god's sake, why not? Don't you want to try it again?' She looks at my face. 'So you *do* want to try it again, but you're, what—'

'This is my stop,' I say suddenly, because I can't talk about this anymore without getting wonderful, awful flashbacks.

I get off the tram with Mai waving impishly to me from the window and walk home. It takes me a while to work out why my clothes are all damp, before I realize it's raining.

I'm so totally wrapped up in myself when I walk into the kitchen that I barely register that Dad's sitting at the kitchen table. Then I realize *Mum's* sitting at the kitchen table as well, which is just peachy.

Dad takes a last swallow of his tea and says, 'Rachel, we'd like you to tell us where you were last night and what you were doing.'

My satchel slides down my arm and onto the floor with a plop. *Mike.*

There's movement in the corner of my eye. I glance over to

see my brother, just peering around the doorway to the kitchen.

'You bastard.' My voice has gone hard as crystal. 'You total—'

Mike hitches fully into the door space. 'Hey, I'm not the one who—'

'I bloody *trusted* you!'

'Rachel!' Mum looks haggard. 'Don't speak to your brother like that, he's got nothing to do with this!'

'We know about everything.' Dad, who hates confrontation more than anything in the world, is gazing straight at me. 'The school called about your absenteeism, you've been skipping your homework sessions, you're fighting with Mum, your brother. We know...we know you stayed out last night, Rachel.'

'If you know that from Mike, then you know that I *fell asleep* in Mycroft's room,' I say, and I'm almost wishing now that it had been different, that Mycroft and I had been up all night ripping each other's clothes off. 'Did he tell you that? And did he tell you that he—'

'Rachel, don't you *dare*.' Mike looks deadly now. The air in the kitchen is suddenly poisonous. 'If you say one more bloody word—'

'*Shut up, the two of you!*' Dad's voice goes through the kitchen like a shotgun blast. He drops his head, rubs at his face. 'God help me. If I'd known that moving away from the country would have this much of an effect on you, on the whole bloody family, I would have—'

'You would have *what*, Dad?' I'm too angry to think straight, to care what I'm saying. 'You would have stayed on in a run-down property that was owned lock, stock and barrel by the *bank?*'

My stomach drops into a big hole in the ground. I can't believe what I just said. And I want to say that I didn't mean it, that it's not true. But I can't, because it *is* true. Why is it that I open my mouth lately and nothing but *horrible shit* comes out?

Mum's face is livid. 'Rachel, you don't know anything about it!'

My hands spasm out. I'm shaking with rage. 'I know plenty about it – I *saw* the bank statements, Mum, I saw *everything!* If you and Dad hadn't done such a shit job of managing the property, we'd still be back in Five Mile!'

———

It's ugly. God, it's so ugly.

Do I have to go into it? I just want to blank it out, the shouting, Mum yelling so hard she started spitting, Dad going *white*, oh shit... The way Mike tried to duck and cover, me screeching at him – then he started roaring his own stuff, stuff that Mum and Dad would probably have reacted to better under calmer conditions.

All of a sudden the fight wasn't just about me, about the fact that I'd acted like a teenager instead of a responsible person who made dinners and cleaned up messes. It became a fight about the whole *family*, and what we were doing here and how we came to get here.

I don't want to remember all the words that were screamed and spat out. I'm not brave enough. I have courage sometimes, in the strangest situations, when there are dead bodies with their throats cut in abandoned hollows of midnight parks. But I'm gutless most of the time, gutless enough to say things that slash and wound with the same violence as a knife across an old man's throat.

I spent hours afterwards lying on my bed, just crying myself stupid. I felt washed out and hollow, like a dam that's burst its walls. Nothing I could do or say was ever going to take back those words that had exploded out of me. Nothing seemed to matter:

not homework waiting to be done, or dinner, or murder investigations...I wanted to lie on my bed forever, letting life undulate around me.

Mike had gone out, the door rattling on its hinges as he slammed it behind him. I knew Mum had gone to bed. I imagined her lying there, staring up at the ceiling like me. Mum and I can be strangely similar sometimes, hiding away when things get too overwhelming. Except we usually hide outside – escape into the far paddocks, walk and walk, with the kangaroo grass and leaf litter under our boots and the rest of the property extending beyond our sight.

We can't do that anymore. We don't even have a place of escape. The only place I can go now is into my head, closing my eyes to flee into memory, or if that's too painful, into sleep...

I don't sleep for long. I only doze long enough for my body to get stiff and cold, lying on top of the doona with my boots still on. When I hear the crow-tap at the window, I jerk into full consciousness. My mind is spinning with images of blood, eerie black figures with shark teeth, wind whipping through long black hair...

Then I hear the mumbled swearing and I realize it's Mycroft. Mycroft is tapping on my window. A light-headed thrill hauls me up – and then I remember why he's out there and I'm in here. I rub my face, walk over and pull the curtain and unlock the latch. Mycroft is standing outside my window, with the square-edged security bars just wide enough for it to look like he's in jail.

But *I'm* the one in the room. I'm the one in jail.

It's still drizzling; the open window lets in dark moist air. Mycroft's absolutely drenched – limp curls dripping run-off down his face, his black T-shirt painted onto his chest. I get a wave of longing so bad it makes me grit my teeth. That kiss has flipped some stupid switch inside me that I can't flip back.

Mycroft grabs the security bars with shivering marble fingers. I snag a towel off my chair and pass it through the bars.

'Mycroft, for god's sake.' My voice is just above a whisper. 'You'll catch your death out there.'

'I've been wet before.' He drapes the towel over his head, stage-whispering back. 'Thought I was gonna have to throw a rock through the window or something. You doing all right?'

'Yeah.' He gives me a look, and I close my eyes. No more pretending. 'I mean, no. I don't know.'

'I was going to come earlier, but I heard all the shouting.'

'You heard that from your place?'

'Sure. I think maybe they heard it down in Brunswick.'

'Oh god.'

'Watts, relax.' Mycroft rubs his hair with the towel, which does nothing at all considering he's still being rained on. 'It's what teenagers are supposed to do, y'know. Fight with their parents. It's normal, apparently.'

I lean against the bars, with the damp chill in my face, the nausea in my gut. 'It wasn't just me. Mike weighed in too. It was... Well, it's a total mess.'

'So... do you want to come over to mine?'

Mycroft's searching my face, and his expression has gone strangely soft. That's when I know I'm not imagining it. Whatever it is I'm feeling – the tension, the spin inside that lifts me up and makes me feel like I'm going to fly into a thousand pieces, all at the same time – he's feeling it too.

A rush of tiny wings zips through my body, but I stand rooted in place.

'I'm not…' My chin trembles, I'm that close to crying. 'Mycroft, I've been banned from your place. I don't know how long for.'

He smiles, but his lip curls down. It's not a happy smile. 'What are they going to do, keep you in chains?'

'Something…' I glance back at my bedroom door. Has anyone heard us, talking through the window at midnight? 'They're threatening to move us away from here.'

'*What?*'

'Mike's leaving, and Mum said we could find a smaller rental closer to her work…' I clench the bars, rest my forehead against the freezing metal. 'This is such a fucking disaster.'

Mycroft leans in, and I startle. His hands are covering my fists, his fingers cold and his palms hot as a pocket sun.

'I let you sleep at my place.' He swallows. 'It's my fault. I could tell them—'

I shake my head.

'It's *not* your fault and you don't need to tell them anything.' The jail-cell struts between us are suddenly unbearable. I yank on them, rattle them in the frame. 'These bloody security bars!'

Mycroft's grin is wonky. 'I guess this is a bad time to tell you I have a dead Jack Russell in my freezer.'

'You… What? You *found Poodle?*'

'Yeah.' His grin gets brighter.

'Is that where you went this afternoon? After…'

After you kissed me. I want to say it, but I just can't. Mycroft ducks his head, apparently wanting to fudge that part as well.

'It took me a while, but yeah, I found him. I mean, I spent hours looking for him and it turned out to be simple. I just had to imagine what I would do if I was a dog.'

It's the first non-fraught thing either of us has said. My eyebrows skyrocket. 'If you were a dog.'

'Exactly.'

'So where was he?'

'Down near the underpass for the tram. I brushed the leaves off and had a look, and there's not a mark on him.'

I frown. 'What, so there's nothing? No throat-slashing, no knife wounds…'

Mycroft shakes his head. 'No wounds at all. That I can see, anyway. He's just kind of floppy and dry and pretty smelly. Which is consistent with five days, under cover, but nothing like a dog that's been slashed and gone off to die.'

My head aches with the effort of making my over-taxed brain work. 'But he *had* gone off to die. And he must have been scared off by something, or he would have stayed with Dave.'

'He didn't get very far. I'm amazed I didn't find him sooner, but he's small. I rooted around in a lot of garbage bins and under the rail platform and stuff before I spotted him.'

I close my eyes, open them. 'So Poodle wasn't cut.'

'That's right.'

'And I really doubt that he died of a heart attack. So whatever it was that killed Dave also killed Poodle.'

'That would follow.'

'So if Dave and Poodle were killed by the same thing, then it must have been…'

Mycroft is standing, shivering and patient in the rain. He's got the same expectant look on his face he had that night at Mai's. He's waiting for me to come to some conclusion he figured out ages ago.

I stare at him. 'You know already, don't you?'

'Yeah.' He nods. 'Something that would kill a man and his dog quickly and simultaneously, not a physical injury. Something that imitates the symptoms of cardiac arrest.'

He's coaxed the realization out of me with these little clues. It still takes me a moment to get a handle on the idea. It seems so preposterous, because who *does* that? Who kills someone like that?

'Mycroft, that's—' I shiver. 'Poison. That's *poison*.'

'Yeah.' His lips are starting to blue up in the cold. 'But it must be something weird, because I called Professor Walsh about Dave's tox report. They didn't find anything. But it *has* to be poison – Watts, do you remember the scene? The photos? There was a piece of paper, a hamburger wrapper, scrunched up under Dave's leg—'

'And whatever Dave ate, *Poodle shared*,' I say.

I'm clutching his arm now and I'm shaking, partly from cold and partly from fierce joy, because *we've done it*. We've figured it out. The sequence of events when a homeless man and his dog share a meal of something given to them, something fatal, which rips through their blood and stops their hearts. Then a person nearby decides to disguise what they've done by doing something even worse, by cutting a still-warm throat, so the blood gushes out in slow spurts...

A tiny light flicks on inside me then. Not quite Mycroft's MCG floodlight – more like a fairy light, a firefly.

'What?' Mycroft peers at my face. 'You've got that look, like when you—'

I shake my head. 'Listen. We had this dog for roundups, her name was Sally...Anyway, she ate fox bait.'

'She was poisoned.'

'That's right. But Mycroft, she made it back from the far side of the property, and then she was under the back porch for hours before she died. It wasn't quick at all. And Dave's heart attack came on before he could even tip over his trolley.'

'And Poodle only made it a hundred meters away.'

I nod. 'Whatever this poison is, it must be incredibly fast-acting.'

Mycroft gazes into space. 'Fast, lethal, hard to detect. That's... that's a biotoxin. An organic poison...' I can see his mind working, hummingbird-quick behind his eyes. He's gripping both my arms through the bars. 'A *biotoxin*, Watts!'

'What does that mean?'

'It means algae, and snakes, and komodo dragons, and loruses, and fish. It means *the zoo*.'

His savage expression reminds me of the look on his face as he stood over Dave's body, saying *Who dies like this? Who did this?*

'Mycroft, you *knew*.' There's wonder in my voice. 'You *knew* the dog was important, right from the beginning. How did you know?'

'Just did.' He scuffs the wall of my house with the toe of his shoe. 'It was logical, wasn't it?'

I bite my lip. I have to give credit where it's due. 'Mycroft, you know I *never* tell you this, but... you're a genius.'

His face is transfigured. It's like a starburst is radiating from inside him, making his whole body glow and his eyes ignite. I'm so happy to see him like this, I wonder why I've put off saying it for so long.

He presses himself against the security bars and reaches in and touches my face, cups my cheek in his hand. His fingers are glacial and damp, and rusty from clinging to the metal, but the warmth in his palm sizzles my skin.

'I'm an academic genius but a social moron.' His voice is a dove's wing, and a tremor runs up my spine. 'Remember when I said—'

Thunder cracks around us suddenly, makes me jump. A white spear of lightening rakes the sky, and I hear the pop of a streetlamp blowing out. The rain starts hammering down in earnest.

'Oh shit.' I push his hand back. 'Mycroft, you'll get saturated out there. Saturated, then *electrocuted*.'

He slips his arms outside, backing away. I see his T-shirt, where he's been pressing against the bars so hard it's left a mark. 'Watts, this is none of my business, but . . . make up with your folks.'

'Mycroft—' Now I'm the one pressed against the bars.

'Make up. Because you've got folks. Because you can.'

I open my mouth to reply, but another storm crack snuffs my voice out. By the time the echoes pass, Mycroft has melted into darkness.

————

'Are your parents really gonna move?'

Mai is sitting on the library bench seat at recess, with Gus beside her. Gus offers me consolatory chips from his packet. I shake my head. I can't quite stomach chips right now, and I don't know the answer to the question.

I talked with Dad, at least. He was in the kitchen when I came out in my pajamas to have breakfast – unavoidable, as I hadn't had anything to eat since my limp school sandwich yesterday. Mum had already frazzled her way off to work. Dad was just sitting there, looking like the sole survivor of some jungle massacre as he nursed a cup of instant mud at the kitchen table.

I asked Dad the question Mai's asking me now. He sighed and shook his head, the same as I'm doing.

'It would make sense,' he said. 'If your brother is set on leaving, then having a two-bedroom house would be cheaper.'

'But you just got the Hills Hoist out...'

Dad looked at me, and I looked into my coffee mug, as if the solution was in the sediment at the bottom.

I grabbed for whatever clothes I could find in my room – cut-offs, shirt, boots – and got to school before the first bell. People were hoisting bags, scuffing their feet on the slow march to home group and the start of Wednesday. How can it only be Wednesday? The world has shifted on its axis while I wasn't looking.

'So your parents really did their blob,' Gus says.

'Yeah.' I hold an apple in my hand, feeling no desire to eat it. 'Actually, we all did our blob. And then I did a load of blobbing around in my room, until I fell asleep, before Mycroft came by to tell me about the dog.'

'So you haven't done the rest of the practice essay Ms Ferguson wants next lesson?'

I stop, close my eyes. This is going to be a shit day. 'No. I totally forgot about it.'

'Thought so.' He grins. 'Then you better take a look at this.'

He pulls some printed sheets out of the back of his notebook and wiggles them in front of me.

'Is this...' I flick my eyes over the sheets. 'Oh my god, you—'

'We worked on it together, Mai and me, after you emailed her last night to say your parents took your phone.'

Mai grins. 'I figured you've got enough problems with your parents, and the fashion-tradge thing – you don't need dramas with practice essays as well. It's not perfect, and it's probably not

257

your phrasing, but we thought it might be better than nothing.'

'Guys, you...' I look from one to the other. 'You guys are made of awesome, you know that, right?'

Mai shrugs. Gus smiles – if his skin wasn't so dark, I'm sure I'd see him blush.

'Just hope it's useful,' Mai says. 'Now stop talking and read it through. You might have a chance to make corrections before Ferguson collects them.'

I'm amazed. This is what it's like to have meat-space friends, I realize. Maybe this won't be such a shit day after all.

We get through English, and I get the cobbled-together essay into Ms Ferguson's eager hand. After lunch I somehow bumble through the first half of double Biology without getting into too much strife, and by two-forty-five I'm feeling as if the day is actually starting to get under control.

I'm hunched over my notebook, scrawling the required responses into the case-study fields, when I hear a scratching at the window.

The scratching turns into a rattling, as the window is pushed open by a large familiar hand. People are looking over. A black-jeaned leg comes over the window ledge and I feel the rush of adrenalin that usually means Mycroft's about to do something totally insane.

He's half in and half out the window, waving papers in his hand. 'Watts, it's—'

He straddles the ledge, pushes the window higher with one shoulder. I get a buzz from looking at his face, his cheeks pink from excitement. But the feeling is overshadowed by panic, because Mycroft is on school grounds while on suspension and that's all kinds of bad.

My chair scrapes back and I rush towards him. 'Mycroft, you can't be here.'

Miss Paulsen strides over in all her triple-chinned glory. 'Mr Mycroft, what in god's name are you doing?'

He tumbles onto the floor in a gangly black sprawl. 'Watts, Maddison is—'

'Mycroft—'

'Watts.' He sits up and grabs my arm. 'Ronald Maddison is dead.'

I gape. 'What?'

'He died earlier this morning. I've been trying to call you, text you—'

'Mum and Dad took my phone,' I say. 'Oh my god.'

Miss Paulsen speaks in a clipped voice. 'Right. I'm calling the principal.'

She waddles back towards the Biology wing office. Every other student in the room is talking, laughing and watching. I help Mycroft stand and he thrusts the papers at me.

'I just found out, I was too bloody busy researching the poison thing, and then I checked the newsfeeds for information on Rosemarina—'

'How did it happen?' I scan the papers.

'How do you think?'

'Heart attack.' I brake hard. 'Jesus. At the zoo?'

'At home. But it won't matter, will it? I mean, they're not going to look at it as a suspicious death. Who would link the murder of a homeless man near the zoo with the death of the director?'

'And that's why she did it. My god – Mycroft, you were right. The vagrant experiments, the syphilis and the, the—'

'She needed to check the dosage.'

259

'Yes.'

We're standing there, holding each other's arms. The outside world has disappeared, until a hard voice from the front of the room wrenches us back.

'Mr Mycroft. Miss Watts.'

Principal Conroy is framed in the doorway, his mouth a ruled line.

'Come with me,' he says.

CHAPTER NINETEEN

Miss Paulsen looks triumphant as we walk out of her room. The whole way back to Conroy's office, I'm glancing at Mycroft and he's glancing at me. We have to get out of here, get out of school somehow and follow up this lead.

But having Mycroft so close, without those bloody security bars, is wonderful. He touches the small of my back as we're ushered into Conroy's office and my shoulders straighten involuntarily.

Conroy takes up position behind his desk. His face is solemn, a formal warning. We perch on seats on the other side. Our school principal leans on his fingers.

'Mr Mycroft, I'll be brief. I'm beginning the paperwork for your expulsion—'

'*What?*' Mycroft gapes, like he's just been winded.

I round on Conroy, furious. 'You can't do that!'

'I can, and I will.'

'*No.*' Mycroft knocks his chair back as he stands. His eyes have a hard furious glitter under his dark brows and his cheekbones are long paper cuts.

'*Yes.*' Conroy stares him down. 'You've breached the terms of your suspension, and this isn't the first time.'

'That's not *fair.*'

'It's very fair. I've held off for as long as I could. Even after the fire incident I stayed my hand, despite getting advice from other staff that you were a pernicious influence.'

I can guess who the other staff member was. I put my hands flat on Conroy's desk. 'He didn't mean to cause trouble. Nothing was damaged in the fire, it wasn't a serious arson attempt—'

'Miss Watts, I'll thank you to stay out of it. You've already earned yourself an after-school detention for your collusion in this unfortunate business.' Conroy stares back at Mycroft. 'Mr Mycroft, your absence from this school is about to become permanent.'

There's a hole in the air where Mycroft's sarcastic verbal gaffes should be. He's standing rigid, hands clenched into fists.

Conroy sighs. 'Mycroft, I've tried. I really have. I thought if we gave you time, and a certain amount of freedom, you'd start to level out. But your behavior has made it impossible for me to keep being lenient.'

'If I get expelled again, the Social Services will step in.'

Mycroft's words are bitten off, taut. His face is darkening as though it's being slowly layered with ash. I remember that although the bonds between him and Angela are bitter, they're still real – he's always thought being with Angela was preferable to other options. A group home, for instance.

Conroy nods. 'It's possible—'

'It's for certain.'

'Your home situation with your aunt has never been—'

'At least she's *family*.'

'I'm sorry, Mycroft. You have a quick and clever mind. But you've never focused it on anything of worth.' Conroy looks tired. 'Go home. I won't call the police, even though that's standard procedure in this kind of case. Consider it my last charitable act.'

For a minute, I think Mycroft is going to refuse to budge. His lips are pale as milk. His eyes are an intense vacancy, like looking into a black hole.

I reach out to him and whisper his name, try to revive him. He jerks back a step, stands and breathes, staring at Conroy for a long moment. Then he spins around and takes long strides out of the room. The door bangs with his departure.

I close my eyes. When I open them, Conroy is looking at me.

'Now, Miss Watts, let's discuss your detention.'

His words wash over me. I think of Ronald Maddison, gasping his last, like a trout flipped onto a riverbank. I wonder how Rosemarina felt when her father died, when the abuse stopped at last, once it was all over. And I'm struck again by the look on Mycroft's face as he stormed out…

I'm rocked by the idea that maybe it's all over for him too.

————

I'm getting all kinds of new life experiences now I've moved to the city, and after-school detention is one of them.

Basically, it's me and three boys and Zoe Michaels from Year Eleven, all assembled in a classroom near the vice-principal's office.

Conroy gives us a lecture about wasting his time and our own, and I seem to get a few extra significant glances. I glare back, which I think earns me more black marks, but I don't really care.

Miss Paulsen does the rest of the supervision. She looks smug the entire time. We have to write out what we did and why we did it, crap like that. I spend a lot of time doing furious crossings-out and underlinings.

It's the longest hour of my life. I spend most of it fretting about where Mycroft went after he left, what damage he's inflicting on himself. If he torched a building because of a fight with me, what will he do now? I chew my nails, imagining horrible scenes with booze, fire, chemicals, box cutters. I chafe, knowing I could be out there making sure he's okay, helping him chase up new leads at the zoo.

At four-thirty, Miss Paulsen delivers another lecture about how she hopes she never sees any of us back here in the future (which I know for a fact is a vain hope in Zoe Michaels's case). After stretching it out for the full nine minutes and thirty seconds, she finally winds up. We can go.

I yank on my satchel, make my way down the hallway towards the outside steps. I push up my sleeves and open the buttons on my flannie for more air. Even the exhaust pollution at the front of the school is a refreshing change, after being stuck in that class-room with the smell of student sweat and stale farts. I'm bracing myself for Mum and Dad's reaction when I finally get home.

A voice cracks the sound of background traffic. 'I'm going to the zoo.'

Mycroft's leaning against the rail of the school fence, out of sight under the gardenia hedge. I take in the tight jeans, black T-shirt, and familiar red hoodie. His lips are still pasty, but his expression is determined. He's made up his mind.

But after this afternoon, I'm angry enough not to care what my parents will say. I'm going to cop hell anyway. May as well make it worth it.

'You want company?'I swing my satchel strap over my head.

'Why else would I be hanging around here?'

'They catch you lurking and they'll call the cops.'

'I'm not on school grounds, so stuff 'em. They can't expel me twice.'

I nod. 'Then let's go.'

———

We catch the four-fifty-one tram. While the shopping district whizzes past, Mycroft briefs me on new developments.

'Maddison died early this morning, right over breakfast. I'd be willing to bet it was after he drank his morning coffee or something like that.'

'And Rosemarina experimented with the poison by trying it out on Dave.'

'She'd want to make sure it looked natural. She'd need some idea of how much poison to use, especially if it's something unusual.'

'And it has to be unusual because…'

'Because it's so fast. Only a biotoxin would act that quickly. And because the autopsy on Dave would have found signs of known toxic substances. Strychnine, digitalis – common poisons leave distinctive traces.'

'And that's why she cut him. So it wouldn't look like a poisoning straight away.'

'But she didn't realize something important.'

'That everything Dave eats, Poodle shares.' My face pales with the memory. 'Poodle died from the poison. Maybe she tried to chase him down, to make it look like it was all part of the same attack.'

'That's probably why he ran off and hid.'

Mycroft's face shows the dark trace of stubble. He's all hollow angles. This isn't just the after-effect of expulsion.

'You were up all night with this, weren't you?'

He rubs his jaw. 'After I found Poodle I thought I'd better do some research. Research takes time.'

I look out the window and make an ugly noise.

'What?'

'He shouldn't have said that. Conroy.' I'm so angry it's making my vision blur.

'That I was a pernicious influence?'

'That you've never focused your mind on anything of worth.'

'Oh.' There's a long pause while Mycroft gazes outside. 'Thanks.'

I have a strong urge to reach up and touch his cheek, but I keep my hands in my lap.

To distract myself, I ask the next obvious question. 'So we're going to the zoo to find out about the poison?'

'Not just the poison. The news article... Is it still in your bag?'

I reach for my satchel, snatch through papers. 'Here. Show me.'

He smooths the paper flat on his upraised knee and reads aloud, one finger tracing the ink lines.

'*Ronald Maddison, fifty-seven, senior director of the Melbourne Zoo in Parkville, has died this morning,* blah blah... and here we go, *...proprietary organization of the Zoo facility was transferred to operations manager Ian Illingham, who was voted into the director's position unanimously during an Extraordinary Meeting of the Board at noon today.*'

'Ian Illingham? The guy who chucked us out yesterday?'

Mycroft nods, his eyes still on the paper. '...*sweeping changes already announced by Illingham, widely acknowledged as the heir-apparent, in which budgetary spending cuts will play a major part*...et cetera. There's more, but I think you get the drift.'

'*Widely acknowledged as heir-apparent.* So Maddison's death benefited more than one person.'

'And Rosemarina *must* have got her poison from the zoo.' Mycroft makes a vicious smile. 'Did you know that Illingham's PhD is in herpetology?'

'That's...that's reptiles.'

'Yes.'

'So you think Illingham gave Rosemarina the poison? I thought he hated her.'

Mycroft's eyes spark. 'No, no, think about it. Remember what your mate John Harrow said? That Rosemarina's behavior reflected badly on her father professionally, in front of the board. Illingham probably considered her useful.'

'She might have stolen the poison. She had access.'

'Not everywhere, I'll bet. And I think with a substance that toxic someone *had* to have given it to her, explained how to use it. Illingham has access and motive.'

I nod, because it makes sense. 'Suspicion wouldn't fall on him straight away. If the police decide to investigate Maddison's death, all the trails are going to lead back to Rosemarina. She has good reason to hate her father.'

'And a history of mental instability.' Mycroft chews his bottom lip. 'But it seems a safe bet for Illingham. I don't think the police have the foggiest idea about any of this. And the poison is so exotic it may as well be untraceable.'

'Doesn't that make it kind of hard for *us* to trace it?'

'We know what we're looking for. Although we need to find out more about the venomous exhibits. And whether Rosemarina has been on the zoo premises lately.'

I frown. 'Mycroft, we can't just waltz in there and start asking around about stuff like that.'

'Strangely enough, we can. Because we have an ally in the zoo.'

'I don't think your aunt is going to—'

'Not *Angela*. John Harrow.'

'John? But he's just a guy who works in the labs.'

'Yes – in the labs near the Reptile House. And he knows Illingham, works with him. We'll have to be a bit circumspect, but I'm sure there's more information there if we dig a little. He can tell us about Illingham's movements. And about the poisonous displays. There are sixteen types of deadly exhibits, including lizards, loris, fish. Given that we know Illingham's a herpetologist, we can probably exclude...'

It suddenly occurs to me that Mycroft hasn't said anything about his expulsion. I watch his face as he talks. His eyelids are violet, almost translucent. Mycroft likes to make people think that his energy and enthusiasm are boundless, but I know that's not true. He can power himself along by force of will, but there's a limit. I hope he isn't reaching it now.

'Mycroft—'

'...so there are six reptiles on display that have venom proven to be cardiotoxic – the banded krait, the Taiwan cobra, both the black and the green mamba, the Gila monster, and the Coastal Taipan. They're all milked regularly, and the venom is stored and transported. Under the right conditions it retains its potency for—'

'*Mycroft.*' I put a hand on his arm. 'What are you going to do?'

He looks at me properly then. His lips are dry and his eyes unfocused, and he knows I'm not talking about the investigation. His mouth opens and closes silently. I wait. Then the tram rolls to a halt, and his glance jitters away.

'This is our stop.'

We pile off into the whizzing shambles that is the corner of Sydney and Brunswick Roads. I go to check my phone for the time, but of course my phone is gone – Mum took it last night. I should have thought to wear a watch.

'Are you hungry?' Mycroft scrunches his hands into his jeans pockets. 'I'm hungry. We've got a few minutes while they kick out all the zoo tourists. I feel like baklava. And maybe a quick coffee.'

He leads me back up the street to a little Greek social club. Through the windows I can see old men smoking and drinking espresso from tiny cups.

Mycroft waves to a man behind the counter, mimes coffee. The bare skin of my legs cringes against the plastic chairs at our wobbly outside table. The proprietor emerges from the doorway with two steaming shots and a plate of sticky pastry.

'Ai, you never come over my way last few weeks, Mycroft.' The man is thick in the waist, with a white tea-towel tied around himself as an apron. 'You don't like baklava anymore, 's that it?'

'I love it, Constantine, you know that. Thought I'd introduce my friend to the best baklava in town. Con, this is Rachel Watts.'

I smile at Constantine, who beams back, his face sooty with afternoon whiskers.

'Best baklava in Melbourne, on the house.' He claps Mycroft on the shoulder. 'Nice to see you with a lady. It's good for a man to spend time on his own, but 's not good to *be* alone, you get what I'm saying?'

'You're a poet philosopher, Con.'

Con throws back his head and laughs, retreats into the shop.

Mycroft grins and puts one huge hand around a tiny cup. 'He's been trying to hook me up with his niece for ages. Try the coffee, it's awe-inspiring.'

Once again, I'm amazed. And not just by the coffee, which is very good. 'How do you do it?'

'Do what?'

'Know everyone in this whole damned city?'

Mycroft shrugs, talks with his mouth full of baklava.

'Not really. Not at all. But it's like you talking about your paddocks, how you know every bump and curve. There's, like, the lay of the land. Streets are like creeks. The people are like homesteaders, who live along the creek.' He cocks an eyebrow and swallows his pastry. 'I thought you'd get that analogy better than "I walk around on my own a lot".'

I grin, but then let my grin fade. We have to talk. I start slowly, because I don't want to hit any raw nerves too soon.

'So...what *are* you going to do?'

Mycroft shrugs. Back-breeze from the traffic blows curls into his face as he flicks honeyed flakes of pastry off his T-shirt. 'Don't know yet.'

'I didn't think they could do that. Expel you midway through your final year.'

'My last school kicked me out in the middle of Year Ten. I guess they can expel you whenever they want.'

'You could try ringing the Education Department...' It sounds limp, even to me. 'Conroy can say you've been disruptive, but come on. It's not like you've been a threat to the student body.'

'You think I should make a case?'

I twist my hair back into a rough knot. '*Yes*. I think you should fight it. Getting suspended is one thing, but getting kicked out of school...'

'Look, school doesn't matter. It only matters because an expulsion would bring in Social Services, and I'm already on their radar.'

'Because of the hospital?'

'Yeah. But, y'know, I've got a place to stay. I'm not getting beaten up or abused. I'm hoping I don't make it too high up the list of priority cases.'

'Could they remove you? From Angela's?'

'Yes, but...' His second gulp empties the coffee cup. 'That's not going to happen.'

'Would it really be so bad?' He's not looking at me, but I keep going. 'Mycroft, you and Angela don't get on. She seems to be struggling to look after you—'

'I don't need looking after.'

'That's not what I mean. Your family is supposed to care for you, provide for you.'

'She pays for school stuff, my phone. She feeds me, puts up with all my shit... There's a lot she's had to put up with.'

'Mycroft, *we* feed you more than Angela does. And being tolerated... it's not enough.'

'It's better than being a state ward. Watts, I've *been* in a group home. When my parents...' He cuts himself off as though the words choke him, and rephrases. 'When the accident happened, nobody could find Angela's contacts, so without a next of kin they put me in a temporary group place. It's the pits, Watts, I'm telling you. I'm not doing that again.'

'But it's only four months! Four months, and then you turn eighteen—'

'So what are *you* going to do?'

He stabs a glance at me, and I realize that I can hardly give advice when my own family life is such a mess.

'Same as you, really. I don't know.' I look away, press the pad of my finger down on the plate, then suck at honey I don't feel hungry for. 'Wait for Mike to figure out what the hell he's doing, I guess. Wait for Mum and Dad to make up their mind about the whole moving idea.'

'So you're just in limbo.'

'Basically.' I drop my hand so I won't chew my nails. 'Look, it's not the same for me as it is for you. I've only just turned seventeen. It's ages before I'm old enough to move out and make my own way.'

Mycroft looks away from his cup, straight at me. 'Are you going to move back to the country?'

My shoulders slump.

'I...I don't think so. I don't know. I mean, I've been thinking about it all the time for the last four and a half months, and now I just...' I rub at the frown lines between my eyes. 'I love the country, it's a part of me. But it's not practical. That's why we moved to the city, because it just wasn't practical to stay in a place with no house and no work available. And...well, I'm just not sure now. It's confusing. There are other reasons.'

'What other reasons?'

'Oh, uni maybe, and...' I meet his eyes. 'Don't you *know*?' I push a hand through my hair, make a shaky laugh. 'Here's me, thinking you're some great detective, and you don't even—'

What cuts me off is Mycroft's hand pulling on my sleeve. He pulls at me until I'm off-balance, leaning closer to him than is gravitationally possible, so I have to put out a hand to stop myself falling off my chair. My hand comes to rest on his knee, and I'm pretty sure that was his intention all along, but I don't have time or inclination to say anything about it because he's leaning forward to kiss me.

It's a soft, sinking kiss, as though we're tasting the honey on each other's lips. It's not like I imagined, nothing wild and uninhibited. It's delicate, and gentle, and delicious. Once again I'm caught up in the wonder of how velvety his lips are, how full, the sensation of the kiss and the taste of him, and this time I don't fight it.

A wildfire travels from where our lips connect to every place in my whole body. I'm hyper-aware, every nerve-ending alight. I can feel my hand squeezing his knee. He reaches up to touch my hair, and when his fingers skim over my ear, I give a little gasp.

My reaction seems to kick off something inside him – his palm curves around my cheek, pressing me closer, and his lips open. The world outside dissolves. I'm completely absorbed in the way we're melting together, until something filters through and I realize it's the sound of cheering.

Mycroft and I break apart, my face going beetroot-red as I realize that the old men inside the social club are clapping, toasting us with raised coffee cups from behind the window.

Mycroft grins, makes a little shooing wave at them. I like the fact that his friends are applauding him, but I wish his hand was still where it was before, touching me.

'Bloody hell.' Mycroft's cheeks are flushed. He scratches through his hair. 'There's no privacy in the world.'

'Not on Sydney Road, anyway,' I say.

'Right.' The color in his face makes him seem less tired as he smiles. Then he gasps and grabs for his phone. 'Shit, it's five-thirty.

We'd better move it, or we'll miss him.'

We abandon our cups and plate, cross at the lights and head towards the familiar path that takes us back to the start – back to Dave's old stamping ground.

CHAPTER TWENTY

Mycroft's long legs move fast and I have to trot to keep up.

'What are we going to do?' I retie my hair, sling my satchel around to the back. 'Once we find out about Rosemarina and the poison, I mean.'

'We call Pickup, and we tell him what we've discovered.'

'Do you think he'll even believe us?'

'Actually, I've already explained part of it.'

I stop dead. 'You've *spoken* to him? To Pickup?'

Mycroft grabs my hand to get me moving again. 'Well, no. Not really. I didn't think he'd take the call, so I texted his phone.'

'You *texted* him?'

'Yeah. He gave us his number, right? I mean, I thought I'd better tell him. Even if he hates me. I told him about Poodle, and that we found a name through the hospital of someone who might have had contact with Dave, someone connected to Maddison. And I might have mentioned something about seeing Harrow at the zoo with the poison idea.'

'You *might have* mentioned—'

'Yeah. Well, Pickup should know, shouldn't he? Saves him from running around, chasing his own tail on the sport-killing theory.'

'Did he text you back?'

'Yes.'

'What did the message say?'

'Well, actually, it was rude. So I deleted it.'

'Right.'

'But I also spoke to Professor Walsh, so at least someone intelligent has information about the poison thing.'

'Covering the bases.'

'Exactly.'

My heart is beating fast from the pace. 'Mycroft, are we doing something stupid? I mean, Rosemarina is still running around out there—'

'But she won't be at the zoo, will she? She'll be busy trying to make everyone believe she's the grieving daughter. And if Pickup has half a brain he'll connect all the dots, and then she'll be busy talking to the cops.' He grins at the logic of it. 'Listen. We've got a suspect, a motive, and a modus operandi. Now all we need to do is figure out the actual method, and we've got the complete package to give our jolly detective friend when he finally pulls his head out of his arse and gets back in touch. I think it's bloody terrific.'

He's definitely lighter, more energized, than when he was on the tram. He's put the threat of expulsion out of his mind, to focus on something concrete – the case, the investigation. Or maybe it was the kissing that improved his mood. I try not to smile; I don't want to get too full of myself just yet.

I raise my eyebrows at him. 'You're feeling pretty pleased with yourself right now, aren't you?'

'Why yes, actually, I am.'

'And does John Harrow know we're coming to meet him?'

'Yup. I phoned the zoo and got through to him earlier.'

'You've set this all up nicely, then.'

He winks at me. 'That's why they pay me the big bucks.'

But the zoo doors are closed when we get there. We run around to the front entrance. I'm getting nervous, until Mycroft makes a case with the lone park attendant at the gate.

'Better be quick,' the woman says. She's pulling on her staff-issue windbreaker, collecting her handbag. 'Everyone else is gone. If you get shut in, you'll be bedding down with the baboons for the night.'

We thank her, and run.

By the time we make it to the labs near Reptile House, John is already padlocking the doors.

'Oh, hi.' He gives the padlock a rattle. 'I've already shut everything up, I didn't think you were coming.'

'Sorry, sorry...' Mycroft puts his hands on his knees, heaving his breath back. 'Sorry, we were held up. We heard about the death of Rosemarina's father this morning. Can you still talk to us?'

'Sure, but it'll have to be fast. And we'll have to go up to my office.' He nods his chin back the way we've come. 'I'm running an experiment, so I'd better be there, hope you don't mind.'

'That's fine.' I squeeze my waist with one hand. 'Thanks for seeing us, John. Hope it's not a bother.'

'No, no problem. Come on up.'

After the mad bolt to the bottom end of the zoo, we have to double back. We make our way up to a small modular hut. A wooden walkway in front takes pedestrians over a tiny rilling stream; the constructed lagoon there looks amazingly natural. Water reeds escape the walkway to poke towards the sky.

'This is where you work?' I'm glancing around at the land-scaping, which is a wonderful improvement on your average office cubicle.

'Yep. Well, here, over near Reptiles, other places.' John waves a hand, grinning. 'It's a bit nicer than most labs, yes.'

A pair of moorhens gives us a wide berth as we follow John past the plastic strips in front of the open door and into the exhibit area. Glass-fronted enclosures are set into the wall, all glowing faintly. John unlocks a door.

'Here we go.' He stands back for us to enter, although it's a bit of a squash. 'Do you want a cuppa? We've got all the comforts of home here.'

'I didn't know you were with the amphibians,' I say.

'I got my degree studying cane toads, can you believe. Nasty things, cane toads. I prefer frogs, although people say you shouldn't discriminate.'

We enter the warmth of his cramped office, There's a tiny work desk beneath a crowded pinboard, and a little handbasin in one corner – for washing off frog slime, I guess. John fills a kettle in an awkward way from the tap, puts it back in its electric cradle, hits the switch.

Mycroft is staring at the backs of the exhibits. The interiors of the enclosures can be viewed from small glass windows on this side. 'Cane toads are poisonous, aren't they?'

John nods. 'Yes. They sweat out a substance called bufotoxin. Kill your dog or cat stone dead, if it ate one. But the toads taste horrible, apparently – I can't speak from experience, you under-stand – so mostly they only get half-eaten and then the pet feels very sick for a while.' He waves a teaspoon. 'The warts thing is an urban myth, you know. You can't get warts from touching a toad. '

I put down my satchel and peer at the exhibits. Mike used to have an aquarium, but the yabbies he dumped in it all died. Now I'm looking at a very upmarket version, with moss and trickling water and twisted sticks designed to create a whole environment. The tiny frogs inside are gorgeous, acid yellow or electric-blue striped, like sour gumdrops. They sit placidly in the green of their fake jungle home.

'Are any of these poisonous?'

'Certainly. Well, they were when we first acquired them.'

Mycroft comes over and looks where I'm looking. '*Phyllobates terribilis*.'

John grins at him. 'That's right. Golden Poison frogs. Also called Poison Dart frogs. They're from Colombia, and they're utterly lethal.'

'Batrachotoxin, right?'

'Very good. Yes, batrachotoxin is an alkaloid poison, and it's exuded from their skin. These guys have been raised in captivity, so their toxin has been neutralized by a change in diet. But if these were wild frogs, you'd have to watch out.'

I grin. 'So if I ate one, it could kill me?'

John shakes his head.

'No need for that. You could just give it a pat.' He squints into the enclosure. 'If these guys were newly caught, you wouldn't even need to touch them. Touching a leaf they crawled on would kill about ten of you.'

'My god.'

John lifts a coffee mug with a picture of a toad on it. The underlying text says *Slime me*.

'Still fancy that cup of tea?' He smiles. 'I promise I've washed my hands since I last touched the exhibits.'

'Yeah, that would be great,' Mycroft says, even as I'm opening my mouth to decline. I glance at him; he's giving John the smile reserved for people who are about to be picked for information.

'Most people who are into reptiles aren't as interested in the amphibians.' John drops a teabag into his mug, reaches for two more. 'I know I'm biased, but I find them just as fascinating as the snakes.'

Mycroft is checking out the residents in another enclosure.

'They milk all the dangerous snakes here, don't they? I read that on the website.' His voice is so off-hand, it takes me a moment to remember he's interrogating.

'Yes. Sugar?' John pours the water, adds the necessities. 'They milk the snakes every fortnight. The dried venom is quite valuable, especially the venom from some of the rarer species, like the inland taipan. They even ship the cobra and viper venoms overseas.'

'You're not the lucky man, then?'

'Me? God, no. I'm not a snake handler by training. We have a special team for that. Here you go.' He hands us each a mug. 'But you didn't come here to talk about frogs and reptiles, did you?'

Mycroft gives him an embarrassed grin that comes across as extremely genuine. 'Not really, sorry. We're still trying to get more information on Rosemarina Maddison. Her father's death sort of puts a whole new perspective on things.'

'Yeah, that was a terrible shock. So did you find Rosemarina?'

Mycroft speaks before I can. 'We went to the art school, but she wasn't in. That was yesterday, and our paper is due tomorrow, so…'

'Writing to deadline.' John sits in a wooden office chair. 'I've had ten years of tertiary education, so I do understand. But you know I can't tell you anything much about her, only what I've heard. Do you really want to put hearsay into your article?'

I make something up on the spot. 'If we can get something to show we're trying, we can make a case for an extension. That would give us time to actually get an interview with Rosemarina.'

I don't like lying to John, but he's our only contact and we need to know more about Rosemarina.

'That's sensible,' John says. He slurps his tea. 'And you're not going to mention my name, are you?'

'Not at all.' I shake my head. 'If you were to tell us something, we could follow it up. So it'll just be us speculating, and then only including stuff we can confirm. Your name won't appear anywhere.'

It's much the same line I used on Gray Jetta, and I feel a bit bad. But it got results last time.

'Okay.' John puts his mug on a benchtop, removes his glasses to wipe off the condensation. 'So what do you want to know?'

Mycroft folds himself into another chair. 'Well, what is her relationship like with her dad?'

I look around while Mycroft and John talk. Mycroft uses the present tense, I note. John replies in the same way, as though Ronald Maddison is still walking around in his posh house.

'Fairly awful, from what I hear. He's not an easy man to get on with. And I did see them have a blazing row once when she came in to visit him.'

'Did she do that a lot? Just drop in at the zoo?'

'Well, it's her father's second home, isn't it? Or I should say *was*. Goodness. Anyway, yes, she used to come to the zoo. I think she was painting a series on the snakes at one point.' John cranes his head to see what I'm doing, right at the moment I pick up a large glass thermometer. 'Ah, please be careful with that.'

'Oh, sorry.' I put the thermometer down.

'That's fine.' John turns back to Mycroft. 'Sorry, what were you saying?'

'What about Mr Illingham? You said he couldn't stand her—'

John waves a hand.

'Well, it's all a bit irrelevant now, with Maddison dead. Just privately, I thought they'd had a fling, Rosemarina and Illingham, and that was why they didn't get along. God, please don't put that in your paper...'

'Rosemarina and Illingham had an affair?' Mycroft's eyebrows come together.

'I believe so – I can't say for sure, of course. But that was the way they interacted. And of course, whatever made Ron Maddison look bad was good for Illingham, so in a way he was probably happy to have her around.' John shifts in his chair so he can glance between me and Mycroft. 'Shouldn't you be more interested in the influences on her art or something?'

I nod and try to sound as if I know what I'm talking about. 'Well, it's people's lives that affect their art, so whatever Rosemarina lived through would color her work. I mean, maybe that's why she started with the graffiti – it wasn't "high art", so she knew it would piss off her dad.'

I can see Mycroft behind John's shoulder. He's frowning at the rubbish I'm spouting, or frowning at me, I don't know which.

I keep talking so John won't turn back to him. 'Either way, it doesn't sound like she's going to be too devastated about her dad's death.'

John lifts an eyebrow. 'Maybe not. In fact, I would have thought the opposite, that she'd be overjoyed. But who knows, really. People are strange...'

I'm standing beside the aquarium with the gum-drop frogs

again. I flap a hand toward them. 'Frogs are easier, I expect.'

'Quite a bit easier.' John stands up, adjusting his gold frames, almost shy-looking. 'Do you like them?'

'They're pretty,' I say. It's true – they are just about the most gorgeous frogs I've ever seen.

John smiles. 'I think so too. Not everyone agrees with me, but I think they're beautiful.'

'Watts…' Mycroft starts, but I make a tiny shooing gesture to him. John seems more at ease discussing frogs than people. Maybe we can draw him out a bit this way. Mycroft could use my conversation with John as a chance to look around. I point at the fluoro-blue stripes on one frog as a distraction.

'If they're so poisonous in the wild, why are they so attractive? I would have thought the colors would attract predators.'

'The color pattern is aposematic. It's a warning pigmentation for predators – like a sign saying *Danger – don't touch.*' John sighs, as if he's happy about it. 'Doesn't seem to work with me, though. To me, they just look like…bright-colored jewels.'

'Cute.'

'Yes. And they're family frogs, too. They live in social groups, almost like mammals, which is quite fascinating.'

I guess it is fascinating, if you're a frog person. John really seems to adore them. When he talks about them, looks at them, this fire ignites behind his eyes.

But something is niggling at me. Something he's just said about the frogs triggers an echo in my memory, and I can't get what it is.

Mycroft's voice cuts through my concentration.

'*Watts.*' He's over near John's desk, shifting from foot to foot. 'We should probably let Mr Harrow finish his experiment and go home. It's late.'

'Oh, right.' That's annoying; I haven't worked out the memory yet. If I had just a few more seconds...I turn to John to wind up the conversation. 'So you said the specimens in the exhibit are non-toxic now?'

John nods. 'Mm, yes. The poison is from a food-based source occurring in the frog's natural environment. We feed them different things here, so they lose their toxicity. It takes a while, but it makes handling them a lot easier, of course.'

'How long does it take?'

'About seven years.'

'*Seriously?*'

'Completely seriously. Until two years ago, we had to handle all the specimens with special gear on. And the tanks too. Anything they touch, really. Batrachotoxin is terrifically dangerous. A fatal dose is equal to about two grains of salt. I've heard of researchers being nearly killed after coming into accidental contact with the moss in the bottom of an enclosure. Here, have a look at this.'

He waves me over three steps, to the other side of the office. Mycroft is glaring at me. I ignore him. There's something here that's important. Maybe if I let John talk it out, the memory echo will come clear.

There's a glass-fronted exhibit case mounted on the wall. Inside it are a bunch of fine wooden spikes. Some of them are broad and flat, some as thin as needles, with bases wrapped in grass-like fiber. They're all suspended on pins, carefully mounted like butterflies in one of those weird sadistic-looking bug collections.

I can feel John behind me as I peer closer. 'What are they?'

'They're darts, bamboo darts, from Colombia. I went over there last year on a research grant, looking at the frogs in their natural habitat. Fascinating stuff. These are what I brought back.

The Choco Embera people use them for hunting. They impregnate the darts with poison by rubbing them against the frogs, and use them in blowpipes. Highly effective.'

'Wow.'

'Yes. These are still potent.' John chuckles to himself. 'I had a hell of a time convincing Customs that it would really *not* be in their best interests to examine these without protective gloves.'

I stare at the blowpipe darts as John's voice mumbles on behind me.

'The Choco Embera have been hunting in the same way for generations. Amazing, really, to think how people live so differently...'

I tune him out a bit. The bamboo is smooth and evenly finished. I'm reminded suddenly of the pathetic blow darts that Mike used to make from old lathing nails, trying to zap the dogs, or the back of my legs, usually spitting all over himself and pissing Mum right off.

I'm thinking of that, I'm thinking of my family, when I realize something.

'Well, it looks like you're still working on acquiring a full collection,' I say, pointing at two empty pins.

It actually takes me a few more seconds to register what this might mean.

Mycroft's voice comes from somewhere behind me. 'Watts. I think he already knows.'

CHAPTER TWENTY-ONE

I swivel my head around.

Mycroft is standing about a meter away. His face is very open, attentive, hands hanging lightly at his sides. He's looking at John.

When I turn farther, I see John too. But what I see first is the shining point of the scalpel John has positioned at my neck.

My eyes bulge at him.

I lurch back, but John's too fast, grabbing my wrist in a rubber vice-grip. He's wearing latex gloves, I notice, and I get a sick feeling in my stomach.

'Please don't try to run, Rachel.' John's voice is completely calm, even as he tightens his grip on my wrist. 'That would be very inconvenient, for everyone concerned.'

'*No.*' I'm gasping. It feels like every breath I take in this city is a gasp. 'Not you.'

'Yes. Me.' He smiles. 'Surprised? It's nice to be surprising. Goodness, your face now is such a picture…'

John's genial smile is pleasant, unassuming. But the smile is like the college-professor glasses and the casual trousers – all a camouflage. In his eyes I see the feral glint, see the *real* John Harrow.

The homicidal one.

I get a sudden uncontrollable shiver. 'You knew. You knew who I was—'

'I saw you,' John says. My blood chills at his tonelessness. 'I saw what happened that night. Two teenagers finding the body, and then the police, all of it. I was watching, you know. I always watch an experiment, to see what happens, see if something goes wrong...'

And I remember Mai saying *What if the murderer was still there?* Suddenly I'm having trouble staying upright, my legs are shaking so badly.

'You recognized us,' Mycroft says.

It gives me a jolt to see his expression, see he hadn't counted on that.

'Yes.' John's voice is eerily quiet. 'And naturally, I kept an eye on the site.'

The room reels as I get my head around what this means. 'Then that day, outside the zoo—'

'Well, when I saw you, Rachel, going all weak in the knees right nearby...' He chuckles. 'That was wonderful luck – I do like to have any loose ends tied up. You really fell in my lap, so to speak.'

All I can manage is a whisper. 'I thought... you were a nice person.'

'I am a nice person.' John's latex-covered thumb strokes my wrist. 'I was nice to you, wasn't I?'

My reaction is completely instinctive – I sob, pull hard at my arm. For a second I've forgotten the knife exists. But it does exist, and when Harrow jerks me back he presses the flat of the blade against my neck.

He smiles. 'Rachel, please. Show some common sense. I could open your artery with no trouble at all. You know I could do it.'

I swallow, because I *do* know. Someone who could poison an old man and slit his throat wouldn't find killing me a problem. Once he's sure he's got my attention, John turns his calm expression on Mycroft.

'When did you work it out?'

Mycroft's face is like cut glass. He's matching John's quiet tone. 'A few minutes ago, when you said that Rosemarina and Illingham had a fling. I remembered something I'd heard, something Rosemarina said. Look, you can have whatever you want, you don't have to hurt her.'

I get that shiver again. I don't know what my face looks like to Mycroft. Probably panicked, fear freezing my expression, while my eyes call out. I put everything I can into my eyes.

John ignores the appeal. 'So you *did* meet our lovely Rose?'

'Yes,' Mycroft says. 'At the school, just like you told us.'

'And did she try out her feminine wiles on you?' John seems to find the idea amusing. 'She loves that first-meeting kiss, doesn't she—'

'Yes,' Mycroft interrupts, his voice flat and unembarrassed. 'That was when she said she only kissed people she had no respect for.'

He's taller than John, and although his eyes are very big and his face is pale, he stares Harrow down. 'Rosemarina doesn't date men. Which is hardly surprising, after what her father put her through. She would never have a romantic relationship with Illingham. So I knew you'd lied.'

'Touché.' John's sneer is dark with malice. He squeezes my wrist and I gasp.

'Don't hurt her,' Mycroft blurts. One fisted hand releases as he reaches out.

'I'll do what I want,' John says. 'Pray continue.'

Mycroft looks from me to John. His jaw works as he swallows. 'A friend of mine said Rosemarina had a visit from a boyfriend when she was in Royal Park hospital. So I knew she'd had contact with *somebody*, a man. I thought it was Illingham, that he was the zoo link... And then just a second ago I saw this near your desk.'

Taking a careful step back, holding Harrow's gaze the whole time, Mycroft reaches out a hand and snags something from the pinboard above the over-papered desk. He holds it up. It's small, half a postcard, but it's unmistakeable – apocalyptic colors behind a black silhouette, a figure with long legs and whipping tendrils of hair.

I think of Mycroft's urgent glares, the way he called my name before... My god, I am such an *idiot*.

John makes a grin which isn't. 'Should have chucked that out, I suppose. I was going to.' He shrugs. 'She's a sweet girl, really. Kind. Talented. And smart. She could see the advantage of us working together.'

I still can't adjust to the change in his face. When did I become so fucking *gullible*?

He suddenly lifts his arm over my head, as though spinning a dance partner, until he's tucked in behind me. His face is snug beside my ear, my arm banded across my chest, so he can hold my wrist in comfort. The scalpel lies flush against my neck, rising and falling with my breath.

Having him this close to me, skin to skin, as though we're embracing, makes me sweat. My eyes flit away desperately.

Mycroft's mouth opens. But there's nothing he can do.

John is whispering into my hair. 'It was easy. I had something *she* wanted, and she had something *I* wanted. It was a useful arrangement. Much like this arrangement here. With my scalpel like *this*, I can make you and your friend do whatever I say, isn't that right?'

I can feel him smiling, the bastard. He uses the tip of the scalpel to scrape back the hair at my throat. I strain away from the contact, swallow hard.

'Is that why you visited Rosemarina in the hospital?' My voice comes out more cracked than I'd like, but at least it's coming out. 'To remind her not to blab about your *arrangement*?'

John laughs.

'Well, as I said, she's a sweet girl, but she's as mad as a cut snake. So I had to make sure of my investment.' He presses his cheek against mine. 'Did you know that with Maddison dead, and Illingham as director, the operations manager position is suddenly open?'

'*That's* what this is about? Your *promotion*?' My voice drips acid. 'Who says Illingham will give you the position anyway?'

John pastes the scalpel to my throat.

'*I* say. I've got the dirt on Illingham, on all his dodgy little business dealings, thanks to Rose. He can dance around on *my* puppet strings now, which will be a nice change.' His hand on my wrist relaxes a fraction. 'And come on, let's face it. No one's really going to mourn Maddison's death, are they? Certainly not his daughter. The world's a better place without him in it.'

Something fork-tongued rattles to life inside me as I listen to John. I might be gullible, I might be naive, but I'm also righteously *pissed off*, and this might be the only chance I get. There's no point in just standing here, waiting to get sliced up.

I release a breath, relax my arm. Then I *yank* as hard as I can, twist out, *away...*

It doesn't work. John's stronger than he looks – he heaves me back, pulls me even closer. His left hand squeezes my wrist so hard my fingers turn to ice.

I can't help it, I yelp at the feeling of my bones being crushed together. Then there's a sharp sting on my cheek, and a trickle of warm wet slides down my face. It feels almost like tears.

'*NO!*' Mycroft's voice breaks into pieces.

'*Stop.*' I feel John's breath, his voice shaking slightly from the effort. 'Stop *doing* that.'

'*The world is a better place*, is that what you tell yourself?' I'm babbling, because, oh god, I'm *stuck* here; I'm stuck to John Harrow like glue. 'A better place for *what*? For people like you? Oh *fuck*, I thought you were nice, and you—'

John says, '*Sshhh...*' straight into my ear. I wail, twist my head to the side. I can't stand it, this closeness—

And it comes to me, the echo in my memory. What John said before about the brilliant aposematic colors of the frogs, combined with an image from my brain: Rosemarina, the glossy black curls and the red dress.

Suddenly I know why he did this. Why the murder, why everything. John doesn't really care about the promotion, that's just a side benefit. The only thing he cares about, the thing he's fixated on, is...

'You wanted her.' The words breathe out of me. '*Aposematic*. Rosemarina is about as aposematic as they come, and you wanted her, you couldn't stand it—'

John sucks in a breath, and his voice goes off like a bomb. *'What do you know, you little BITCH?'*

He tugs me in, brings the scalpel up so the point is hovering in front of my right eye.

'Stop!' Mycroft has his hand out, edging closer, his face white as paper. *'Please.* It's okay...It's okay. She didn't mean it, did you, Watts?'

He gives me a hard desperate glance. His face is so freaked I go even more wooden in Harrow's grip. I don't say anything.

Mycroft keeps talking to cover the pause. 'Batrachotoxin. I discounted it initially, when I learned the frogs in the exhibit had lost their toxicity. But it was perfect, wasn't it? Batrachotoxin affects the heart like digitalis. Arrhythmia, fibrillation, cardiac arrest. Almost impossible to detect. And it's off-the-charts lethal, so fast, very fast. I'm sure she would have wanted something fast-acting, wouldn't she?'

John seems to calm a little, although his grip doesn't change by so much as a millimeter. 'Yes. I said she was kind, didn't I? Rose *is* kind. Kinder to her father than he ever was to her. She told me she couldn't bear it anymore. He was going to have her declared incompetent, she would have been at the house all the time, at his mercy...'

'I understand,' Mycroft says. 'I really do.'

'A man like that deserves to die,' John whispers.

Mycroft nods carefully. 'And now Ronald Maddison has got what he deserved. She probably put the dart in his coffee or something, right? Something only her dad would touch.' He swallows hard on the next part. 'But first you needed to know if the darts would still work, didn't you?'

John fixes his gaze on Mycroft.

'He was a nobody.' His voice is soft thunder in the office. 'I'd see him on my way to work, near the train station. Just sitting there, under that bloody tree. He was old. I didn't want to hurt anybody young, who had a life. Anybody who mattered.'

The air outside the tiny office window is glowing in the pink lick of sunset. The world is going dark. Harrow's voice is right beside my ear, so I hear it too well. *Anybody who mattered.*

I close my eyes as the feeling boils up out of me. There's a tremble in my legs, in my shoulders. It could be a reaction to having a scalpel blade against my face, but that's only part of it.

'*He wasn't a nobody.*' My words are too loud, too shaky. 'He was a *person*. His name was Dave Washburn, and he had a *life*—'

'*Watts,*' Mycroft whispers. I can see how scared he is. He starts talking, stuttering, his desire for calm warring with the fear. 'W-when we showed up, looking for Rosemarina, you knew straight away that we were checking it out.'

'Yes,' John says. When he snorts, I feel it on my neck. 'You make a fine pair of detectives, I must say.'

I clear my throat. 'Then ... why did you send us to Hundertwasser?'

Harrow smiles. He's recovered his rational exterior. 'Consider it an experiment. I did wonder whether Rose would give anything away. I mean, if she talked to you, goodness knows what she'll say to the police. I might have to have a quiet chat with her later ...'

'She didn't say anything,' Mycroft says quickly. 'Not about you. Not about the test case.'

The test case. My stomach hollows out as I realize he means Dave. And he's speaking a language Harrow understands, because Harrow laughs in response.

'Well, good for her. The test was my own idea, of course. Rose didn't approve. But I think it worked out well. I was worried, naturally, but I knew I'd done a good job. I'd been thorough.'

'The hamburger wrapper,' I grind out.

'Nothing you could get off it,' John says. 'I used gloves. I rubbed the dart right through the meat. And the cutting was so close to the time of death—'

'You did a good job,' Mycroft says. 'The police were completely fooled.'

'Thank you.'

I feel John grinning next to my face and have an immediate urge to be sick. No, I can't be sick, not now.

'But you forgot about Poodle,' I whisper.

John sighs. 'That bloody dog. That was a pest. He snapped at me, you know.'

'Good for him.' I think about Poodle, baring his teeth at a piece of cardboard.

'You don't have to do this.' Mycroft's soft voice resonates, not quite pleading, in the quiet office. He is trying to mollify the crazy person in the room, instead of aggravating him, which I seem intent on doing.

'It would be nice if that were true.' John sighs again, as if he really wishes it were so.

'But it *is* true.' Mycroft tries for a jaunty expression and fails. 'It's just like you said. You were thorough. And the police are honestly barking up the wrong tree – they're following up the first death as a sport killing.'

He says 'death', not 'murder' – a desperately diplomatic choice of words I would have slipped up on.

'It doesn't matter.' John stares at him. 'You two know.'

'But we're just *kids*.' Mycroft's voice is horribly unsteady as he attempts a laugh. 'Nobody's going to believe a couple of—'

John cuts him off. 'You found the body. You traced Rosemarina.

And now you've come here. Do you honestly expect me to trust that you won't run straight to the police?'

Mycroft's eyes dart from me to Harrow. I realize he's trying to figure out whether to tip our hand. Should we tell Harrow that the police know where we are, that they could already be on their way? Or would this inflame him further?

If we say we're just solo-investigating, satisfying our own curiosity…Well, surely that would mean he'd feel that we were expendable?

But suddenly I know it doesn't matter. My mind scuttles back to that conversation – so long ago! – in Mai's room. *Live or die – Every breath is a choice.* Harrow has already made his choice. We're just stringing it out by conversing with him. He made his decision before we arrived at the zoo this afternoon; actually, he made it a lot further back than that.

My cheek is hurting and I suddenly feel very tired. 'So what now? Are you going to jab us with another poison dart or something?'

John licks his lips. 'Goodness me, no. That would be a waste. And what would I do with two dead teenagers in my office? No, let me…' He blinks rapidly, then he gives a short, barking laugh. 'Right. Oh yes. I think I've got a much better idea.'

He releases my wrist. My breath catches as the blood returns to my fingers. Before I can take advantage, John grabs me by the back of the neck.

'First of all, your phones,' he says. 'Put them on the desk.'

'I don't have one,' I say dully. 'My parents confiscated it.'

John presses the scalpel in as he frisks me, and I yelp.

'Excellent. Mr Mycroft?'

With so much reluctance it's as if Harrow's asking him to cut off his arm, Mycroft peels his phone out of his jeans pocket. He places it carefully on the benchtop to his right.

John nods and smiles. 'Wonderful. Now, this is the part you'll like. We're all going for a little walk. Mr Mycroft, you'll walk in front. Rachel and I will be close behind you. I'm going to hold the scalpel right here, near her armpit, so if either of you tries anything, poor Rachel will bleed out like a proper stuck pig. Let's go.'

The world outside the door is cool, with a light breeze, whereas the office was soupy and airless. The zoo is quiet in the dusk, with only the faint sound of animals. There's nobody nearby. No security, no evening tours, no park attendants – nobody at all.

Mycroft walks in the lead. He keeps looking over his shoulder at me and Harrow. I'm willing him to *do* something, *anything*. I could distract Harrow, and Mycroft could help pull me away. Something like that. This could be our only chance, and he's wasting it. He's worried I'll get cut. He's calculated the statistical probability of me getting cut, and decided it's not worth it.

I don't *care* about getting cut; I don't care about statistics. I want to get *out* of this. It might be a risk, but whatever Harrow has in mind is sure to be worse.

But I never get my chance. Too quickly, we're at the base of the ramp that travels over and above the lion enclosure. John pushes me to the right of the ramp, into the shrubbery, and keeps pushing all the way up to the fence. When we stop in front of the box-squared wire I just gape, because is he *kidding*?

'*Lions*. You're going to put us in with the *lions*.'

'That fence is fifteen feet high.' Mycroft's face is disbelieving.

John smiles, short and tight. 'I'm sure you'll manage it. Especially if your girlfriend here will get her throat cut unless you comply.'

'I'm never going to get over that fence,' Mycroft says.

For some reason, I can't stop thinking that Harrow called me Mycroft's girlfriend, and Mycroft didn't deny it. The stupid things you think when you're about to *die*.

I look John Harrow square in the eyes. 'Nobody will ever believe we've done this on purpose.'

'Of course they will. You're teenagers.' John grins. 'Teenagers do crazy risk-taking things. Stupid things.'

'Not *this* stupid.'

Mycroft turns suddenly. 'The police know we're here. They'll know we wouldn't do something like this.'

But I'm thinking of the word *TWAT*, written in fire across the side of a building. Will they really know?

John's mouth becomes mocking. 'All the more reason to get this over with quickly, then. I must say, it'll be interesting to see how the new zoo director handles the shocking deaths of two idiot kids who thought they could break into the lion pen.'

'Your mate, Rosemarina, is probably in police custody even as we speak.' Mycroft's voice is controlled.

'You don't know that.' But John looks unnerved. He presses the scalpel blade against my throat and I suck in a breath. He turns flinty eyes on Mycroft. 'Now shut up and climb.'

Mycroft chews on his bottom lip. He turns and puts his hands on the fence.

I have a shocking premonition then, a memory of my boots washed in blood. 'Mycroft, *don't*.'

Mycroft looks at me over his shoulder. He looks at Harrow.

'He doesn't have a choice,' John says. 'Do you?'

I watch as Mycroft climbs the fence. It's worse, knowing how much he hates heights, when he gets to the top. I can see his white face as he eases himself over the inward-curving wire.

He shuts his eyes for a moment, then swings forward over the wire to shove his fingers into it, monkey-bars fashion. His fingers clench and he scrabbles with his toes, but it's no use – his height and weight and fear all combine to drag him down. He ends up half-sliding down the other side of the fence. He lands heavily on the grass, with a thump and a painful gasp of breath.

'*Mycroft!*' I pull against the shackle of Harrow's fingers at my nape. My voice is frantic, when I want so badly not to let Harrow know how scared I am.

Mycroft doesn't answer me. He's kneeling, his head hanging between his straightened arms, palms flat against the ground. The way he's doing that makes me frightened and when he lifts his head, I can see why. He must have hit something when he tumbled. He's opened up the old gash on his eyebrow; a blood flower is blooming all around it.

I make a noise, a choked-off moan. Mycroft wipes blood out of his eye, and when he glances at me I know just how he feels. Vulnerable. Powerless.

John's voice breaks the moment. 'Now you, Rachel. You can help your little friend fight off the lions, or you can watch him bleed, here against the fence.'

I glare at him so hard it's a wonder there are no holes smoking in his face. 'You know, I used to think that Mycroft was a bit mental, but he's not a patch on *you.*'

Harrow gives me a shark grin. 'Here, I'll make it easier for you,' he says, raising the scalpel.

Mycroft gives a strangled cry. His long fingers push through the wire, reaching out, and his face is desperate, so I miss what happens when Harrow actually cuts me.

The scalpel is so sharp that at first there's just this sensation of…airiness, as if someone opened the door and let in a draft. Then the stinging starts. When I look down, there's a wide red gash, like the world's worst paper cut, from above my elbow to halfway down my forearm.

I hiss and clap my hand onto it, but touching it makes it hurt more. The nick on my cheek is a flea bite in comparison. Blood trickles between my fingers, flows down in a series of thin red lines. I can feel it dripping off the little bone on the outside of my wrist.

I look up at Harrow with genuine loathing. 'That fucking *hurts!*'

He gives me a cheery smile. The smile fades, and he pushes me at the fence. 'Now up and over you go.'

I hate him, really *hate* him then. This scheming lying, murdering, betraying *arsehole*, with his pathetic glasses and his frog obsession. Maybe he was a nice person, once. Now I see the insane glister of his eyes, and I can't find anything in them that's worth saving.

'Chop chop.' Harrow shoves me in the back. 'Maybe you'll get lucky. Maybe the cats will decide you're on the side of the angels.'

Mycroft and I are pressed together, with the wire between us. Blood is beaded in Mycroft's eyelashes. He's lacing his fingers into mine and shaking his head.

He glances back over his shoulder, back to me. 'Watts—'

Harrow cuts him off. 'Do you need a leg up?'

I turn my head and give Harrow my iciest expression. 'I don't want anything from you.'

I start climbing the fence.

The wire cuts into my fingers and I'm having trouble getting the toes of my boots into the holes. I breathe hard against the pain in my arm.

I get a sudden wash of vertigo on the very top edge – I understand why Mycroft closed his eyes; it's as though I'm sailing over the tops of the trees nearby – and then I'm sliding over the rolled wire, grabbing, finding only harsh edges that rip at my fingers. I try to steady my descent but it doesn't work. I feel Mycroft grab for my legs, and then I'm tumbling on top of him, so we both end up heaped together on the grass.

I shake my head to clear it. When I glance up through the wire, Harrow is smiling hugely.

'Well, I'd better go tidy up in my office – your bag, his phone, and so on. And then I can come back to observe.' He gives a friendly little wave. 'But if the cats get to you before I return…well, bye-bye, Rachel. It's a shame the way it worked out, but it was nice to have met you. It's reassuring to know that naiveté still exists in the world.'

I scramble up to the fence and put all my brother's lessons to work when I spit at Harrow through the wire. But I miss – he's already walking away. I'm trembling with anger. I thrust my fingers through the holes and scream at him.

'*You fucking fuck! You murdering—*'

Which is as much as I get out before Mycroft's body presses against me and his hand clamps across my mouth. I fight it for a second, until I hear his whisper near my ear.

'I don't think we should make too much noise.'

It's the shake in his voice that rams some sense into me. My anger jerks away, leaving me wobbly-legged, and I shut up like a tap that's been turned off. I turn around in Mycroft's arms, press my back against the fence and look.

It's getting darker by the second. In the oyster-pink light I see an expanse of grassy enclosure, about half the size of the school sports oval. There are trees, giant logs, and great boulders that are sunning spots. I can smell this horrible reek, like cat's wee magnified by the power of ten. *I am in a pen full of lions.*

'No yelling. Right.' My voice is quavering. I feel grimy, and I can smell my own sweat, the stink of my fear above the smell of lion. 'Where are they?'

'I don't know. I can't see them yet.'

I swallow. 'This is bad.'

'Yes, this is very bad.' Mycroft rubs an unsteady hand over his face. There's a red smear down the side of his cheek now. 'You know, lions sleep twenty hours a day, so maybe we'll get lucky. Maybe they'll all be too tired—'

He's interrupted by a sound from the far corner, shrouded by shrubbery and small landscaped hills. I don't want to see what's over there, but I can hear it now. A gentle rumble of thunder, which from a house-cat's throat would sound like a purr. From a lion's throat it sounds like the doors of hell grinding open.

That's when I really start to shake.

CHAPTER TWENTY-TWO

I'm shaking and shaking, and I can't stop.

'Mycroft—'

'We've got to bandage your arm,' he whispers. 'The smell of blood—'

Bandage it with what? I want to say. *And what about your head?* Nothing comes out of my mouth. I can't stop looking over to where the noise came from, and god, I can't stop *shaking*.

Mycroft grabs my arm, and I have to close my eyes for a second.

'Oh shit, this is really…' His fingers jitter against my skin. 'I can't stop the bleeding. Fuck. Hold still.'

I'm trying, but my whole body is shuddering. I hear the gnash of a zipper.

Mycroft's wrapping something tightly around my arm, so tight it stings. His voice is all corrugations. 'It's not true, what Harrow said. You're not naive.'

'I'm an idiot.' I press my head against the wire. 'A stupid, gullible—'

'No. You're open. But that's not a flaw, it's…' He fumbles as the noise sounds again. 'We would never have gotten to know each other, if you weren't open like that. D'you see what I'm saying?'

His blue eyes burn into me. I realize that he's used his T-shirt – he's pulling his hoodie back on over his bare chest. I think, hysterically, *Well, at least I get to see Mycroft semi-naked before I die*, which makes me feel even worse.

I check the shrubbery for signs of movement. Then a thought occurs to me, something so obvious it's a wonder it didn't pop up before.

'We've got to climb back out.'

Mycroft shakes his head. 'The way the fence curves inward, we can't get over without—'

The rumbling comes again. It's joined by another sound, identical to the first. There's more than one lion making that sound.

Mycroft freezes. Then he pushes me around to the fence. 'We're climbing back out. Now. Hurry.'

The fence wire bites into my fingers. Mycroft has his hands on my bum, helping me up, and I don't say a thing about it. When I get to the curved bit, I realize I'll have to reach out almost half the length of my body to get any purchase. I don't want to say *This isn't going to work*, but it's clear that it isn't, even as I'm stretching out my arm.

But I've got to try. I reach, slip off, reach again, my breath heaving out of me. I've caught it. I squeeze the wire with my fingers, it's digging into my skin. I'm using my right hand, which was dumb, because that's the one with the cut – my grip is weaker and my hand is already slippery with blood. Then I'm hanging by my fingers, I get my left hand over and—

I just *can't*. I can't do it. My fingers slide, convulse. Then I'm holding air. I fall back onto Mycroft a second time, only this is harder, because I'm not able to hold back any of the weight.

My ribs hurt from the fall. When I feel grass under my cheek again, I think I really might start crying. But I can't do that, we haven't got time for that.

I roll up to sitting. 'Mycroft—'

He's wincing, one hand pressed against his cut. The blood is flowing more freely now, dripping out from between his fingers.

'Oh, shit.' I crawl closer, wipe at the blood with a corner of my makeshift arm-bandage. It's so soaked with red that all I manage to do is make more of a mess.

'Forget it,' he says hoarsely. 'Come on, I'll lift you. We have to try again—'

But when he heaves himself up, he staggers. I have to hold him. He leans against the fence, looking as if he's going to throw up.

'You can't lift me,' I say. 'You can barely stand.'

I cast around the area nearby. We're not lions – we can use our intelligence and our opposable thumbs and move stuff. We could stand on something. But all the logs are enormous, and the boulders are boulders, and the only useful things I can see are halfway across the pen.

Another rumble sounds. It turns into a full-blown lion *roar*. It's like listening to a plane taking off. I am in a pen with *roaring lions*.

'Come on.' I tug on Mycroft's jacket. 'I'll lift you. I'm strong, really strong, Mike and Dad always say I'm stronger than they are—'

'Rachel, I'm sorry.' Mycroft's voice is tattered. He's sagging against the fence. 'God, I'm so sorry. I screwed up. I didn't mean to, I didn't realize—'

Part of me registers that his eyes are blinking, his pupils badly dilated. He cups my face in his big hands – the nick on my cheek stings under his thumb.

But the foremost thing I'm aware of is that he said 'Rachel'. He *said my name*, and that makes me more terrified than anything, since I first realized that Harrow had a scalpel at my throat.

'*Don't you dare.*' My voice comes out a shivering wail. 'Don't you *dare* say that to me, not now, not—'

And it's while I'm cussing him out that I see the small CCTV camera suspended above us, pointed straight in to view the pen. It seems crazy that I didn't think of it before: they would monitor the behavior of the largest carnivores in the zoo, wouldn't they? Of course they would. Especially given that people have tried to break into the enclosure before.

Liquid fire gushes through my veins, probably a combination of exhaustion and stress and pure terror. I grab Mycroft by the front of his jacket, push him hard against the fence.

'Stay here and be ready!' I'm panting, as if I've run a marathon. 'Be ready for what?'

I don't reply, just push at his chest one more time – maybe for luck, maybe to feel one last human contact – and then I do something utterly certifiable.

I run, stagger really, farther into the pen. Everything inside me wants to run in the opposite direction, but I aim for somewhere close to the middle. I have to skirt a huge boulder and I slip on the grass. I push off my hands in the dirt, scramble a few steps closer to the center. Closer to a bunch of lions than any sane person should be.

I don't look towards the lions. I don't look back at Mycroft either – I don't want to see his face. I just move farther into the camera's range. Then I raise my arms, bare and bandaged, and I start waving.

I flap my arms like crazy; I do star jumps; I leap up and down. I don't yell or scream, because my mouth has gone too dry to spit, and because I don't think the camera does audio. But I try to make myself look as un-lionlike as possible.

'*Watts!*'

Mycroft's garbled cry makes me turn. His eyes flick away, to somewhere over my shoulder, and I *know*.

For one horrible second, I freeze. Then my head turns slowly, as if I'm fighting my own movement.

I see motion, color. A flicker of brown and gold behind a hillock to my right. The flicker becomes a furry edge, which becomes a mass, which becomes a ruff. There's a moment when I think the lion hasn't seen me, isn't going to emerge. Then I understand it was just shifting position to get up onto the hillock, and I see bunched muscles beneath dun-colored fur and *I am looking at a lion*.

It's all so familiar and so incredible – the mane, the golden eyes, the strong stiff tail, the liquid musculature beneath the skin. And this is not a lion on a documentary, and this is not Aslan, or Simba, or any of that crap. This is a *wild animal*, and it is standing six meters away, and there is no fence, no protective barrier, no TV screen to shield me. This is *real*, and I realize that Mycroft and I are going to die.

And then I turn and run.

Every primal instinct in my mind is screaming not to turn my back on a predator, but the flight reaction takes over. As I bolt down the small hill towards Mycroft, I shriek at him.

'Come on! Leg up!'

He stands paralyzed for a moment against the fence, then he hunkers down, puts his hands forward with the fingers interlaced, making a cup for my foot.

I burn down the slope and I don't stop. When I reach Mycroft, I step one foot into his cupped hands, using my momentum to push myself up in a leap. Mycroft heaves as I straighten my leg – I make a wild cry and fling myself up and out. I grab the inward-curling edge of the fence with both sets of fingers in the wire. It's as though we've been practicing for the gymnastics team or something, the timing is so perfect.

The wire cuts into my fingers, but there's so much adrenalin in my body I'm anaesthetized to it. I drag myself up, taking grasping handfuls of wire and pulling with both arms while my legs scramble in space. Just at the fulcrum of balance, when it's either fall or get over, I make a groaning, gasping *AARRGGHH!* and then I'm here. I'm at the top.

My arms, and my fingers, and my lungs, and my ribs, they all hurt like hell. I squiggle around on my stomach on the rolled top-edge of the wire until I'm turned about.

Now my shoulders are hanging into the pen and my legs are hanging out. The balance is so precarious that if I don't grab on to the wire for dear life I'll fall back in again, but with a wriggle I steady myself. Then I take a handful of wire with my slippery right hand and extend my left down as far as it can go.

'Take my hand!' I yell. 'Climb up and grab me, come on!'

Mycroft's face is pale as the moon in this dark light. Then movement from the lion distracts me. It's pacing slowly back and forth on its hill, making smaller and tighter turns, working itself up to something.

'Mycroft, *come on!*'

This next bit all happens so fast I can hardly take it in. I'm dangling over the top of the fence, with my right hand holding on and my left hand reaching for Mycroft. My right arm feels as if it's about to separate from my body. I'm yelling at him, and the lion is pacing closer, with short twisting steps.

Mycroft grabs the wire and starts scrambling, although his runners are so big the toes won't go into the wire-holes. He's clinging, and gasping, and then there's shouting from behind me, on the safe side of the fence.

My mind shrieks, *Oh no, Harrow's come back, he's come back with the scalpel,* and then the voice registers.

'Hold on! Don't bloody move! *Get him out!*'

At least that's what I think Detective Pickup says, but it's all a big confused mess of yelling, because there are other voices too. I scrape my chin painfully when I turn my head to see, and there's Pickup, galloping through the shrubbery, his suit jacket flapping, and then I'm screaming, *'Get us the fuck out of here!'*

Something bangs against the fence, from the safe side. It shakes through my body, so I have to grip harder with my right hand, and I moan. Then I feel a paper-light touch on the tips of my left fingers.

Mycroft is halfway up, his arm stretched to its limit. He brushes my fingers again, and his face is fraught with fear and last-ditch despair. He's so close, so close, so even though my body feels it's being ripped in two, I strain farther to reach him.

Someone grabs my leg, and my foot hits something solid, and it must be a ladder or a cherry picker. There's a big, heavy body beside me against the fence, and it's Pickup, and we are both reaching for Mycroft.

And there's a lot of shouting, and Mycroft is gasping, and I feel his hand, grip for it. My palm is slick with sweat, but there are more hands now and he's being held by his right hand as he holds the fence wire with his left, and his feet dangle and kick the air. My breath is coming in great damaged heaves. We've just managed to get enough purchase to start hauling him up when there's a flash of brown and gold fur below, and something yanks on him from the opposite direction.

I scream, because I'm being pulled forward, and I'm losing balance, and *I'm losing him.* Mycroft makes this choking terrified pain-filled noise, and I never want to hear another noise like that, not ever. And his eyes roll back, and Pickup yells, '*Shoot it! Shoot it!*' right in my ear. There's a massive report, like an explosion, and then I've got Mycroft's whole arm, and the sudden change in direction overbalances me. Mycroft sort of slithers over the edge of the fence as we all half-stumble, half-fall, and it turns out to be a ladder and not a cherry picker. But we land mostly on Pickup and a cushioning of shrubs, so that's okay.

I black out for a second, or maybe zone out in a weird shock-reaction way. When I come back, I'm not in a pen full of lions anymore – I'm lying on the ground between the shrubs and the footpath, and Mycroft is lying next to me, and there are a lot of people moving around.

I look at Mycroft's leg and it's red from below the knee, mostly red but some bone-white as well, and his shoe is gone. I scramble up onto one elbow, and start patting him with my right hand, on the chest, on the face, just gentle pats. My fingers leave soft red smears everywhere, like ink-spots.

His lips are white, like fish meat. I think he's asleep, but then he opens his eyes.

'Fucking *lions.*'

His voice is barely above a whisper. I'm crying, for some reason, but I swallow and nod at him anyway.

His eyes drift closed, then open again. 'I think I'd like a holiday now. I think I'd like that expulsion now,' he says.

I nod and cry and groan, all at the same time. He looks so tired. I wonder if I look tired like that.

There's a bulk looming over us suddenly, and Mycroft opens his eyes again. We stare up at Pickup, who has his suit jacket open in front and his shirt spotted with blood, and one arm holding his other arm. He seems to be frowning with the effort of not letting it hurt.

'Tell me,' he says to Mycroft. His voice is low and rough and very gentle.

'Harrow,' Mycroft breathes. 'It was Harrow.'

Pickup nods, and Mycroft nods, and I don't have the energy to nod. Then Mycroft moves his hand to touch my fingers.

'Rachel.' His whisper is as soft as cottonwool, and he's doing that thing again, the name thing, and I'm starting to freak out about how white he is.

'Here. I'm here.'

'Rachel, I think I dropped my cigarettes in the lion pen. If it's not too much trouble, could you go and get them for me?'

His grin is faint, so I guess that's why my reaction is hysterical. But when I realize that my laugh doesn't really sound like a laugh, and my eyes are streaming and my throat is gummed up, I stop. That's when Mycroft's eyes start rolling again, and I can't help it, I grab for him and my hand leaves great red splotches now, and my voice has a weird panicky quality.

'Mycroft.' And when he doesn't come back, I shake him. '*James*. James, *please*—'

I hear myself on repeat, saying *'James! James!'* and I wonder why I sound so high-pitched, screaming really, and then there are people, and a sharp pain in my arm.

And if you think that being given an intramuscular sedative is anything like the movies, where you feel a jab and then your vision pinpoints down to nothing as you float away, think again.

It's like being hit on the back of the head with a shovel.

CHAPTER TWENTY-THREE

Well, we didn't die. I should clear that up right away.

I thought I was dead there for a while, I passed out so suddenly. And when I woke up I was somewhere extremely white and dimly lit and quiet. I thought maybe I was in some sort of after-life, until I saw my dad beside me. His head was lowered – I could see his coarse dark hair, so different to mine.

I said 'Dad', and his face shot up. His eyes and nose were all red-rimmed, as if he had a cold. But he was there, and he was real. He squeezed my hand on the stiff white bedsheet, which hurt, although I only found out later that was because I had twenty-one stitches in my arm.

'*Rachel.*' He blinked, and his chin was wobbling. 'Rachel, oh Jesus, god, sweetheart—'

Then Mike and Mum were standing behind him. Mike had his arm around Mum's shoulders.

The room was foggy; I couldn't keep my eyes focused. Everything swam in and out as if I was underwater. I thought of something Mycroft had said once about goldfish time, and then I *remembered*.

'Where is he?' I started to throw off the sheets and get up, like that was really going to happen. '*Where is he*? Oh god, he—'

Dad pushed me back gently and started talking, saying things like, 'He's fine, love, he's fine, they operated a few hours ago, and he's okay—' and suddenly I felt so much better, even though trying to sit up had made me feel sick. I felt so much better I think I passed out again.

The next time I woke up, it was morning. I could hear voices – a gruff gravelly voice, and two other voices I knew better than my own. But I didn't hear what they were saying, because Mike was beside the bed.

He looked really awful, gray and stubbled, like he needed a coffee more than anything else in the entire world. But he smiled, and sighed out hugely, and brushed some hair out of my face that I hadn't even known was bothering me.

'Jesus, Rache, you really take the cake,' he said, and then he kept talking. 'I broke my track record, Rache, and I'm *sorry*, I'm so sorry. But they asked me, they were worried about you, and *I* was worried about you, because you're *my sister*, Rache, you're my little...' and then his face crumpled, and I thought, *oh my god, he's going to cry*.

I lifted my hand and touched his arm. That was when I discovered I had a long, tight bandage from my elbow to my wrist, and tape on quite a few of my fingers. It was hard to maneuver my hand in the right direction. Then Mike said, 'Come here, you goose,' and he kissed my cheek and held my hand, grinning.

When I smiled back, I felt the band-aid over the nick on my cheek. I tried to lift my other hand, and discovered I had a new bandage over the old splinter wound, and an IV line attached to my wrist – in fact, I discovered all sorts of inconvenient things at that moment. And then Detective Pickup's grizzled face and blazing hair and bulbous nose appeared on my other side, along with the rest of him, and my parents, who were holding arms, clinging together tightly.

Pickup had a dazzling white sling over a fresh shirt, and his jacket was humped over his shoulders. He was looking at me with an expression that was half-annoyed and half-perplexed and half-proud, although that was three halves, which didn't make sense.

'Thought you'd like to know that we caught up with John Harrow. He led us a bit of a dance through the zoo back areas, but we got him in the end. I've given your belongings to your parents – they were in Harrow's office. We also tried to arrest Rosemarina Maddison, but she's disappeared.' Pickup cleared his throat. 'So even though it was very foolish, what you did, you're both being officially credited with solving the two murders, of David Washburn and Ronald Maddison. As well as—'

'You hurt your arm,' I said, but my throat was so dry it came out like a wheeze, and I couldn't talk anymore until Mike gave me some water from a paper cup.

'Dislocated shoulder,' Pickup said roughly. Everything the man did was rough, as though instead of filing all his sharp edges down, he sharpened them. Is that what homicide detectives have to do to keep their souls?

'Sorry,' I said. 'I landed on you.'

'It'll come good.' Pickup's eyes softened for a moment. 'Your lad will come good, too.'

I felt my eyes pricking, and I had to blink really hard. 'God, is he—'

'He's okay, Rache.' Mike smoothed my hair. 'He had a rough trot, but he's gonna be okay. Might have a bit of a limp for a while, the doctor says, but basically he's all right.'

I sank into my pillows for a second, then I opened my eyes again. 'I want to see him.'

'Rache—'

'Let her go and see him.' It was Dad who spoke. 'We can get her there.'

But of course when I tried to get up I was so dizzy I spewed, which was charming, so I negotiated going in the afternoon. While I was drifting in and out between sleeping and waking, Mike fed me little pieces of information until I had the whole story.

Apparently, even though Pickup had sent Mycroft a rude text message in reply to all the information, he was still enough of a thorough bastard to actually check out what Mycroft had said. Which is how he managed to get Rosemarina Maddison's name connected to the hospital and the fact that her father had just mysteriously died. Professor Walsh had confirmed that it was extremely unlikely both Dave and his dog could have died simultaneously of heart attack, and even more unlikely that Ronald Maddison would make the trifecta of zoo-related heart attack deaths.

So Pickup went to Hundertwasser to bring in Rosemarina. But all he discovered there was an art display: a carefully angled collection of canvases propped on easels, a hideous Hall of Mirrors detailing who Rosemarina Maddison was and what her father had done to her. The sole and final exhibition of the Patronymic series, an explanation in embers.

Nestled in the collection, front and center, was a painting of a shark-toothed girl holding a dagger that dripped poison-green – Rosemarina's revenge, and her release.

That was when Pickup realized we might be in trouble. Speeding up Royal Parade to the zoo, he texted Mycroft and got no response, so he *knew* we were in trouble. By the time he and the rest of the unit got there, I was climbing out of the lion pen, and it was actually *Angela* who'd seen us, or rather seen me, on the CCTV screens when she was cleaning the admin rooms, so really we had her to thank for the ladder and everything.

Mike reassured me that the lion had only been grazed when Pickup's officer shot at it and scared it away, but by the time Mike got to that part, the almost-death-by-lion part, I didn't want to hear any more and I *had* to see Mycroft. There was nothing my stupid recovering body, or any other body, could do to dissuade me. So Dad got me a wheelchair, and Mum helped me slowly lever myself out of bed. Dad took me two doors down; somehow, Mycroft and I had ended up neighbors even in hospital.

The biggest shock wasn't the metal bed, with the sheets tented up over his leg. The biggest shock was that Angela was there. She was sitting in the corner, with her bag in her lap and her fingers to her lips, as if she wished she was smoking. She was as thin as a praying mantis, her hair falling out of her ponytail in lank strands. Her chair was at such a distance that if Mycroft looked from the bed, he'd be unlikely to see her.

She didn't startle when we arrived, just glanced at us and stood up.

I cut in front of Dad's awkward pause. 'You don't have to go.'

'It's all right,' she said. Her arms hugged her body so tight I was worried she'd implode.

'Thank you.' I blinked at her. 'You saw us on the camera. If it hadn't been for you—'

'It was an accident. I just saw it by accident. You were waving your arms, and jumping—' She hiked up her bag, 'Anyway, it's over.'

'Will you be here when he wakes up?'

Angela didn't say anything. Her eyes pierced me, and my mind jumped from her face to her sister's, in the photos. To Mycroft's. I couldn't help but glance at him. The pause seemed to stretch on forever, and then I realized that it would never end, so I spoke.

'He looks very like his mum.' As soon as the words came out I knew they were the wrong ones.

'I have to go,' Angela said.

I was too tired to do anything but nod, and she didn't wait for my nod anyway, just left. Dad leaned down to look at me.

'You all right?'

'Yeah.'

'Normal for her, is it?'

'I don't know.'

Then he pushed me over to the bed, and I could see Mycroft close up. I could see his long body, stretched under the sheet; I could see his face. His hair on the pillow was a shocking dark jungle and everything about him was gaunt. His eyelids were a deep purple, his cheekbones just blades. His hands lay motionless, one on the sheet, one on his chest – long wax-sculpted fingers, some of them wrapped with tape where the fence wire had cut through his skin.

I'd wanted to come, to make sure he was okay, just to reassure myself he was still there. Suddenly I regretted the decision. I'd never seen him so still. Even times I'd seen him asleep, even when he passed out, after the lion cage, he never looked as still as this. It just seemed so wrong. He could have been dead. I had to close my eyes and open them, to control the dizziness that came over me.

They'd cleaned up the cut on his eyebrow, taped it with butterfly closures. His swollen lips were chapped, dry. There was a scrape of paper-tape adhesive on his jaw. I realized it was from the tape they'd used to keep him intubated, while they were operating. Somehow it was this one detail that set me off.

I started crying. I reached out to Mycroft's hand, pulled back, put my hand on the sheet beside his fingers, squeezed the sheet instead. I couldn't keep my head up, I was crying so hard. The tears were bowing me over, bowing me low. Dad came around in front of me and knelt on the ground, so I could put my face on his shoulder and let my body heave. I made this noise, it was so... god. I just didn't know I could sound like that.

I kept gasping, 'Oh god, I'll wake him up.' And Dad was patting my back, stroking my hair, saying, 'He's out of it, love, he's sleeping off the anesthetic. He won't wake up, it's fine,' and that would set me off again for some reason.

Somewhere in all that mess Dad held my shoulders, wiped my face with a tissue from Mycroft's nightstand.

'Rachel... we could go back,' he said. While I was sitting there with my mouth open and my vision watery, he rattled on. 'If that's what you really want, if it'll make you feel better...' and I knew he wasn't talking about returning to my room.

I could only gape at him, tears trickling out of me.

He squeezed my shoulders. 'We could make do, if we had to. We don't have to stay—'

I tucked my face into his shoulder and held on tight. Because there could be no retreat after this. Whatever I said would make it real, would make it forever.

And I said, 'We should stay. I want to stay. Daddy, I'm sorry.'

Then I did some more crying, until I was exhausted, exhausted of tears and just so *tired*; I had never been so tired. Dad got off his knees and sat in a chair by Mycroft's bed, and we sat there, listening to the beeping machines.

I got up the courage to take Mycroft's hand on the sheet. His fingers were cold, and I squeezed them and just held on.

CHAPTER TWENTY-FOUR

Six days later I'm perched on the railing of the wire fence outside Mycroft's house, waiting for him to come home.

Mai came over in the morning, wearing a T-shirt with a picture of the Cowardly Lion, and a worried frown. 'Too soon?'

I had to laugh. 'Tell me what you said on the phone is true.'

'It's absolutely definitive.' She dumped her backpack on my bedroom floor. 'Conroy's already conceded extenuating circumstances. He's reduced Mycroft's expulsion to another five-day suspension, but Mycroft has already spent his suspension time in hospital. So, effectively, he's off sick. He can come back to school whenever he wants.'

'You are incredibly, incredibly brilliant,' I said. 'Have I said you're incredibly brilliant?'

'Yes, but you can say it again if you like.'

Instead of saying it again, I gave her a big hug.

She stayed for a while and helped me pick out something to wear. We talked for a long time about stupid stuff – music, books, the Furies, whether girls dress up for guys or for themselves – because we'd already talked out all the other stuff days before. Apparently there's still an open spot on the Furies if I want it. Mai pointed out that all the gear is supplied by the club. She said that anyone who can climb out of a lion pen, with actual lions in it, is a shoo-in for roller derby.

Gus and Mai had come with me to see Mycroft in the hospital. I think they were both a bit embarrassed to be in the room when Mycroft and I saw each other again for the first time after his surgery, but they were pretty good about it.

Mai sat me down and brushed my hair and did my eyes with kohl. Not too much, because, as she pointed out, we didn't want a radical departure from my *au naturel* look. She had to do the eyeliner – my arm doesn't quite bend properly at the elbow, because of the bandage. But I'm getting the stitches out on Monday. The nurse said I'll have a faint silver line when everything has finally healed up, so fine I'll hardly notice.

So Mai stayed until after lunch, and then I dithered around helping Mike type up some job applications. Graham Jetta said he would give Mike a recommendation for some janitorial work at the hospital. I even thought about taking Mike in to see Alicia Azzopardi. He deserves more than just being a janitor, but he said he has to have something regular.

'I mean, there's no point is there, just pissing along with short-term stuff if I want to stay.' He flicked one of the applications on the kitchen table.

My fingers paused on the keyboard. 'You want to stay, though. Right?'

'Of *course* I want to stay. What, you think I wanna go back and hang out under the gum trees, nothing but Jack Daniels and Coke, and Jimmy Barnes on the radio, to keep me company on a Friday night?' He frowned at me. 'So what about you? You gonna stay?'

'Sure,' I said.

Mike saw my shrug. '*Sure*, what's that mean? What are you gonna do?'

'I don't know. Study, I guess. Apply for some courses for next year.'

'Like what, the ag stuff?'

'Maybe.'

He sat back in his chair with this amused expression. 'Look, Rache, I hate to be the one to break it to you, but people with your marks don't apply for ag courses.'

I squinted at him. 'What do they apply for?'

'Medicine.'

'Medicine.' The idea made me stop typing. 'Do you think?'

'I *know*. I'm your brother.' He frowned at the papers spread over the kitchen table. At the laptop I was typing his CV on. At me. 'What I *don't* get is why girls wear all that shit on their face. Rache, he knows what you look like. Wash it off.'

I'd been feeling so weird in the eye makeup and the carefully selected clothes that I went into the bathroom and scrubbed everything off. Then I went to my room and changed back into my boots, and the jeans and white T-shirt that I'd had on at breakfast, and felt much more comfortable.

Now finally it's five-thirty, and I'm not expecting Mycroft until six, but the taxi coming up the street is definitely slowing, not passing, and it's not Dad. I get off the fence, and then, my god, he's here.

I help him with his backpack as he struggles out of the cab. He looks more solid, stronger in the shoulders, as if he's put on a little

322

weight eating regular meals in hospital. He has an enormous hard plastic brace is on his left leg. It's bright red, in case his foot goes missing and he has to search for it or something. His crutches are almost as tall as I am.

Mycroft smiles down the street, taking in Mum at the fence of our place, Mike next to her, giving a wave. Mum's arms are crossed, but she isn't frowning.

'You've got the full cheer squad there.' Mycroft staggers a bit on the edge of the footpath and I have to help him get his crutches into place.

'Mm,' I say. 'I'm under heavy supervision. But I can help you get into the house. Come on.'

We have to take our time, struggling all the way to his room. At the door, he balances on his crutches to reach for the doorhandle at the same time that *I* reach for the doorhandle. We fuddle in space for a second, but it doesn't last and I get the door open so he can clunk his way inside. We stand in the middle of the Stranger's Room for a minute as he looks around at all his junk.

His eyes come back to mine. 'Rachel—'

I interrupt him, even though I hate doing it. 'Look, I can't stay.'

His face falls. I hurry onto the next part.

'I mean, I'm still not allowed to stay here. In your room. With just you and me.' I keep going in a jolly way. 'But, hey, I thought of a solution to that, so if you'll just bear with me for a second…'

I rush over to the window and hitch the curtains back as far as they'll go, letting so much sunlight into the room it feels like another country. I undo the latch and heave the window up to its limit, then I rush back and grab Mycroft's office chair. I push him into it gently. He sits down with a careful thump and a wince.

'What are you—'

'One second!' I say cheerily.

I put his crutches on the bed and say, 'Lift your foot.' Eventually he gets it, that I'm driving him over to the window. I swivel him into position and he laughs, low in his throat.

He laughs more when I squeeze in front of him and climb out the window.

'Rachel, what are you doing?'

I clamber onto the park bench that I got Mike to help me move into place right underneath Mycroft's window, out on the buckled porch at the front of his house. I give Mum and Mike a wave; Mike gives me the thumbs-up, and he and Mum finally stop rubber-necking and go inside.

Then I poke the top half of me into Mycroft's room. I leave the bottom half of me outside, so my parents can ensure I'm not breaking the – let's face it – seriously dumb rule.

'So you're officially *not* in my room,' Mycroft says. His eyebrows lift to high heaven.

'That's right.' I'm kneeling on the bench seat with my head and shoulders inside and my arse sticking out. With my hands planted on the window ledge I am slightly taller than he is in the chair, which has got to be a first. 'What do you think?'

'What do I think?' Mycroft bites his bottom lip and snorts. 'Well, I think—'

That's all he gets out. Because the lip-biting thing is too much for me, so I put one hand on the arm of his chair and one hand where it's always, *always* wanted to go – laced through his hair, his amazingly dark and curly hair. His thick soft locks twine through my fingers and I pull his face towards mine.

This kiss is different, because it's the first kiss where we don't have anything to hold back, or anything to hide. Maybe it's different because it's the first kiss when we don't have an audience. And my god, it's like a jump-start from the mains.

Mycroft doesn't have time to gasp. His fingers float up to my cheek, my ear, feather along my neck. I was already smoldering before we began; now I just burst into flames. His lips are something I want to sink into and there's nothing holding me back this time. I indulge myself completely, until I have to pull back for half a second so we can both inhale.

'I think it's worth remembering that I just came out of hospital—' Mycroft breathes. But he's staring at my lips and I reel him in again.

We started fast and urgent – now we kiss slowly. I remember the first time, the science experiment, the whole world reduced to sensation, and it's like that again. My body is melting into gold. I can feel every place we connect, every place we dissolve into each other. I wonder if kissing Mycroft is always going to be like this, and if it is, *sign me up*. Why oh why weren't we doing this sooner?

Mycroft's hands lift to my shoulderblades, kneading and squeezing. If we weren't in such a weird position our bodies would be clasped together. I let my fingers caress his head and I have wanted to do that *forever*.

His fingers wander, curl around the nape of my neck. He unravels the knot of my hair. My hair sweeps down like a theater curtain and he makes *the noise*, the low noise in his throat, a satisfied, turned-on kind of noise. Which is when I realize that even though my body feels white-hot, we haven't even *started*.

I'm putting as much weight as I can on the arm of Mycroft's chair. He's angled sideways, so his foot doesn't hit the wall. But the angles make it better somehow – our lips fit together perfectly.

He tastes like sheet lightning – I want to touch more of him.

I lean my hips on the window ledge, lift my hand off the chair and slide it across to his chest and squeeze, as if I'm testing for firmness, and yes, it's very firm indeed. I clasp his shoulder, caress the side of his neck. I'm warring over whether I can move my lips from his mouth to his neck, which is so smooth and soft it's criminal, but I *can't decide*, everything on offer is so goddamned good.

Mycroft is making deep husky sounds which make my toes curl up, and his hands are stroking down my sides. My back is a bow over the window ledge, my chest straining forward. Then somehow Mycroft's fingers are sliding under my T-shirt, where the hem is sagging open from my leaning. His big hands cup my hips and his thumbs brush small arcs on the skin of my stomach, either side of my belly button. I make a mewling kind of noise, and I think...I think...maybe I can't think anymore.

And then he's pushing me back gently. Our mouths disconnect with a small suck and he's panting, as if he's about to pass out. He says, 'God, *Rachel*—' and slides one hand into my hair and pulls me to him again. 'This is going to drive me crazy,' he whispers as we lean on each other and breathe and shake for a minute, while I recover the power of speech.

'Apparently,' I say at last, my voice coming out trembly and soft, 'apparently I'll be allowed back into your room when I've proven myself trustworthy.'

When Mycroft laughs, I can feel it against my hand. 'I don't even know what to say to that.'

I rub my face into the place where his neck meets his shoulder. 'The stupid thing is, there's more we could get up to now than when I was over here all the time. And in eight months I'll be eighteen, and I'll cross some invisible arbitrary line that only my parents can see, and I'll be able to do whatever I want. Go crazy.'

'Eight months is a long time,' Mycroft says.

He sounds frustrated. Also tantalized, somehow, as if there's such a wealth of possibilities in eight months with a window ledge between us it's making him curious and excited to see how creative we can be.

I nudge him. 'I'll be off house arrest sooner than that. And you can always come over to my house.'

'I've got a better idea,' he says.

He pushes me back and suddenly he's standing up from the chair, poking his head and shoulders out the window, and I figure it out fast. I'm laughing as I help him maneuver his whole long self through the window. We bump his foot once but it's not bad, and then he's sitting out on the porch of his house, on the bench seat with me.

His foot, with the enormous red brace-thing, sticks out in front as he relaxes against the back rest. He really is too big for this stupid bench seat. We sit and hold hands, watching Summoner Street settle into late afternoon.

I clasp his hand tightly. 'Did you notice anything about the yard when we came in?'

'Not really.' He smiles, his eyes diving straight into me. 'I wasn't looking at anything except you.'

He's not looking at anything except me now, either. I grin and bump his shoulder. 'So much for being a master of observation. Check out the yard.'

His eyebrows lift as he finally notices. 'I can see the garden path.'

He's being a bit generous, calling the cracked strip of concrete from the gate to the porch a garden path, but I'm not going to argue. 'Dad mowed your lawn. He got that bloody Hills Hoist

327

out at our place, so I think he's decided to move his attention elsewhere.'

'Wow.' He looks nonplussed. 'Will you thank him for me?'

'Thank him yourself. He'll be over soon. He said he's going do some weeding in your backyard before dinner.'

'This just gets weirder and weirder. Who's making dinner?'

'Mike. He's not working, so he's got more time than me now. But I felt a bit sorry for him, so I said we could take it in turns.' I snort and roll my eyes. 'God knows how the meal will turn out. But I think it's a ruse, he just pretends he's an incompetent cook. He can do a barbeque all right.'

'So you'll be having barbequed sausages every alternating night for the next however-long.'

'Exactly.'

'Great.' Mycroft seems entertained by the idea, and maybe interested in the prospect of eating some of the sausages. 'Was your dad serious about giving me a lift to the funeral tomorrow?'

'Yeah, of course. We can fit five in the taxi. You'll just have to squash up next to me.'

Mycroft grins. 'You can sit in my lap.'

'God, I'm never going to live that down, am I?'

'Not if I have any say in the matter.' His hand pulls at mine and he leans to nuzzle my ear, under my hair.

I get a bright, sizzling flash inside – I can't get over how incredible it is to be doing this, just touching him, being touched in return. It makes me feel like doing it over and over, to make sure I'm not imagining things.

I put my other hand against his chest. 'We'll have to be on our best behavior tomorrow. No touchy-feely in the cab, or you'll be getting a ride back with Detective Pickup.'

328

Mycroft pulls away reluctantly. 'Is he going to be there?'

I nod and glance out into the street. Someone has put Hilltop Hoods on the stereo, away down the block.

'The department's looking after the funeral costs. And yeah, I think he wants to see it through.' I only have to blink and Dave appears to me in my mind's eye, having a laugh over a cuppa. 'Gray Jetta will be there as well. I think Dave would like it.'

Mycroft's face is soft in the dusky rose of afternoon. 'I think he'd like it too. So has Pickup said any more about the hunt for Rosemarina?'

'No. Just that it's ongoing. It's not like he gives me regular updates or anything.'

'I don't think they'll ever catch up with her.' Mycroft's eyes are musing on the street as he squeezes his sore leg. 'She and Anna could be anywhere by now.'

'I'm glad.' My voice is firm. 'If anyone deserved to get away, it's her.'

I imagine Rosemarina in her boots and her red dress, drinking Caribbean roast in some Parisian cafe, painting by the Seine. Cuddling up to Anna in a big white bed in some Tuscan villa. The picture might be way off, but it still makes me smile.

Mycroft's tug on my hand brings my attention back home. 'What about the court case?'

I look down. 'Don't know. Don't care.'

'They'll call us as witnesses, you know.'

I pull Mycroft's hand over, so I can smooth his thumbnail. All the tape, on his fingers and mine, is gone now. 'I've been talking to Pickup about giving video evidence. So I don't have to go into the courtroom.'

'You sure?'

'Yeah. I think I am.' I look up at his face. 'You want to go in, though, don't you?'

'Yes.' Mycroft's expression turns fierce as he stares out into the street, at something else. Not a Tuscan villa. 'I want to see Harrow squirm.'

He looks back at me, the fierceness melting, and surprises me by swapping the hand-holding for putting his arm around my shoulders. I hug back for a second before I remember something important.

'Oh, wait, I've got to show you something.' I wriggle out of his arm and pull a folded-up paper from my jeans pocket.

'What something? What's that?'

'No, let me read it.' I grin. I've been looking forward to seeing his reaction. 'Are you ready?'

'Ready for what, exactly?'

'Shush. Okay.' I scan down the lines until I find the ones I want. 'Okay, listen: *Dear Diogenes, further to the matter of lividity explored in your article earlier this month, I seek to consult with you on a matter recently brought to the attention of the Stockholm Police—*'

'You're shitting me,' Mycroft says. He tries to snatch the paper but I yank it out of his reach.

'Let me finish! – *to the attention of the Stockholm Police, please return email if you find the matter of interest, signed Detective Inspector Olaf Albeson*. And wait, there's more – blah blah, *referring to my enquiries regarding your research on micro-abrasions, please contact me through the email address at this link* – that one's from Perth – and this one says, *would you be interested in taking the matter further, your most recent information on vagrant homicides or sport killings is of great interest in a case currently being pursued by the department, please contact—*'

'That's...that's not possible.' Mycroft's eyebrows are so scrunched up his eyes almost disappear.

I shrug and hand him the paper. 'It's all up at the website. You can check it yourself if you don't believe me.'

'How is that possible?'

He's staring at the limp piece of paper, utterly amazed, I honestly don't know why. His expression is such a mixture of *everything*, with his eyes darting all over the place, that I take pity on him and stop laughing.

'Your fame is spreading. You know what Pickup would say.'

Mycroft rubs his face with one hand.

'Yeah – stay home, listen to pop music, do homework, like a normal teenager. But Jesus Christ, this is...' He waves the paper in the air, then turns to me. 'It's not *my* fame, by the way. If you hadn't archived everything, climbed that bloody scaffolding, pulled me out of the lion pen—'

'God, don't talk about it.'

'Rachel...' He puts the paper in his lap and reaches for my hand. 'Don't hang on to what Harrow said about naivety, okay? Don't let him change you. Stay you. Stay open.'

'I will,' I say.

'He's just one person in this huge city...'

I put a finger over his lips.

I've thought about it already and I refuse to let one cut go bone-deep. I won't put up walls, but I really *don't* want to talk about it, any more than I want to see Harrow in the courtroom – in *any* room, ever again. I keep flipping to that moment when Mycroft's eyes rolled back and he just faded, right in front of me...

But this is not a flashback moment. I think it's all going to take

331

a little while to settle and I'm in no hurry. Right now, I'm just happy to grab Mycroft's hand and change the subject.

'So, Mai told me you're going back to school. Does that mean you're going to stay on here, with Angela?'

His face closes down a bit. I realize that maybe I've changed to the wrong subject, but we have to talk about it sometime.

'I suppose.' He makes a stiff shrug. 'It's not like she's been around much to discuss it. But yeah, I guess. I'm set up here.'

I come out with it. 'Angela sat with you. At the hospital.'

'She didn't.' He looks shocked.

'I saw her.' I trace his fingers with my thumb again, to soften my next suggestion. 'Maybe you two could start cutting each other a bit of slack. It might make the next four months more bearable.'

'I guess.' Mycroft makes a face. 'Or there's always the share-house notices down on Smith Street.'

'You'll have to keep it in mind for next year, anyway,' I point out.

'Would you be interested?' he asks suddenly.

'In share-housing? With you?'

He's making an effort to look casual. 'We could invite Mai and Gus, split it four ways.'

I blink and stare. Now *I'm* shocked. And excited. And terrified. And kind of…

I think for a moment, narrow my eyes at his innocent expression. 'Is there a Baker Street address in Melbourne?'

'In Richmond. Off Victoria Street—'

I'm laughing. 'Oh my god, you are *so* predictable—'

'It's near the tram and everything. It'd be perfect!' He gives me a sly grin. 'You know, you haven't said my name since I came home.'

'*Don't* start.' I groan, because I've been wondering when he would bring this up again. 'Seriously, it's confusing – don't *laugh*! I've had you in my head with one name for so long—'

'Go on then,' he says. 'I like it.'

'I can't!' I push at his arm, rake my hair out of the way. 'I'm saving it up.'

'For life-threatening situations?' He's doing the smile thing on me. 'For near-death experiences?'

'For throes of passion,' I say with a smirk.

'Mm, I like the sound of that. Let's try it out now, shall we?'

I squeal as he pulls me until I'm lying over his lap. I'm laughing and my hair is spread out under my head, spilling over his knees. He's got one hand in my hair and one hand squeezing my hip, his thumb sliding into the loop on the waistband of my jeans. He lowers himself forward, and he's smiling, his lips forming that sweet shape.

I whisper, *'James...'* – which is all the incentive he needs to kiss me.

The gate creaks.

'Hey there, you two. Public displays of affection, and all that.'

I jerk my hand out of Mycroft's hair and sit up, pressing my lips together. 'Hey, Dad. Well, it's not like we can go *inside*.'

Dad's got his old tool belt hanging off his waist. He's like a paunchy gunslinger, although the tools are just secateurs and gardening gloves now.

He rolls his eyes at me. 'Yeah yeah, I've heard this argument before. How's things, Mycroft? Glad to be home?'

Mycroft tries to get the *I've been kissing your daughter* look off his face. 'Yes indeed, Mr Watts, I certainly am.'

'And I suppose you two would rather just sit there and not help me with the weeding?'

I decide to go all out and snuggle up to Mycroft's shoulder. 'Thanks for the offer, Dad, but I think here's more comfortable.'

Dad sighs. 'Ah well, your loss. So – dinner. Looks like Mike's overestimated with the sausages again. You two be up for that, eh? Helping us get through an excess of burnt sausages?'

'I'll have two,' I say, then I stop. Mycroft says nothing. I look at his face, look back to Dad. 'Be over later, okay?'

Dad waves his secateurs. 'No worries. Okay, the weeds are getting desperate. See you for dinner in an hour.'

As soon as Dad's walked past the porch and into the squeezeway, I turn to Mycroft. I make my expression light.

'Should we go? With that thing on your leg, it'll take us an hour to get you down the street and in the door of my place.' I watch him chew on his lip. I don't want to sound too eager, but I think it bleeds into my voice anyway. 'Do you want to come?'

He ducks his head. 'Yeah, I want to come.'

'So come.' I take his hand again. My voice is butterfly-soft. 'James, come.'

'You're doing the name thing on me,' he says, with a fake groan. Or maybe it's a real groan.

'Yes, I am.' I'm unrepentant. But I know what this means for him. 'Are you up for this?'

'I don't know,' he admits.

That is all right; that is perfectly understandable. This is not insignificant. I squeeze his fingers, smooth them down, as if I'm stroking the lines on his forehead.

'It'll be okay,' I say. 'They're just people.'

'Help me up,' James says, and my heart lifts.

He uses my hand, pushing off the bench seat to stand. Somewhere down past Summoner Street a siren wails away to nothing, tram bells clang, music sounds joyful and quiet. The exhaust pollution mingles with the scent of new-mown grass and burning sausages.

We stand there on his front porch as the day darkens and the world turns to velvet. For the first time, there's no doubt inside me. Every breath is a choice, and I chose, and I feel a strong, slow calm, the reward for making the right one.

I look out into the street, catch the lay of the land, the home-steads along each creek and tributary bend, the tall blocks of the high country in the distance, all radiating with a universal glow as the stars emerge. The headlights and the streetlights and the house lights – all the stars, winking. The move and wheel and turn: people going to work, people returning to their homes, the morning and the close of the long day. All the tiny individual lights, the galaxy of souls inside the city, the teeming, bustling, populated city...

The place where I live now.

ACKNOWLEDGMENTS

Without these people, this book wouldn't exist, and I would still be scribbling in cafes.

So big hugs, and huge thanks...

To Geoff, who is my everything, and to my amazing boys – Ben, Alex, Will and Ned.

To Catherine Drayton, my awesome agent, for believing and taking a chance. To Eva Mills – who's been there from the start – and Hilary Reynolds at Allen & Unwin, for being so *lovely*, and for making this real. To Liz Bray, Lisa White and the Sydney sales and publicity team for providing such fantastic support.

And special thanks to Alison, Tara, Sylvia and the whole team at Tundra for introducing Rachel and James to an extraordinary world of new friends, and for making the ride so smooth.

To PD (Phillipa) Martin, without whom this novel would never have gotten beyond a few pages scrawled in a notebook, and to the folk from the Popular Fiction course, especially Alisdair Daws, criminal accomplice.

To the women from Sisters in Crime (Melbourne), who are the real deal.

To Cath Crowley, for encouragement I needed to hear, for pointing me in the right direction, and for writing such lovely words of praise.

To Celia, Julie-Anne and Simon, Nadine and Grant, and Denis – who proofread the first draft and noticed that I'd attributed 'My Sharona' to the wrong band, among other things, and who spurred me on.

To Lisa, Louiseann, Jane, Andy, and other friends who've helped me along the way, and to Deborah, for writing support and wisdom on raising four sons.

To Robyn, Marion, Jess and the team at Castlemaine Library – you guys are the best. And to friends I've made through Castlemaine Word Mine, who heard *Every Breath* for the first time.

To Professor David Williams, forensic pathologist at Townsville General Hospital, who advised me on forensic facts (any errors or artistic license taken with these facts are entirely my own).

To my late father-in-law, Brian, who read more crime novels than I've had hot dinners, and to my extended family, Deb, Mike and John.

To my own family – Mum and Dad, and Sarah, Lucy and Jared – who told me to keep at it. And to my friends, both in Castlemaine and Melbourne (especially the Bittangabee Crew!), who have all listened to me bang on and put up with me.

And to Lorna Ferguson, English teacher and poet, much missed.

ABOUT THE AUTHOR

Ellie Marney was born in the tropical northeast of Australia, and has lived in Indonesia, Singapore and India. Now she writes, teaches, talks about kid's literature at libraries and schools, and gardens when she can, while living in a country idyll (actually a very messy wooden house on ten acres with a dog and lots of chickens) near Castlemaine, in north-central Victoria. Even though she often forgets things and lets the housework go, her partner and four sons still love her.

Ellie's short stories for adults have won awards and been published in various anthologies. *Every Breath* is her first novel for young adults.

EVERY WORD

Rachel is still getting used to the idea of Mycroft as her boyfriend when he disappears off to London to investigate a carjacking death. Rachel has family, friends and exams to keep her busy at home... so of course she follows him over there and into a whole storm of trouble. Get ready to see more sparks fly in this second stylish, sophisticated thriller about the teen crime-fighting pair.